DEATH MATCH

Also by Lincoln Child
in Large Print:

Co-authored with Douglas Preston
The Ice Limit
Still Life with Crows

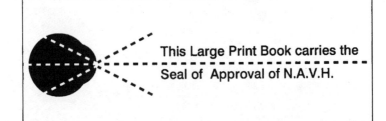

DEATH MATCH

Lincoln Child

WHEELER
PUBLISHING

Published in 2004 by arrangement with Doubleday, a division of the Doubleday Broadway Publishing Group, a division of Random House, Inc.

Wheeler Large Print Hardcover.

The text of this Large Print edition is unabridged. Other aspects of the book may vary from the original edition.

Set in 16 pt. Plantin by Minnie B. Raven.

Printed in the United States on permanent paper.

Library of Congress Cataloging-in-Publication Data

Child, Lincoln.
    Death match : a novel / by Lincoln Child.
      p. cm.
    ISBN 1-58724-709-7 (lg. print : hc : alk. paper)
    1. Marriage brokerage — Fiction.   2. Suicide victims — Fiction.   3. Mate selection — Fiction.   4. Suicide pacts — Fiction.   5. Large type books.   I. Title.
PS3553.H4839D43 2004b
  813'.54—dc22
                                   2004045832

To Veronica

As the Founder/CEO of NAVH, the only national health agency solely devoted to those who, although not totally blind, have an eye disease which could lead to serious visual impairment, I am pleased to recognize Thorndike Press★ as one of the leading publishers in the large print field.

Founded in 1954 in San Francisco to prepare large print textbooks for partially seeing children, NAVH became the pioneer and standard setting agency in the preparation of large type.

Today, those publishers who meet our standards carry the prestigious "Seal of Approval" indicating high quality large print. We are delighted that Thorndike Press is one of the publishers whose titles meet these standards. We are also pleased to recognize the significant contribution Thorndike Press is making in this important and growing field.

Lorraine H. Marchi, L.H.D.
Founder/CEO
NAVH

★ Thorndike Press encompasses the following imprints: Thorndike, Wheeler, Walker and Large Print Press.

ACKNOWLEDGMENTS

Many people lent their expertise to the writing of this book. I'd like to thank my friend and editor at Doubleday, Jason Kaufman, for his assistance in countless ways, large and small. Thanks also to his colleagues, Jenny Choi and Rachel Pace.

Kenneth Freundlich, Ph.D., provided invaluable insight into psychological testing and administration. Thanks also to Lee Suckno, M.D., Antony Cifelli, M.D., Traian Parvulescu, M.D., and Daniel DaSilva, Ph.D., for their medical and psychological expertise. Cezar Baula and Chris Buck helped with chemical and pharmaceutical details. Once again, my cousin Greg Tear was both a vital sounding board and a fount of ideas. And ongoing thanks to Special Agent Douglas Margini for his assistance with law enforcement aspects of the book.

A special thanks to Douglas Preston for his support and encouragement throughout the writing of this book, and for supplying a crucial chapter.

I'd also like to thank Bruce Swanson, Mark Mendel, and Jim Jenkins, for their guidance and friendship.

Last, I want to thank those without whom my novels could never exist: my wife, Luchie; my daughter, Veronica; my parents, Bill and Nancy; and my siblings, Doug and Cynthia.

It goes without saying that the characters, corporations, events, locales, entities, pharmaceutical products, psychological apparatus, governmental bodies, computing devices, and the rest of the clay out of which this novel was fashioned are all fictitious, or are used fictitiously. The Eden Incorporated of this book — though it may exist some day — is at present a caprice of my imagination.

ONE

It was the first time Maureen Bowman had ever heard the baby cry.

She hadn't noticed right away. In fact, it had taken five, perhaps ten minutes to register. She'd almost finished with the breakfast dishes when she stopped to listen, suds dripping from her yellow-gloved hands. No mistake: crying, and from the direction of the Thorpe house.

Maureen rinsed the last dish, wrapped the damp towel around it, and turned it over thoughtfully in her hands. Normally, the cry of a baby would go unnoticed in her neighborhood. It was one of those suburban sounds, like the tinkle of the ice cream truck or the bark of a dog, that passed just beneath the radar of conscious perception.

So why had she noticed? She dropped the plate into the drying rack.

Because the Thorpe baby never cried. In the balmy summer days, with the windows thrown wide, she'd often heard it cooing, gurgling, laughing. Sometimes, she'd heard

9

the infant vocalizing to the sounds of classical music, her voice mingling in the breeze with the scent of piñon pines.

Maureen wiped her hands on the towel, folded it carefully, then glanced up from the counter. But it was September now; the first day it really felt like autumn. In the distance, the purple flanks of the San Francisco peaks were wreathed in snow. She could see them, through a window shut tight against the chill.

She shrugged, turned, and walked away from the sink. All babies cried, sooner or later; you'd worry if they didn't. Besides, it was none of her business; she had plenty of things to take care of without messing in her neighbors' lives. It was Friday, always the busiest day of the week. Choir rehearsal for herself, ballet for Courtney, karate for Jason. *And* it was Jason's birthday; he'd demanded beef fondue and chocolate cake. That meant another trip to the new supermarket on Route 66. With a sigh, Maureen pulled a list from beneath a refrigerator magnet, grabbed a pencil from the phone stand, and began scrawling items.

Then she stopped. With the windows all closed, the Thorpe baby must really be cranking if she could hear . . .

Maureen forced the thought from her mind. The infant girl had barked her shin or something. Maybe she was becoming colicky, it wasn't too late for that. In any case, the

Thorpes were adults; they could deal with it. The Thorpes could deal with anything.

This last thought had a bitter undertone, and Maureen was quick to remind herself this was unfair. The Thorpes had different interests, ran in different circles; that was all.

Lewis and Lindsay Thorpe had moved to Flagstaff just over a year before. In a neighborhood full of empty nesters and retirees, they stood out as a young, attractive couple, and Maureen had been quick to invite them to dinner. They'd been charming guests, friendly and witty and very polite. The conversation had been easy, unforced. But the invitation had never been returned. Lindsay Thorpe was in her third trimester at the time; Maureen liked to believe that was the reason. And now, with a new baby, back full-time at work . . . it was all perfectly understandable.

She walked slowly across the kitchen, past the breakfast table, to the sliding glass door. From here, she had a better view of the Thorpes'. They'd been home the night before, she knew; she'd seen Lewis's car driving past around dinnertime. But now, as she peered out, all seemed quiet.

Except for the baby. God, the little thing had leather lungs . . .

Maureen stepped closer to the glass, craning her neck. That's when she saw the Thorpes' cars. Both of them, twin Audi A8s,

11

the black one Lewis's and the silver one Lindsay's, parked in the breezeway.

Both home, on a Friday? This was seriously weird. Maureen pressed her nose up against the glass.

Then she stepped back. *Now listen, you're being exactly the kind of nosy neighbor you promised you'd never be.* There could be any number of explanations. The little girl was sick, the parents were home to tend to her. Maybe grandparents were arriving. Or they were getting ready to go on vacation. Or . . .

The child's cries had begun to take on a hoarse, ragged quality. And now, without thinking, Maureen put her hand on the glass door and slid it open.

Wait, I can't just go over there. It'll be nothing. I'll embarrass them, make myself look like a fool.

She looked over at the counter. The night before, she'd baked an enormous quantity of tollhouse cookies for Jason's birthday. She'd bring some of those over; that was a reasonable, neighborly thing to do.

Quickly, she grabbed a paper plate — thought better of it — replaced it with a piece of her good china, arranged a dozen cookies on it, and covered them with plastic wrap. She scooped up the plate, made for the door.

Then she hesitated. Lindsay, she remembered, was a gourmet chef. A few Saturdays before, when they'd met at their mailboxes, the woman had apologized for being unable to chat because she had a burnt-almond ganache boiling on the stove. What would they think of a homely plate of tollhouse cookies?

You're thinking about this way, way too much. Just go on over there.

What was it, exactly, she found so intimidating about the Thorpes? The fact they didn't seem to need her friendship? They were well educated, but Maureen had her own cum laude degree in English. They had lots of money, but so did half the neighborhood. Maybe it was how perfect they seemed together, how ideally suited to each other. It was almost uncanny. That one time they'd come over, Maureen had noticed how they unconsciously held hands; how they frequently completed each other's sentences; how they'd shared countless glances that, though brief, seemed pregnant with meaning. "Disgustingly happy" was how Maureen's husband termed them, but Maureen didn't think it disgusting at all. In fact, she'd found herself feeling envious.

Steadying her grip on the plate of cookies, she walked to the door, pulled back the screen, and stepped outside.

It was a beautiful, crisp morning, the smell of cedar strong in the thin air. Birds were piping in the branches overhead, and from down the hill, in the direction of town, she could hear the mournful call of the South-west Chief as it pulled into the train station.

Out here, the crying was much louder.

Maureen strode purposefully across the lawn of colored lava and stepped over the border of railroad ties. This was the first time she'd actually set foot on the Thorpes' property. It felt strange, somehow. The back-yard was enclosed, but between the boards of the fence she could make out the Japanese garden Lewis had told them about. He was fascinated by Japanese culture, and had translated several of the great haiku poets; he'd mentioned some names Maureen had never heard of. What she could see of the garden looked tranquil. Serene. At dinner that night, Lewis had told a story about the Zen master who'd asked an apprentice to tidy his garden. The apprentice had spent all day at it, removing every last fallen leaf, sweeping and polishing the stone paths until they gleamed, raking the sand into regular lines. At last, the Zen master had emerged to scru-tinize the work. "Perfect?" the apprentice asked as he displayed the meticulous garden. But the master shook his head. Then he gathered up a handful of pebbles and scat-tered them across the spotless sand. "*Now* it is perfect," he replied. Maureen remembered how Lewis's eyes had sparkled with amuse-ment as he told the story.

14

She hurried forward, the crying strong in her ears.

Ahead was the Thorpes' kitchen door. Maureen stepped up to it, carefully arranged a bright smile on her face, and pulled open the screen. She began to knock, but with the pressure of her first rap the door swung inward.

She took a step.

"Hello?" she said. "Lindsay? Lewis?"

Here, in the house, the wailing was almost physically painful. She hadn't known an infant could cry so loud. Wherever the parents were, they certainly couldn't hear her over the baby. How could they be ignoring it? Was it possible they were showering? Or engaged in some kinky sex act? Abruptly, she felt self-conscious, and glanced around. The kitchen was beautiful: professional-grade appliances, glossy black counters. But it was empty.

The kitchen led directly into a breakfast nook, gilded by morning light. And there was the child: up ahead, in the archway between the breakfast nook and some other space that, from what she could see, looked like a living room. The infant was strapped tightly into her high chair, facing the living room. The little face was mottled from crying, and the cheeks were stained with mucus and tears.

Maureen rushed forward. "Oh, you poor thing." Balancing the cookies awkwardly, she fished for a tissue, cleaned the child's face. "There, there."

But the crying did not ease. The baby was pounding her little fists, staring fixedly ahead, inconsolable.

It took quite some time to wipe the red face clean, and by the time she was done Maureen's ears were ringing with the noise. It wasn't until she was pushing the tissue back into the pocket of her jeans that she thought to follow the child's line of sight into the living room.

And when she did, the cry of the child, the crash of china as she dropped the cookies, were instantly drowned by the sound of her screams.

TWO

Christopher Lash stepped out of the cab and into the tumult of Madison Avenue. It had been half a year since he was last in New York, and those months seemed to have softened him. He hadn't missed the acrid diesel plumes belching from serried rows of buses; he'd forgotten the unpleasantly burnt aroma of the sidewalk pretzel stands. The throngs of passersby, barking into cell phones; the blat of horns; the angry interplay of cars and trucks — it all reminded him of the frantic, senseless activity of an ant colony, exposed from beneath a rock.

Taking a firm grip on his leather satchel, he stepped onto the sidewalk and inserted himself deftly into the crowds. It had been a long time, too, since he'd carried the satchel, and it felt foreign and uncomfortable in his hand.

He crossed Fifty-seventh Street, letting himself be carried along by the river of humanity, and headed south. Another block, and the crowds eased somewhat. He crossed

17

Fifty-sixth, then slid into an empty doorway, where he could pause a moment without being jostled. Placing his satchel carefully between his shoes, he gazed upward.

Across the street, a rectangular tower rose into the sky. There was no number, or corporate lettering, to betray what lay within. They were rendered unnecessary by the logo that — thanks to countless high-profile news reports — had recently become almost as familiar an American icon as the golden arches: the sleek, elongated infinity symbol that hovered just above the building's entrance. The tower rose to a setback, halfway up its massive flank; higher, decorative latticework ran around the structure like a ribbon, setting off the top few floors. But this simplicity was deceptive. The tower's skin had a richness, a sense of depth, almost like the paintwork on the most expensive of cars. Recent architectural textbooks called the building "obsidian," but that wasn't quite correct: it had a warm, pellucid glow that seemed almost drawn from its environment, leaving the surrounding buildings cold and colorless by comparison.

Dropping his gaze from the facade, he fished into the pocket of his suit jacket and pulled out a piece of business stationery. At the top, "Eden Incorporated" was embossed in elegant type beside the infinity logo; "deliver by courier" was stamped at the bottom.

He reread the brief message below.

Dear Dr. Lash:
I enjoyed speaking with you today, and I'm glad you could come on such short notice. We'll expect you Monday at 10:30 a.m. Please give the enclosed card to one of the security personnel in the lobby.

Sincerely,

Edwin Mauchly
Director, Facilitation Services

The letter yielded up no more information than it had the other times he'd read it, and Lash returned it to his pocket.

He waited for the light to change, then picked up his satchel and made his way across the street. The tower was set back extravagantly from the sidewalk, creating a welcoming oasis. There was a fountain here: marble satyrs and nymphs disporting themselves around a bent, ancient figure. Lash peered curiously through the curtain of mist at the figure. It seemed a strange centerpiece for a fountain: no matter how he stared, he could not quite determine whether it was male or female.

Beyond the fountain, the revolving doors were kept in constant motion. Lash stopped again, observing this traffic intently. Almost everyone was entering, not leaving. But it was almost ten-thirty, so it couldn't be employees he was seeing. No, they must all be clients; or, more likely, would-be clients.

The lobby was large and high-ceilinged, and he paused again just inside. Although the surfaces were of pink marble, indirect lighting lent the space an unusual warmth. There was an information desk in its center, of the same obsidian as the building's exterior. Along the right wall, beyond a security checkpoint, lay a long bank of elevators. New arrivals continued to stream by him. They were a remarkably heterogeneous crowd: all ages, races, heights, builds. They looked hopeful, eager, perhaps a little apprehensive. The excitement in the air was palpable. Some headed toward the far end of the lobby, where twin escalators climbed toward a wide, arched passage. CANDIDATE PROCESSING was engraved above the passage in discreet gold lettering. Others were moving toward a set of doors below the escalators marked APPLICATIONS. And still others had gravitated to the left side of the lobby, where Lash caught the flicker of myriad movements. Curious, he drifted closer.

Across a wide swath of the left wall, floor to ceiling, large flatscreen plasma displays had been set edge to edge in a huge matrix. On each screen was the head shot of a different person, talking to the camera: men and women, old and young. The faces were so different from each other that, for a moment, Lash sensed but could not place the commonality they shared. Then he realized: every face was smiling, almost serene.

Lash joined the crowd who had assembled, mute and staring, before the wall of faces. As he did so, he became aware of countless voices, apparently coming from speakers hidden among the screens. Yet through some trick of sound projection, he found it easy to isolate individual voices in three-dimensional space, to match them with faces on the screens. *It completely turned my life around,* a pretty young woman on one of the screens was saying, seeming to speak directly to him. *If it wasn't for Eden, I don't know what I would've done,* a man on another told him, smiling almost confidentially, as if imparting a secret. *It's made all the difference.* On yet another screen, a blond man with pale blue eyes and a brilliant smile said, *It's the best thing I've ever done. Period. End of story.*

As he listened, Lash became aware of another voice: low, just on the edge of audibility, little more than a whisper. It was not coming from any of the screens, but seemingly from all around. He paused to listen.

Technology, the voice was saying. *Today, it's used to make our lives easier, longer, more comfortable. But what if technology could do some-*

thing even more profound? What if it could bring completion, bring utter fulfillment?

Imagine computer technology so advanced it could reconstruct — virtually — your own personality, the essence of what makes you unique: your hopes, desires, dreams. The inmost needs that not even you may be aware of. Imagine a digital infrastructure so robust it could contain this personality construct of yours — with its countless unique facets and characteristics — along with those of many, many other people. Imagine an artificial intelligence so profound it could compare your construct with these multitudes of others, and — in an hour, a day, a week — find that one person, that sole individual, that is your perfect match. Your ideal soulmate, uniquely fitted by personality, background, interests, countless other benchmarks to be your other half. To make your life complete. Not just two people who happen to share a few interests. But a match where one person complements the other in ways so profound, so subtle, it could never be imagined or anticipated.

Lash continued to watch the endless sea of faces before him while listening to the disembodied, sonorous voice.

No blind dates, it went on. *No singles parties, where your choice is limited to a handful of random meetings. No evenings wasted on incompatibility. Rather, a proprietary system of profound sophistication. This system is now. And the company is Eden.*

The service is not cheap. But if there is even the slightest dissatisfaction, Eden Incorporated offers a full refund, guaranteed for life. Yet out of the many, many thousands of couples Eden has brought together, not one has requested a refund. Because these people — like those on the screens before you — have learned there is no price that can be put on happiness.

With a start, Lash looked away from the screens and down at his watch. He was five minutes late for his appointment.

Walking across the lobby, Lash drew out a card and handed it to one of the uniformed guards. He was given a signed pass and cheerfully directed toward the bank of elevators.

Thirty-two stories above, Lash stepped into a small but elegant reception area. The tones were neutral, and there was the faintest rush of industrial pink noise. There were no signs, directories, formal guides of any kind: just one desk of polished blond wood, an attractive woman in a business suit behind it.

"Dr. Lash?" she asked with an engaging smile.

"Yes."

"Good morning. May I see your driver's license, please?"

This request was so strange that Lash did not think to question it. Instead, he pulled out his wallet and fished for his license.

"Thank you." The woman held it briefly

over some scanning apparatus. Then she handed it back with another bright smile, rose from her chair, and motioned him toward a door in the far wall of the reception area.

They passed down a long corridor, similar in decor to the room they'd just left. Lash noticed many doors, all unlabeled, all closed. The woman stopped before one of them.

"In here, please," she said.

As the door closed behind him, Lash looked around at a well-appointed room. A desk of dark wood sat upon a dense carpet. Several paintings hung on the walls, beautifully framed. Behind the desk, a man now rose to greet him, smoothing his brown suit as he did so. Lash shook the proffered hand, typing the man from old habit as he did so. He looked to be in his late thirties: fairly short, dark complexion, dark hair, dark eyes, muscular but not stocky. Swimmer, perhaps, or tennis player. His bearing spoke of someone self-confident, considered; a man who would be slow to act but, when acting, would do so decisively.

"Dr. Lash," the man said, returning his gaze. "I'm Edwin Mauchly. Thanks for coming."

"Sorry I'm late."

"Not at all. Take a seat, please."

Lash sat down in the lone leather chair that faced the desk while Mauchly turned toward a computer monitor. He typed for a moment, then stopped. "Give me just a minute here, please. It's been four years since I gave an entrance interview, and the screens have changed."

"Is that what this is?"

"Of course not. But there's some similar initial processing to be done." He typed again. "Here we are. The address of your Stamford office is 315 Front Street, Suite 2?"

"Yes."

"Good. If you could just fill out this information for me, please."

Lash scanned the white card that was slid across the desk: date of birth, social security number, half a dozen other mundane details. He took a pen from his pocket and began jotting on the form.

"You used to give entrance interviews?" he said as he wrote.

"I helped design the process, as an employee of PharmGen. That was early on, before Eden became an independent company."

"What's it like?"

"What is what like, Dr. Lash?"

"Working here." He slid the card back. "You'd think it would be magic. Listening to all those testimonials in the lobby, anyway."

Mauchly glanced at the card. "I don't blame you for being skeptical." He had a face that managed to look both candid and reticent at the same time. "Two people's feelings for each other, what can technology do about that? But ask any of our employees. They see it work, time after time, *every* time. Yes, I guess magic is as good a word for it as any."

On the far side of the desk, a telephone rang. "Mauchly," the man said, tucking the phone beneath his chin. "Very well. Good-bye." He replaced the phone, then rose. "He's ready for you, Dr. Lash."

He? Lash thought to himself as he picked up his satchel. He followed Mauchly back out into the corridor, to an intersection, then into a wider, plushly appointed hallway that ended in a set of brilliantly polished doors. Reaching them, Mauchly paused, then knocked.

"Come in," came a voice from beyond.

Mauchly opened the door. "I'll speak with you again shortly, Dr. Lash," he said, motioning him inside.

Lash stepped forward, then stopped again as the door clicked closed. Before him stood a long, semicircular table of dark wood. Across it sat a lone man, tall and deeply tanned. He smiled, nodded. Lash nodded back. And then, with a sudden shock of recognition, he realized the man was none other than John Lelyveld, chairman of Eden Incorporated.

Waiting for him.

THREE

The chairman of Eden Incorporated rose from his seat. He smiled, and his face broke into kindly, almost grandfatherly lines. "Dr. Lash. Thank you so much for coming. Please, take a seat." And he motioned toward the long table.

Lash took a seat across from Lelyveld.

"Did you drive in from Connecticut?"

"Yes."

"How was the traffic?"

"I was parked on the Cross Bronx about half an hour. Otherwise, okay."

The chairman shook his head. "That road is a disgrace. I have a weekend place not far from you myself, in Rowayton. These days I usually take a helicopter. One of the perks." He chuckled, then opened a leather portfolio that lay beside him. "Just a few formalities before we get started." He took out a sheaf of stapled pages and passed it across the desk. It was followed by a gold pen. "Would you mind signing this, please?"

Lash looked at the top page. It was a

nondisclosure agreement. He flipped quickly through the pages, found the signature line, signed.

"And this."

Lash took the second proffered document. It appeared to be some kind of guarantee of confidentiality. He turned to the back page, signed.

"And this, if you please."

This time, Lash simply signed without bothering to review the verbiage.

"Thank you. I do apologize, I hope you understand." Lelyveld returned the sheets to the leather portfolio. Then he placed his elbows on the desk, resting his chin on tented fingers. "Dr. Lash, you understand the nature of our service, I believe?"

Lash nodded. There were few who didn't: the story of how Eden had grown, over just a handful of years, from a research project of brilliant computer scientist Richard Silver to one of the highest-profile corporations in America was a favorite of financial news services.

"Then you probably won't be surprised when I say that Eden Incorporated has *fundamentally* improved the lives of, at last count, nine hundred and twenty-four thousand people."

"No."

"Almost half a million couples, with thousands more added each day. And with the

28

opening of satellite offices in Beverly Hills, Chicago, and Miami, we've dramatically increased our service range and our pool of potential candidates."

Lash nodded again.

"Our fee is steep — $25,000 per applicant — but we have never yet been asked for a refund."

"So I understand."

"Good. But it's important you also understand our service does not end on the day we bring a couple together. There is a mandatory follow-up session with one of our counselors, scheduled three months later. And after six months, couples are requested to join encounter groups with other Eden couples. We carefully monitor our client base — not only for their benefit, but to improve our service, as well."

Lelyveld leaned slightly toward Lash, as if to impart a secret across the massive table. "What I'm about to tell you is confidential and trade secret to Eden. In our promotional material, we speak of providing a perfect match. The ideal union between two people. Our computer intelligence compares roughly *one million* variables from each of our clients to those of other clients, looking for a match. With me so far?"

"Yes."

"I'm speaking in gross simplifications here. The artificial intelligence algorithms are the result of Richard Silver's ongoing work, as well as countless man-hours spent researching the behavioral and psychological factors. But in short, our scientists have determined a specific threshold of matching variables necessary to declare a fit between two candidates." He shifted in his chair. "Dr. Lash, if you compared these million factors in an average happily married couple, how closely do you think that couple would match each other?"

Lash thought. "Eighty, maybe eighty-five percent?"

"That's a very good guess, but I'm afraid it's way off. Our studies have shown the average happily married American couple matches in the range of only *thirty-five percent.*"

Lash shook his head.

"You see, people tend to be seduced by superficial impressions, or physical attractions that by themselves will be practically meaningless in a few years. Today's relationship services and so-called Internet dating sites — with their crude metrics and simplistic questionnaires — actually encourage this. We, on the other hand, use a hybrid computer to find two *ideal* partners: people for whom a million personal traits are in synch." He paused. "Not to delve too deeply into proprietary matters, but there are varying degrees of perfection. Our staff has determined a specific percentage — let's just say it's over ninety-five — that guarantees an ideal match."

"I see."

"The fact remains, Dr. Lash — and forgive me if I remind you of the confidentiality of this information — that during the three years Eden has been offering this service, there have in fact been a small number of uniquely perfect matches. Matches in which *all one hundred percent* of the variables between two people have been in synch."

"One hundred percent?"

"A uniquely perfect match. Of course, we don't inform our clients as to the precise exactness of their match. But over the lifetime of our service, there have been six such statistically perfect matches. 'Supercouples,' as they're referred to in-house."

So far, Lelyveld's voice has been measured, assured. But now he seemed to hesitate slightly. The grandfatherly smile remained on his face, but an undertone of sadness, even pain, was introduced. "I've told you that we do post-monitoring of all our clients . . . Dr. Lash, I'm afraid there's no pleasant way to say this. Last week, one of our six uniquely perfect couples —" he hesitated, then went on "— committed double suicide."

"Suicide?" Lash echoed.

The chairman glanced down, consulted some notes. "In Flagstaff, Arizona. Lewis and

31

Lindsay Thorpe. The details are rather, ah, unusual. They left a note." He looked up again. "Can you understand now why we've requested your services?"

Lash was still digesting this. "Perhaps you could spell it out."

"You're a psychologist specializing in family relationships, particularly marital relationships. The book you published last year, *Congruency*, was a remarkable study on the subject."

"I wish more book buyers had felt that way."

"The peer reviews were all quite enthusiastic. In any case, in addition to being utterly perfect for each other, the Thorpes were both intelligent, capable, well adapted, *happy*. Clearly, some tragedy must have befallen this couple after their marriage. Perhaps a medical problem of some sort; perhaps the death of a loved one. Maybe it had to do with financial issues." He paused. "We need to know what changed in the dynamic of their lives, and why they took such an extreme action as a result. If by some remote chance there's a latent psychological tendency operating here, we should know so we can prescreen for it in the future."

"You've got a team of in-house mental health professionals, right?" Lash asked. "Why not use one of them?"

"Two reasons. First, we want an impartial

person to look into the matter. And second, none of our staff has your particular credentials."

"Which credentials do you mean?"

Lelyveld smiled paternally. "I'm referring to your prior occupation. Before you went into private practice, I mean. Forensic psychologist with the FBI, part of the Behavioral Science team operating out of Quantico."

"How did you know about that?"

"Dr. Lash, please. As a former special agent, you no doubt retain behind-the-scenes access to places, people, information. You could undertake such an investigation with great discretion. Were we to investigate ourselves, or request official assistance, there might be questions. And there is no point in causing our clients — past, present, and future — unnecessary concern."

Lash shifted in his chair. "There was a reason I left Quantico for private practice."

"There's a newspaper account of the tragedy in your dossier. I'm very sorry. So it doesn't surprise me you're not eager to leave the comfort of that practice, even temporarily." The chairman opened the leather portfolio, removed an envelope. "Hence the amount of the enclosed."

Lash took the envelope and opened it. Inside was a check for $100,000.

"That should cover your time, travel, and expenses. If more is needed, let us know.

Take your time, Dr. Lash. Thoroughness, and a subtle approach, are what's required here. The more we know, the more effective we can make our service in the future."

The chairman paused a moment before speaking again. "There is one other possibility, however remote. And that is one of the Thorpes was unstable, had a prior history of mental problems they were somehow able to conceal from our evaluation. This is highly, *highly* unlikely. However, if you are unable to find an answer over the course of their married life, you may have to look into their past as well."

Lelyveld closed the portfolio with an air of finality. "Ed Mauchly will be your primary point of contact for this investigation. He's put together a few things to get you started. We can't release our own files on the couple, of course, but they wouldn't be of much interest to you anyway. The answer to this riddle lies in the *private* lives of Lewis and Lindsay Thorpe."

The man fell silent again, and for a moment Lash wondered if the meeting was over. But then Lelyveld spoke again, his voice quieter now, more intimate. The smile had faded. "We have a very special feeling for all of our clients, Dr. Lash. But to be honest, we feel particularly strongly about our perfect couples. Whenever a new supercouple is found, word ripples throughout the company, despite our best attempts to keep it private. They're very rare. So I'm sure you can understand how painful and difficult this news was to me, especially since the Thorpes were our very first such couple. Luckily their deaths were kept out of the papers, so our employees have so far been spared the sad news. I'd be personally grateful for any light you can shed on what, precisely, went wrong in their lives."

When Lelyveld stood and extended his hand, the smile returned, only now it was wistful.

FOUR

Twenty-four hours later, Lash stood in his living room, sipping coffee and gazing out the bay window. On the far side of the glass lay Compo Beach, a long, narrow comma of sand almost devoid of waders and walkers this weekday morning. The tourists and summer renters had left weeks before, but this was the first time in a month he'd taken the time to really look out the window. He was struck by the relative emptiness of the beach. It was a clear, bright morning: across the sound, he could make out the low green line of Long Island. A tanker was passing, a silent ghost heading for the open Atlantic.

Mentally, he went over again the preparations he'd made. His regular private therapy and counseling sessions had been cancelled for one week. Dr. Kline would cover for the groups. It had all been remarkably easy.

He yawned, took another sip of coffee, and caught sight of himself in a mirror. Deciding what to wear had been a little more difficult. Lash had always disliked fieldwork, and his upcoming appointment felt a little too much like old times. But he reminded himself it would speed things up enormously. People didn't just deviate into aberrant behavior, especially something as exotic as double suicide. Something must have happened in the two years since the Thorpes got married. And it wouldn't be subtle: some minor life upheaval, say, or a drift toward serious depression. It would be massive, obvious in hindsight to those who'd been around them. He might, in fact, understand what went wrong in their lives by the end of the day. With luck, he could have the case study written up tomorrow. It would be the quickest $100,000 he'd ever earned.

Turning from the window, he let his eyes roam over the room's features: a baby grand, bookcase, couch. Lack of furniture made the room appear larger than it was. The house had a spare, ordered cleanliness he'd cultivated in the years since he'd moved in. The simplicity had become part of his personal armor. God knew the lives of his patients were complicated enough.

Lash glanced once more at his reflection, decided he looked the part, and went out the front door. He looked around, cursed good-naturedly when he noticed that the delivery man had forgotten to leave the *Times* in his driveway, then headed for his car.

An hour's worth of wrestling with I-95

traffic brought him to New London and the low silver arch of the Gold Star Memorial Bridge. Exiting the freeway, he made his way toward the river and found parking on a side street. He thumbed once more through a sheaf of papers on the passenger's seat. There were black-and-white head shots of the couple, a few printed sheets of biographical information. Mauchly had given him precious little data on the Thorpes: address, dates of birth, names and locations of beneficiaries. But it, along with a few telephone calls, had been enough.

Already, Lash felt a stab of remorse for the small deception he was about to perpetrate. He reminded himself it might well yield insight that would prove critical to his investigation.

In the backseat was his leather satchel, well padded now with blank sheets of paper. He grabbed it, exited the car, and — after a final self-inspection in the front windshield — started toward the Thames.

State Street lay dozing beneath a mellow autumn sun. At its foot, beyond the fortresslike bulk of the Old Union railroad station, the harbor glittered. Lash walked down the hill, stopping where State Street ran into Water. There was an old hotel here, a Second Empire with a hulking mansard roof, that had recently been converted into restaurants. In the closest window he made out a sign for The Roastery. A public location, near the water, had seemed best. It had a low threat-factor. Lunch had seemed inappropriate, under the circumstances. Besides, recent inpatient studies at Johns Hopkins showed that grieving people were more responsive to external stimuli during the morning hours. Midmorning coffee seemed ideal. It would be calm, conducive to talk. Lash glanced at his watch. Ten-twenty, on the dot.

Inside, The Roastery was all he'd hoped for: high tin ceilings, beige walls, a low hum of conversation. The delicious fragrance of freshly ground coffee hung in the air. He'd arrived early to make sure he got a suitable table, and he chose a large round one in a corner near the front windows. He took the seat facing the corner; it was important for the subject to feel in control of the situation.

He'd barely had time to place the satchel on the table and arrange himself when he heard footsteps approaching. "Mr. Berger?" came a voice.

Lash turned around. "Yes. You're Mr. Torvald?"

The man had thick, iron-gray hair and the leathery sunburnt skin of a man fond of the water. His faded blue eyes still bore the dark circles of heartbreak. Yet his resemblance to the picture Lash had just viewed in his car was remarkable. Older, masculine, shorter hair; otherwise, it could have been Lindsay Thorpe, returned from the dead.

Out of long habit, Lash betrayed no expression. "Please, take a seat."

Torvald settled himself into the corner chair. He looked briefly around the restaurant, without interest, then settled his gaze on Lash.

"Allow me to convey my deepest condolences. And thank you very much for coming."

Torvald grunted.

"I realize that this must be a very difficult period for you. I'll try to make this short —"

"No, no, it's all right." Torvald's voice was very deep, and he spoke in short, staccato sentences.

A waitress approached their table, offered them menus.

"I don't think we'll need those," Torvald said. "Coffee, black, no sugar."

"Same for me, please."

The woman nodded, swirled, and left them in peace. She was attractive, but Lash noticed Torvald did not even glance at her departing form.

"You're an insurance readjustor," Torvald said.

"I'm an analyst for a consulting firm employed by American Life." One of the first pieces of information Lash sought out on the Thorpes had been their insurance policies.

Three million dollars each, payable to their only daughter. As he'd anticipated, it was a quick and relatively easy way to get neutral access to the closest relatives. He'd gone to the trouble of having phony business cards printed up, but Torvald didn't ask to see one. Despite his obvious pain, the man retained a habitual air of gruff command, as if he was used to having orders quickly obeyed. A naval captain, perhaps, or a corporate executive; Lash had not dug deep into the family background. Corporate executive seemed more likely, though: given the amount Eden charged for its service, it was likely daddy had helped bankroll Lindsay Thorpe.

Lash cleared his throat, put on his best sympathetic manner. "If you wouldn't mind answering just a few questions, it would be very helpful to us. If you find any of them objectionable, or if you feel it necessary to stop for a while, I'll certainly understand."

The waitress returned. Lash took a sip of his coffee, then opened the satchel and pulled out a legal pad. "How close were you to your daughter as she was growing up, Mr. Torvald?" he began.

"Extremely."

"And after she left home?"

"We spoke every day."

"Overall, how would you characterize her physical health?"

"Excellent."

"Did she take any medications on a regular basis?"

"Vitamin supplements. A mild antihistamine. That's about it."

"What was the antihistamine for?"

"Dermatographia."

Lash nodded, made a notation. A skin condition that caused itchiness: his next-door neighbor had it. Completely benign. "Any unusual or serious diseases or childhood illnesses?"

"No, none. And this would all be in the applications she originally filled out with American Life."

"I understand that, Mr. Torvald. I'm simply trying to establish some independent frame of reference. Did she have any living siblings?"

"Lindsay was an only child."

"Was she a good student?"

"Graduated magna cum laude from Brown. Got her master's in economics from Stanford."

"Would you call her shy? Outgoing?"

"Strangers might think her quiet. But Lindsay always had more friends than she needed. She was the kind of girl who had many acquaintances, but was very choosy about her friends."

Lash took another sip of coffee. "How long had your daughter been married, Mr. Torvald?"

"Just over two years."

"And how would you characterize the marriage?"

"They were the happiest couple I've ever seen, bar none."

"Can you tell me about the husband, Lewis Thorpe?"

"Intelligent, friendly, honest. Witty. Lots of interests."

"Did your daughter ever mention any problems between herself and her husband?"

"You mean, fights?"

Lash nodded. "That, or other things. Differences of opinion. Conflicting wishes. Incompatibilities."

"Never."

Lash took another sip. He noticed Torvald had not touched his own cup.

"Never?" He allowed the slightest hint of incredulity to enter his voice.

Torvald rose to the bait. "Never. Look, Mr. —"

"Berger."

"Mr. Berger, my daughter was . . ." For the first time, Torvald seemed to hesitate. "My daughter was a client of Eden Incorporated. You've heard of them?"

"Certainly."

"Then you'll know what I'm getting at. I was skeptical at first. It seemed like an awful lot of money for some computer cycles, a statistical roll of the dice. But Lindsay was firm." Torvald leaned forward slightly. "You have to understand, she wasn't like other girls. She knew what she wanted. She was never one to settle for second best. She'd had her share of boyfriends, some of them really nice boys. But she seemed to get restless, the relationships didn't last."

The man sat back abruptly. It was by far the longest statement he'd made so far. Lash made a notation, encouragingly, careful not to meet Torvald's eyes. "And?"

"And it was different with Lewis. I could tell from the very first time she mentioned his name. They hit it off from the first date."

Lash looked up just as a faint smile of reminiscence crossed the old man's face. For a moment the sunken eyes brightened, the tense jaw relaxed. "They met for Sunday brunch, then somehow ended up Rollerblading." He shook his head at the memory. "I don't know whose crazy idea that was, neither of them had ever tried it. Maybe it was Eden's suggestion. Anyway, within a month, they were engaged. And it just seemed to get better. Like I said, I've never seen a happier couple. They kept discovering new things. About the world. About each other."

As quickly as it had come, the light left Torvald's face. He pushed his coffee cup away.

"What about Lindsay's daughter? What

kind of an impact did she have on their life?"

Torvald fixed him with a sudden gaze. "She *completed* it, Mr. Berger."

Lash made another notation, a real one this time. The interview was not progressing quite as he'd expected. And the way the man pushed away his cup made Lash think he might be limited to just a few more questions.

"To the best of your knowledge, have there been any recent setbacks in the life of your daughter or her husband?"

"No."

"No unexpected difficulties? No problems?"

Torvald stirred restlessly. "Unless you call the approval of Lewis's grant and the arrival of a beautiful baby girl problems."

"When was the last time you saw your daughter, Mr. Torvald?"

"Two weeks ago."

Lash took a sip of his coffee to conceal his surprise. "Where was this, may I ask?"

"At their house in Flagstaff. I was on my way back from a yacht race in the Gulf of Mexico."

"And how would you characterize the household?"

"I would *characterize* it as perfect."

Lash scribbled another note. "You noticed nothing different from previous visits? No appetite loss or gain, perhaps? Changes in sleep patterns? Lack of energy? Loss of interest in hobbies or personal pursuits?"

"There was no affective disorder, if that's what you're getting at."

Lash paused in his scribbling. "Are you a clinician, Mr. Torvald?"

"No. But before her death, my wife was an occupational therapist. I know the signs of depression when I see them."

Lash put the legal pad to one side. "We're just trying to get a grasp of the situation, sir."

Suddenly, the older man leaned toward Lash, bringing their faces very close. *"Grasp?* Listen. I don't know what you or your firm hope to learn from this. But I think I've answered enough questions. And the fact is there's not a damn thing to grasp. There *is* no answer. Lindsay wasn't suicidal. Neither was Lewis. They had everything to live for, *everything."*

Lash sat silently. This was not just grief he was seeing. This was *need:* a desperate need to understand what could not possibly be understood.

"I'll tell you one thing more," Torvald said, his face still close to Lash's, speaking low and fast now. "I loved my wife. I think we had just about as good a relationship as a married couple could ever hope to have. But I'd have cut off my right arm without a thought if that could've made us as happy as my daughter and Lewis were together."

And with that, the man pushed back, rose from the table, and left the restaurant.

FIVE

Flagstaff, Arizona. Two days later.

The carport was already taken up by two Audi A8s, so Lash left his rented Taurus at the curb and started up the flagstone walk. Brown pine needles crunched underfoot. 407 Cooper Drive was an attractive bungalow with a broad low roof and fenced backyard. Beyond the fence the hillside fell away, revealing a panorama of downtown, faintly blurred by morning mist. Behind and to the north rose the purple-and-brown bulk of the San Francisco Peaks.

Reaching the front door, Lash tucked several large envelopes under one arm and sounded his pocket for the key. He fished it out, white evidence tag dangling from its chain. The chief of the Phoenix field office had been a classmate in the drab gray dorms of Quantico and fellow-sufferer on the obstacle courses of the Yellow Brick Road, and owed him several favors. Lash had turned one of them in for the key to the Thorpes' house.

47

He glanced up, noticing the security camera bolted beneath the eaves. It had been installed by the previous owner of the house and was deactivated for the police investigation. Since the house would go on the market once the investigation was officially closed, the system remained off.

Lash looked down again, fitted the key to the door, and unlocked it with a twist of his hand.

Inside, the house had that peculiar watchful, listening quality he found in homes that had seen unnatural death. The front door opened directly onto the living room, where the bodies had been found. Lash walked forward slowly, looking around, noting the location and quality of the furniture. There was a butternut-colored leather sofa with matching armchairs, an antique armoire, an expensive-looking flatscreen television: clearly, the Thorpes weren't hard up for cash. Two beautiful silk rugs had been arranged over the wall-to-wall carpeting. One still bore powder traces from the medical examiner's team. This unexpected sight stirred memories of the last crime scene he'd witnessed, and he moved quickly onward.

Beyond the living room, a hallway ran the width of the house. To his right was a dining room and kitchen; to his left, what looked like a couple of bedrooms. Lash dropped his envelopes on the sofa and walked down as far as the kitchen. It was as well appointed as the living room. There was another door here, with a view of the narrow side yard and the neighboring house.

Lash moved back up the hallway in the direction of the bedrooms. There was a nursery, all blue taffeta and lace; a master bedroom, its night tables littered with a typical assortment of paperback novels, medicine bottles, and television remotes; and a third room, which was apparently a guest room doubling as a study. He paused at this last room, looking around curiously. Japanese woodblock prints of thinnest rice paper decorated the walls. On a desk sat several framed photographs: Lewis and Lindsay Thorpe, arm in arm in front of a pagoda; the Thorpes again, standing on what looked like the Champs-Elysées. In each photo, the couple was smiling. He'd seen smiles like that before, rarely: simple, unfeigned, undiluted happiness.

He moved to the far wall, which was completely taken up by bookshelves. The Thorpes had been eclectic, voracious readers. Two upper shelves were completely taken up with textbooks in varying degrees of decrepitude; another with trade journals. Below these were several shelves of fiction.

One shelf in particular caught Lash's eye. The books here seemed to be given preferential treatment, bookended by statues of carven jade. He glanced over the titles: *Zen and the Art of Archery*, *Advanced Japanese*, *Two Hundred Poems of the Early T'Ang*. The shelf above it was empty except for an un-framed picture of Lindsay Thorpe riding a merry-go-round, surrounded by children, laughing as she stretched her arm toward the camera. He picked it up. On the back had been scrawled, in a masculine hand:

I wish I were close
To you as the wet skirt of
A salt girl to her body.
I think of you always.

He carefully replaced the photo, exited the study, and returned to the living room.

Outside, the morning mist was quickly burning off, and slanted bars of sunlight now lay across the silk rugs. Lash moved to the leather sofa, pushed the envelopes aside, and sat down. He'd done this many times before, as an agent with the Investigative Support Unit: gone through a house, trying to get a feel for the pathology of its occupants. But that had been very different. He'd been doing criminal personality profiles for NCACP, studying the personal hells of mass mur-derers, serial rapists, "blitz" attackers, socio-paths. People, and houses, who had absolutely nothing in common with the Thorpes.

He'd come here in search of clues to what had gone wrong. Over the last three days, he had performed what clinicians referred to as a psychological autopsy, conducting discreet interviews with family members, friends, doctors, even a minister. And what had at first seemed like an easy case formulation quickly turned otherwise. There were none of the stressors, the risk factors, normally associated with suicide. No history of prior attempts. No history of psychiatric disorders. Nothing that should have triggered one, let alone two, suicides. On the contrary, the Thorpes had everything to live for. And yet, in this very room, they had written a note, tied dry cleaning bags around their heads, embraced on the carpet, and asphyxiated themselves in front of their infant girl.

Lash pulled one of the two envelopes toward him, ripped it open with the edge of a finger, and dumped the contents onto the couch: documentary evidence compiled by the Flagstaff police. There was a thin packet of glossy photographs held together with a clip, and he leafed through them — scene-of-crime photos of the husband and wife, together in death, rigid on the beautiful carpet. He put down the eight-by-tens and picked up a photocopy of the suicide note. It read simply, "Please look after our daughter."

A thicker document lay nearby: the official police incident report. Lash turned its pages slowly. Neither husband nor wife had left the house since the night before their bodies were discovered. The tapes of the external security cameras revealed nobody else had come to the house in the interim. The silent alarm was triggered only by a curious neighbor the next morning. At the back of the report was a transcript of an interview with this neighbor.

OFFICIAL TRANSCRIPT
PROPERTY OF
FLAGSTAFF POLICE DEPARTMENT

Docket:	AR-27
Case No.:	04B-2190
OIC:	Det. Michael Guierrez
Int. Officer:	Sgt. Theodore White
Subj:	Bowman, Maureen A.
Date / Time:	9/17/04 14:22

==================================

EZ-Scrip Transcription Follows

==================================

IO Please make yourself comfortable. My name is Sergeant White, and I'll be conducting the interview. If you would please state your name for the record.

S   Maureen Bowman.

IO Your address, Ms. Bowman?

S   I live at 409 Cooper Drive.

IO How long have you known Lewis and Lindsay Thorpe?

S   Since they moved into the neighborhood. Not all that long, a year and a half, maybe.

IO Did you see much of them?

S   Not really. They were very busy, what with the new baby and all.

IO Did they have many regular visitors?

S   None that I noticed. There were some people from the lab that Lewis was friendly with. I think they came over for a couple of dinner parties. After the baby was born, the grandparents visited a couple of times. Things like that.

IO And how did the Thorpes seem?

S   How do you mean?

IO As neighbors, as a couple. How did they seem?

S   They were always very pleasant.

IO Did you ever observe any problems? Arguments, raised voices, anything of the sort?

S   No, never.

IO Were they ever in any kind of difficulty that you were aware of? Money, for example?

S   No, not that I know. We never really spent that much time together, as I said. They were always very pleasant, very happy. I don't think I've ever seen a couple happier.

IO What, precisely, made you go over to the Thorpe residence this morning?

S The baby.

IO I'm sorry?

S The baby. She was crying, wouldn't stop. The baby had never cried before. I thought maybe something was wrong.

IO Describe, for the tape, what you found, please.

S I — I went in the kitchen door. The baby was there.

IO In the kitchen?

S No, in the hallway. The hallway leading from the dining room.

IO Ms. Bowman, please describe everything you saw and heard. In detail, please.

S Okay. I could see the baby, ahead, past the kitchen. She was screaming, her face was red. There weren't any lights on, but it was a bright morning, I could see everything clearly. There was some kind of opera playing.

IO Playing where?

S On the stereo. But the baby was crying so loudly. I could barely think. I moved ahead to comfort her. That's when the living room came into view. That's when I saw . . . oh, God . . .

10 Take as long as you need, Ms.
   Bowman. You'll find tissue to your
   right, on the table, there.

Lash put the transcript aside. He didn't
need to read any more: he knew exactly what
it was Maureen Bowman saw.

I don't think I've ever seen a couple happier.
It was just about the same thing, word for
word, Lindsay Thorpe's father had told him,
with those hollow, haunted eyes, at the restaurant in New London. The same thing everybody had told him since.

What had gone wrong with this couple?
What had happened?

Lash's experience with pathology had two
very distinct periods: first as a forensic psychologist with the FBI, studying violence
after the fact; and then later, as a specialist
in private practice, working with people to
make sure violence never became a necessary
option. He had worked very hard to keep the
two worlds separate. Yet here in this house
he felt them drawing together.

He dropped his gaze to the other envelope:
the one imprinted *Property of Eden Inc. Proprietary and Confidential.* He unwound the
sealing thread, opened the flap. Inside were
two unlabeled videotapes. Lash slid them out,
balanced one in each hand for a moment.
Then he rose and walked to the television

console. He turned it on, inserted one of the tapes.

A date resolved on the black screen, followed by a long scroll of numbers. And then a face appeared suddenly, larger than life: brown hair, penetrating hazel eyes, handsome. It was Lewis Thorpe, and he was smiling.

The first step in any application to Eden was to sit before a camera and answer two questions. Besides the scant biographical information, these initial tapes of the Thorpes were the only material Mauchly had supplied him with.

Lash turned his attention to the tape. He had watched it and its mate several times before. Here in the Thorpes' own house he would watch them one last time, in hopes the surroundings would somehow render up the connection that so far had eluded him. It seemed a vain hope, but he was running out of options — and spending a lot more time — than he had ever intended.

"Why are you here?" an off-camera voice was asking.

Lewis Thorpe had a frank, disarming smile. "I'm here because something is missing in my life," he said simply.

"Describe one thing you did this morning," the off-camera voice said. "And why you think we should know about it."

Lewis thought for just a moment. "I finished translating a particularly difficult haiku," he said. He waited, as if for a response. When none came, he went on. "I've been translating the work of Bashō, the Japanese poet. People always think translating haiku must be easy, but in fact it's really, really hard. It's so dense, yet so simple. How do you capture that wealth of meaning?" He shrugged at the camera. "It's something I started doing in grad school. I'd taken a lot of Japanese courses, and I was really taken with Bashō's book, *Narrow Road to the Interior*. It's the story of this journey he took through Japan's northern interior four hundred years ago. But, of course, it's also about his own . . . Anyway, it's a short work, laced with haiku. There was one in particular, a famous one, that I struggled with, kept putting off. This morning, on the taxi coming here, I finally finished it. Sounds funny, doesn't it, since it's only, what, nine words long?" He stopped.

It was hard to reconcile the handsome face with that other one, shown in the police photos: the yawning mouth, the wide unseeing eyes, the dark lolling tongue.

Sudden fade to black. Lash withdrew the tape, slotted in the other.

Another scribble of numbers. Then Lindsay Thorpe appeared on the monitor, thin and blonde and deeply tanned. She looked a trifle more nervous than Lewis had. She licked her lips, traced an errant hair away from her eyes with a finger.

57

"Why are you here?" the off-camera voice asked again.

Lindsay paused for a moment, looked away. "Because I know I can do better," she replied after a moment.

"Describe one thing you did this morning. And why you think we should know about it."

Lindsay looked back at the camera. And now she smiled too, displaying perfect, gleaming teeth. "That one's easier. I took the plunge, bought my round-trip ticket to Lucerne. There's this special tour group taking a one-week hike through the Alps. It's kind of expensive, seemed like a bit of an extravagance, especially on top of the fee for . . ." Her smile turned a little shy. "Anyway, I finally decided I was worth it. I recently ended this relationship that just hadn't been working out, and I wanted to get away, maybe get a little perspective on things." She laughed. "So I put the ticket on my Visa this morning. Nonrefundable. I leave the first of next month."

The tape ended. Lash removed it and shut off the player.

Five months after these interviews, the Thorpes were married. They moved here not long after. The most perfect couple anyone could remember.

Lash dropped the tapes into the envelope and started for the door. As he opened it he

58

paused to turn back, asking once again for an answer. When the house remained silent, he shut and locked the door carefully behind him.

SIX

Cruising at thirty-five thousand feet on his way back to New York, Lash inserted his credit card into the seatback slot, plucked the air-to-ground phone from its handset, and stared at it a moment. *What does an expert do when something makes no sense?* he thought. *Simple. You ask another expert.*

His first call was to directory information; the second to a number in Putnam County, New York.

"Weisenbaum Center," came a clipped, efficient voice.

"Dr. Goodkind, please."

"Who may I say is calling?"

"Christopher Lash."

"Just a minute."

Among private psychologists, the Norman J. Weisenbaum Center for Biomedical Research was both revered and envied for the quality of its neurochemical studies. As Lash waited through ethereal, New Age music, he tried to picture the center in his mind. He knew it was located on the Hudson

River about forty-five minutes north of Manhattan. No doubt beautiful, with impeccable architecture: the center was a darling of both hospitals and pharmaceutical companies, and was lavishly funded.

"Chris!" came Goodkind's cheery voice. "I can't believe it. I haven't heard from you in, what, six years?"

"Must be that long."

"How are you enjoying private practice?"

"The hours are better."

"I'll bet. I always wondered when you'd give up riding with the cavalry, settle down in some nice, lucrative town. You're practicing in Fairfield, right?"

"Stamford."

"Yes, of course. Close to Greenwich, Southport, New Canaan. All full of rich, dysfunctional couples, no doubt. Excellent choice." Old U. Penn classmates like Goodkind had been divided in their opinions on Lash joining the FBI. Some seemed envious. Others shook their heads, unable to comprehend why he'd willingly take on such a stressful, physically demanding, potentially dangerous job when his doctorate entitled him to something a lot cushier. When he did leave the FBI, he'd been careful to let them believe greed was the motivating factor — rather than the tragedy that so abruptly ended both his law enforcement career and his marriage.

"You hear much from Shirley?" Goodkind asked.

"Nope."

"Shame you two split up. It didn't have to do with, what, that Edmund Wyre business, did it? I read about that in the paper."

Lash was careful to keep his voice from betraying the pain that, even three years later, mention of that name could evoke. "No, nothing like that."

"Horrible. Horrible. Must've been rough on you."

"Wasn't easy." Lash began to feel sorry he'd called. How could he have forgotten Goodkind's curiosity, his love of prying into the personal affairs of others?

"I picked up that book of yours," Goodkind said. "*Congruency*. Excellent stuff, though of course you were writing for the unwashed."

"I wanted to sell more than a dozen copies."

"And?"

"Sold two dozen, at least."

Goodkind laughed.

"I read your recent article, too," Lash went on. "In the *American Journal of Neurobiology*. 'Cognitive Reappraisal and Agenerative Suicide.' Nicely argued."

"One thing about my position here at the center is I can specialize in the research of my choice."

"I was also interested in some of your other recent papers. 'Reuptake Inhibitors and Elder Suicide,' for example."

"Really?" Goodkind sounded surprised. "I had no idea you were keeping such close tabs."

"I infer from the articles that, in addition to the lab research, you've interviewed quite a number of suicide attempters?"

"Well, I haven't had a chance to talk with too many suicide *completers*." Goodkind chuckled at his little joke.

"Including survivors of double suicides?"

"Of course."

"Then there's something I'm looking into that might interest you. In fact, I could use your advice. These friends of a patient of mine, a couple. Committed double suicide recently."

"Successfully?"

"There are some unusual aspects to the pathology."

"Such as?"

Lash pretended to hesitate. "Well, what if we turned it around, and you speculated — based on your research, of course — what the motivating factors might have been. Perform a psychological autopsy on the couple. I'll fill in the blanks."

There was a brief silence. "Sure, why not. What were their ages?"

"Early thirties."

"Employment history?"

"Stable."

"Psychiatric history? Mood disorders?"

"None known."

"Suicidal ideation?"

"No."

"History of prior attempts?"

"None."

"Substance abuse?"

"The autopsy bloods were clean."

Another pause. "Is this a joke?"

"No. Go on, please."

"The couple's relationship?"

"Warm and loving, by all accounts."

"Major losses of any kind?"

"No."

"Family history?"

"Negative for depression, schizophrenia, any mental illness, in fact."

"Any other life stressors? Significant changes?"

"No."

"Any health issues?"

"Both received glowing physicals within the last six months."

"Anything I should know? Anything at all?"

Lash paused. "They'd recently had a child."

"And?"

"Normal and healthy in every way."

There was a long silence. Then, Lash heard laughter over the line. "This is a joke, right? Because these aren't double suicides you're describing. This is Captain America and Wonder Woman."

"Is that your considered opinion?"

Goodkind's laugh slowly died. "Yes."

"Roger, you've got a unique perspective on suicide. You're a biochemist. You not only talk to suicide attempters, you study their motivation on a molecular level." Lash shifted in his seat. "Is there any commonality among people that might predispose them — no matter how happy they appear — to suicide?"

"You mean, like a suicide gene? I wish it were that easy. There's research that's shown some genes may — *may* — code for depressive tendencies. Just as there are genes that code for heavy eating, sexual preferences, eye or hair color. But predicting suicide? If you're a betting man, stay away from that one. You've got two deeply depressed people. Why does one commit suicide and another doesn't? In the end there's no way to predict. Why did Miami Beach police report a rash of suicides last month, while Minneapolis had a historic dip? Why did Poland have a dramatically high rate of suicide in the year 2000? Sorry, pal. When you get right down to it, it's just a roll of the dice."

Lash ingested this. "A roll of the dice."

"Take it from an expert, Chris. And you can quote me on that."

SEVEN

After the dry high-altitude air of Flagstaff, New York City felt damp and miserable. Lash wore a heavy raincoat as he approached the reception desk in Eden's lobby for the second time in five days.

"Christopher Lash to see Edwin Mauchly," he told a tall, thin man behind the counter.

The man tapped a few keys. "Do you have an appointment, sir?" he asked with a smile.

"I left him a message. He'll be expecting me."

"One moment, please."

As he waited, Lash turned to gaze around him. There was something different about the lobby today, but he wasn't quite sure what it was. Then he realized there was no line of prospective applicants this morning. The twin escalators leading to Application Processing were empty. Instead, a smaller flow of traffic was headed for the security checkpoint. They were all couples, many hand in hand. Unlike the anxious, hopeful faces he'd seen his last visit, these people were smiling, laughing, chattering loudly. After showing laminated cards at the checkpoint, the couples moved on to a large set of doors and vanished out of sight.

"Dr. Lash?" the man at the desk said.

Lash turned back. "Yes?"

"Mr. Mauchly is waiting for you." The man slid a small ivory passcard emblazoned with Eden's infinity logo across the desk. "Please show this at the elevator station. Have a pleasant day."

When the elevator doors opened onto the thirty-second floor, Mauchly was waiting. He nodded to Lash, then led the way down the corridor to his office.

Director of Facilitation Services, Lash recalled as he followed Mauchly. *Whatever the hell is that?* Aloud, he asked: "Why all the happy faces?"

"Sorry?"

"Downstairs, in the lobby. Everybody was grinning as if they'd won the lottery or something."

"Ah. Today is class reunion."

"Class reunion?"

"That's our term for it. Part of our client contract calls for a mandatory six-month re-valuation of the couples we've brought together. They return for a day of one-on-one sessions, encounter groups, the like. For the most part, quite informal. Our researchers find the back-end data helpful in refining the selection process. And it allows us to watch for any signs of incompatibility, warning signals, between couples."

"Seen any?"

"None to date." Mauchly opened the door, ushered Lash inside. If he was curious, it did not show in his dark eyes. "Would you care for any refreshment?"

"No thanks." Lash slipped his satchel from his arm and took the indicated chair.

Mauchly sat down behind his desk. "We didn't expect to hear from you so soon."

"That's because there's not much to tell."

Mauchly raised his eyebrows.

Lash leaned over, unfastened his satchel, and pulled out a document. He straightened its edges, then placed it on the desk.

"What is that, Dr. Lash?" Mauchly asked.

"My report."

Mauchly made no move to pick it up. "Perhaps you could summarize it for me."

Lash took a deep breath. "There are no indicators for suicide in either Lewis or Lindsay Thorpe. None at all."

Mauchly folded one muscular arm over the other, waited.

"I've spoken to family, friends, doctors. I've examined their credit histories, financial records, employment status. I've called in favors from federal and local law enforcement. This was as functional, stable a couple — a *family* — as you'll ever find. They could have

68

been poster children for that wall of happy faces down in your lobby."

"I see." Mauchly's lips pursed into what might have been a frown. "Perhaps there were prior indicators that —"

"I looked there, too. I checked school records, interviewed teachers, spoke with former classmates. Nothing. And no psychiatric history, either. In fact, the only hospital visit was by Lewis, who broke a leg skiing in Aspen eight years ago."

"Then what is your professional opinion?"

"People don't just commit suicide for no reason. Especially double suicide. There's something missing here."

"Are you implying —"

"I'm not implying anything. The police report reads suicide. What I mean is, I don't have enough *information* to form an opinion on why they did what they did."

Mauchly glanced at the report. "It appears you've done a thorough investigation."

"What I need is in this building. Your evaluations of the Thorpes might give me the psychological data I need."

"You must know that's out of the question. Our data is confidential. Trade secrets are involved."

"I've already signed a nondisclosure agreement."

"Dr. Lash, it's not my call to make. Besides, it's unlikely you'd find anything in our test results you have not already found on your own."

"Perhaps. Perhaps not. That's why I've also prepared this." Lash withdrew a small envelope and placed it atop the sheaf of papers.

Mauchly cocked his head inquiringly.

"It's a breakdown of my expenses. Time billed at my usual consultation rate of $300 an hour. I didn't charge overtime. Airplane tickets, hotel rooms, rental cars, meals, it's all there. Just a shade over $14,000. If you'll initial the amount, I'll write you out a check for the balance."

"What balance would that be?"

"The rest of the hundred thousand you gave me."

Mauchly reached for the envelope, withdrew the folded sheet inside. "I'm not sure I understand."

"It's quite simple. Without more information from you, there's nothing I can say except Lewis and Lindsay Thorpe were just as perfect a couple as your computer thought they were. I didn't earn a hundred thousand to tell you that."

Mauchly studied the paper for a moment. Then he replaced it in the envelope and put it back on the table. "Dr. Lash, would you excuse me for just a moment?"

"Of course."

Mauchly stood and, with a polite nod, left the room, closing the door behind him.

It was perhaps ten minutes before Lash heard the door open again. He turned to see Mauchly standing in the corridor.

"This way, if you please," he said.

Mauchly led Lash to a new elevator. It descended briefly, then opened onto a featureless corridor. The walls, floor, and ceiling were all painted the same shade of pale violet. Mauchly led the way down the corridor, then stopped to open a door the same color as the walls and ceiling. He gestured Lash to enter first.

The space beyond was long and dimly lit. From a narrow floor, the walls angled outward at a forty-five-degree angle to waist level, where they became abruptly vertical. It felt to Lash like staring down a funnel.

"What kind of place is this?" he asked, walking forward.

Mauchly closed the door and pressed a button on a nearby control panel.

There was a low whirring noise, and Lash took an involuntary step toward the center. On both sides, a dark curtain drew back along the angled walls at his feet. And now Lash realized that they were not walls at all, but windows, looking down into two large rooms: one to his left, the other to his right. They were standing on a catwalk, suspended above and between the two identical rooms: conference rooms containing large, oval tables. Perhaps a dozen people were seated around each. There was no sound but Lash could see from their gestures they were talking animatedly.

"What the hell —" he began.

Mauchly gave a dry laugh. Yellow light from the conference rooms lit his face from below, giving his smile a disconcerting cast. "Listen," he said, pressing another button.

The room was suddenly filled with a babel of voices. Mauchly turned to the panel, adjusted a knob, and the volume decreased.

Lash realized he was hearing the conversations of the people in the room below. Another moment and he realized they were all couples who had been brought together by Eden. They were joking, sharing reminiscences about the experience.

"I've told seven, maybe eight friends about it," a man was saying. He was in his early forties, black, wearing a dark suit. A woman was sitting close beside him, head resting on his shoulder. "Three have already applied. A couple more are saving up. One of them's even thinking of turning in his Saab for a used Honda to raise the fee. That's desperation."

"We haven't told anybody," said a young woman across the table. "We like keeping it a secret."

"It's a blast," her husband added. "People are always telling us how great we are for each other. Just last night a couple of the guys cornered me at the gym. They complained their wives were all bitches, wondered how I was lucky enough to find the last nice girl on Long Island." He laughed. "How could I tell them Eden brought us together? It's too much fun taking the credit myself."

This brought a burst of assenting laughter from the group.

Mauchly reached for the dial again, and the laughter faded out. "Dr. Lash, I believe you feel I'm being intentionally coy about all this. That is not the case. It's not that we don't trust you. It's simply that secrecy is the only way to protect our service. There are any number of would-be competitors who will do *whatever* it takes to obtain our testing techniques, our evaluation algorithms, anything. And remember, the secrecy is not just for *us*." He gestured toward the other room below them, turned another knob.

". . . if I'd known just what was in store for me, I don't know if I'd have had the *cojones* to take that eval," a tall, athletic-looking man in a crewneck sweater was saying. "It was a brutal day. But now that it's seven months behind me, I know it was the best thing I ever did."

"I went to a typical online dating service once, a couple of years back," another added. "Couldn't have been more unlike Eden. Crude. Low-tech. They only asked a few questions. And guess what the first one was: Are you interested in a casual or a serious relationship? Can you believe it? I was so insulted I walked out the door right then!"

"I'll be paying off the loan for years," said a woman. "But I'd have paid twice as much. It's like they say on that wall in the lobby. What price can you put on happiness?"

"Anybody here ever fight?" somebody else asked.

"We disagree," a silver-haired woman at the far end responded. "Wouldn't be human if we didn't. But it just helps us learn more about each other, respect each other's needs."

Mauchly turned off the sound again. "You see? It's for *them*, as well. Eden provides a service nobody's ever dreamed of before. We can't take any chance, no matter how small, of compromising that service." He paused. "Now listen. I'm bringing in someone you can talk to, ask a few questions. But you must understand, Dr. Lash: *he doesn't know.* Morale at Eden is exceptionally high. People are very proud of the service they provide. We cannot undermine that, even with an unrelated tragedy. Understood?"

Lash nodded.

As if on cue, a door opened at the far end of the room and a figure in a white lab coat stepped forward.

"Peter, there you are," Mauchly said. "Come and meet Christopher Lash. He's doing some random follow-up checks on a few of our clients. For statistical purposes."

The man came forward with a shy smile. He was little more than a youth, really. There was an abundance of carrot-colored hair above his forehead that bobbed slightly as he shook Lash's hand.

"This is Peter Hapwood. He's the evaluation engineer that did the one-on-one with the Thorpes when they came back for their class reunion." Mauchly turned to Hapwood. "Do you remember Lewis and Lindsay Thorpe?"

Hapwood nodded. "The supercouple."

"Yes. The supercouple." Mauchly turned his hand toward Lash, palm extended, as if inviting questions.

"In the one-on-one with the Thorpes," Lash asked the young engineer, "did anything stand out in particular?"

"No, nothing. Not that I can remember."

"How did they seem?"

"They seemed happy, like everybody else on their return interview."

"How many couples have you interviewed? On their six-month return, I mean?"

Hapwood thought a moment. "A thousand. Maybe twelve hundred."

"And they've all been happy?"

"Without exception. After all this time, it still seems uncanny." Hapwood shot a quick look at Mauchly, as if wondering whether he'd said something inappropriate.

"Did the Thorpes say anything about their lives since meeting each other?"

"Let me think. No. Yes. They'd recently moved to Flagstaff, Arizona. I remember Mr. Thorpe saying he was having a little trouble with the altitude — he was a jogger, as I recall — but they both loved the area."

"Anything else come up in the questions?"

"Not really. I just went through the standard question set. Nothing got flagged."

"What standard set is that?"

"Well, we start with the mood-setting items, just to establish a comfort level, by —"

"I don't think such specifics are necessary," Mauchly said. "Any other questions?"

Lash felt the opportunity slipping away from him. And yet there were no other questions left. "You don't recall anything they said, or mentioned, out of the ordinary? Anything at all?"

"No," Hapwood replied. "Sorry."

Lash's shoulders sagged. "Thanks."

Mauchly nodded at Hapwood, who headed for the far door. Halfway there, he stopped.

"She hated opera," he said.

Lash looked at him. "What?"

"Ms. Thorpe. When they came into the consultation room, she apologized for being late. On the way here, she refused to take the first cab they hailed because the driver was blaring opera from his radio. She said she couldn't stand it. Took them ten minutes to find another." He shook his head at the memory. "They were laughing about it."

He nodded to Lash, then Mauchly, and left the room.

Mauchly turned, spectral in the glow of the rooms below, and raised a bulky manila envelope. "The results of the Thorpes' inkblot tests, administered during their evaluations. It's the only test we give that isn't proprietary, that's why I am able to share it."

"Big of you." Frustration gave an edge to Lash's voice he didn't intend.

Mauchly regarded him mildly. "You must understand, Dr. Lash. Our interest in what happened to the Thorpes is as a case study only. This is a tragic event, one that's especially painful to us because a supercouple was involved. But it's an isolated occurrence." He handed the folder to Lash. "Look these over at your convenience. It's our hope you'll continue to investigate, search for any personality issues we should keep in mind for future evaluations. But if you still want to quit the job, we'll accept the brief you've already prepared. In any case, the money is yours to keep." He gestured toward the door. "And now, with your permission, I'll see you back to the lobby."

EIGHT

The afternoon shadows were lengthening when Lash pulled into the Greenwich Audubon Center, parked, and started down the wood-chipped path leading to Mead Lake. He had the place to himself: the school groups had left hours before, and the weekend birders and nature photographers wouldn't gather until the weekend. The dampness of the morning had given way to limpid sunlight. Around him, open woodlands melted away into fastnesses of green and brown. The air was heavy with the scent of moss. As he walked, the traffic on Riversville Road grew fainter. Within minutes, it was replaced entirely by birdsong.

He had left the offices of Eden Incorporated intending to drive straight back to his Stamford office. The week he'd allowed for this assignment was up, and he now had to decide what, if anything, was to be done about next week's arrangements. But halfway home he'd found himself leaving the New England Thruway and driving, almost aimlessly, through the shady lanes of Darien, Silvermine, New Canaan, the stomping grounds of his youth. The Thorpes' inkblot tests lay, untouched, in an envelope on the passenger seat. He'd driven on, letting the car decide where to go. And it ended up here, at the nature preserve.

It seemed as good a place as any.

Ahead of him the pathway forked, leading to a series of bird blinds overlooking the lake. Lash selected one at random, climbed the short ladder into the boxlike structure. Inside it was warm and dark. A long horizontal slit at the rear offered a clandestine view of the lake. Lash peered out at the waterbirds, ducking and bobbing, oblivious to his presence. Then he took a seat on the wooden bench and placed the bulky manila envelope beside him.

He did not open it right away. Instead, he reached into a jacket pocket and pulled out a tiny volume: *Narrow Road to the Interior*, by Matsuo Bashō. He'd seen copies for sale on the counter of a Starbucks in Sky Harbor International, and the coincidence seemed too great not to pick one up. He thumbed through the translator's introduction, found the opening lines.

The moon and sun are eternal travelers. Even the years wander on. A lifetime adrift in a boat, or in old age leading a tired horse into the years, every day is a journey, and the journey itself is home.

He put the book aside. What had Lewis Thorpe said about the poetry of Bashō: so dense, yet so simple? Something like that.

Lash had many professional rules, but the preeminent one was Keep your distance from your patients. It was a rule he'd learned the hard way, profiling at the FBI. So why had he allowed himself to become so fascinated with Lewis and Lindsay Thorpe? Was it simply the mystifying nature of their deaths? Or was there some special allure in the perfection of their marriage? Because by every account he'd been able to obtain, their marriage had, in fact, been perfect — right up to the moment they put dry-cleaning bags over their heads, embraced, and slowly lost consciousness in front of their infant daughter.

Normally, Lash did not permit personal introspection. It led nowhere, dulled his objectivity. But he decided to allow himself another observation. He had not chosen this place at random, after all. This sanctuary, this pathway — and, in fact, this very blind — had been the spot where, three years before, Shirley said she never wanted to see him again.

Every day is a journey, and the journey itself is home. Lash wondered what kind of a journey the Thorpes had embarked on. Or for that matter, what kind of a journey he himself was undertaking to discover their secret. It was a journey his better judgment told him to resist even as his feet led him farther down the path.

He passed his hand wearily across his eyes, reached for the bulky envelope, and tore it open with a tug of his index finger.

Inside were just over a hundred sheets of paper: the results of Lewis and Lindsay Thorpe's inkblot tests, administered by Eden during their application process.

As a high school student, Lash had been fascinated by inkblots; by the idea that seeing objects in random smudges could say something about you. It wasn't until graduate school, when he studied test administration — and took the test himself, as all psych students were required to do — that he realized how profound a tool of psychodiagnosis it could be. Inkblots were known as "projective" tests because — unlike highly structured, objective written tests like the WAIS or MMPI — the concept of right and wrong was ambiguous. Looking for images in an inkblot required bringing deeper, complex areas of personality to bear.

Eden used the Hirschfeldt test, a choice Lash wholeheartedly approved. Though indirectly based on Exner's refinement of the original Rorschach, the Hirschfeldt test had several advantages. There were only ten Rorschach inkblots, and these were kept secret by psychologists: it would be easy for a person to memorize the "right" responses to such a small number of blots. Each administration of the Hirschfeldt test, on the other hand, drew from a catalogue of five hundred catalogued blots — far too many to memorize. Thirty blots were shown, rather than ten, generating a deeper response pool from the subject. Unlike the Rorschach, where half of the inkblots were in color, all of the blots in the Hirschfeldt test were black and white; its supporters thought color to be an unimportant distraction.

Lindsay Thorpe's test results came first. Lash paused a moment to imagine her in the examination room. It would be quiet, comfortable, free of distraction. The test administrator would be sitting slightly behind her; face-to-face examinations were to be avoided. Lindsay Thorpe would not see the inkblots until the moment the examiner laid them upon the table before her.

The ground rules of the test were as guarded as the blots themselves. Any question she asked would be met with a preformulated response. Lindsay would not know that *everything* she said about the blots, relevant or not, would be written down and scored. She would not know that her responses were being timed with a silent watch:

the quicker her responses, the better. She would not know that she was supposed to see more than one thing in each card; seeing only one was suggestive of neurosis. And she wouldn't know that — though the test administrator would deny it if asked — each card *did* in fact have a "normal" response. If you saw something original, and could justify it, you'd get points for creativity. But seeing something nobody else saw in an inkblot usually implied psychosis.

Lash turned to the first blot. Below it, the administrator had recorded Lindsay's responses verbatim.

1 of 30   Card 142

Free Association:
1. It looks like a body. Those white things in the middle look like lungs, kind of.
2. This thing at the bottom looks like an upside-down pelvic bone.
3. ⬇ It looks kind of like a mask. Yes, a mask.

4. And, down at the bottom, there's a little bat.

Inquiry:
1. (Repeats.)
2. (Repeats.)
3. Yes, a mask. Those two white blobs at the top are the eyes. The blobs in the middle are the nose, and the one at the bottom is the mouth. It's creepy, like a devil mask.
4. Down at the bottom, a bat. You can see the two leathery ears, the out-stretched wings. It looks like it's flying.

There were two steps to viewing each card: a free-association phase, where the subject stated his or her first impressions of the card, and an inquiry phase, where the examiner would ask the subject to justify their impressions. Lash noticed, from the arrow marked on the third free association, that Lindsay had on her own volition turned the card upside down and kept it that way. That was a sign of independent thinking: if you asked whether you could turn the card over, you got a lower score. Lash recognized this blot, and Lindsay had hit most of the typical responses: a mask, a bat. No doubt the examiner would have noted Lindsay's reference to the devil, an extraneous remark that would need to be scored.

The next sheet in the pile was the examiner's scoring sheet for this first card:

Card	No.	Loc.	Resp. #	Determinants	Form Factor	Specials
1	1	B S	6	H1, M+	OK	
	2	D	21	H, Ma-	OK	
	3	B S	1	I, Ffr2	OK	MOR
	4	D	4	Am, A-, (If)	OK	

Lash quickly reviewed the way Lindsay's four responses had been typed and scored. The examiner had done a thorough job. Despite the years since he'd last administered a Hirschfeldt test, the arcane codes came back to him: *B* stood for a response encompassing the whole blot; *D* for a response to a commonly noted detail. Human and animal forms, anatomy, nature, and the rest were all noted. In all four responses, Lindsay's form factors had been marked OK: a good sign. She saw more images in the white spaces than usual, but not enough to cause any concern. In the "specials" category — where examiners listed deviant verbalizations and other no-nos — Lindsay received only one mark, MOR, for morbid content: no doubt for her characterization of the image as a "devil mask" and "scary."

He moved on to the second blot:

Again, the examiner had carefully listed Lindsay's responses.

Free Association:
5.   It looks like a Christmas ornament.
6.   Those things at the top are like pairs of insect antennae.
7.   ↓ From this angle, the antennae look like crab legs.

Inquiry:
5.   Well, it's rounded like those ornaments that hang from the boughs. Right? The part at the top is where the hook goes.
6.   Yes. They're feathered with papillae, like the antennae of certain insect species.
7.   (Repeats.)

Again, Lash recognized this blot. Lindsay Thorpe's responses were all within normal.

Lash looked back idly at the blot. Suddenly, he stiffened. Completely unexpectedly, a series of associations flashed through his own mind as he stared: a quickly spreading sea of red across a white carpet; a dripping kitchen knife; the grinning mask of Edmund Wyre, handcuffed and in leg irons, as he was arraigned before a sea of shocked faces.

God damn Roger Goodkind and his curiosity, Lash thought as he put the blot quickly aside.

He leafed brusquely through the other twenty-eight blots, finding nothing out of the ordinary. Lindsay was characterized as a well-adjusted, intelligent, creative, rather ambitious person. He knew this already. The faint hope that had again stirred within him began to fade.

There was still one more item to examine. He turned to the structural summary page, where all Lindsay Thorpe's scores were put through a series of ratios, frequency analyses, and other algebraic convolutions to determine particular personality traits. One of these sets of traits was known as "special indications," and it was to this Lash turned his attention.

Section VIII. Special Indications (H. 28)

H.28a.	SZ	— (1/10)
H.28b.	HVG	— (3/12)
H.28c.	S-Cluster	— (0/8)
H.28d.	RH-2	— (0/9)
H.28e.	MRZ	— (1/15)
H.28f.	N-Calc	— (2/11)
H.28g.	PS-Neg	— (0/8)

The special indications were red flags. If more than a set number of responses fell under a specific indicator — SZ for schizophrenia, for example — it was flagged positive. One of the special indications, S-Cluster, measured suicide potential.

Lindsay Thorpe's S-Cluster showed negative; in fact, she was coded as displaying zero out of eight possible suicide indicators.

With a sigh, Lash put Lindsay's results aside and picked up her husband's.

He had just finished ascertaining that Lewis Thorpe's suicide cluster was as low as Lindsay's when a beep sounded from his jacket pocket. Lash drew out his cell phone. "Yes?"

"Dr. Lash? It's Edwin Mauchly."

Lash felt mild surprise. He didn't give out his cell number to anybody, and he certainly didn't recall giving it to Eden.

"Where are you right now?" Mauchly's voice sounded different: clipped, brusque.

"Greenwich. Why?"

"It's happened again."

"What's happened?"

"There's been another one. Another double-suicide attempt. A supercouple."

"*What?*" Surprise vanished beneath a wave of disbelief.

"The couple's name is Wilner. Larchmont residents. They're en route to Southern Westchester now. From your location, you should be able to make it in —" there was a brief pause "— fifteen minutes. I wouldn't waste any time."

And the line went dead.

NINE

Southern Westchester County Medical Center was a cluster of brick buildings on the outskirts of Rye, just over the New York border. As Lash screeched into the ambulance entrance, he could see that the ER was unusually quiet. Just two vehicles sat together in the shadows beyond the glass admitting doors. One was an ambulance; the other a long, low, hearse-like vehicle bearing the seal of the county medical examiner. The rear doors of the ambulance were open, and as Lash trotted across the blacktop he glanced toward it. An EMS technician was at work with a bucket and sanitizer, swabbing the interior. Even from twenty yards Lash caught the coppery tang of blood.

The smell brought him up short, and he glanced hesitantly up at the building's dark-red bulk. He had not been inside an emergency room in three years. Then, recalling the urgency in Mauchly's voice, he forced himself forward once again.

The waiting area seemed subdued. Half a

dozen people sat in plastic chairs, staring vacantly at walls or filling out forms. A small knot of policemen stood in one corner, talking among themselves in low tones. Quickly, Lash headed for the door marked SQUAD ROOM, opened it, felt along the wall for the button that opened the automatic doors into the emergency room.

The doors whispered open onto a far different scene. Several orderlies were at work, scrambling with equipment trays. A nurse walked by, liters of blood clutched in her arms. Another followed with a crash cart. Three EMS technicians were standing at the nurses' station, not speaking. They looked dazed. Two were still wearing pale-green gloves heavily smeared with blood.

Lash scanned the area for a familiar face. Almost instantly he spotted the chief resident, Alfred Chen, walking toward him. Normally, Chen moved with the slow, stately grace of a prophet, a smile on his Buddha-like face. Tonight, Chen was moving quickly, and the smile was gone.

The resident's eyes were on a metal clipboard in his hands, and he didn't bother looking up at Lash. As Chen passed, Lash stuck out an arm. "Alfred. How's it going?"

Chen stared blankly for a moment. "Oh. Chris. Hi." The smile made a brief appearance. "Could be better. Listen, I —"

"I'm here to see the Wilner couple."

Chen looked surprised. "That's where I'm headed. Follow me."

Lash swung in beside the resident.

"Are they patients of yours?" Chen asked.

"Prospective."

"How'd you hear about it so fast? They just got here five minutes ago."

"What happened?"

"Suicide pact, according to police. Pretty thorough job of it, too. Radial vein, opened lengthwise from wrist to forearm."

"In the bath?"

"That's the strange part. They were found in bed together. Fully clothed."

Lash felt the muscles of his jaw tighten. "Who found them?"

"Blood came through the ceiling of the condo below theirs, and the owner called the police. They must have been there for hours."

"What's their condition?"

"John Wilner bled out," Chen puffed. "Dead on the scene. His wife is alive, but just barely."

"Any kids?"

"No." Chen glanced down at the sheet. "But Karen Wilner is five months pregnant."

Ahead, the nurse with the crash cart disappeared behind a drawn curtain. Chen followed, Lash at his heels.

The space beyond was so crowded that at first Lash could not see the bed. Somewhere, an EKG was bleating out a dangerously fast pulse. There was a torrent of voices, talking over each other, calm but urgent.

"Heartbeat's at 120, out of sinus tach," a woman said.

"Systolic's at 70."

An alarm sounded abruptly, adding its drone to the babel.

"Hang more plasma!" This voice was louder, more insistent.

Lash slipped along behind the blue-garbed figures, back against the curtain, working toward the head of the bed. As he squeezed into position between two racks of diagnostic equipment, Karen Wilner finally became visible.

She was like alabaster, so pale Lash could see an incredible tracery of starved veins around her neck, across her breasts, down the sweep of her arms. Her blouse and bra had been cut away, and her torso swabbed clean, but she was still wearing a skirt and it was here the whiteness ended. The fabric was soaked through with blood. Twin IVs, turned wide open, were notched into her inner elbows: one of plasma, the other of saline. Below these, tourniquets were placed around her forearms, and doctors were at work, trying to suture the ruined veins.

"We've got vasospasm," said a nurse, one hand to the patient's forehead. Karen Wilner's eyes remained closed, and she did not respond to the pressure of the nurse's hand.

Lash slipped in closer, knelt down beside the motionless face.

"Ms. Wilner," he murmured. "Why? Why did you do it?"

"What are you doing?" the nurse demanded. "Who is this guy?"

The bleat of the EKG machine had slowed to a lazy, irregular rhythm. "Bradycardia!" a voice called. "Pressure's down to 45 over 20."

Lash drew closer. "Karen," he said, more urgently. "I need to know why. *Please*."

"Christopher, move away," Dr. Chen warned from the far side of the bed.

The woman's eyes fluttered open; closed; opened again. They were dry and even paler than her skin.

"Karen," Lash repeated, placing a hand on her shoulder. It felt like marble.

"Make it stop," she said, the words more breath than voice.

"Make what stop?" Lash said.

"That sound," the woman replied, almost inaudibly. "That sound in my head."

Her eyes slipped closed again, and her head lolled to one side.

"We're losing her!" a nurse cried.

"What sound?" Lash said, bending closer. "Karen, *what sound?*"

He felt a hand land on his shoulder, pull him back. "Away from the bed, mister," said an orderly. His eyes glittered black above the white gauze of his mask.

Lash retreated between the racks of equipment. The EKG was now droning a high, incessant note. The nurse scrambled forward with the crash cart.

"Charged?" asked Dr. Chen as he took the paddles.

"One hundred joules."

"Back!" called Chen.

Lash watched Karen Wilner's body stiffen as electricity coursed through it. The driplines hanging from the IV racks whipsawed violently back and forth.

"Again!" Chen cried, paddles raised in the air. For a moment, his gaze met Lash's own. Brief as it was, the glance said everything.

With one final, searching look at Karen Wilner, Lash turned and left the emergency bay.

TEN

This time, when Edwin Mauchly ushered
Lash into the Eden boardroom, the table was
full. Lash recognized some of the faces:
Harold Perrin, ex-chairman of the Federal
Reserve Board; Caroline Long of the Long
Foundation. Others were unfamiliar. But it
was clear the entire board of Eden Incorporated was assembled before him. The only
person missing was the company's reclusive
founder, Richard Silver: although the man
had rarely been photographed in recent years,
it was clear none of the faces assembled here
belonged to him. Some looked at Lash with
curiosity; others with grave concern; still
others with an expression that was probably
hope.

John Lelyveld sat in the same chair he'd
occupied at the first meeting. "Dr. Lash."
And he waved at the sole vacant seat.
Mauchly quietly closed the door to the
boardroom and stood before it, arms behind
his back.

The chairman turned to a woman at his

right. "Stop the transcription, if you please, Ms. French." Then he looked back at Lash. "Would you care for anything? Coffee, tea?"

"Coffee, thanks." Lash studied Lelyveld's face as the man made brisk introductions. The benevolent, almost grandfatherly manner of the prior meeting was gone. Now the Eden chairman seemed formal, preoccupied, a little distant. *This is no longer a coincidence,* Lash thought, *and he knows it.* Directly or indirectly, Eden was involved.

The coffee arrived and Lash accepted it gratefully: there had been no time for sleep the night before.

"Dr. Lash," Lelyveld said. "I think everyone would be more comfortable if we got straight to the matter at hand. I realize you haven't had much time, but I wonder if you could bring us up to speed on anything you've learned, and whether —" he paused to glance around the table "— whether there's any explanation."

Lash sipped his coffee. "I've spoken with the coroner and local law enforcement. On the face of it, everything still points to the original conclusion of double suicide."

Lelyveld frowned. Several chairs away, a man who'd been introduced as Gregory Minor, executive vice president, moved restlessly in his seat. He was younger than Lelyveld, black-haired, with an intelligent, penetrating gaze. "What about the Wilners themselves?" he asked. "Any indications to explain this?"

"None. It's just like the Thorpes. The Wilners had everything going for them. I talked to an emergency room intern who knew the couple. They had great jobs: John an investment banker, Karen a university librarian. She was pregnant with their first child. No history of depression or anything else. No apparent financial difficulties, no family tragedies of any kind. The autopsy bloods were clean. It will take a thorough investigation to be certain, but there seems no evidence to indicate suicidal tendencies."

"Except the bodies," Minor said.

"The evaluator at their class reunion here made a similar report. They seemed just as happy as the rest of the couples." Lelyveld glanced at Lash. "You used the phrase 'on the face of it.' Care to elaborate?"

Lash took another sip of coffee. "It's obvious the suicides in Flagstaff and Larchmont are related. We're not dealing with coincidence. And so we need to treat these incidents as what, at Quantico, we termed 'equivocal death.' "

"Equivocal death?" Caroline Long sat to his right, her blond hair almost colorless in the artificial light. "Explain, please."

"It's a type of analysis the Bureau pioneered twenty years ago. We know the victims, we know how they died, but we don't yet know the *manner* of death. In this case, double suicide, suicide-homicide — or homicide."

"Homicide?" said Minor. "Just a minute. You said the police are treating these deaths as suicides."

"I know."

"And everything you've observed agrees with that finding."

"That's correct. I mention equivocal death because what we have is an enigma. Every *physical* sign points to suicide. But every *psychological* sign points away from it. So we can't close our minds to any possibility."

He looked around the table. When nobody spoke, he went on.

"What are those possibilities? If we're dealing with homicide, then it has to be somebody who knew both couples. A rejected suitor, perhaps? Or somebody who was rejected as an Eden client by your winnowing process and now holds a grudge?"

"Impossible," Minor said. "Our records are kept under the most stringent security. No rejected applicant knows the identities or addresses of our clients."

"They could have met in the lobby, the day they both applied. Or one of the couples could have bragged about their experience at Eden to the wrong person."

Lelyveld shook his head slowly. "I don't think so. Our security and confidentiality procedures begin the moment somebody steps into the building. They're transparent for the most part, but they would forestall the kind of casual interaction you describe. As for the other, we caution our couples against any boastfulness. It's one of the things we monitor at the class reunions. And both the Thorpes and the Wilners were discreet about how they met."

Lash drained his coffee. "All right, then. Back to suicide. Maybe there's something inherently wrong with the makeup of a supercouple. Some psychopathology in the relationship, but very deep and subtle, something that wouldn't show up in the usual screenings at your — what do you call them? — class reunions."

"That's nonsense," said Minor.

"Nonsense?" Lash raised his eyebrows. "Nature abhors perfection, Mr. Minor. Show me a rose without at least a minor blemish. Pure gold is so soft as to be unworkable, useless. Only fractals are perfect, and even they are fundamentally asymmetrical."

"I think what Greg means is that, even if such a thing were possible, we would have learned about it," Lelyveld said. "Our psychological assets run extremely deep. Such a phenomenon would have been picked up in our evaluations."

"It's just a theory. In any case, homicide or suicide, Eden is the key. It's the one thing, the *only* thing, these couples have in common. So I need to understand the process better. I want to see what the Thorpes saw, what the Wilners saw, as your clients. I want to know just how they were selected as perfect couples. And I'll need access — *unrestricted* access — to their files."

This time, Gregory Minor rose to his feet. "That's out of the question!" He turned to Lelyveld. "You know I've had reservations from the first, John. Bringing in somebody from the outside is dangerous, destabilizing. It was one thing when we were dealing with an isolated incident, something that affected us tangentially. But with what happened last night — well, the security risk is too great."

"It's too late," Caroline Long replied. "The risk goes beyond company secrets now. You of all people, Gregory, should understand that."

"Then forget security for the moment. It just doesn't make sense bringing somebody like Lash inside the Wall. You read his jacket, that messy business just before he left the FBI. We have a hundred psychologists on staff already, all with impeccable credentials. Think of the time and effort it would take to get him up to speed. And for what? Nobody knows why these people died. Who's to say there's reason to think it will happen again?"

"You want to take that chance?" Lash retorted angrily. "Because there's one thing I can tell you with absolute certainty. You've caught a huge break. These two double suicides happened *on different coasts*. And in the case of the Wilners particularly, so close to home, you've managed to keep things low key, out of the press. So nobody's picked up on the coincidence. But if a *third* couple decides to go out the same way, there won't be a chance in hell of keeping your precious company out of the news."

He sat back, breathing heavily. He raised his coffee cup, remembered it was empty, set it back down again.

"I fear Dr. Lash is right," Lelyveld said, his voice soft. "We must understand what's going on and put a stop to it, one way or another — not just for the sake of the Thorpes and the Wilners, but for Eden as well." He glanced at Minor. "Greg, I think Dr. Lash's objectivity here is an asset rather than a liability. He may not yet understand the process, but he comes to it with a fresh eye. Of the dozen candidates we considered, he has the best qualifications. We already have his confidentiality agreement on file. I say we put bringing him inside to a vote." He took a sip from a glass of water by his elbow, then raised his hand into the silence.

Slowly, another hand went up; then another, and another. Soon, all hands had been raised except those of Gregory Minor and another man in a dark suit beside him.

"The motion is passed," Lelyveld said. "Dr. Lash, Edwin here will get the process started for you."

Lash stood up.

But Lelyveld wasn't through. "You're being given unprecedented access to Eden's inner workings. You've requested — and been granted — a chance to do what nobody with your knowledge has done before: experience the process as an actual applicant. You'd do well to remember the old saying Be careful what you wish for."

Lash nodded, turned away.

"And Dr. Lash?" Lelyveld's voice came again.

Lash turned back to face the chairman.

"Work quickly. Quickly."

As Mauchly opened the door, Lash heard Lelyveld say, "You may resume transcribing the minutes of the meeting, Ms. French."

ELEVEN

Kevin Connelly walked across the broad blacktop lot of the Stoneham Corporate Center, making for his car. It was a Mercedes S-class, low-slung and silver, and Connelly was careful to park it far from other vehicles: it was worth the extra walk to avoid dings and scratches.

He unlocked the door, opened it, and slid onto the black leather. Connelly loved fine cars, and everything about the Mercedes — the solid thunk of the door, the cradling sensation of the seat, the low throb of the engine — gave him pleasure. The AMG performance package had been worth every penny of the twenty grand it added to the sticker price. There had been a time, not so long ago, when the drive home itself would have been the highlight of his evening.

That time was gone.

Connelly eased across the lot and slid onto the feeder road for Route 128, mentally plotting his route home. He'd stop by Burlington Wine Merchants for a bottle of Perrier-Jouet, then visit the adjoining florist for a bouquet. Fuchsias this week, he decided; she wouldn't be expecting fuchsias. Flowers and champagne had become a staple of his Saturday evenings with Lynn: the only mystery, she liked to joke, was the color of roses he'd bring home.

If someone had told him, just a few years before, what a difference Lynn would make in his life, he would have scoffed. He had an exciting and challenging job as CIO for a software development company; he had plenty of friends and more than enough interests to occupy his free time; he made a lot of money and never had problems meeting women. And yet, on some almost subconscious level, he must have known something was missing. Otherwise he would never have visited Eden in the first place. But even after enduring the grueling evaluation, even after shelling out the $25,000 fee, he'd had no inkling of how Lynn would make his life complete. It was as if he'd been blind all his life, never understanding what he'd been missing until the gift of sight was suddenly granted.

He pulled onto the freeway and merged with the weekend traffic, enjoying the effortless acceleration of the big engine. The strange thing, he remembered, was how he'd felt that night of their first meeting. For the first fifteen minutes, maybe even more, he'd thought it was a huge mistake; that somehow

Eden had blundered, maybe mixed up his name with somebody else's. He'd been warned in his exit interview this was a common initial reaction, but that made no difference: he'd spent the first part of the date looking across the restaurant table at a woman who looked nothing like what he expected, wondering how quickly he could get back the twenty-five grand he'd dropped on the crazy scheme.

But then, something had happened. Even now, no matter how many times he and Lynn had joked about it in the months that followed, he couldn't articulate just what it was. It had crept up on him. Over the course of the dinner he'd discovered — often in ways he could never have expected — interests, tastes, likes and dislikes they shared. Even more intriguing were areas where they differed. It was as if, somehow, each filled gaps in the other. He'd always been weak in foreign languages; she was fluent in French as well as Spanish, and explained to him why language immersion was more natural than memorizing a textbook. She'd spent the second half of the dinner speaking only in French, and by the time his crème brûlée arrived he marveled at how much he was managing to understand. On their second date, he learned Lynn was afraid to fly; as a private pilot, he explained how to cope with fear of flying and offered to take her up for desensitization flights in the Cessna he co-owned.

He shifted lanes, smiling to himself. These were crude examples, and he knew it. Truth was, the way their personalities complemented each other's was probably too subtle and multifaceted to detail. He could only compare it to the other women he'd known. The real difference, the *fundamental* difference, was that he'd known her close to two years — and yet he was as excited now at the prospect of seeing her as he'd been in the first flush of new love.

He wasn't perfect; far from it. Eden's psychological screening had made his own faults all too clear. He tended to be impatient. He was rather arrogant. And so on. But somehow, Lynn canceled these things out. He'd learned from her quiet self-assurance, her patience. And she had learned from him, as well. When they'd first met, she was quiet, a little reserved. But she'd loosened up a lot. She was still quiet at times — the last couple of days, for example — but it had grown so subtle that nobody but he would have noticed.

Although he'd never have admitted it to anybody, the thing he'd been most worried about, going into Eden, was the sex. He was old enough, and he'd had enough relationships, for bedroom marathons to be less important to him than they once were. He was by no means a Viagra candidate, but he found he now had to feel deeply about a woman before he could really respond. This had been an issue in his prior relationship: the woman had been fifteen years his junior, and her sexual hunger, which as a young stud he would have found desirable, had been a little intimidating.

It proved a non-issue with Lynn. She'd been so patient and so loving — and her body was so wonderfully sensitive to his touch — that the sex was the best of his life. And, like everything else about the marriage, it only seemed to get better with time. He felt an electric tickle of lust as he thought about their upcoming anniversary. They were going to spend it at Niagara-on-the-Lake, in Canada, where their honeymoon had been. *Just a few more days,* Connelly thought as he slowed for his exit. If there was anything on Lynn's mind, the spray of the Maid of the Mist would soon drive it far, far away.

TWELVE

At 8:55 Sunday morning, Christopher Lash pushed through a revolving door and entered the lobby of Eden Incorporated, surrounded by dozens of other hopeful clients. It was a crisp, sunny autumn day, and the pink granite walls blazed with light. Today he'd left the satchel at home. In fact, other than his wallet and his car keys, the only thing in Lash's pockets was a card Mauchly had given him at their last meeting reading simply: *Candidate Processing, 9 a.m. Sunday.*

As he walked toward the escalator, Lash mentally reviewed the test preparations he'd been coached on at the Academy, over a decade ago. Get a good night's sleep. Eat a breakfast high in carbs and low in sugar. No alcohol or drugs. Don't panic.

Three out of four, he thought. He was tired, and despite the mammoth Starbucks espresso he'd had on the drive in, he found himself craving another. And though he was far from panicked, he was aware of feeling uncharacteristically nervous. *That's okay,* he reminded himself: a little tension kept you alert. But he kept recalling what the man said at the class reunion he'd observed: *If I'd known just what was in store for me, I don't know if I'd have had the* cojones *to take that evaluation. It was a brutal day.*

He put this aside as he approached the escalator. Amazing to think that demand for Eden's services was so great it had to process its applicants seven days a week. He stepped on, looking curiously at the people ascending the twin escalator to his left. What had been going through Lewis Thorpe's head when he rode this same escalator? Or John Wilner's? Were they excited? Nervous? Scared?

As he watched, he saw two people on the adjoining escalator — a middle-aged man and a young woman, a few riders apart — exchange a brief glance. The man nodded almost imperceptibly at the woman, then looked away. Lash thought of what the chairman had said: security was subtle but ever-present. Were some of these would-be applicants really Eden operatives?

Reaching the top of the escalator, Lash passed beneath the wide archway and entered a passage decorated with cheery promotional posters. Faint parallel lines had been etched into the floor, creating a series of wide lanes leading down the passage. They had the effect of making the applicants — of their own accord, or through subtle orchestration —

spread apart and walk side by side. Ahead, each lane terminated in a door. A technician in a white coat stood before each. Lash could see the person at the end of his lane was a tall, slender man of about thirty.

As Lash approached, the man nodded and opened the door behind him. "Step inside, please," he said. Lash glanced around and noticed attendants at the other doors doing the same. He stepped through his doorway.

Ahead lay another hallway, very narrow, unrelievedly white. The man closed the door, then led the way down the featureless hall. After the airy lobby and the wide approach corridor, this space felt claustrophobic. Lash followed the man down the passage until it opened into a small, square room. It was as white as the hallway. Its only features were six identical doors set into the surrounding walls. Instead of a handle, each door had a small white card reader bolted to its face. One door in the far wall had a placard designating it a unisex bathroom.

The man turned toward him. "Dr. Lash," he said. "I'm Robert Vogel. Welcome to your Eden evaluation."

"Thanks," said Lash, shaking the proffered hand.

"How are you feeling?"

"Fine, thanks."

"We've got a long day ahead of us. If at any time you have questions or concerns, I'll do my best to address them."

Lash nodded as the man slipped a hand into his lab coat and pulled out a palmtop computer. He plucked a stylus from its groove and began scrawling on the pad. After a moment, he frowned.

"What is it?" Lash asked quickly.

"Nothing. It's just —" the man seemed surprised. "It's just that you're showing up as pre-approved for the evaluation. I've never seen that before. You had no initial screening?"

"No, I didn't. If it's a problem —"

"Oh, no. Everything else checks out." The man recovered quickly. "You do understand, of course, that you won't be formally accepted as a candidate until after today's evaluation?"

"Yes."

"And that if you are not accepted, your application fee of $1,000 is nonrefundable?"

"Yes." There had been no application fee, of course, but the man didn't have to know everything. Lash was relieved: clearly, Vogel didn't know his real purpose in being here. Lash had told Mauchly emphatically that he wanted to be treated as a real candidate, see everything the Thorpes and the Wilners had seen.

"Any questions before we begin?" When Lash shook his head, Vogel drew a card from around his neck, strung on a long black cord.

Lash looked at it curiously: it was pewter-colored, with an iridescence that did not completely hide the gold-green of microprocessing inside. Eden's infinity logo was embossed on one side. Vogel ran the card through the reader by the nearest door, and it sprang open with a click.

The room beyond seemed little wider than the hallway. There was a digital camera on a tripod inside, and a painted X on the floor beyond the camera.

"Please stand on the cross and look at the lens. I'm going to ask you two questions. Answer them as completely and as truthfully as you can." And Vogel took up position behind the camera. Almost immediately, a tiny red light glowed on its upper housing.

"Why are you here?" Vogel asked.

Lash hesitated for just a moment, remembering the tapes he'd watched in the Flagstaff house. *If I'm going to do this at all,* he thought, *I should do it right.* And that meant honesty, avoiding easy or cynical answers.

"I'm here because I'm searching for something," he replied. "For an answer."

"Describe one thing you did this morning, and why you think we should know about it."

Lash thought. "I caused a traffic jam."

Vogel said nothing, and Lash went on.

"I was on I-95, coming into the city. I've got an E-ZPass unit for the windshield so I don't have to pay cash at the tunnels and toll roads. I get to the bridge leading into Manhattan. It took a little time, because one of the three lanes at the toll plaza was down. The reader scans my card. But for some reason, the wooden gate doesn't lift. I sit for a minute until an attendant comes. She tells me my E-ZPass is invalid. That it was revoked. But that's not the case, I'm fully paid up. The thing had worked fine half a dozen times just this week. Clearly their system was messed up. But she insists I pay the six dollars to get across the bridge in cash. I say no, I want her to fix the error. Meanwhile, now there's only one good lane onto the bridge. The line behind me is growing longer. People are honking. She insists. I stick to my guns. A cop takes notice, starts to walk over. Finally she calls me an unpleasant name, opens the gate manually, and lets me through. I give her my most endearing smile as I pass."

He stopped, wondering why this of all things had come to mind. Then he realized it was, in fact, in character. If he'd been here for himself, for real, he'd have said something equally mundane. It wasn't like him to cough up a teary-eyed story about how he'd embarked on a quest for the woman of his dreams.

"I guess I mention this because it reminds me of my father," Lash went on. "He was very combative over the little things, as if it was a personal grudge match between him and life. Maybe I'm more like him than I realized."

He fell silent, and after a moment the red light went out.

"Thank you, Dr. Lash," Vogel said. He stepped away from the camera. "And now, if you'd follow me, please?"

They returned to the small central hallway, and Vogel swiped his card through the reader of the adjoining door. The room beyond was larger than the first. It contained a chair and a desk, on which sat a small Lucite cube holding sharpened pencils. Once again, the room was unrelievedly white. The ceiling was entirely covered in squares of frosted plastic. All these little rooms, identical in color and lack of decoration, each being used for a single purpose: they seemed to Lash almost like a genteel version of an interrogation suite.

Vogel motioned Lash to sit down. "Our tests run on a clock, but only to make sure that you complete the necessary battery by the end of the day. You have one hour, and I think you'll find it plenty of time. There are no right or wrong answers. If you have any questions, I'll be just outside." He laid a large white envelope on the desk, then left the room, closing the door quietly behind him.

There was no clock, so Lash removed his watch and laid it on the table. He picked up the envelope, upended it into his hand. Inside was a thin test manual and a blank score sheet:

EDEN INC.
Proprietary and confidential

ANSWER SHEET
SIDE 1 — BEGIN ON THIS SIDE

MARKING INSTRUCTIONS

Please answer each of the questions below by shading in one of the following five responses on the attached score sheet:

- ○ strongly agree
- ○ agree
- ○ neutral
- ○ disagree
- ○ strongly disagree

Please do not skip any questions, and make sure your answers are clearly marked. Make no unnecessary or stray marks. If you decide to change an answer, completely erase the prior answer before shading in a new one.

Wrong: ○
Wrong: ♀
Right: ●

==============
ehk90000000049a

Lash scanned the questions quickly. He recognized its basic structure: it was an objective personality test, the kind made famous by the Minnesota Multiphasic Personality Inventory. It seemed an odd choice for Eden; because such tests were primarily used as psychoanalytical diagnostics, they arranged personality into a series of scales, rather than ferreting out particular likes and dislikes. This seemed an unusually long test, too: while the MMPI-2 consisted of 567 questions, this test had precisely one thousand. Lash decided this was probably due to authentication factors: such tests always included a number of redundant questions to make sure that the subject was answering consistently. Eden was being extra-cautious.

He became aware of the ticking of his watch. With a sigh, he took one of the pencils from the Lucite cube and turned to the first question.

1. I enjoy watching large parades.

Lash did, so he shaded in the ○ in the "agree" column.

2. I sometimes hear voices other people claim not to hear.

A smoking gun if ever he'd seen one. *No right or wrong answers — yeah, sure.* If he answered in the positive, the ranking on his schizophrenia scale would increase. He shaded in the "strongly disagree" O.

3. I never lose my temper.

Lash recognized this question type by its use of the word "never." All personality tests contained so-called validity scales: questions that could indicate whether the test-taker was lying, or exaggerating, or faking something like bravery (for police department applicants) or mental illness (for disability compensation). Lash knew that if you claimed too often never to feel fear, never to have told a fib, never to be moody, your lie scale would become elevated and your test thrown out as invalid. He shaded in the "disagree" O.

4. Most people tell me I'm an outgoing person.

This question skewed toward the extrovert/introvert scale. In such tests, extroversion was looked upon as a favorable trait. But Lash preferred his privacy. He again shaded the "disagree" circle.

The pencil point snapped and he cursed under his breath. Five minutes had already passed. If he was going to do this, he'd have to take the test like a typical person, filling in the answers instinctively rather than analyzing each one. He reached for a fresh pencil and reapplied himself to the task.

By ten o'clock, he had completed the battery of questions and been given a five-minute break. Then Vogel seated him again at the desk, left for a moment, and returned with another white envelope and the coffee Lash had requested: decaffeinated, the only kind offered. Lash opened the new envelope and found it contained a battery of cognitive intelligence tests: verbal comprehension; visual-spatial; a memory battery. Once again, the tests were longer and more thorough than he'd experienced before, and by the time he was done it was nearly eleven.

Another five-minute break; another cup of decaffeinated coffee; and a third white envelope. Rubbing his eyes blearily, Lash opened it and pulled out the stapled pamphlet within. This time, the test consisted of a long set of incomplete sentences:

I wish my father_____

My second favorite food is_____

My greatest mistake was_____

I feel that children are_____

I'd like it if other people_____

I believe that mutual orgasm_____

I feel that red wine_____

I would be completely happy if only____

Some areas of my body are very_____

Mountain hiking in spring is_____

The book with the greatest influence on me was_____

Here they were at last: the personal, intimate questions that had been noticeably lacking from the first test. Once again, Lash guessed there were close to a thousand. As he scanned the unfinished sentences, his instincts — both professional and personal — warned him to be disingenuous. But he reminded himself half-measures would not work here: if he was to fully understand the process, he had to experience it with the kind of commitment that the Wilners and the Thorpes had made. He took a fresh pencil, considered the first sentence, then completed it:

I wish my father had taken the time to praise me more often.

It was almost twelve-thirty by the time he

filled in the last sentence, and Lash felt the beginnings of a headache creeping along his temples and behind his eyes. Vogel came in with a long, narrow sheet in his hand, and for a terrible moment Lash thought another test was coming. Instead, it was a lunch menu. Although he felt little appetite, he dutifully made his choices and handed it back to Vogel. The man suggested Lash take a bathroom break, then stepped out of the room, leaving the door open.

By the time Lash returned, Vogel had brought in a folding chair and placed it perpendicular to his own. Where the cube of pencils had been was now an oblong box of black cardboard.

"How are you feeling, Dr. Lash?" Vogel asked as he sat in the folding chair.

Lash passed a hand across his eyes. "Sandbagged."

A smile flitted briefly across Vogel's face. "It seems grueling, I know. But our studies have shown that a single, intensive day of evaluation yields the best results. Please sit." He opened the box, revealing a stack of large cards face down.

The moment he saw a small number printed on the top card, Lash knew what lay ahead. He'd been so engrossed in the first three tests he'd almost forgotten about what he himself had examined in the blind just a few days before.

"We're now going to do an inkblot test, known as the Hirschfeldt. Are you familiar with it?"

"More or less."

"I see." Vogel drew out a blank control sheet from the box, made a notation. "Let's begin. I'll show you the inkblots, one by one, and you tell me what they look like." He lifted the first card from the box, turned it over, and placed it on the table, facing Lash. "What might this be?"

Lash looked at the picture, trying to empty his mind of prior associations — especially the terrible images that had jumped unbidden into his mind back at the Audubon Center. "I see a bird," he said. "Up at the top. It's like a raven, the white part is its beak. And the whole card looks like a warrior, Japanese, a ninja or samurai. With two swords in scabbards — you can see them sticking out there, left and right, pointed downwards."

Vogel scribbled on the control sheet, taking down — Lash knew — his remarks verbatim. "Very good," he said after a moment. "Let's go on to the next one. What might this be?"

Lash worked his way through the cards, fighting a growing weariness, trying always to make the responses his own rather than what he knew to be common replies. By one o'clock, Vogel had finished both the response and inquiry phases of the test, and Lash's headache had grown worse. As he watched Vogel put the cards away, he found himself wondering about all the other applicants who had streamed into the building this morning: were they all squirreled away somewhere on this floor, in their own little testing suites? Had Lewis Thorpe felt as exhausted as he himself did now, as tired of staring at the blank white walls?

"You must be hungry, Dr. Lash," Vogel said as he closed the box. "Come on. Your lunch is waiting."

Though he felt no hungrier now than before the inkblots, Lash followed him across the small central space to one of the doors in the far wall. Vogel swiped his card through the reader, and the door sprang open to reveal yet another white room. This, however, had prints on three of its walls. They were simple, well-framed photographs of forests and seacoasts, bereft of people or wildlife, yet Lash's gaze rested hungrily on them after the sterile emptiness of the morning.

His lunch was laid out on a crisp linen tablecloth: cold poached salmon with dill sauce, wild rice, a sourdough roll, and coffee — decaffeinated, of course. As he ate, Lash felt his appetite return and the headache recede. Vogel, who had left him to dine in peace, returned twenty minutes later.

"What next?" Lash asked, dabbing at his mouth with a napkin. He held out little hope his question would be answered, but Vogel surprised him.

"Just two more items," Vogel said. "The physical examination and the psychological interview. If you've finished, we can proceed immediately."

Lash laid the napkin aside and rose, thinking back again to what the man in the class reunion had said about his own day of testing. So far it had been tiring, even enervating, but nothing worse. A physical exam he could handle. And he'd given enough psychological interviews to know what to expect.

"Lead on," he said.

Vogel ushered Lash back out into the central space and pointed at one of the two blank doors not yet opened. Vogel swiped his card through the reader, then began scratching something into his palm device with the plastic stylus. "You may proceed, Dr. Lash. Please remove your clothes and put on the hospital gown you'll find inside. You can hang your things on the door hook."

Lash entered the new room, closed the door, and looked around as he began undressing. It was an examination room, small but remarkably well equipped for its size. Unlike the previous rooms, there were plenty of items here, but most were of a kind Lash would have preferred not to see: probes, curette and syringe packets, sterile pads. A faint smell of antiseptic hung in the air.

Lash had no sooner donned the gown before the door opened again and a man stepped in. He was short and dark-complexioned, with thinning hair and a bottle-brush moustache. A stethoscope hung from the side pocket of his white coat.

"Let's see," he said, examining a folder in his hand. "Dr. Lash. Medical doctor, by chance?"

"No. Doctorate in psychology."

"Very good, very good," the doctor said, putting the folder aside and pulling on a pair of latex gloves. "Now just relax, Dr. Lash. This shouldn't take more than an hour."

"An hour?" Lash said, but fell silent when he saw the doctor poking his finger into a jar of petroleum jelly. *Maybe $100,000 isn't such an outrageous fee, after all,* he thought to himself.

The doctor's estimate proved correct. Over the next sixty minutes, Lash endured a more comprehensive and painstaking physical examination than he'd ever thought possible. EKG and EEG; echocardiogram; samples of urine, stool, mucus membranes, and the epithelial lining of his mouth; an extensive background medical history of both himself and two generations of forebears; checks of reflexes and vision; neurological testing and fine motor control; an exhaustive dermatological examination. There was even a point when the doctor gave him a glass beaker and, leaving the room, asked for a sample of Lash's ejaculate. As the door closed, Lash stared at the tube — chill in his fingers — and felt a sense of unreality creep over him. *Makes sense,* a small voice said in his head. *Infertility or impotence would be an important concern.*

Some time later, he told the doctor he could come in again, and the examination resumed.

"Just the blood work now," the doctor said at last, arranging a tray containing at least two dozen small glass tubes, currently empty. "Please lean back on the examining table."

Lash did so, closing his eyes as he felt a rubber tube tightening above his elbow. There was a cold swab of Betadine, a brief probing fingertip, then the sting of a needle sliding home.

"Make a fist, please," the doctor said. Lash did so, waiting stoically while at least half a pint of blood was drawn. At last, he felt the tension of the rubber release. The doctor slipped out the needle and applied a small bandage in one smooth motion. Then he helped Lash into a sitting position. "How do you feel?"

"I'm okay."

"Very well. You may proceed to the next room."

"But my clothes —"

"They'll be waiting here for you at the

close of the interview."

Lash blinked, digesting this a moment. And then he turned away, toward the central cubicle.

Vogel was there, once again scribbling something on his digital device. He looked up as Lash emerged from the examination room. The normally unflappable face now held an expression Lash couldn't quite read.

"Dr. Lash," Vogel said as he slipped the device back into his lab coat. "This way, if you please." But Lash needed little guidance: there was only one door in the suite that had not yet been opened, and he could guess where the final interview would take place.

When he turned toward it, he found the door already ajar. And the room beyond was unlike any of the others he had seen that day.

THIRTEEN

Lash hesitated in the doorway. Ahead lay a room almost as small as the others, simply furnished: a chair in the center with unusually long armrests; a metal cabinet beside it; a table with a laptop near the rear wall. But Lash's attention was drawn immediately to the leads that snaked away from the chair to the laptop. He'd sat in on enough interrogations to recognize the setup as a lie detector.

A man was seated behind the table, reading from a folder. Seeing Lash, he stood and came around the table. He was tall and cadaverously thin, his head covered with iron-gray hair, closely cropped. "Thank you, Robert," the man said to the hovering Vogel. Then he closed the door and wordlessly motioned Lash toward the center chair.

Lash complied, feeling disbelief as the man attached clips to his fingertips, fitted a blood pressure cuff to his wrist.

The man moved out of Lash's vision for a moment. When he returned, he was holding a red cap in one hand. A long, rainbow-hued ribbon cable was affixed to one side. Dozens of clear plastic discs, each about the size of a dime, had been sewn into the cloth. *Two dozen, to be exact,* Lash thought grimly. He recognized it as a "red cap," adult headgear for the Quantitative EEG test, or QEEG, which monitored the frequencies of brain activity. It was usually used for neurological disorders, dissociation, head trauma, and so forth.

This was not like any psych interview he had ever heard of.

The man injected conducting gel into each of the twenty-four electrodes, attached the cap to Lash's head, and fitted ground leads to each of his ears. Then he returned to the table and attached the ribbon cable to the laptop. Lash watched, the cap on his head feeling uncomfortably snug.

The man sat down and began typing. He peered at the screen, typed again. He had not shaken Lash's hand or acknowledged him in any way.

Lash waited, numb, feeling exposed and undignified in his hospital gown. He knew from experience that, at heart, psych evaluations were often battles of wit between shrink and patient. One was trying to learn things that, many times, the other did not want to have known. Perhaps this was just some unique form of that game. He remained silent, waiting, trying to clear the fatigue from his head.

The man shifted his gaze from the laptop to the folder on his desk. Then, at long last, he lifted his head and looked Lash directly in the eyes.

"Dr. Lash," he said. "I'm Dr. Alicto, your senior evaluator."

Lash remained silent.

"As senior evaluator, I'm privy to a little more background information than Mr. Vogel. Information, for example, that would indicate your prior job no doubt familiarized you with a lie detector test."

Lash nodded.

"In that case we'll dispense with the usual business of demonstrating its effectiveness. And are you also familiar with the neuro-feedback device I've placed on your head?"

Lash nodded again.

"As a clinician, you're probably curious about its use in this environment. You know lie detectors only measure heart rate, blood pressure, muscle tension, and so forth. We've found the factor-analyzed data from the QEEG an excellent complement. It allows us to go far beyond the normal 'yes' and 'no' responses of a lie detector."

"I see."

"Please keep your arms motionless on the armrests and your back straight. I'm going to ask some baseline questions. Answer only yes or no. Is your name Christopher Lash?"

"Yes."

130

"Do you currently reside at 17 Ship Bottom Road?"

"Yes."

"Are you thirty-nine years old?"

"Yes."

"Now I'm going to show you a playing card. Whatever color it is, red or blue, I want you to tell me the *opposite* color. Understand?"

"Yes."

Alicto picked up a deck of cards, withdrew a red card, held it up. "What color is this card?"

"Blue."

"Thank you." Alicto put the deck away. "Now then. Have you completed today's tests in as honest and complete a manner as possible?"

The man was looking at him with a quizzical, almost dubious expression. "Of course," Lash said.

Alicto looked back down at the folder, let the silence build a moment. "Why are you here, Dr. Lash?"

"I should think that would be obvious."

"Actually, it's not obvious at all." Alicto flipped over some pages in the folder. "You see, I've never done an evaluation on a psychologist before. For some reason, they never become Eden candidates. Internists, cardiologists, anesthesiologists by the truckload. But never psychologists or psychotherapists. I have a theory about that. But in any case, I've been going over your test results of the morning, particularly the personality inventory." He raised a scoring sheet, giving Lash the merest glimpse:

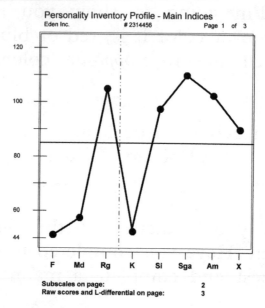

Personality Inventory Profile - Main Indices

Eden Inc.   # 2314456   Page 1 of 3

Subscales on page: 2
Raw scores and L-differential on page: 3

"It's intriguing, to say the least." Alicto replaced the sheet in the folder.

Normally, psychometric evaluators would not reveal information like this to subjects. Lash wondered why Alicto was treating him in an almost cavalier way. "If you want to know more about my taste in movies, or if I prefer cognac to whisky, you should be concentrating on the preference test."

Alicto glanced at him. "See, that's another thing," he said. "Most candidates are cooperative, eager to help, candid. Sarcastic responses are most unusual and, frankly, a matter of concern."

Annoyance began bubbling up through the haze of weariness. "In other words, you intimidate your candidates and they act like sycophants in return. I can see how that would be gratifying to one's ego. Particularly if that ego had been inadequately nurtured in earlier life."

A flash of something — irritation, or perhaps suspicion — flickered in Alicto's eyes. As quickly as it had come, it was gone again.

"You seem angry," he said. "What is it about my questions that makes you angry?"

It occurred to Lash this very line of questioning could already be providing the responses Alicto was searching for. He fought back his annoyance. "Look," he said in as reasonable a tone as he could muster. "It's hard to feel cooperative when strapped to a lie detector, wearing nothing but a biofeedback cap and a hospital gown."

"Actually, most candidates appreciate the lie detector, once they've gotten over the initial surprise. They find it reassuring to know that any partner they are matched with has been as honest as they've been."

Alicto's calm voice added to the unreality of the situation. Lash's anger faded and grogginess again took its place. "Why don't we get on with the evaluation?" he asked.

"What makes you think all this isn't part of the evaluation, Dr. Lash? I'm evaluating you as a complete person in real time, not as the faceless body that completed those tests this morning. But very well, back to the personality inventory. While your scales for falsehood and median response are good, your remedial skews abnormally high."

Lash remained silent.

"As you know, that implies you are limiting disclosure of negative information about yourself: trying to make a good impression, or trying to minimize personal problems."

Lash waited, cursing himself for completing the tests candidly.

"Some of your clinical scales are most unusual for an Eden candidate. For example, your social introversion scale is high, as is your individual control scale. Taken together, these indicate a loner personality; someone who has perhaps had bad experiences in relationships. Such a person would not be motivated to take such a complete — and expensive — step as coming to us." He glanced up from the folder. "Understand, Dr. Lash, that I would not usually share such technical details with a candidate. But your being a fellow psychologist . . . well, it's a unique opportunity."

A unique opportunity to watch me squirm, Lash thought.

"Such items alone would be of concern to me as an Eden evaluator. But there are also elements of the test — may I be frank here? — that reveal distinct pathonomonic signs. Red flags, if you will." Another turning of pages. "For example, your amorality and self-alienation scales are unusually high. Your depression scale, though not exactly high, is well above modal. Your vulnerability scale — that is, your degree of sensitiveness to surrounding events — is also high, despite your individual control scale: an anomaly I can't immediately explain. This all seems like a dangerous cocktail, Dr. Lash. Something I would urge you to have looked at and, if necessary, treated in a clinical setting."

Alicto closed the folder with an air of finality and turned to the laptop. "Just a few more questions, Dr. Lash. I promise you this won't take long."

Lash nodded. Weariness threatened to engulf him.

"How long have you been in private practice?"

"Almost three years."

"And your specialty?"

"Family relationships. Marital relationships."

"And your own marital status?"

"I'm single."

"Widowed?"

"No. Divorced. As you know."

"Just another control question for the lie detector. Your heartbeat is accelerating, Dr. Lash. I would advise you to breathe slowly. When were you divorced?"

"Three years ago."

"What was that like for you?"

"I was married. Now I'm not."

"And you left the FBI for private practice around the same time." Alicto looked up from the screen. "It would seem that quite an interesting nexus of events took place three years ago: a divorce, a highly dramatic career change. Would you care to elaborate on why the divorce took place?"

Lash felt himself tense. *Does he know about Wyre? Is he just baiting me?* Aloud, he answered, "No."

"Why is it so difficult for you to talk about?"

"I just don't see the relevance."

"No relevance? For a potential client?"

"I'm here about my future, not my past."

"One is shaped by the other. But very well. Let's stay in the past a little longer. Elaborate a little on what you did for the FBI, if you please."

"I was with the Investigative Support Unit out of Quantico. I examined murder scenes, drew up psychological autopsies of the victim and unsub — the perpetrator. I'd look for commonalities between them, look for cause, draw up a profile of the killer and coordinate with NCAVC."

"How did you feel about doing that kind of work?"

"It was challenging."

"And were you good at your job?"

"Yes."

"Then why did you leave?"

It seemed an effort just to blink. "I grew tired of trying to figure out what had gone wrong with people after they were dead. I thought I could be more useful helping them when they were still alive."

"Understandable. And, no doubt, you saw some terrible things."

Lash nodded.

"But they didn't affect you?"

"Of course they affected me."

"What kind of a toll, exactly, did they take on you?"

"Toll?" Lash shrugged.

"So they didn't disturb you in any *pathological* way. They ran off your back, so to speak. They didn't affect your work or yourself."

Lash nodded again.

"Could you answer aloud, please, Dr. Lash?"

"No, they did not."

"I ask because I've read a few studies on agent burnout. Sometimes, when people see terrible things, they don't address them as they should. Instead, they bury them, try to ignore them. And, in time, they come to live in a constant state of darkness. It's not their fault: it's the culture of the workplace. Showing pity, weakness, is frowned upon."

Lash said nothing. Alicto glanced over at

the laptop screen, made a notation on the folder. He paused, glancing over the sheets. Then he raised his head again.

"Was there any particular assignment in your prior job that precipitated your decision to leave? Some unusually unpleasant case, say? Some error or lapse of judgment on your part? Something, maybe, that spilled over into your private life?"

Despite the weariness, this question sent an electric twinge through Lash. *So he does know, after all.* He glanced quickly at Alicto, who was regarding him intently.

"No."

"I'm sorry?"

"I said, no."

"I see." Alicto glanced at the screen again, made another notation. Then he leaned back from the laptop. "That concludes the interview, Dr. Lash," he said, coming around the table and removing the cap and the finger clips. "Thank you for your patience."

Lash stood up. The world rocked slightly and he steadied himself on the chair.

"Are you getting enough sleep?" Alicto asked. "Because I've observed you seem to be more than usually tired."

"I'm fine."

But Alicto was still looking at him closely, with what — now that the interview was concluded — seemed to be genuine concern.

"You know, sleeplessness can be common in cases of —"

"I'm *fine,* thank you."

Alicto nodded slowly. Then he turned away, raised his hand toward the door.

"What now?" Lash asked.

"You can put on your clothes. Vogel will see you out."

Lash could hardly believe his luck. After what had gone before, he was sure the psychological interview would take hours. Most lie detector tests were protracted affairs, the same questions repeated over and over in slightly altered form. But this had taken just thirty minutes. "You mean, I'm done?"

"Yes, you're done." And the way Alicto said it made Lash hesitate.

"I'm very sorry," said Alicto. "But in light of the results I'm going to have to recommend against your candidacy."

Lash stared.

"There's no point delaying the bad news. I hope you'll understand. We have to always look at the big picture, what's best for our clients as a whole, rather than the feelings of a single candidate. It's difficult. We'll provide you with some exit literature. Candidates who are declined often find reading it helps get over any feelings of rejection they might naturally have. I'm sure Vogel explained the initial fee is nonrefundable, but there will be no further charges. Take care, Dr. Lash —

and bear in mind what I said about the red flags."

And — for the first and last time — Alicto offered his hand.

FOURTEEN

Although it is three in the morning, the bedroom is bathed in merciless light. The two windows facing the deck of the pool house are rectangles of unrelieved black. The light seems so bright the entire room is reduced to a harsh geometry of right angles: the bed, the night table, the dresser. The light sucks color from the room: the wooden veneer of the dresser, the paisley comforter, the broken mirrors, are bleached to the color of bone. All that remains is the red covering the walls.

There is very little blood on the victim; remarkably little, under the circumstances. She lies naked on the carpet like a porcelain doll, alone beneath a circle of sodium vapor lights. Fingers and toes, carefully cut away at the first joint, are arranged like a halo around the head of the corpse.

There is a murmur of background voices, the low susurration of a crime scene being worked:

"Anal probe reads 83.9 degrees. Dead

approximately six hours. Lack of rigor's commensurate with this estimate."

"Got any latents?"

"Latents is all we got."

"Security system is central station, but the line was cut at the house foundation. Like with the Watkins girl."

"Any entrance or egress yet?"

"The squad's working it."

Captain Harold Masterton, tall and heavily built, breaks away from a knot of Poughkeepsie police and walks across the room, carefully circling the bank of lights, hands in his pockets.

"Lash, you're not looking so hot."

"I'm fine."

"So what do you know?"

"I'm still assessing. There are contradictory elements here, things that don't make sense in the context."

"Fuck the context. You've got enough support personnel crunching numbers back in Quantico to man a football team."

"You've got the partial profile already."

"The partial profile didn't stop him from killing a second time."

"I identify them. I don't catch them. That's your job."

"Then give me enough to find him, for Christ's sake. He's written his damn autobiography twice now. He bled out two women just to get enough ink. There it is,

right in front of our noses. He's handing himself to you on a fucking plate. So when are you going to hand him to me? Or is he going to have to write it a third time?"

And Masterton gestured toward the wall, which was covered in neatly drawn block letters, crimson and recently dried, an endless litany of desperate words: I WANT TO BE CAUGHT. DON'T LET ME KEEP CUTTING THEM. I DON'T LIKE IT. THE SAINTS TELL ME TO CUT THEM BUT I DO NOT WANT TO BELIEVE . . .

Lash rose from his bed and went to the door, opened it, and walked toward the living room. The curtains of the picture window were thrown wide. Beyond, moonlight daubed the creamy breakers with a pale blue phosphorescence. The furniture was illuminated with the half-light of a Magritte painting. He sat down on the leather couch and hunched forward, arms resting on his knees, gaze still on the sea.

Earlier, as Vogel had directed him through a series of nondescript hallways and out a side door onto Fifty-fifth Street, he had been aware primarily of rage. He had walked in a red fog to his parking garage, conducting gel still drying on his scalp, throwing away the exit literature Vogel apologetically pressed into his hands. But as the evening wore on — as he'd eaten a light supper; checked his phone messages; conferred with Kline, the psychologist who was covering his practice — the anger ebbed, leaving an emptiness in its place. And when at last he could put off going to bed no longer, the emptiness began to give way to something else again.

And as he sat staring out at the sea, Dr. Alicto's words came back yet again. *You saw some terrible things. But they ran off your back. They didn't affect your work or yourself.*

Lash closed his eyes, unable to shake the lingering sense of disbelief. Going into Eden that morning, he had anticipated a great many things. But the one thing he had not anticipated was rejection. True, he'd gone through it simply as an exercise: the monochromatic Vogel; the annoying, faintly alarming Dr. Alicto — they had not known the real reason he was there. But that didn't ease his failure. And now he'd come away from the process, not with clearer insight into the Wilners or the Thorpes, but with Dr. Alicto's low, mellifluous voice buzzing in his head.

Sometimes, people don't address the terrible things they see. They bury them in a deep place. And they come to live in a constant state of darkness . . .

During his years of analyzing and treating others, Lash had carefully abstained from directing that same searching light upon himself: from thinking about what drove him forward or held him back; about his motivations, good or bad. And yet now, here in the dark, those were the only thoughts coming into his head.

Was there any particular assignment in your prior job that precipitated your decision to leave? Some error or lapse of judgment on your part? Something that spilled over into your private life?

Lash stood up and made his way down the hall to his bathroom. He flicked on the light, opened the cupboard beneath the sink, and knelt down. There, under the extra bottles of shampoo and the blister-packs of razor blades, was a child's shoe box. He reached for it, removed the cover. The little box was half full of small white tablets: Seconal, appropriated for him by a sympathetic fellow-agent years before, during a raid on a money launderer's townhouse. When he'd moved to this house, he'd meant to flush them down the toilet. Somehow, he never had. And the sleeping pills had sat there, inhabiting the dark space beneath the sink, almost forgotten. They were three years old, but Lash was fairly certain they hadn't expired. He grabbed a handful, held them in his palm, stared at them.

And then he dropped them back into the box and replaced it inside the cupboard. That would return him to the bad days, to the months just before — and just after —

he left the Bureau. It was a place he did not ever want to revisit.

He rose and washed his hands, raising his face to the mirror as he did so.

Since he'd moved here, gone into private practice, sleep had returned. He could give up this case tomorrow, get back to his regular round of consultations. He could sleep well again.

And yet, somehow, he knew he could not do that. Because even now, as he looked in the mirror, he could see the ghostly outline of Lewis Thorpe, looking back at him through the wash of videotape: always, always, asking the same question . . .

. . . *Why?*

Lash dried his hands. Then he went back to his bedroom, lay down again, and waited — not for sleep, because sleep would not be coming — but simply for the morning.

FIFTEEN

The next morning, when Lash stepped out of the elevator onto the thirty-second floor, Mauchly was waiting for him.

"This way, please," he said. "What have you learned about the Wilner couple?"

Not one for small talk, thought Lash. "Over the weekend, I managed to speak to their doctor, Karen Wilner's brother, John Wilner's mother, and a college friend who'd spent a week with them last month. It's the same story as the Thorpes. The couple was almost *too* happy, if such a thing is possible. The friend said the one disagreement she'd witnessed had been minor — about which movie they should see that night — and it dissolved into laughter within a minute."

"No indications for suicide?"

"None."

"Hmm." Mauchly steered Lash through an open door and into a room where a worker in a white coat waited behind a counter. Mauchly reached for a stapled document on the counter, handed it to Lash. "Sign this, please."

147

Lash leafed through the long document. "Don't tell me this is another confidentiality agreement. I've signed more than one of these already."

"That was when you were privy only to general knowledge. Things have changed. This document just spells out in greater detail the extent of the punitive damages, civil and criminal liabilities, and the like."

Lash dropped the document onto the counter. "Not very reassuring."

"You must understand, Mr. Lash. You are the first non-employee to be given access to the most sensitive details of our operation."

Lash sighed, took the proffered pen, and signed his name in two places indicated by yellow flags. "I'd hate to see the kind of screening your employees have to go through."

"It's much more stringent than the CIA's. But our pay scales and benefits are uniquely high."

Lash handed the document to Mauchly, who passed it to the man behind the desk. "What wrist do you wear your watch on, Dr. Lash?"

"What? Oh, the left one."

"Then would you please extend your right arm?"

Lash did so, and was surprised when the worker behind the desk slipped a silver band around his right wrist, tightening it with what

148

looked like a miniature band wrench.

"What the *hell?*" Lash jerked his arm away.

"Strictly a security precaution." Mauchly raised his own right wrist, displaying an identical bracelet. "It's coded with your unique identifier. While you wear that, scanners can track your movements anywhere inside the building."

Lash rotated the thing around his wrist. It was tight, but not uncomfortably so.

"Don't worry, it will be cut off when your work here is complete."

"*Cut* off?"

Mauchly, who so rarely smiled, smiled faintly now. "If it was easy to remove, what would be the point? We've tried to make it as unobjectionable as possible."

Lash glanced again at the smooth, narrow bracelet. Although he disliked jewelry — he'd even refused to wear a ring during his marriage — he had to admit the discreet-looking silver band was vaguely attractive. Especially for a manacle.

"Shall we?" Mauchly said, ushering Lash back into the hall and leading him to a different bank of elevators.

"Where are we going?" Lash said as the elevator began to descend.

"Where you requested. Following the Thorpes and the Wilners. We're going inside the Wall."

SIXTEEN

For a moment, Lash simply stared at Mauchly. The chairman's words came back to him: *You're being given unprecedented access to Eden's inner workings. You've requested — and been granted — a chance to do what nobody with your knowledge has done before.*

"Inside the Wall," he said. "I heard that same expression used in the emergency board meeting."

"It's quite literal. This tower is actually made up of three separate buildings. Not only for security, but for safety — in an emergency, the three structures can be completely isolated by security plates."

Lash nodded.

"The front section of the Eden tower is what our clients see: the testing suites, breakout areas, screening rooms, conference halls, and the like. The rear structure is where the real work goes on. Physically, it's larger. There are six entrance checkpoints. We're headed for Checkpoint IV."

"You mentioned three buildings."

"Yes. Atop the inner tower is the penthouse. Dr. Silver's private quarters."

Lash glanced at Mauchly with new interest. So little was publicly known about the secretive founder of Eden, the brilliant computer scientist behind its technology, that simply hearing he lived here — that there was a good chance he was close at hand — seemed a revelation. Lash found himself wondering what kind of a person Silver was. An eccentric, Howard Hughes figure, emaciated and addicted? A despotic Nero? A cold, calculating arch-tycoon? Somehow, the mere lack of information served to increase his curiosity.

The elevator doors slid back to reveal a wider corridor. Lash could see that it ended in what looked like a wall of glass. A large Roman number IV glowed above it. People were queued before the glass wall, almost all of them wearing white lab coats.

"Most of the checkpoints are on the lowest levels of the building," Mauchly said as they joined the end of the line. "Makes access easier at the start and the close of the working day."

As the line shuffled slowly forward, Lash got a better look at what lay beyond the glass: a short hexagonal corridor, like a horizontal honeycomb, brightly lit, with another glass wall at the far end. As he watched, the near wall slid open; the person at the head of the line walked through; and the wall slid closed again.

"You didn't bring along any mechanical devices, did you?" Mauchly asked. "Voice recorder, PDA, anything like that?"

"I left everything at home, as you requested."

"Good. Just follow my lead. Once the guard has verified your bracelet, just walk slowly through the checkpoint."

They had reached the head of the line. Two guards wearing beige-colored jumpsuits flanked the glass. Everything — the guards, the checkpoints, the bracelet, all the fanatical baggage of security — seemed out of scale. But then, Lash recalled what the company's revenue had been the prior year. And Mauchly's words: *Secrecy is the only way to protect our service. There are any number of would-be competitors who will do whatever it takes to obtain our testing techniques, our evaluation algorithms, anything.*

As Lash watched, Mauchly held his left hand beneath a scanner set into the wall. A blue light shone onto his skin, and the bracelet flashed. With a faint hiss, the glass wall slid away and Mauchly walked into the brilliant space beyond. The near wall closed, then the far wall opened. Once Mauchly was through the chamber and both doors had shut, the guards motioned Lash forward.

He held his bracelet beneath the scanner,

felt his wrist grow warm under its beam. The glass wall slid back and he moved into the chamber.

Immediately, the wall whispered back into place behind him. The light inside the checkpoint chamber was so bright, and it reflected so brilliantly off the white surfaces, that Lash was only dimly aware there was more to this honeycomb chamber than bare walls. As he walked forward, he was aware of shapes protruding from the walls, painted the same white as their surroundings and hard to make out. There was a faint humming noise, like the purr of a distant generator. This was more than a corridor — it was a conduit linking two separate towers.

Then the glass wall at the far end slid open and he stepped out. There was a lone guard here, who nodded at Lash as he emerged. Lash nodded back, looking around curiously. "Inside the Wall" did not look particularly different from the Eden he had already seen. There were a variety of signs: *Telephony A–E*, *Online Surveillance*, *Advanced Data Synthesis*. People moved along the corridors, talking in low voices.

Mauchly stood to one side, waiting. As the inner glass wall slid shut behind Lash, he stepped forward.

"What was all that about?" Lash nodded at the chamber he'd just passed through.

"It's a scanning corridor. Just to make sure

you're not bringing anything in or out. The instruments, software, information, everything on the inside must stay inside."

"Everything?"

"Everything except a few tightly controlled datastreams."

"But all the real processing takes place here, on the inside. Right? There must be an outrageous amount of number-crunching going on."

"More than you could ever imagine." Mauchly pointed at a large panel, set low into one wall. "Data conduits like this link all the areas inside the Wall. They're basically wiring trunks that connect every internal system to all the others."

Mauchly stepped to one side and gestured toward a figure Lash had not noticed before. "This is Tara Stapleton, our chief security technician. She'll be your advisor while you're inside."

The woman stepped forward. "Dr. Lash," she said in low, quiet voice, extending her hand.

Lash took it. Stapleton was a tall brunette with serious eyes who, he decided, couldn't yet have reached thirty.

"Our first stop is this way," Mauchly said as they started down one of the wide corridors. "Tara has just been briefed on exactly why you're here. But of course nobody else knows. Your cover story's that you're preparing an efficiency report for the board's five-year plan. I think you'll be surprised at just how dedicated, and motivated, our people are."

Lash glanced at Tara Stapleton. "Is that true?"

She nodded. "We have all the best equipment. We have a proprietary technology far beyond anything else. What other job lets you make such a difference in other people's lives?" Despite the enthusiastic words, the delivery seemed rote, without nuance, as if her mind was elsewhere.

"Remember those class reunions I had you listen in on?" Mauchly asked. "Everyone on staff is required to witness them twice a year. It helps remind us of what we're working for."

They had arrived at a set of double doors labeled DATA GATHERING–INTERNET–GALLERY. Mauchly placed his bracelet beneath the scanner and the doors slid back. He motioned Lash ahead.

Lash found himself on a balcony above a room busy as the trading floor of the New York Stock Exchange. Except that, while the Stock Exchange always seemed to Lash like barely contained chaos, the huge space below had the precise, calm flow of a beehive. People sat at desks, staring at computer screens, while others gathered at data centers, pointing up at monitors or speaking into telephones. Oversize videoscreens covered the walls, showing feeds from Reuters and other wire services, CNN, local and foreign newscasts.

"This is one of our data-gathering centers," Mauchly said. "There are several other research and surveillance subsections in the building, all similar to this one."

"It seems like an awfully big operation," Lash murmured as he gazed at the activity below.

"We tell our clients their single day of testing is the most important stage in the matching process, but actually it's just a small part. Following the evaluation, we monitor all aspects of an applicant's behavior patterns. It can take a few days, or a month, depending on the width of the datastream we get back. Lifestyle preferences, taste in clothes and entertainment, spending habits: everything is tracked. For example, this center tracks an applicant's Internet use. We monitor what sites are visited, how they're moused, then we integrate the clickstream data with the other information we're gathering."

Lash looked at him. "How is that possible?"

"We have agreements with the major credit agencies, telephone and ISP providers, cable and satellite TV, and the like. They allow us to monitor their bandwidth. And we in turn provide them with certain metrics — generalized, of course — for spotting trends. And we have our own surveillance specialists on board, of course. The omnipresence of computers in daily life is part of what makes our business possible, Dr. Lash."

"Makes me almost afraid to touch mine," Lash said.

"All monitoring is transparent. Our clients have no idea their Web surfing, credit card charges, and phone records are being tracked. It gives us a far more complete picture than we could gather any other way. It's one of the things that separates us from the other, far more primitive social-networking services that have sprung up in our wake. And needless to say, the data we gather remains within these walls. That's another reason why we seem so secretive to you, Dr. Lash: our first mandate is to ensure our clients' privacy."

He waved his hand at the activity below. "Once the Thorpes completed their personal evaluations, their datafiles would have been distributed to centers like this for monitoring. It would have been the same for the Wilners. Or you, for that matter, had you been selected as a candidate."

Here, Mauchly paused. "By the way, I'm sorry about that. I've read the exit reports of Vogel and Alicto."

"Your Dr. Alicto seemed to have a personal grudge against me."

"No doubt it seemed that way. The senior examiner does have some leeway in how he conducts an interview. Alicto is one of our best examiners, but he's also one of the most unorthodox. In any case, it was not a real evaluation in the sense that you were a candidate. I hope that lessens the sting somewhat."

"Let's move on." Lash felt vaguely uncomfortable about having his less-than-stellar performance analyzed before Tara Stapleton.

Mauchly ushered Lash out of the gallery and down the long, pale-hued corridor, stopping at last before a heavy steel door marked by a biohazard symbol and the label RADIOLOGY AND GENETICS III. Once again, Mauchly opened the door with his security bracelet. Beyond was a large room full of gray-painted lockers. "Bluesuits" for biomedical and hazmat duty hung from metal dollies. The far wall of the room was made of clear Plexiglas, and its sealed entrance portal sported several warnings. *Clean-Room Environment Beyond,* read one; *Sterile Clothing and Procedures MANDATORY. Thank You For Your Cooperation.*

Lash walked up to the glass and looked through curiously. He could see gloved and suited figures bending over a variety of complex equipment.

"That looks like a DNA sequencer," he said, pointing at a particularly large console in a far corner.

Mauchly came up beside him. "It is."

"What's it doing here?"

"Part of our genetics analysis."

"I don't see what genetics has to do with a service like yours."

"Many things, actually. It's one of Eden's most sensitive areas of research."

Lash waited expectantly, letting the silence lengthen. At last, Mauchly sighed.

"As you know, our application process isn't limited to psychological evaluations. During the initial physical, any candidates who present with significant physical problems, or appear to be at high risk for future problems, are disqualified."

"Seems harsh."

"Not at all. Would you care to meet your perfect mate, only to have her die a year later? In any case, after the physical, the candidate's blood is further screened — here and at other labs inside the Wall — for a variety of genetic disorders. Anybody with a genetic predisposition for Alzheimer's, cystic fibrosis, Huntington's chorea, and such are also disqualified."

"Jesus. Do you tell them why?"

"Not directly, no — it might attract attention to our trade secrets. Besides, rejection can be traumatizing enough. Why compound it with anxiety over something that might not develop for years — if at all — and that's untreatable in any case?"

Why, indeed? Lash thought.

"But that's just the beginning. Our most important use of genetics comes in the matching process itself."

Lash looked from Mauchly, to the lab workers moving busily beyond the Plexiglas wall, and back to Mauchly again.

"You're no doubt more familiar with evolutionary psychology than I am," Mauchly said. "In particular, the concept of gene spreading."

Lash nodded. "The desire to send your genes on to future generations under the best possible conditions. A fundamental impulse."

"Precisely. And the 'best possible conditions' usually means a high degree of genetic variability. What a technician might call an increase of heterozygosity. It helps ensure strong, healthy progeny. If one mate is blood type A, with a relatively high susceptibility to cholera, and the other mate is blood type B, with a heightened susceptibility to typhus, their child — with blood type AB — is likely to have a high resistance to both diseases."

"But what does this have to do with what's going on in there?"

"We keep very close tabs on the latest research in molecular biology. And we're currently monitoring several dozen genes that influence the choice of an ideal mate."

Lash shook his head. "You surprise me."

"I'm no expert, Dr. Lash. But I can offer

one example: HLA."

"I'm not familiar with it."

"Human leukocyte antigen. In animals it's known as MHC. It's a large gene that lives on the long arm of chromosome 6, and affects body odor preferences. Studies have shown that people are most attracted to mates whose HLA haplotypes were *least like their own.*"

"Guess I should be reading *Nature* more carefully. Wonder how they demonstrated that?"

"Well, in one test, they asked a control group to sniff the armpits of T-shirts worn by the opposite sex, and to rank them in order of attractiveness. And the scents the group universally preferred were of people whose genotypes were *most different* from their own."

"You're kidding."

"No, I'm not. Animals also display this preference for mating with partners whose MHC genes are opposite their own. Mice, for example, make the determination by sniffing the urine of potential mates."

This was greeted by a brief silence.

"Personally, I prefer the T-shirt," Tara said.

It was the first time in several minutes that she'd spoken, and Lash turned to look at her. But she wasn't smiling, and he was uncertain whether she'd meant it as a joke.

Mauchly shrugged. "In any case, the genetic preferences of the Wilners and the Thorpes would be pooled with the other information we'd gathered on them: monitoring data, test results, the rest."

Lash stared at the gowned workers on the far side of the glass. "This is amazing. And I'll want to see those test results in due time. But the real question is *how*, exactly, did the two couples get together?"

"That's our next stop." And Mauchly led the way back into the hallway.

A confusing journey through intersecting corridors; another brief ascent in an elevator; and then Lash found himself before another set of doors labeled simply: PROVING CHAMBER.

"What is this place?" Lash asked.

"The Tank," Mauchly replied. "After you, please."

Lash stepped into a room that was large, but whose low ceiling and indirect light gave it a strangely intimate atmosphere. The walls to the left and right were covered with various displays and instrumentation. But Lash's attention was drawn to the rear wall, which was completely dominated by what seemed some kind of aquarium. He paused.

"Go ahead," Mauchly said. "Take a look."

As Lash drew closer, he realized he was looking at a vast translucent cube, set into the wall of the chamber. A handful of technicians stood before it, some scribbling notes into palmtop computers, others simply observing. Inside the cube, innumerable ghostly apparitions moved restlessly back and forth, colors shifting, flaring briefly when colliding with other apparitions, then dimming once again. The faint light, the pale translucence of the entities within, gave the cube an illusion of great depth.

"You understand why we call it the Tank," Mauchly said.

Lash nodded absently. It *was* an aquarium, of sorts: an electromechanical aquarium. And yet "Tank" seemed too prosaic a name for something with such an otherworldly beauty.

"What *is* this?" Lash asked in a low voice.

"This is a graphic representation of the actual matching process, occurring in real time. It provides us with visual cues that would be much harder to analyze if we were scanning through, say, reams of paper printouts. Each of those objects you see moving within the Tank is an avatar."

"Avatar?"

"The personality constructs of our applicants. Derived from their evaluations and our surveillance data. But Tara can explain it better than I."

So far, Tara had stayed in the background. Now, she came forward. "We've taken the concept of data mining and analytics and stood it on its head. Once the monitoring period is over, our computers take the raw applicant data — half a terabyte of information — and create the construct we call the avatar. It's then placed in an artificial environment and allowed to interact with the other avatars."

Lash's gaze was still locked on the Tank. "Interact," he repeated.

"It's easiest to think of them as extremely dense packets of data, given artificial life and set free in virtual space."

It was strange, almost unnerving: to think that each of these countless gossamer-like specters, flitting back and forth in the void before him, represented a complete and unique personality: hopes and needs, desires and dreams, moods and proclivities, manifested as data moving through a matrix of silicon. Lash looked back at Tara. Her eyes shone pale blue in the reflected light, and strange shadows moved across her face. A faraway look had come over her. She, too, seemed mesmerized by the sight.

"It's beautiful," he said. "But bizarre."

Abruptly, the faraway look left her eyes. "Bizarre? It's brilliant. The avatars contain far too much data to be compared by conventional computing algorithms. Our solution was to give them artificial life, let them make the comparisons *on their own*. They're inserted into the virtual space, and then excited, much in the way atoms can be. This prompts the avatars to move and interact. We call these interactions 'contacts.' If the two avatars have already intersected in the Tank, it's a stale contact. But if this is the *first* encounter between two avatars, it's a 'fresh contact.' Each fresh contact releases a huge burst of data, which basically details the points of commonality between the two."

"So what we're looking at right now are all of Eden's current applicants."

"That's correct."

"How many are there?"

"It varies, but at any one time there could be up to ten thousand avatars. More are added constantly. There could be almost anybody in there. Presidents, rock stars, poets. The only people . . ." she hesitated. "The only people not allowed are Eden personnel."

"Why's that?"

Tara's reply did not address this question. "It takes approximately eighteen hours for any one avatar to make contact with all the others in the Tank. We call that a cycle. Thousands upon thousands of avatars intersecting with every other, releasing a massive torrent of data — you can imagine the kind of computing horsepower required to parse the data."

Lash nodded. There was a low beeping behind him, and he turned to see Mauchly raising a cell phone to his ear.

"Anyway," Tara went on, "when a match is determined, the two avatars are removed from the Tank. Nine times out of ten, a match is made within the first cycle. If there is no match, the avatar is retained in the Tank for another cycle, then another. If an avatar hasn't found a match within five cycles, it's removed and the candidate's application is voided. But that's only happened half a dozen times."

Half a dozen times, Lash thought to himself. He glanced over at Mauchly, but he was still on the phone.

"But under normal circumstances, you could take one of these avatars, put it back in the Tank a year from now, and another match would be found. A *different* match. Right?"

"That's a sensitive issue. Our clients are told that a perfect match has been found for them. And it's true. But that isn't to say we couldn't find an equally perfect match for them tomorrow, or next month. Except in the case of the supercouples, of course — those really *are* perfect. But we don't tell our clients about degrees of perfection, because that might encourage window shopping. Once we've found a match, that's it. End of story. Their avatars are removed from the Tank."

"And then?"

"The two candidates are notified of the match. A meeting is set up." As she said this, her expression once again grew distant.

Lash turned to the Tank, staring at the

thousands of avatars gliding back and forth within, weightless and alien. "You mentioned the need for computing horsepower," he murmured. "That seems an understatement. I didn't know any computer could handle such a job."

"Funny you should say that." It was Mauchly speaking this time, slipping the phone back into his jacket pocket. "Because there's one person in this building who knows more than anyone else about that. And he's just asked to make your acquaintance."

SEVENTEEN

Five minutes brought them to a sky lobby: a two-story space on the thirtieth floor, surrounded by banks of elevators. One end opened onto an employee cafeteria, and Lash could see workers clustered around dozens of tables, talking and eating.

"We have ten cafeterias here on the inside," Mauchly said. "We discourage people from leaving the building for lunch or dinner, and the excellent free food helps."

"Lunch *or* dinner?"

"Or breakfast, for that matter. We've got technicians working shifts round the clock, especially in the data-gathering sections." Mauchly made for an elevator at the end of the nearest bank. It was set apart from the others, and a guard in a beige jumpsuit was posted before it. When the guard saw them approach, he stepped aside.

Mauchly turned to Tara. "You've got the latest code. Go ahead." And he indicated a keypad beside the elevators.

"Where are we headed?" Tara asked.

"The penthouse."

There was a quick intake of breath, quickly checked. Tara punched in a code and, a moment later, the doors opened.

As he stepped inside the elevator, Lash sensed something was different. It wasn't the walls, which had the same glossy wood grain as the others in the building; it wasn't the carpeting, or the lighting, or the safety railing. Suddenly he realized what it was. There was no pinhole security camera in this car. And there were only three buttons on the instrument panel, all unmarked. Mauchly pressed the topmost button, placed his bracelet beneath the scanner.

The elevator rose for what seemed forever. At last it opened onto a brilliantly lit room. But this was not the artificial light Lash had seen elsewhere in Eden: this was sunlight, streaming in from windows that filled three of the four walls. He stepped forward onto a sumptuous blue carpet, looking around in wonder. Through the wall of glass, the dense cityscape of mid-Manhattan lay beneath a cloudless sky. To his left, and right — at what seemed great distances — other windows afforded unbroken vistas of Long Island and New Jersey. Instead of the fluorescent lighting panels of the floors below, beautiful cut-glass fixtures hung from the ceiling, unnecessary in this explosion of daylight.

Lash remembered seeing, from street level,

the figured grille that set off the tower's topmost floors. And he recalled Mauchly's words: *The tower is made up of three separate buildings. Atop the inner tower is the penthouse.* This aerie that crowned the corporate tower could only be one thing: the lair of its reclusive founder, Richard Silver.

Except for the elevator door, the entire fourth wall was covered in rich mahogany bookcases. But they were not the leatherbound volumes one would expect in such a setting; there were cheap science fiction paperbacks, yellowing and broken-backed; technical journals, clearly well thumbed; oversize manuals for computer operating systems and languages.

Tara Stapleton had walked across the wide floor and was staring at something before one of the windows. As his eyes grew used to the light, Lash became aware that dozens of objects — some large, some small — were arranged in front of the huge plates of glass. He stepped forward himself, curious, stopping before a contraption almost the size of a telephone booth. Rising from its wooden base was a complex architecture of rotors, stacked horizontally on spars of metal. Behind the rotors was a complex nesting of wheels, rods, and levers.

He moved to the next window, where what looked like the metal guts of some giant's music box lay on a wooden stand. Beside it was a monstrous device: a cross between an ancient printing press and a grandfather clock. A large metal crank was visible on one side, and its face was covered with flat, polished metal discs of all sizes. Large spools of paper sat on a wooden tray between its legs.

Mauchly seemed to have disappeared, but another man was approaching them from across the room: tall, youthful-looking, with a vast mop of red hair rising from a square forehead. He was smiling, and his watery blue eyes peered out through thin silver frames with a friendly sparkle. He wore a tropical shirt over a pair of worn jeans. Though Lash had never seen the man before, he instantly recognized him: Richard Silver, the genius behind both Eden and the computer that made it possible.

"You must be Dr. Lash," the man said, extending his hand. "I'm Richard Silver."

"Call me Christopher," Lash said.

Silver turned toward Tara, who had turned wordlessly at the man's approach. "And you're Tara Stapleton? Edwin's told me great things about you."

"It's an honor to meet you, Dr. Silver," she replied.

Lash listened to this exchange in surprise. *She's the chief security tech. But she's never met him before.*

Silver turned back to Lash. "Your name

rings a bell, Christopher, but I can't quite place it."

Lash said nothing, and after a moment, Silver shrugged. "Ah, well. Perhaps it will return to me. In any case, I'm curious about your theoretical orientation. Given your prior job, I'd guess you belong to the cognitive behavioral school?"

This was the last thing Lash expected to hear. "More or less. I'm eclectic, I like to pick and choose from other schools as well."

"I see. Such as behavioral? Humanist?"

"More the former than the latter, Dr. Silver."

"It's Richard, please." Silver smiled again. "You're right to pick and choose. Cognitive behavioral psychology has always been fascinating to me because it lends itself to information processing. But on the other hand, strict behaviorists feel all behavior is learned. Right?"

Lash nodded, surprised. Silver did not fit his image of what a brilliant recluse should look like.

"You've got a remarkable collection here," he said.

"My little museum. These devices are my one weakness. Such as that beauty you were just examining: Kelvin's Tide Predictor. It could predict the high and low tides for any future date. And note the paper drums at its base: perhaps the first instance of hardcopy output. Or how about the device on the stand beside it? Built more than three hundred and fifty years ago, but it can still do all the arithmetic, subtraction, multiplication, division of today's calculators. It's fashioned around something called the Leibniz Wheel, which went on to jumpstart the adding machine industry."

Silver walked along the wall of glass, pointing out various machines and explaining their historical importance with relish. He asked Tara to walk with him, and as they proceeded he praised her work, asked if she was happy with her position at the company. Despite the short acquaintance, Lash found himself warming to the man: he seemed friendly, free of arrogance.

Silver stopped before the huge device Lash first noticed. "This," he said almost reverently, "is Babbage's Analytical Engine. His most ambitious work, left incomplete at his death. It's the precursor to the Mark I, Colossus, ENIAC, all the really important computers." And he stroked its steel sides with something like affection.

All of the ancient artifacts, perched as they were before staggering vistas of midtown Manhattan, were still remarkably out of place in this elegant room. Then abruptly, Lash understood. "They're all thinking machines," he said. "Attempts at creating devices to do the mental computations of humans."

Silver nodded. "Exactly. Some of them —" he waved at the Analytical Engine "— keep me humble. Others —" he gestured across the room, where a much more modern 128K Macintosh sat on a marble plinth "— give me hope. And still others keep me honest." And he pointed toward a large wooden box with a chessboard set into its front.

"What's that?" Tara asked.

"That's a chess-playing computer, built in France during the late Renaissance. Turned out the 'computer' was really just a pint-sized chess whiz who squeezed himself inside the machine and directed its movements. But come, let's sit down." And he led the way to a low table surrounded by leather chairs. It was littered with periodicals: the *Times*, the *Wall Street Journal*, issues of *Computerworld* and the *Journal of Advanced Psychocomputing*.

As they sat, Silver's smile seemed to falter. "It's great to make your acquaintance, Christopher. But I wish the circumstances were more pleasant."

He sat forward, head slightly bowed, hands clasped together. "This has come as an awful shock. To the board, and to me personally." And when Silver looked up, Lash saw anguish in his eyes. *It's rough,* he thought. *The company this man formed, its good works, put into mortal danger.*

"When I think of those couples, the Thorpes, the Wilners . . . well, words fail

174

me. It's incomprehensible."

Then Lash realized he'd been wrong. Silver wasn't thinking about the company: he was thinking about the four dead people, and the cruel irony that had suddenly ended their lives.

"You have to understand, Christopher," Silver said, looking down again at the table. "What we do here goes beyond a service. It's a responsibility, like the responsibility a surgeon feels when he approaches a patient on the operating table. Except for us, the responsibility goes on *the rest of their lives.* They've entrusted their future happiness to us. That's something that never occurred to me when I first had the idea-germ for Eden. So now it's our duty to learn what happened, whether . . . whether or not we had any role in the tragedy."

Once again, Lash felt surprise. This was a frankness he had not seen from anybody on the Eden board save perhaps the chairman, Lelyveld.

"I realize the Wilner deaths took place just days ago. But have you learned anything useful?" Silver looked up with an almost pleading expression in his eyes.

"It's as I told Mauchly. There are absolutely no indications for suicide in the months leading up to their deaths."

Silver held his gaze briefly, then looked away. For a ridiculous moment, Lash feared the computer genius would burst into tears.

"I hope to be going over Eden's own psych evaluations of the couples shortly," Lash said quickly, as if to reassure Silver. "Perhaps I'll know more then."

"I want all of the resources of Eden put behind this," Silver replied. "Tell Edwin I said so. If there's anything I or Liza can do, please let me know."

Liza? Lash thought a little vaguely. *You mean, Tara? Tara Stapleton?*

"Do you have any theories?" Silver asked in a quiet voice.

Lash hesitated. He didn't want to bring up any more bad news. "They're only theories at this point. But unless there's some unknown emotional or physiological agent at work here, the signs are pointing increasingly at homicide."

"Homicide?" Silver echoed sharply. "How is that possible?"

"As I said, so far I'm only working the theories. There's a small chance somebody on the inside is involved: one of your employees, or ex-employees. But it's far more likely the suspect is somebody rejected by your selection process."

An odd look came over Silver's face: the look of a child who has just been rebuked for something he didn't do. It was a look of hurt innocence.

"I can't believe it," he murmured. "Our security protocols are so stringent. Tara here can verify that. I've been assured —" He broke off.

"Like I said, so far it's just a theory."

Another silence settled over the table; this one longer than the first. Then Silver stood up.

"I'm sorry," he said. "I guess I've been keeping you from more important things." And as he extended his hand, some of his smile's warmth returned.

From out of nowhere, Mauchly reappeared. He ushered both Tara and Lash toward the elevator.

"Christopher?" came Silver's voice. And Lash turned to see Silver standing by the Analytical Engine.

"Yes, sir?"

"Thank you for coming up. It's reassuring, knowing you're assisting us. I'm sure we'll be meeting again, soon."

And as the elevator door slid open, Silver turned away, his face thoughtful, his hand once again stroking, almost absently, the metal flank of the ancient computer.

EIGHTEEN

By the time Lash pulled into his driveway it was almost seven-thirty, and the curtain of night was dropping over the Connecticut coastline. He turned off the engine and sat for a moment, listening to the tick of cooling metal. Then he stepped out and walked wearily to the house. He felt drained, as if the sheer volume of technological marvels he'd seen today had temporarily dulled his capacity for wonder.

The house smelled of the lingering smoke from a Sunday fire. Lash turned on the lights and made his way back to the small office that adjoined his bedroom, the weight of the bracelet on his wrist still strange. He picked up the phone and dialed; discovered there were fifteen waiting messages; then sat down, steeling himself for the task of plowing through them.

It took surprisingly little time. Four had been telemarketers and six others were simply hang-ups. There was, in fact, only one message that had to be dealt with right away.

He reached for his address book, then dialed the home number of Oscar Kline, the covering psychologist.

"It's Kline," came the clipped voice.

"Oscar, this is Christopher."

"Hey, Chris. How's it going?"

"It's going."

"Everything all right? You sound tired."

"I am tired."

"I'll bet you were up all night, working on this research project you're being so secretive about."

"Something like that."

"Why bother? I mean, you don't need the fame — not after that book of yours. And you don't need the money, God knows you live like a monk in that Westport cloister."

"It's hard to drop something like this once you've gotten involved. You know how these things are."

"Well, there's one good reason I can think of. Your practice. After all, this isn't August, patients expect us to be around. You miss one session, fine. But two? People get restless. There were a couple of loudmouths in group today, troublemakers."

"Let me guess. Stinson."

"Yes, Stinson. And Brahms, too. You miss another, it's going to get serious."

"I know. I'm trying hard to get this wrapped up before that happens."

"Good. Because otherwise I'm going to

have to off-load some of them onto Cooper. And that wouldn't be a pretty sight."

"You're right, it wouldn't. I'll be in touch, Oscar. Thanks for everything."

As Lash hung up and began to walk away, the phone rang again. He turned back, picked it up. "Hello?"

With a sharp *click*, the line went dead.

Lash turned away again, yawning, forcing himself to think about dinner. He walked into the kitchen and opened the refrigerator, in hope some meal might put itself together. Nothing did. And with his brain shutting down, Lash opted for the easiest solution: he'd phone the Chinese place on the Post Road.

As he reached for the phone, it rang again.

He picked it up. "Hello?"

This time, there was a listening silence on the line.

"Hello?"

Another click as the line went dead.

Lash slowly replaced the phone, then stared at it, thinking. He'd been so wrapped up in the events at Eden he hadn't noticed all the little annoyances that were once again creeping back into his life. Or perhaps he *had* noticed them, but simply hadn't wanted to address them. His newspaper, missing three days out of four. The mail, missing from his mailbox. The repeated hang-ups, eight today alone.

180

He knew exactly what this meant, and he knew what had to be done to stop it.

The prospect filled him with gloom.

The drive to East Norwalk took less than ten minutes. Lash had made it only once before, but he knew Norwalk well, and the landmarks were familiar. The area he found himself in was what civic leaders euphemistically called a neighborhood in transition: close by the new Maritime Center, but also near enough to the poorest sections to require bars on the doors and windows.

Lash pulled over to the curb and double-checked the address: 9148 Jefferson. The house looked like all those that surrounded it: Craftsman-style; small, just two rooms over two; stucco front with a detached garage in the rear. This particular lawn might be less tended than those around it, but all the houses shared a certain shabbiness under the pitiless glare of the streetlight.

He stared at the house. This could be handled in one of two ways: with compassion, or with firmness. Mary English had not responded well to compassion. He'd been compassionate with her last year, during the marital therapy sessions with her husband. Mary had seized upon that compassion, fixated upon him. She had developed an infatuation, an obsession, that ironically led to her divorce: the very thing Lash had been trying to forestall. It had also led to a protracted stalking — telephone hang-ups, mail missing or thumbed through, tearful late-night ambushes outside his office — that had taken a restraining order to stop.

Lash sat a moment longer, preparing himself. Then he opened the door, came around the car, and walked toward the house.

The sound of the doorbell echoed hollowly through the rooms beyond. As the chimes died away, silence briefly returned. Then, the tread of feet descending stairs. The outside light came on, and the eyehole cover was scraped away. A moment later, the thud of the deadbolt; the barred door pulled back; and there was Mary English, blinking out into the glow of the streetlight.

She was still wearing her work clothes, but she had clearly been interrupted in washing up: her lipstick was gone, but the mascara remained. Although it had been only a year since the last therapy session with her husband, she now looked far older than her forty years — there were hollows beneath her eyes the makeup couldn't hide, and a tracery of fine lines ran away from the corners of her mouth. Her eyes went wide with recognition, and in them Lash read a complex mix of emotions: surprise, pleasure, hope, fear.

"Dr. Lash!" she said a little breathlessly. "I — I can't believe you're here. What is it?"

Lash took a deep breath. "I think you

know what it is, Mary."

"No, I don't know. What's happened? Do you want to come in? Have a cup of coffee?" And she held the door open for him.

Lash remained in the doorway, trying to keep his voice cool, his face expressionless. "Mary, please. This will only make it worse."

She looked at him, uncomprehending.

For a moment, Lash hesitated. Then he remembered how it had been the first time he'd confronted her, on this same stoop, and he forced himself on.

"Denial won't help, Mary. You've been harassing me again — phoning my house, tampering with my mail. I want you to stop it, please, and stop it now."

Mary did not speak. But as she looked at him, she seemed to age even more. Her eyes slowly fell away from his, and her shoulders slumped.

"I can't deal with this again, Mary. Not right now. So I want you to agree to stop this before it escalates again. I want you to *say* you'll stop this, say it to my face. Please, don't force my hand."

At this, she looked up again, her eyes glittering with sudden anger.

"Is this some kind of cruel joke?" she spat at him. "Look at me. Look at my *house*. There's barely a stick of furniture in it. I've lost custody of my child. It's a struggle just to see him alternate weekends. Oh, *God . . .*"

As quickly as it had come, the anger receded. Tears traced muddy lines of mascara. "I've complied with the judge. I've done everything you asked."

"Then why is my mail missing again, Mary? Why all the hang-up calls?"

"You think that's *me?* Do you think I could bring myself to do that, after all that's happened . . . after what your judge did to my life, to my —" Further words were choked off by a sob.

Lash hesitated, not quite sure what to say. The anger, the sadness, seemed genuine. But then again, borderlines like Mary English *did* feel anger, misery, depression. It was just misdirected. And they were very good at dissembling, at twisting things back on you, making you, not them, the guilty party . . .

"How could you come here like this, hurt me this way?" she sobbed. "You're a psychologist, you're supposed to *help* people . . ."

Lash stood in the doorway, silent and increasingly uncertain, waiting for the emotions to play themselves out.

The sobs ceased. And a moment later, her shoulders straightened.

"How could I possibly have ever been attracted to you?" she asked in a quiet voice. "Back then, you struck me as a man who cared, who had it all together. A man with a little sense of mystery." She brusquely wiped away a tear. "But you know what I decided, lying here awake at night, alone, in my empty house? Your mystery is the mystery of a man who's got *nothing* inside. A man who's got nothing of himself to give."

She reached behind her, fumbled with a box of tissues on the hall table, cursed when she found it empty. "Get out of here," she said quietly, without meeting his gaze. "Get out of here, *please*. Leave me be."

Lash stared at her. By old habit, half a dozen clinical replies came to mind. But sorting through them, none seemed appropriate. So he simply nodded and turned away.

He started the car, did a U-turn, retraced his route down the street. But before he got to the corner, he pulled over to the curb and stopped. In the rearview mirror, he could see that the front light of 9148 Jefferson had already been extinguished.

What had Richard Silver said, in that vast room floating sixty stories above Manhattan? *It's reassuring, knowing you're assisting us.* Here, staring out into the dark, Lash felt no such reassurance.

NINETEEN

The following morning, as he walked from a Manhattan parking garage, Lash stopped outside a magazine shop, set into the base of a vast apartment house and drowned in the shade of the facing buildings. He stepped inside, his eye quickly scanning the headlines of local and national newspapers: the *Kansas City Star*, the *Dallas Morning News*, the *Providence Journal*, the *Washington Post*. He breathed a small sigh of relief on finding no stories detailing double suicides among happily married couples. Leaving the shop, he turned right on Madison Avenue, heading for the Eden building. *Now I know how Louis XVI must have felt*, he thought; getting up each morning under the shadow of the axe, never knowing if this was to be the day of ultimate revelation.

Though he remained tired, he felt a little better about the night before. Borderlines like Mary English were excellent liars, actors in their own way. He'd done the right thing. He'd have to keep a close eye for future signs

186

of stalking, just in case.

He arrived in the lobby a little early but Tara Stapleton was already there waiting for him. She was wearing a dark skirt and sweater, without jewelry of any kind. She smiled briefly, and they exchanged a few pleasantries about the weather, but she seemed as remote as she had the day before.

Leading him past the security perimeter and down a wide unmarked corridor, Tara instructed him in crisp sentences on the finer points of getting in and out of the inner tower. Although there were two entrance portals at Checkpoint I, the morning crush of employees meant a five-minute wait. Tara spoke very little, so Lash listened discreetly to the conversations going on around him. There was excited chatter about a memo that had circulated recently, reporting client applications were up thirty percent. There was remarkably little talk about last night's ball game or how the morning commute had gone. It was as Mauchly said: these people genuinely loved what they did.

Once past the checkpoint, Tara showed Lash to an office reserved for him on the sixteenth floor. The door had no key, but was opened by a bracelet scanner. The office was windowless, but pleasantly bright and large, with a desk and table, a large empty bookcase, and a computer, also sporting a scanner. The only other feature was a small panel, set low in one wall, allowing access to the inner tower's omnipresent data conduit.

"I've arranged to have all the results for the Thorpes and Wilners brought to you," she said. "We'll have the data terminal online for you this morning, and I'll show you how to access records as needed. You'll need to scan your bracelet before you can log on. Here's my extension and cell number if you need to reach me." She placed a card on the table. "I'll come back for you at lunch."

Lash pocketed the card. "Thanks. Where can I find coffee around here?"

"There's a staff cafeteria down the hall. The bathroom's that way, too. Is there anything else?"

Lash dropped his leather satchel on one of the chairs. "Could I have a whiteboard, please?"

"I'll have one sent in." With a nod, she turned gracefully and left the room.

For a moment, Lash stared thoughtfully at the space where she'd stood. Then he stowed his satchel inside one of the desk drawers and made his way to the cafeteria, where a Junoesque woman behind the counter cheerfully brought him a large espresso. He took it gratefully, sipped, found it excellent.

No sooner had he returned to his office and made himself comfortable than a technician knocked on the open door. "Dr. Lash?"

"Yes?"

The man wheeled in what looked like a black evidence locker, set on a steel cart. "Here are the documents you requested. When you've finished your examination, call the number stamped on the cartons and someone will pick them up."

Lash lifted the heavy locker and placed it on the table. It was sealed with white tape that read HIGHLY CONFIDENTIAL AND PROPRIETARY — NOT TO LEAVE EDEN INTERNAL.

He closed the door to the office. Then he slit the tape and snapped open the lid. Inside were four large accordion files, each bearing a name and a number:

THORPE, LEWIS A.   000451823
TORVALD, LINDSAY E.   000462196
SCHWARTZ, KAREN L.   000527710
WILNER, JOHN L.   000491003

Each was sealed with white tape and bore an identical label:

EDEN CONFIDENTIAL MATERIAL
INTERNAL USE ONLY
L-3 AUTHORIZATION REQUIRED

NOTE: HARDCOPY WITHIN. DIGITAL MEDIA ALSO AVAILABLE.
USE REQUISITION AT-4849

Lash reached for Lewis Thorpe's file. Then he hesitated: no, he'd leave Lewis Thorpe for last. Instead, he opened Lindsay Thorpe's file and upended it onto the table. A flood of paper streamed out, much of it testing sheets and result forms, but also a thick spiral-bound packet that made little sense:

CODING SHEET FOLLOWS
Note: Summarization only

header
=====

telephony metrics — quantization
assembly period: 27 Aug 02/09 Sep 02
datastream: nominal
homogenization: optimal —
data location (hard): 2342400494234
   first access sector 3024-a
   compartmentalization algorithm set
chief operator: Pawar, Gupta
scrub chief: Korngold, Sterling
data gathering supervisor: Rose, Law-
rence

hexadecimal source follows

234B	3A32	5923	9F43	5032	5225	60D2	6522	6A1D	5934
59C9	322D	4034	25C5	2344	5982	3F40	2354	0C81	2119
2B92	C598	0423	58A0	8981	2099	0901	4309	5852	19B5
5931	0904	88F9	0123	550D	0492	4E90	0499	0982	1258
5AB8	293F	5014	0E94	4C0F	1039	0589	3E09	5915	03E1
2903	854A	4910	C252	3414	0539	932E	3210	54AA	4913
2234	590C	2340	0D82	7899	3981	777F	3291	0948	A972
4933	0D81	4802	29E1	0913	5A0B	1501	08D1	4848	9083

It appeared to be some kind of machine-code summary of Lindsay's telephone habits during her surveillance period. Readable or unreadable, it wasn't the data he was interested in. Lash put this aside and picked up the test forms. They looked precisely like the tests he had taken just days before; the sight sent a fresh surge of mortification through him. He sipped his espresso, riffled through the pages, glancing at the little black circles Lindsay Thorpe had filled in so industriously. Her answers seemed to fall within normal ranges, and a quick glance at the scoring sheets confirmed this. His eye fell at last on the senior evaluator's report.

Lindsay Torvald shows all signs of being well-adjusted socially, with a normative personality profile. Appearance, demeanor, behavior during and between the tests was within normal limits. Attention span, speech articulation, comprehension, and verbal skills were all within the top 10th percentile. Tests showed little abnormal scatter or skew, and validity scales were high across the board: the applicant seemed exceptionally candid and forthright. The projective inkblot test indicated creativity and a vivid imagination with only slight morbidity factors. The personality profile showed slight tendencies toward introversion but well within acceptable levels, especially given the strong indicators for self-confidence. The intelligence battery was also strong, particularly in the areas of verbal comprehension and memory; computation skills were weaker, but still the overall score gives the applicant a Full Scale IQ of 138 (modified WAIS-III).

In short, all quantifiable metrics suggest Ms. Torvald would make an excellent candidate for Eden.

R. J. Steadman, Ph.D.
August 21, 2002

There was movement in the corridor outside his door; a technician wheeled a whiteboard into his office. Lash thanked him, watched him leave. Then he put the report aside and reached for the testing forms once again.

By noon, he had studied the test results for three of the applicants. No smoking guns, no signs of incipient pathology. Across the board, the signs of depression, the suicide indexes, were extremely low. Lash replaced the stacks of paper into their respective folders; stood; stretched; then went down to the cafeteria for another espresso.

He walked back to his temporary office more slowly than he had left it. There was only one folder left: Lewis Thorpe's. Thorpe, who specialized in invertebrate biology and enjoyed translating the poetry of Bashō. Lash had spent several nights rereading *Narrow Road to the Interior*, putting himself in Lewis's shoes, trying to feel what he'd felt in the testing suite, in that sun-filled Flagstaff living room where he had died under the gaze of his own infant child.

Eagerly — yet a little warily — Lash broke open the seal on the fourth folder.

It took less than half an hour to realize that what he most feared was, in fact, true. Lewis Thorpe's test results showed him to be as normal and well adjusted as the rest. They showed an intelligent, imaginative, ambitious man with a healthy self-regard. No indicators for depression or suicide.

Lash slumped back in his chair and let the senior evaluator's report fall from his hands. The tests he'd fought so hard to get brought him no closer to an answer.

There was a knock at his door, and he looked up to see Tara Stapleton leaning in, her long, intent face framed by thick auburn hair.

"Lunch?" she asked.

Lash gathered Lewis Thorpe's papers together and stuffed them back into the folder. "Sure."

Already, the cafeteria down the hall felt like an old friend. It was bright and almost festive, and more crowded now than it had been on his two earlier visits. He fell in line at the buffet rail, helped himself to another espresso and a sandwich, then followed Tara to an empty table near the rear wall. She'd taken only a cup of soup and some tea, and as Lash watched she tore open a packet of artificial sweetener and poured it into the cup. Her reserved, preoccupied silence remained. But right now, that seemed all right: he wasn't eager to field a lot of questions about how his investigation was going.

"How long have you worked at Eden?" he asked after a moment.

"Three years. Since just after its founding."

"And it's as great a place to work as Mauchly says?"

"It always has been."

Lash waited as she stirred her soup, a little uncertain what she meant by this. "Tell me about Silver."

"How do you mean."

"Well, what's he like? He wasn't at all what I expected."

"Me, neither."

"I take it this was the first time you've met him face to face."

"I saw him once before, at the first anniversary celebration. He's a very private person. Never leaves his penthouse, as far as anybody knows. Communicates by cell or videophone. It's just him up there. Him and Liza."

Liza. Silver had mentioned that name, too. At the time, Lash had thought it a slip of the tongue. "Liza?"

"The computer. His life's work. What makes Eden possible. Liza's his one true love. Kind of ironic, really, given the nature of our business. He does most of his communicating to the board and the staff through Mauchly."

Lash was surprised. "Really?"

"Mauchly's his right-hand man."

Lash noticed that somebody was looking at him from across the cafeteria. The youthful face, the bright thatch of hair, seemed familiar. Then he realized who it was: Peter Hapwood, the evaluation engineer Mauchly had introduced him to the day of the class reunions. Hapwood smiled, waved. Lash waved back.

He returned his attention to Tara, who was once again stirring her soup. "Tell me more about Liza," he said.

"It's a hybrid supercomputer. Nothing else like it in the world."

"Why?"

"It's the only large computer built entirely around a core of artificial intelligence."

"And how did Silver come to build it?"

Tara took a sip of tea. "You hear rumors. Stories, really. I don't know exactly how true any of them are. Some people say Silver had a lonely, traumatic childhood. Others say he was coddled, doing differential equations at the age of eight. He's never talked about it on record. All anybody knows for sure is, by the time he got to college, he was doing pioneering work in AI. Brilliant, genius-level stuff. His graduate work centered around a computer that could learn for itself. He gave it a personality, made its problem-solving algorithms more and more sophisticated. Eventually, he proved a computer that can teach itself could solve problems far more difficult than any hand-coded computer. Later, to finance further research, he farmed out Liza's processing cycles to places like the Jet Propulsion Laboratory, the Human Genome Project."

"And then he had his brainstorm. Eden, with Liza as the computational core. And the rest, as they say, is history." Lash took a sip of coffee. "So what's Liza like to work with?"

There was a pause. "We never get near the core routines or intelligence. Liza's physical plant is in the penthouse, and only Silver has access. Everybody else — scientists, technicians, even the computer programmers — uses the corporate computer grid and Liza's data abstraction layer."

"Liza's *what?*"

"A shell that creates virtual machines within the computer's memory space." Tara paused again. More and more pauses were creeping into her sentences. Then, abruptly, she stood up.

"I'm sorry," she said. "Could we talk about this some other time? I have to go."

And without another word she turned and left the cafeteria.

TWENTY

When Mauchly walked into the office around four, Lash was standing before his white-board. The man moved so silently Lash didn't notice him until he was by his side.

"Christ!" Lash jumped, dropping his marker.

"Sorry. Should have knocked." Mauchly glanced at the bulletin board. "Race, age, type, personality, employment, geographics, victims. What's this?"

"I'm trying to type the killer. Assemble a profile."

Mauchly turned his placid gaze on Lash. "We still don't know there's a killer."

"I've gone over all your records. There's nothing psychologically wrong with the Thorpes or the Wilners, zero clinical evidence of suicide. It would be a waste of time to explore that avenue further. And you heard what Lelyveld said in the boardroom: we don't *have* time."

"But there's no signs of murder, either. The Thorpes' security camera, for one thing.

It didn't show anybody entering or leaving the house."

"It's a lot easier to cover up a murder than to cover up a suicide. Security cameras can be interfered with. Alarms can be bypassed."

Mauchly thought about this. Then he looked back at the writing on the board. "How do you know the killer is in his late twenties or early thirties?"

"I don't. That's the baseline for serial killers. We have to start with the pattern, and refine from there."

"And how about this: that he's either well employed or has access to money?"

"He killed people on opposite coasts within a week of each other. That's not the modus operandi of a drifter or a hitchhiker: their killing patterns chart erratically across short distances."

"I see. And this?" Mauchly pointed to the scrawled words, TYPE: UNKNOWN.

"That's the troubling part. Usually, we type serial killers as organized or disorganized. Organized killers control their crime scenes and their victims. They're smart, socially acceptable, sexually competent. They target strangers, hide their corpses. On the other hand, disorganized killers know their victims, act suddenly and spontaneously, feel little or no stress during the crime, have few work skills, leave the victim at the scene of the crime."

"And?"

"Well, if someone murdered the Thorpes and the Wilners, he exhibits traits of both the organized and disorganized killer. There's no coincidence here: he'd have to know the victims. Yet he left them at the scene, like a disorganized killer. But again, the scene isn't in the least bit sloppy. Such inconsistencies are extremely rare."

"How rare?"

"I never came across a serial killer like it."

Except once, came the voice in his head. He quickly pushed the voice far away.

"If we can get a fix on this guy," Lash went on, "we can compare it against criminal records. Look for a match. Meanwhile, have you thought about keeping a sharp eye on the other four supercouples?"

"We can't do a close surveillance for obvious reasons. And we can't provide adequate protection until we know exactly what's going on. But yes, we're already getting teams in place."

"Where are the rest located?"

"All across the country. The closest couple, the Connellys, live north of Boston. I'll have Tara get you brief reports on all of them."

Lash nodded slowly. "You really think she's the right person for me to work with?"

"Why do you ask?"

"She doesn't seem to like me. Or else she's dealing with some issues that are distracting her."

"Tara's going through a hard time. But she's the best we have. Not only is she chief security tech — which gives her access to every system — but she's unique in having worked both the security and computer engineering sides of the company."

"*If* she gets with the program."

Mauchly's cell phone went off, and he quickly raised it. "Mauchly." A pause. "Yes, of course, sir. Right away."

He replaced the cell phone. "That was Silver. He wants to see us, and right now."

TWENTY-ONE

The day had grown dark and overcast, and the elevator doors opened onto a view far different than Lash had witnessed the day before. Only a handful of the cut-glass ceiling fixtures threw small pools of light across the vast room. Beyond the windows lay a gray stormscape of skyscrapers. The museum-like collection of thinking machines lay before them, hulking objects set against a lowering sky.

Richard Silver was standing by the bank of windows, hands clasped behind his back. At the elevator's chime he turned.

"Christopher," he said, shaking Lash's hand. "Nice to see you again. Something to drink?"

"Coffee would be nice."

"I'll get it," said Mauchly, moving toward a wet bar set into one of the bookcases.

Silver motioned Lash to the same table they'd sat at the day before. The magazines and newspapers were gone. Silver waited for Lash to sit, then took a chair across from

202

him. He was wearing corduroys and a black cashmere sweater, sleeves pulled up his fore-arms.

"I've thought a lot about what you told me yesterday," he said. "About these deaths not being suicide. I didn't want to believe it. But I think you were right."

"I don't see any other possibility."

"No, I didn't mean that. I meant what you said about Eden being involved, either way." Silver looked past Lash, his expression troubled. "I've been too wrapped up in my own projects, here in my ivory tower. I've always been more fascinated by pure science than applied science. Trying to build a machine that can think, learn, *solve* problems on its own: that's where my heart's always been. Exactly what problems interested me less than the *capability* of solving them. It wasn't until the idea for Eden came along that I grew personally involved. Finally, a task to which Liza was worthy: human happiness. Even so, I've kept removed from the day-to-day process. And I see now this was a mistake."

Silver stopped, his gaze focused again on Lash. "I'm not sure why I'm telling you this."

"People tell me I've got a face that inspires confidences."

Silver laughed quietly. "Anyway, I finally decided that, if I've been uninvolved in the past, there *was* something I could do. Now."

"What's that?"

Mauchly returned, coffee in hand, and Silver stood. "If you'll come with me?"

He led the way to a far corner, where the glass windows that ran around three sides of the room met the bookcases of the fourth. Here, Silver's collection of computing machines appeared to run to the musical: a Farfisa Combo; a Mellotron; and a modular Moog synthesizer, all patch cords and low-pass filters.

Silver turned to him. "You said the killer was most likely a rejected Eden candidate."

"That's what the profile suggests. Perhaps a schizoid personality that couldn't accept rejection. There's a smaller chance the killer dropped out of the program *after* acceptance. Or was one of those clients not matched within your five-cycle window."

Silver nodded. "I instructed Liza to parse all accessible applicant data, looking for anomalies."

"Anomalies?"

"It's a little hard to explain. Imagine creating a virtual topology in three dimensions, then populating it with applicant data. Compress the data, compare it. It's almost like the avatar matching Liza does every day, done in reverse. See, our applicants have *already* been psychologically vetted; they should all skew to tightly bounded norms. I was looking for applicants whose behavior, personality, lie *outside* those norms."

"Deviants," Lash said.

"Yes," Silver looked pained. "Or people whose behavior patterns were out of sync with their evaluations."

"How did you do this so quickly?"

"Actually, I didn't. I instructed Liza on the nature of the problem, and she developed the methodology on her own."

"Using the data from applicant testing?"

"Not only that. Liza also called on data trails left by rejected applicants and voluntary dropouts in the months or years since their original applications."

Lash was shocked. "You mean, data gathered *after* they weren't potential clients anymore? How is such a thing possible?"

"It's called activity monitoring. It's practiced by many large corporations. The government does it, too. We're just a few years ahead of everybody else. Mauchly's probably shown you some of its elementary uses already." Silver smoothed the front of his sweater. "In any case, Liza flagged three names."

"*Flagged?* As in, already?"

Silver nodded.

"But there must have been a tremendous amount of data —"

"Approximately half a million petabytes. It would have taken a Cray a year to parse.

Liza completed it in hours." And he gestured at something near the wall.

Lash stared with fresh amazement at something he'd assumed was another antique from Silver's collection. A standard computer keyboard sat on a small table, before an old-fashioned monochrome VDT terminal. A printer stood to one side.

"This is it?" Lash said incredulously. "This is Liza?"

"What did you expect?"

"I didn't expect this."

"Liza herself, or her computational plant, occupies the floors directly below us. But why make an interface more complicated than it has to be? You'd be surprised how much I can accomplish with just this."

Lash thought about the computing feat Liza had just completed. "No, I wouldn't."

Silver hesitated. "Christopher, you'd mentioned another possibility. That the killer was somebody on our own staff. So I also instructed Liza to search for anything unusual, *internally*." His expression grew tight, as if in physical pain. "She flagged one name."

Silver turned to the small table, picked up two sheets of folded paper, and pressed them into Lash's hand.

"Good luck — if that is indeed the right word."

Lash nodded, turned to go.

"Christopher? One other thing."

Lash glanced back.

"I know you understand why I gave this Liza's highest priority."

"I do. And thanks."

He let Mauchly lead the way to the elevator, considering Silver's last words. The same thought had also been running through his own head. The Thorpe couple had died on a Friday, eleven days before. The Wilners had died the following Friday. Serial killers liked consistency and pattern.

They had three days.

TWENTY-TWO

"Four names," Mauchly said.

He was staring at the table in Lash's office. The two sheets of paper Silver provided lay on it, unfolded.

"Any idea why Liza flagged these four in particular?" Tara asked from across the table.

Mauchly picked up the sheet on which a single name had been printed. "Gary Handerling. Doesn't ring a bell."

"He's part of the scrub crew," Tara said.

"The what?" said Lash.

"Data scrub. They're in charge of data storage and security."

Mauchly glanced at her. "You've started the internal trace on him?"

"It should be completed within twelve hours."

"Highest degree of confidentiality?"

"Of course."

"Then I'd better get started on the three clients." Mauchly picked up the other sheet. "I'll have Rumson in Selective Gathering do complete workups."

"What'll you tell him?" Tara asked.

"That we're running some random prototyping on a few obsoletes. Just another system test."

Obsoletes, Lash thought to himself. Eden-speak for disqualified candidates. *Guess that makes me an obsolete, too.*

"Dr. Lash, we should have the results back by midmorning tomorrow. We'll meet then, run them by your profile." Mauchly checked his watch. "It's almost five. Why don't you two head home. We've got a long day tomorrow. Tara, if you wouldn't mind taking Dr. Lash through the checkpoint, make sure he doesn't get lost on the way out?"

By the time they pushed through the revolving doors onto the street, it was quarter past five. Lash stopped at the fountain to button his coat. The clamor of Manhattan, almost forgotten in the hushed spaces of the Eden tower, reasserted itself with a vengeance.

"I don't see how anyone could get used to that," Lash said. "Going through those checkpoints, I mean."

"You can get used to anything," Tara replied, slinging a satchel over one shoulder. "See you tomorrow."

"Hold on a minute!" Lash trotted to keep up with her. "Where are you going?"

"Grand Central. I live in New Rochelle."

"Really? I live in Westport. Let me drop you off."

"That's okay, thanks."

"Then let me buy you a drink before you head home."

Tara stopped and looked at him. "Why?"

"Why not? It's a thing coworkers do sometimes. In civilized countries, I mean."

Tara hesitated.

"Humor me."

She nodded. "Okay. But let's go to Sebastian's. I don't want to catch anything later than the 6:02."

Sebastian's was a sprawl of white-covered tables on the upper level of Grand Central, overlooking the main passenger terminal. The cavernous space had been completely restored in recent years, and was more beautiful than Lash ever remembered seeing it: creamy walls rising to a ceiling of groined vaults, green spandrels, and constellations of glittering mosaic. The voices of countless commuters, the squawk of the dispatch loudspeaker calling out arrivals and departures, mingled together in an oddly pleasing patchwork of background noise.

The two were shown to a small table perched directly in front of the railing. Within moments, a waiter bustled up. "What can I get you?" he asked.

"I'll have a Bombay martini, very dry, with

a twist," Tara said.

"A vodka Gibson, please." Lash watched the waiter thread his way back through the tables, then turned to Tara. "Thanks."

"For what?"

"For not ordering one of those horrible martinis *du jour*. Somebody I was dining with the other week ordered an apple martini. Apple. What an abomination."

Tara shrugged. "I don't know."

Lash looked over the railing at the streams of commuters. Tara was silent, twisting a cocktail napkin between the fingers of one hand. He looked back at her. Hazy light slanted down, catching the gentle curve of her auburn hair. Her eyes, framed by perfect high cheekbones, looked serious.

"Want to tell me what's up?" he asked.

"Up with what?"

"With you."

She wrapped the napkin around one finger, twisted it tight. "I agreed to a drink, not a psychiatric session."

"I'm not a psychiatrist. Just a guy trying to get a job done, with your help. Only you don't seem too eager to help."

She glanced up at him for a minute, then returned her attention to the napkin.

"You seem preoccupied. Disinterested. That doesn't bode well for our working relationship."

"Our temporary working relationship."

"Exactly. And the better we work together, the more temporary it will be."

She dropped the napkin on the table. "You're wrong. I'm *not* disinterested. It's been — a rough couple of days for me."

"Then why don't you tell me about it?"

Tara sighed, her gaze wandering toward the soaring vault overhead.

"I'm buying. It's the least you can do."

Their drinks arrived, and they sipped a moment in silence.

"Okay," Tara said. "No reason you shouldn't know, I guess." She took another sip. "I didn't learn about any of this until yesterday, when Mauchly called to tell me I'd be your liaison while you were inside the Wall. That's when he told me about the problem."

Lash remained silent, listening.

"The only thing is, just this Saturday, I got the nod from Eden."

"The nod?"

"That's what we call getting notification your match has been found."

"Your *match?* You mean that you . . ." He stopped.

"Yeah. I'd been a candidate."

Lash stared at her. "I thought Eden employees weren't allowed to be candidates."

"That's always been the policy. But a few months ago they started a pilot program to phase in employee applicants, based on merit and seniority. In a pool with other Eden employees, not the general pool."

Lash sipped his drink. "I'm not sure I see why the policy was needed in the first place."

"The staff shrinks recommended it from day one. They called it the 'Oz effect.'"

"As in, pay no attention to the man behind the curtain?"

"Exactly. They thought employees wouldn't make desirable candidates. See, we know too much of what goes on, *how* things go on, behind the scenes. They thought we'd be cynical." Then she leaned toward him suddenly, an intensity in her face he hadn't seen before. "But you have no idea what it's like, day after day. Bringing people together. Sitting in the dark behind one-way glass, watching couples at class reunions talk about how wonderful everything had become. How Eden changed their lives, *completed* their lives. I mean, if you've already got someone and you're happy, maybe you can rationalize. But if you don't . . ." She let the sentence hang in the air, unfinished.

"You're right," Lash said. "I don't have any idea what it's like."

"I carried that letter around with me all weekend. I must have read it a hundred times. Matt Bolan, in our biochemistry section, was the match. I've never met him, but I'd heard the name. They'd made a dinner reservation for us this coming Friday. One If

By Land, Two If By Sea."

"In the Village. Beautiful place."

"Especially this time of year." For a moment, Tara's expression brightened. Then it clouded again. "Then, first thing yesterday, I get the call from Mauchly. He tells me about the supercouples, the double suicides. Would I be kind enough to shepherd you around."

"And?"

"And right before I meet you, I send an email to the Applications Committee withdrawing my name as a candidate."

"What?"

Tara's eyes blazed. "How was I supposed to go ahead, knowing what I know? And worse, what I *don't* know?"

"What are you saying? That the application process is flawed?"

"I don't *know* what I'm saying!" she cried. Frustration brought an edge to her voice. "Can't you see? The process *can't* be flawed, I work with it every day, I *see* it perform miracles over and over. But then, what happened to those two couples?"

As quickly as it came, the violent emotion dissipated. Tara sank back. "Anyway, how can I go forward now? If Eden is about anything, it's about lifetime commitment to a relationship. Can I begin such a relationship with a secret I can never reveal?"

The question hung in the air. Tara lifted her drink.

"There you have it," she said with a dry laugh. "I've had a lot on my mind. Happy now?"

"I feel anything but happy."

"Just please don't bring it up again. I'll be fine."

The waiter reappeared. "Another round?"

"Not for me," Lash said. The cocktail might have been a mistake: tired as he was, he'd probably fall asleep at the wheel halfway home.

"Me neither," Tara said. "I've got to catch my train."

"Just the check, please," Lash told the waiter.

Tara watched the man recede toward the bar, then looked back at Lash. "All right. Your turn. I heard you tell Dr. Silver that your orientation was cognitive behavioral."

"That was your first time in the penthouse, too. You never told me what you thought of the place."

"We're talking about you now, not me."

"As you wish." The waiter returned with the check; Lash fumbled for his wallet, dropped a credit card onto the leather folder. "Cognitive behavioral, that's correct."

Tara waited until the waiter had scooped away the bill. "I must have dozed off during our psych orientations. What does that mean?"

"It means I don't focus on unconscious

conflicts, on whether somebody got enough hugs from his mother at age two. I focus on what a person's thinking, what his ruleset is."

"Ruleset?"

"Everybody lives by a set of internal rules, whether they know it or not. You understand enough of a person's rules, you can understand, predict, their behavior."

"Predict. I assume that's what you did for the FBI."

Lash finished off his drink. "Something like that."

"And if this — this turns out to be the work of a killer, will you be able to predict what he'll do next?"

"Hopefully. But the profile is extremely contradictory. Anyway, maybe that won't be necessary. We'll know tomorrow morning." As he spoke, Lash became aware of the waiter standing at his elbow.

"Yes?" Lash said.

"I'm sorry, sir," the waiter said. "But this card has been declined."

"What? Run it again, please."

"I already ran it twice, sir."

"That's impossible, I just sent in a check last week . . ." Lash opened his wallet. It was as he feared: he was only carrying one credit card. He sounded his pocket for cash and found two dollars. *Half asleep and forgot to go to the damn ATM,* he thought.

He replaced his wallet and looked sheepishly at Tara. "Would you mind picking this up?" he asked.

She looked at him.

"I'll pay you back tomorrow."

And then, suddenly, her blank expression dissolved into a grin. "Forget it," she said, dropping a twenty on the table. "It's worth it just to see that smug psychoanalyzing look wiped off your face." And then she laughed: briefly, but loud enough to turn heads halfway to the entrance of Sebastian's.

TWENTY-THREE

By the time Lash broached the Eden lobby Wednesday morning, threaded the complex network of security, and gained the sixteenth floor, it was almost nine-thirty. He walked down the pale violet corridor, bypassing his darkened office and heading directly to the cafeteria.

"A jumbo espresso, right?" asked Marguerite, the counter woman who seemed to know everyone's needs before they did.

"Marguerite, your espresso is the best in the tri-state area. I was dreaming about it the whole drive in."

"Sugar, the amount of caffeine you ingest, they could put a set of wheels on you and you'd drive yourself."

Lash sipped, sipped again. The hot liquid warmed his tired limbs and accelerated his heart. He smiled at Marguerite, then made his way back down the corridor.

He'd been slow to rise, feeling a lethargy that had little to do with weariness. The desperate urgency of their search seemed, ironically, to have a retarding effect on him. All his former field experience told him this wasn't the way to work the case. You didn't sit in an office, poring over computer transcripts. Sure, they were helpful enough in classification and profiling. But when you were hunting a suspected killer who might be about to strike again, you pounded the pavement, hunted up leads, talked to family and eyewitnesses. Sitting in a skyscraper, far from bodies and murder sites, gathering data, seemed like lunacy.

Yet Eden's unmatched ability to gather data was all they had.

Reaching his office, Lash saw through the door pane that one entire wall was now hidden behind stacks of evidence lockers. He barely had time to step inside and place his cup on the desk before Mauchly entered, Tara Stapleton at his side.

"Ah, there you are, Dr. Lash," Mauchly said. "As you can see, the gathering process finished earlier than expected."

Tara smiled at Lash. As she moved to the terminal and scanned her bracelet, Mauchly closed the door and lowered the blinds. "Let's begin with the three obsoletes."

"What if we don't find our killer?"

"Then we'll move on to the Eden employee, Handerling. Though that seems a remote possibility."

"Whatever you say." Lash was highly skilled

219

at reading people, but Mauchly remained an enigma. His seemed a monochrome personality, unburdened by mood or even emotion.

"Let's get started," Tara said. For the first time, she had a brisk, eager air about her. The prospect that filled him with lassitude seemed to give her energy.

They took seats around the table. Lash sipped his coffee while Mauchly broke open the first of three summary folders, put the contents on the desk.

"Grant Atchison," Mauchly said, reading from the top sheet. "Completed initial application July 21, 2003. Age twenty-three, male Caucasian, graduated Rutgers with a bachelor in economics, residing at 3143 Auburn Street, Perth Amboy, New Jersey."

"Is that his own home, or his parents'?" Lash asked.

Tara had taken up a few of the sheets and was riffling through them. "Parents."

"So far, so good."

"Employed at a chemical dye plant in Linden." Mauchly turned over a sheet. "Passed our initial screening, came in for applicant evaluation in August. Was rejected by the senior evaluator, Dr. Alicto."

Lash waited for Mauchly to glance up at him. But the man's eyes remained on the summary sheets.

"Reason?" Tara asked.

"A lot of false answers on the tests, for one

thing. Validity scales were way off baseline." Mauchly read from the sheet. " 'Difficulties with impulse control, emotional turbulence, anhedonia.' It goes on."

"He was in Arizona during the week the Thorpes died," Tara said.

"How do you know that?" Lash asked.

"Any of half a dozen ways. Guy buys an e-ticket, gets entered into the airline database. Pays for it with a credit card, gets into the credit card database. Rents a car in Phoenix, gets into the car rental database." She shrugged as if it was common knowledge.

"Yes, but here's a problem." Mauchly was looking at the last page of the summary. "There are reports here of a recent medical condition: bloods sent to Enzymatics for a workup, there's traffic on the insurance carriers network." He glanced at Tara. "Care to dig a little deeper?"

"Sure thing." Tara walked over to the terminal behind Lash's desk and began to type. "The guy was admitted to Middlesex County Hospital two and a half weeks ago. Renal problems. Had to remove a kidney."

"Length of stay?"

More typing. "He's still there. Complications from surgery."

Lash listened to this interchange in growing disbelief.

"So much for Mr. Atchison." Mauchly gathered the papers, returned them to the folder, then laid it aside and broke the seal on another. "The second obsolete's name is Katherine Barrow. Completed application December 20, 2003. Age forty-six, female, Caucasian, high school equivalency degree, resides in York, Pennsylvania. Religion filled out as 'druid.' Owns a shop called Feminine Magic in Lancaster County. Apparently sells candles, incense, herbal remedies."

"What does her evaluation say?" Tara asked as she returned to the table.

"Never made it that far. There was a security incident after filing the initial application. Lingered in the lobby, tried to approach several male applicants. There was an intervention, and she became disorderly."

"Tut-tut," said Tara.

Mauchly leafed through the summary. "Credit card vouchers and hotel records place her in Sedona, Arizona, when the Thorpes were killed. She was attending a seminar on crystals." He put down the summary, looked at Lash. "How common are female serial killers?"

"More common than people think. Dorothea Puente killed as many as nine of the lodgers in her boarding house during the late eighties. Mary Ann Cotton left a trail of dead husbands and children behind her. Over ninety percent are white. They're frequently health-care providers or other 'black widows' that have been quietly killing for decades.

Age forty-six would fit the pattern. Does she have any family?"

Mauchly looked down at the gathered sheets. "No."

"Look for signs of an isolated existence, no criminal record, possible abuse as a wife or harsh discipline as a child."

"Never married," Mauchly went on. "Runs the shop by herself — I see no reports of any employees in the Department of Labor database. No criminal record."

Lash, watching, could only shake his head. He'd already seen — firsthand — the incredible volume of data Eden assembled on its clients. And yet this ability to peer so deeply into the life of somebody who'd been summarily rejected years before was unsettling.

"Looks like we might have strike two," Tara announced. "There may be no criminal record, but there's a medical history here of substance abuse. She's been in and out of detox the last six months." She picked up some additional sheets, returned to the computer. "Barrow checked herself into a rehab clinic outside of New Hope early Saturday morning."

"The Wilners died Friday night," Mauchly said. "York's only a two-hour drive from Larchmont."

Tara was typing again. "Upon admittance, she was found to have near-toxic levels of fentanyl in her system. The admitting clinician said she'd passed out in the guest lot of the clinic, been asleep for hours."

"Nobody could commit two murders with a bloodstream full of fentanyl," Lash said.

Tara sighed.

For a moment, nobody spoke. Then Mauchly put the papers aside and broke open the third and last folder.

"James Albert Groesch," he began. "Age thirty-one, male Caucasian, no religious affiliation, dropped out of vocational college after two years. Resides in Massapequa, New York. Postal employee. Passed initial screening. Returned for applicant evaluation, failed by the senior evaluator."

"Reason?" Lash asked.

"Alarming test results. The personality inventory showed defective socialization, ambivalence to close relationships, potential sexual maladjustment, incipient misogynic tendencies."

"Misogyny? Why would such a person want what Eden has to offer?"

"You tell me, Dr. Lash. Not everybody comes to us with healthy reasons. That's one of the things our evaluations screen out." Mauchly scanned the report. "The evaluator states that, upon learning of being declined, Groesch grew threatening. He made angry statements about Eden, about — let's see here — 'phony perfection,' 'artificial happiness.' He implied it was all a government plot, recruiting women to spy on men, infiltrate their households. Security was called and the employee who'd vetted Groesch's initial screening was disciplined."

"Groesch was hiking in the Grand Canyon prior to the death of the Thorpes," Tara said, examining the overview. "Spent two nights at Phantom Ranch. Flew from Flagstaff to Phoenix, then back to La Guardia, the day after their bodies were discovered."

So all three had been in or around Flagstaff at the time of the deaths, Lash thought. No doubt one of the filters Liza had used in assembling the list.

"There's something else," Tara said. "Groesch's evaluation took place on August 2, 2002."

"And?" said Lash.

"That was also the day of Karen Wilner's evaluation."

A chill settled over the room.

"Defective socialization," Lash murmured. "Sexual maladjustment."

He turned toward Mauchly. "Anything else there? Anything that says this *couldn't* be our boy?"

Mauchly looked back at the overview. He scanned it briefly, then passed it to Tara. She turned over the pages, shook her head.

A brief but electric tingle surged through Lash. The weariness he'd felt was gone. There was a color photograph of Groesch lying among the papers, and he picked it up. A burly man with close-cropped blond hair and a huge handlebar moustache glared back at him.

"Let's break out the picks and axes," Tara said. "Time for some data mining."

Wordlessly, Mauchly stood and walked toward the far wall, where the evidence lockers were stacked. He brought three to the table, unsealed the first. Inside, Lash saw credit card statements; telephone records; transcripts of what looked like Internet URLs.

"Tara, would you contact the CCTV group and coordinate?" Mauchly asked. "Have them start running recognition algorithms in Massapequa, Larchmont, Flagstaff. And see who's satellite liaison today. Have them spin up their archives, just in case."

"Sure thing." Tara stood, picked up the telephone.

Mauchly reached into the open locker, pulled out two enormous stacks of papers, and began leafing through them. "It appears Mr. Groesch made numerous calls to his mother in the weeks leading up to the four deaths. We'll have to pinpoint any calls he made on the two days in question — that could prove instructive. Hmm. He also joined several primitive Internet matchmaking services over the last couple of months. In each case, he seems to have filled out the forms differently, lying about his age, place of residence, interests. He also seems to have visited some rather unusual websites lately: a site that describes how to make poisons, another specializing in graphic photographs of murders and suicides." He glanced up. "Does this fit with your profile, Dr. Lash?"

It was overwhelming, the level of detail Eden seemed able to pull effortlessly out of the air. "How are you able to do all this?" Lash asked.

Mauchly looked up at him again. "All what?"

"Assemble all this information. I mean, these people didn't even become your *clients*."

Mauchly's lips thinned briefly in what might have been a smile. "Dr. Lash, bringing two people together in perfect unity is only half our business. The other half is, shall we say, informational awareness. Without the latter, we could never do the former."

"I know. But I've never seen anything close to it, even at the Bureau. It's almost as if you can reconstruct people's entire lives."

"People think their daily activities are invisible," Tara said. "Not so. Every time you surf the Web, software cookies track where you've been, every click of your mouse while you were there. Every email you send goes through a dozen hosts before reaching its destination. Spend a day in any large city, and your image is captured by hundreds of closed-circuit television systems. All that's lacking is an infrastructure robust enough to gather it all. That's where we come in. We share our information with commercial database providers, selected government agencies, ISP vendors, junk-mail distributors, and —"

"Junk mail?" Lash said in surprise.

"Junk mail outfits have some of the most sophisticated data algorithms around. It isn't the untargeted bulk people think. Same with telemarketers. Anyway, all this data on you is collected and stored. Stored *forever.* Our problem isn't getting enough data: we usually gather too much."

"It's like Big Brother."

"Perhaps it seems that way," said Mauchly. "But with our help, hundreds of thousands of clients have found happiness. And now we might also stop a murderer."

There was a knock on the door; Tara rose from the keyboard to open it. A man in a lab coat handed her an ivory-colored folder. Tara thanked him, closed the door, and opened the folder. She stared at the contents a minute.

"Shit," she said under her breath.

"What is it?" Mauchly asked.

She handed him the folder wordlessly. Mauchly glanced at it a minute. Then he turned to Lash.

"Our team ran a facial recognition search through our archive of surveillance images," he said. "We already knew Groesch was around Flagstaff when the Thorpes died, so Tara limited the search to his whereabouts the night of the Wilners' deaths. The search picked up these images."

He handed some photographs to Lash. "Here he is, at an ATM at 3:12 p.m. And here again, running a traffic light at 4:05. And again, buying cigarettes at a liquor store at 4:49. Again at 5:45, shopping for jeans."

Lash looked at the photos. They were glossy eight-by-tens, similar to the SOC evidence photos he'd seen at the Bureau. The resolution was remarkably good, and there was no mistaking the blond man with the handlebar moustache for anybody but James Groesch.

He handed back the pictures with mounting excitement. "Go on."

Mauchly pointed to a stamped label on the outside of the folder: MASSAPEQUA, INNER RING, 9/24/04.

As quickly as it had come, the excitement died away. "So he was in Massapequa while the Wilners bled out in Larchmont," Lash said.

Mauchly nodded.

Lash heaved a sigh. He glanced at the clock: it was just ten-thirty.

"What now?" he asked.

But he already knew the answer. Now came their last potential suspect. Gary Handerling. Eden's own.

TWENTY-FOUR

"It shouldn't take long to clear Handerling," Mauchly said. "Our background checks and psych batteries for prospective employees are even more exhaustive than for clients. I'm a little surprised Liza even flagged him." The air of disappointment in the office was almost palpable.

"What's the procedure?" Lash asked. He sipped his espresso, found it cold, drained it anyway.

"We have passive monitoring devices in every workstation and cubicle. Keystroke loggers, so forth. It's no secret, they're more a preventive measure than anything." Mauchly opened a different file: a thin manila folder containing only a few sheets. "Gary Joseph Handerling. Thirty-three years old. Formerly employed as data technician for a Poughkeepsie bank. Currently resides in Yonkers. Divorced, no children. Background check turned up nothing except some visits to his high school guidance counselor after breaking up with his first girlfriend."

Tara chuckled.

"Passed his psych evaluation within the nominal benchmarks. Scored high on his leadership and opportunistic scales. Hired by Eden in June of 2001 and put on a revolving internship. Worked six months in Systems Support. Transferred to Data Gathering in January 2002. Finished his internship by moving to Data Scrubbing in August. Given good marks on all performance reviews. Singled out for his high level of motivation and his interest in learning more about the company."

A damn Eagle Scout, thought Lash.

"Became head of his scrub crew last February. Eligible for promotion out of Data Scrubbing, but seems happy in his position." Mauchly raised his eyes toward Lash. "Fit any profile you know of?" His voice was tinged with a whisper of irony.

Lash felt defeated. "Not really. Some sociopaths are remarkably good at hiding in plain sight. Look at Ted Bundy. The guy's age, race, marital status jibe with an organized serial killer. But the consistent employment history goes against the profile. Then again, nothing about these deaths is standard." He thought a moment. "Is he up to date on his car payments and credit cards? Organized serial killers can be obsessive about not missing payments, not sticking out."

Mauchly looked back at the folder. "Tara,

can you check the credit agencies, cross-check with the DMV records?"

"Sure. What's his SSN?"

"200-66-2984."

"Just a moment." Tara tapped at the keys. "Everything spic-and-span. No late charges on any cards, going back eighteen months. Car payments up to date."

Mauchly nodded.

"Pretty decent driving record, too. Only two points on his license."

"How'd he get those?" Lash asked, more out of habit than any real curiosity.

"Speeding ticket, probably. Let me check WICAPS."

The room fell silent save for the patter of keystrokes.

"Yup," Tara said after a moment. "Excessive speed in a residential zone. Recent, too: September 24."

"September 24," Lash repeated. "That was the day —"

But Tara interrupted. "The location was Larchmont."

Larchmont.

"That was the day the Wilners died," Lash finished.

For a second, the office was still as the three exchanged glances. Then Mauchly spoke.

"Tara," he said in a very quiet voice. "Can you secure this terminal? I don't want anybody looking over our shoulder."

Tara turned back to the keyboard, typed a series of commands. "You've got it."

"Let's start with his credit card records," Mauchly said. "See if he's been anywhere interesting in the last month." His voice remained slow, almost sleepy.

"Interfacing with Instifax now." More typing. "He's been a busy little boy. Lots of restaurant bills, mostly in the city and lower Westchester. Strange: a couple of motel charges, too. One in Pelham, another in New Rochelle." She looked up. "Why would he be paying for motel rooms fifteen minutes from his apartment?"

"Keep going," Mauchly said.

"Here's a recent plane ticket: Air Northern. Car rental of just over a hundred bucks. Another lodging charge for one Dew Drop Inne. And here's an Amtrak charge, too. And what looks like an advance hotel reservation for this coming weekend."

"Where?"

"Just a minute. Burlingame, Massachusetts."

"Get onto EasyTrak. Let's check out those tickets."

"On it." Tara paused, waiting for her screen to refresh. "The plane ticket was a round trip to Phoenix. Leaving La Guardia September 15, returning September 17."

"The Thorpes died on September 17,"

Mauchly said. "You mentioned a Dew Drop Inne. Where's that located?"

The staccato hammer of keys. "Flagstaff, Arizona."

Lash felt an electric tingle.

Slowly, almost casually, Mauchly stood up and came around the table. "Can you bring up the keystroke logs for Handerling's terminal over, say, the past three weeks?"

Lash found himself standing and, like Mauchly, approaching the screen.

"Here we are," Tara said. Lash saw a torrent of data scroll up the screen: every keystroke Handerling's typed over the last fifteen business days.

"Run it through the sniffer." Mauchly glanced at Lash. "We'll pass it through an intelligent filter, look for anything he typed that seems suspicious."

"The way the government combs email and phone calls, looking for terrorists?"

"They license the technology from us."

"Nothing out of place," Tara said after a moment. "Sniffer comes up clean."

"What job did you say this guy has?" Lash asked.

"Data Scrub handles the secure archiving of client data, post-processing."

"Post-processing. You mean, once a match is made."

"That's correct."

"And you said he has a leadership position.

Could that give him access to sensitive, personal data?"

"We slice client data across several scrub teams to minimize such access. It's theoretically possible. But if he'd been snooping around, it would have shown up in his keystroke logs."

"Could he have accessed the data from a different terminal?"

"Terminals are coded by identity bracelet. If he'd used a different terminal, we'd know about it."

The room fell silent. Mauchly stared at the screen, arms folded across his chest.

"Tara," he said. "Run frequency analysis against the keystrokes. See if he deviated from his normal work at any time."

"Give me a minute." The screen refreshed, and a series of parallel columns appeared: dates, times, obscure acronyms meaningless to Lash.

"Nothing stands out," Tara said after a moment. "It all seems routine."

Lash found himself holding his breath. Was it going to happen again: would they find themselves at the threshold of a breakthrough, only to reach another dead end?

"If anything, *too* routine," Tara added.

"How so?" Mauchly asked.

"Well, look at this. Each day, from precisely 2:30 to 2:45, the exact same commands are repeated."

"What's unusual about that? It could be some daily activity, like freshening an archive."

"Even those vary a little: new datasets, different backup locations. But here, even the volume names are the same."

Mauchly peered at the screen for a long moment. "You're right. For fifteen minutes each day, the keystrokes are precisely identical."

"*And* they're typed at precisely the same time each day." Tara pointed at the screen. "Down to the second. How likely is that?"

"So what's it mean?" Lash asked.

Mauchly glanced at him. "Our employees know their work is monitored. Handerling knows that if he tried anything obvious — like disabling the keystroke logger, for instance — he'd come under immediate attention. Looks like he's found a way to throw up a smokescreen, perhaps run a macro of innocuous commands while he's actually doing something else."

"He may have found a vulnerability in the system," said Tara. "Some loophole or flaw he's exploiting."

"So is there some way we can see what he was really up to during those fifteen minutes?" Lash asked.

"No," said Mauchly.

"Yes," said Tara.

They looked at her.

"Maybe. We also use video cameras to take screen captures of all management terminals, right? They're infrequent, and random. But maybe we'll get lucky."

She typed a fresh flurry of commands, then paused. "Looks like there's been only one recent screen capture from Handerling's terminal during that fifteen-minute block. On September 13."

"Can you print it out, please?" Mauchly asked.

She moused a few commands and the printer on the desk began to hum. Mauchly grabbed the sheet as it fed out and they looked at the blurred image:

EDEN — PROPRIETARY AND CONFIDENTIAL
RESULTS OF SQL QUERY AGAINST DATASET
   A$4719
OPERATOR: UNKNOWN
TIME: 14:38:02.98 SEPT 13 04
CPU CYCLES: 23054

Thorpe, L.	Flagstaff, AZ
Wilner, J.	Larchmont, NY
Connelly, K.	Burlingame, MA
Gupta, P.	Madison, WI
Revere, M.	Jupiter, FL
Imperiole, M.	Alexandria, VA

END QUERY

"Oh, Jesus," Tara breathed.

"Those other names," Lash said. "Super-couples?"

Mauchly nodded. "All six to date."

But Lash barely heard him. His mind was racing now. *Serial killers are creatures of habit* . . .

Staring at the list, he remembered something — something chilling.

"You mentioned an Amtrak ticket," he said to Tara. "And an advance motel reservation?"

Tara's eyes suddenly widened. She turned back to the keyboard.

"A reservation on the Acela to Boston. This coming Friday morning."

"And the motel location?"

"Burlingame, Massachusetts."

Mauchly stepped away from the terminal. The dispassionate demeanor was gone. "Tara, I want you to get a record of Handerling's phone calls. Both from his desk and his apartment. Will you do that?"

Tara nodded, picked up the phone.

"Thank you." Mauchly started for the door, turned back. "Now, Dr. Lash, you'll have to excuse me. There are several things I need to do."

TWENTY-FIVE

In many ways, the scene was like the others: the room in disarray, the mirrors broken, the bedroom curtains swept back as if inviting the night to witness the outrage. And yet in others it was very, very different. The woman lay in an embarrassment of blood, flowing from the ruined body in a terrible corona. And in the merciless glare of the crime lights the walls shone white, naked, devoid of any scrawled messages.

Captain Masterton glanced up from the corpse. His face had the pinched look of a cop under pressure from all directions.

"I was wondering when you'd get here, Lash. Say hello to victim number three. Helen Martin, aged thirty-two."

Masterton kept staring at him. He seemed about to make another biting comment on the thinness of Lash's profile. But he merely shook his head in disgust.

"Christ, Lash, you're like a zombie. Every time I see you, you look a little worse."

"We'll go into that some other time. How long has she been dead?"

"Less than an hour."

"Any indication of rape? Vaginal penetration?"

"The ME's on his way, but there doesn't appear to be any. No signs of a burglary gone wrong, either. Just like the others. But we caught a bit of a break this time. A neighbor called in the commotion. No description of a vehicle, but we've already got cars stationed at major intersections, freeway on-ramps. Maybe we'll catch a break."

The crime scene was still so fresh the local cops were just beginning to work it: snapping photos, dusting for prints, chalking the body. He stood there, staring down at the body. There it was again: that maddening sense that everything was out of place. It was like a jigsaw puzzle with the wrong pictures pasted onto the pieces. It didn't fit, and even when it did it didn't look right. He knew, because he'd been putting it together and taking it apart in his mind, over and over and over, for days. It was like a fire burning in his head, consuming all his thoughts, devouring his sleep.

The body was brutalized in what was clearly a blitz attack. That was the hallmark of a socially defective killer. And yet

240

the house was secluded, backing up on woods, private: this was no crime of opportunity, no blitz attack. And then there were the broken mirrors, which normally indicated a killer's discomfort with creating such a scene. But such killers also covered their victims, hid their faces: this woman was naked, her limbs arranged with a ghastly provocativeness. And yet again this crime was not about sex. It was not about robbery. And this time, there was not even the ritual halo of severed toes and fingertips to lend a compulsive taint to the murder.

To build a profile, you had to get into the head of the murderer, ask questions. What had happened in this room? Why did it happen this particular way? Even mass-murderers had their twisted logic. But there was no logic here, no foundation on which to build an understanding.

His eyes traveled over the walls of the bedroom. In the previous two murders, they had been covered with rambling, half-coherent rants: a bloody mélange of contradiction.

This time, the walls were blank.

Why?

His eyes stopped on the big picture window facing the woods behind the house. As before, the blinds were thrown wide, revealing a pane of black that re-

flected the sodium lights back at him. It was hard to be sure in the painful glare, but he thought he could make out faint smudges on the glass, black upon black.

"Masterton. Can you direct those lights away from the window?"

The ME had just arrived, and the captain had moved across the room to confer with him. He looked over.

"What was that, Lash?"

"Those lights there, by the window. Turn them this way."

Masterton shrugged, spoke to Ahearn, his second in command.

As the glare of the light hit him, the window fell into shadow. He stepped forward, Masterton following now. High up on the glass, a few large words were scrawled in bloody finger-paint:

I'VE GOT WHAT I NEED NOW. THANK YOU.

"Oh, shit," he murmured.

"He's done," Masterton said, coming up, Detective Ahearn at his shoulder. "Thank God, Lash. It's finished."

"No," he replied. "No, it's not. It's just beginning . . ."

Lash sat up in bed, wide awake, waiting for the memories to fade. He glanced at the clock: half past one. He stood up, then hesitated, sinking back to the side of the bed.

Four nights in a row, with perhaps as many

242

hours of sleep to show for all of them. He couldn't afford to show up at Eden semiconscious; not tomorrow, he couldn't.

He rose again and — without giving himself a chance to reconsider — went to the bathroom, pulled out the box of Seconal, grabbed a small handful, and washed them down with a mouthful of water. Then he returned to bed, arranged the covers carefully, and gradually slipped into dark dreams.

It was the sound of church bells that woke him; the bells of his wedding, pealing from the dust-bleached mission of Carmel-by-the-Sea. And yet the bells were too loud somehow, and they went on and on, refusing to stop.

Lash forced his eyes open, realized it was the telephone. When he sat up, the room reeled. Closing his eyes, he lay back once again, feeling blindly for the phone.

"Yes," he said, voice thick.

"Dr. Christopher Lash?"

"Yeah."

"This is Ken Trotwood from New Olympia Savings and Loan."

Lash forced his eyes open again, glanced at the clock. "Do you know what time —"

"I know it's early, Dr. Lash. I'm very sorry. But we haven't been able to reach you any other way. You haven't responded to our letters or calls."

"What are you talking about?"

"It's about the mortgage on your house, which we hold. You're behind in your payments, Dr. Lash, and we must insist on immediate payment, with penalty interest."

Lash fought to think clearly. "You've made some kind of mistake."

"It doesn't appear so. The residence in question is number 17 Ship Bottom Road, Westport, Connecticut."

"That's my address, but —"

"According to my screen, sir, we've sent three letters and tried to call you half a dozen times. Without success."

"This is crazy. I haven't gotten any notices. Besides, my mortgage payment is automatically deducted from my bank account."

"Then perhaps there's been some kind of problem at your bank. Because our records show you're more than five months delinquent. And it's my job to inform you that if payment is not made immediately, we'll be forced to —"

"No need for threats. I'll look into it immediately."

"Thank you, sir. Good morning."

And the line went dead.

Good morning. As Lash sank back wearily, his eyes strayed toward the window, where the faintest glimmers of pre-dawn glow had begun to temper the unequivocal blackness of night.

TWENTY-SIX

"What's this guy supposed to have done?" asked the federal agent sitting behind the wheel.

"Under investigation for four possible homicides," Lash replied.

Rain drummed on the roof and ran down the windows in heavy streams. He drained his coffee cup, considered ducking into the nearby deli for another, looked at his watch and decided against it. Ten after five already, and human relations records indicated Gary Handerling almost always left work promptly.

He looked down at the glossy photograph of Handerling on the seat beside him, taken that morning by a closed-circuit camera at Checkpoint I. Then he gazed across Madison Avenue toward the Eden tower. Handerling wouldn't be hard to spot: tall and lanky, save for a softening around the belly, with thinning blond hair and a yellow windbreaker that stood out in a crowd. Even if Lash missed him, one of the other teams was sure to spot him.

Lash's gaze returned to the photo. Handerling didn't look like a serial killer. But then again, so few of them did.

The front passenger door opened and a heavyset man in a dripping blue suit climbed in. When he turned to glance into the rear of the car, the scent of Old Spice reached Lash ahead of the face. He'd known another Fed was going to ride with them, but he was surprised to recognize John Coven, a fellow agent he'd worked with on a few early cases.

"Lash?" Coven said, looking equally surprised. "That you?"

Lash nodded. "How you keeping, John?"

"Can't complain, I guess. Still treading water as a GS-13. Another five years and I'll be down in Marathon, fishing for tarpon instead of scumbags."

"Nice." Like many other agents, Coven was obsessed with the countdown to retirement and a government pension.

Coven looked at Lash curiously. "I heard you were off the Job. In the private sector, making a mint for yourself."

Coven knew Lash had left the FBI, of course; and he would also know the reason. He was just showing tact.

"I am," Lash replied. "This is a temporary thing. Moonlighting for some serious change."

Coven nodded.

"Isn't this kind of an unusual TDY for

246

you?" Lash asked, politely reversing the line of inquiry.

Coven shrugged. "Not anymore. These days, it's alphabet soup. What with all the shakeups and reorganizations, everybody's in bed with everybody else. You never know who you'll be working with: DEA, CIA, Homeland Security, local law enforcement, Girl Scouts."

Yes, but not a private corporation, Lash thought. Using the FBI for hired muscle was something new in his experience.

"Only thing strange was that this came down from the chief's office," Coven said. "Didn't go through the normal channels."

Lash nodded. He remembered Mauchly's words: *We share our information with selected government agencies.* Apparently, the cooperation went both ways.

He had seen very little of either Mauchly or Tara Stapleton all day. He'd arrived late, being forced to spend the better part of the morning untangling a hugely complex web of red tape, bank forms, credit agency reports, and bureaucratic mix-ups to correct his mortgage statement and restore various credit cards. Mauchly had stopped by his office just before lunch with a large packet under his arm. Handerling, he said, had picked up his train ticket for the following evening. A phone call he'd made from his desk that morning indicated he was meeting a woman after work. Surveillance was being arranged, and Mauchly wanted Lash to take part. The night before, he'd gently rebuffed Lash's urgings that they contact the police without delay. "He's not an immediate danger," Mauchly had said. "We need to gather more evidence. Don't worry, he's being carefully watched."

He'd dropped the packet — Handerling's job application, employee evaluation, prior history — on Lash's desk. "See if this fits your profile," he said. "If it does, please put together a brief character analysis for us. That could prove very useful."

And so Lash had spent the afternoon going over Handerling's records. The man was clever: with hindsight, Lash could see subtle evidence he'd carefully coached himself on psych tests. Questions meant to raise red flags had all been answered neutrally. The validity scales were acceptably low across all tests, in fact *equally* low, implying Handerling recognized which questions were testing for fakery and answered them all the same way.

Such intelligence and planning were earmarks of the organized killer. And in fact Handerling would be nothing else if he was posing as a model Eden employee. The disorganized elements in the killings, Lash decided, were explained by the unique nature of the victims. It was clear the six super-couples to date were almost cult figures within Eden. But in somebody with feelings of inadequacy or anger — somebody who'd had an abusive mother, say, or bad luck in personal relationships — they might become touchstones for jealousy, even the acting-out of misdirected rage.

It wasn't that Handerling knew the Thorpes and the Wilners, so much as that he knew *of* them, through his position at Eden. And that was very interesting indeed. It meant a new subdivision of serial killer, not previously identified: a byproduct of the information age, a killer who trolled databases to find ideal victims. It would make a hell of an article in the *American Journal of Neuropsychiatry*: an article that would curl the toes of his old friend Roger Goodkind.

The squawk of a radio came from the front seat. "Unit 709. In position."

Coven picked up the radio, holding it low so it would not be visible outside the car. "Roger." He turned toward Lash. "We didn't get much of a briefing. What's the setup, exactly?"

"This guy Handerling's supposed to meet a woman after work. Beyond that, we don't know much."

"How's he traveling?"

"Unknown. Could be foot, subway, bus, whatever. And —" Lash stopped suddenly. "There he is. Coming out the revolving door now."

Coven switched on the radio. "This is 707. All units, be advised suspect is exiting the building. White male, about six foot two, wearing a yellow windbreaker. Stand by."

Handerling stopped to gaze up and down Madison Avenue. His windbreaker flexed as he raised a large umbrella over his head. Lash resisted the urge to stare at his face. It had been years since he'd last been on a surveillance, and he found his heart beating uncomfortably fast.

"That's our man, there," said Coven, nodding his head in the direction of a corner newsstand.

"The one with the red umbrella and the cell phone?"

"Yup. You wouldn't believe how much easier cell phones have made surveillance. These days, it's normal to see someone on the street talking into their hand. And these Nextel devices have walkie-talkie features built in, so we can broadcast to the entire group."

"Other foot surveillance resources?"

"At the subway entrance and that bus stop, over there."

"This is 709," came a voice over the radio. "Suspect in motion. Looks like he's going to hail a cab."

Lash allowed himself a sidelong glance out the window. Handerling had moved toward the street with a long, loping gait. The man darted out an arm, index finger extended, and a cab nosed obediently to the curb.

Coven grabbed his radio. "This is 707. I've got the eye; 702, 705, we're rolling."

"Roger," came a chorus of voices.

The driver swung the brown sedan out into traffic, a few vehicles behind the taxi.

"Suspect turning eastbound onto Fifty-seventh," Coven said, still holding the radio in his lap.

"How many takeaway vehicles?" Lash asked.

"Two others. We'll sit on him a while, take it a block at a time."

The taxi moved slowly, fighting the rain and the crosstown traffic. One wheel splashed through a deep pothole, sending a brown spray over the sidewalk. At Lexington Avenue, it turned again, brusquely cutting off a minivan.

"Turning south on Lex," Coven said. "Maintaining twenty-five miles per hour. I'm going to relinquish. Anybody?"

"This is 705," came the voice. "I've got the eye."

Lash glanced out the rear window and noticed a green SUV pulling up in the adjoining lane. Through the rain, he could make out Mauchly sitting in the front passenger seat.

Coven's driver pressed on the gas, accelerating smoothly past the taxi and down

Lexington Avenue. It was standard surveillance practice, Lash knew: have as many vehicles as possible involved so the suspect won't think he's being followed. In a few blocks, they'd make a turn, circle back, and join the rear of the line.

"Seven-oh-five, roger," Coven glanced back. "So, Lash, what's it like in the private sector?"

"I can't get speeding tickets fixed anymore."

Coven grinned, told the driver to turn onto Third Avenue. "Ever miss the Bureau?"

"Don't miss the pay."

"I hear that."

"Unit 705," the radio squawked. "Suspect turning east onto Forty-fourth. Vehicle stopping. I'm going to pass him, who's picking up the eye?"

"This is 702. We've pulled over at the far corner. Maintaining visual contact."

Coven's driver pushed the sedan forward now, bullying his way through first one intersection, then another.

"Seven-oh-two," came the voice. "Suspect has exited the vehicle. He's entering a bar called Stringer's."

"Seven-oh-seven," Coven replied. "Roger that. Keep a visual on the entrance. Seven-fourteen, we need you at Stringer's. Forty-fourth between Lex and Third."

"Roger."

Minutes later, their sedan nosed into a no-parking zone on Forty-fourth. Lash glanced out the window. Judging by the garish awning and knots of twenty-somethings outside, Stringer's was a pickup bar for young professionals.

"Here they come now," Coven said.

Lash looked at an unfamiliar young couple coming down the street, holding hands and sharing an umbrella. "Is that foot surveillance?"

Coven nodded.

The couple disappeared inside the bar. A minute later, Coven's cell phone rang.

"Seven-oh-seven," he said.

Lash could hear distinctly the voice that came through the tiny speaker. "We're at the bar. Suspect is at a rear table. He's with a white female, heavyset, five foot six, wearing a white sweater and black jeans."

"Roger. Stay in touch." Coven put the phone aside, then looked into the rear of the sedan. His eye landed on Lash's empty coffee cup.

"Another?" he asked. "I'm buying."

Within half an hour, Lash was completely caught up on Bureau gossip: the Lothario who was playing around with the section chief's wife; the annoying new red tape out of Washington; the weak leadership in the upper echelons; how unbelievably green the latest batch of new jacks were. Infrequently, reports came in from the agents watching Handerling from the bar.

Then came a moment when talk faltered, and Coven glanced at his driver. "Hey, Pete. How about getting us a couple more coffees?"

Lash watched the agent get out of the car and trot toward a deli down the block.

"Caught a break with this rain," Coven said.

Lash nodded. He looked in the rearview mirror: on the far side of the street and half a block back, he could just make out the dim form of Mauchly's SUV.

Coven was shifting restlessly in the front seat. "So tell me, Chris," he said after a moment. "This place you're moonlighting, Eden. What's it like?"

"Pretty remarkable," Lash replied guardedly. If Coven was getting curious about the tail, fishing for more information, he'd need to be careful what he said.

"I mean, can they really *do* it? Are they as good as everybody says?"

"They've got a great track record."

Coven nodded slowly. "There's this guy in my golf foursome, an orthodontist. Something of a Gloomy Gus, never married. You know the type. We were always trying to fix him up with somebody, but he hated the singles scene. It became a running joke on the links. Anyway, he went to Eden about a year ago. You wouldn't know him now, he's a different person. Married to a really nice woman. Great body, too. He doesn't talk about it much, but any idiot can see how happy he is. Even the bastard's golf game has improved."

Lash listened without comment.

"Then there's this chief I know, over in Operations. Harry Creamer, remember him? Anyway, his wife died in a car accident couple of years back. Good guy. Well, he's remarried now. Never seen anybody happier. Rumor is, he went to Eden, too."

Coven turned around again, and Lash could see a kind of desperate eagerness in his eyes. "I'll be honest with you, Chris. Things aren't so hot between me and Annette. We've been drifting apart ever since we learned she can't have kids. So I look at my golf buddy, I look at Harry Creamer, and I start thinking twenty-five thousand bucks isn't all that much money. Not in the long run, it isn't. I mean, why live a half-assed life? It's not like you get a second chance if you fuck it up the first time." He paused a second. "I was wondering if you knew whether —"

The cell phone chirped. "Seven-oh-seven, this is unit 714, you read?"

Instantly, the professional veneer settled back over Coven. He reached for the phone. "This is 707, go ahead, 714."

"Suspect's having some kind of argument with the woman. They're on their way out."

"Roger, 707 out."

At that moment, the door of Stringer's opened and a woman emerged, walking quickly, shrugging into a raincoat as she went. Then Handerling pushed his way through the doors and went after her.

"All units, suspect on foot," Coven said into his radio, cracking open the car window as he did so. The woman was shouting at Handerling over her shoulder: Lash made out the words "fucking low-life snoop" before the rest was drowned in the passing traffic.

Handerling put out a hand to stop her and she brushed it away. When he reached out again she turned, raising her arm to slap him. Handerling dodged the blow and pushed her roughly toward a shop front.

"Let's take him," Coven said.

Lash quickly ducked out the back and followed Coven across the street. From the corner of his eye he saw the agent named Pete come out of the deli, a cup in each hand. When he saw Coven on the move, he dropped the coffees in a trash can and joined the pursuit.

Within seconds, Handerling was surrounded. "Federal agents," Coven barked, showing his shield. "Back off, mister. Hands at your sides."

The anger on the woman's face was replaced by fear. She retreated a few steps, then turned and ran.

"You want secondary surveillance on the girl?" Pete asked.

"No." It was Mauchly who answered. He stood behind them in the rain, Tara at his side. "Mr. Handerling, I'm Edwin Mauchly of Eden. Will you come with us, please?"

Handerling had gone white. His lips were working silently, and his eyes darted left and right. Half a dozen more men in suits were trotting toward them now, whether federal agents or Eden security Lash did not know.

"Mr. Handerling," Mauchly said again. "This way, if you please."

Handerling straightened. For a moment, he gathered himself to bolt, and the circle tensed.

Then all at once he seemed to deflate. His shoulders drooped visibly. And he nodded, stepped forward, and allowed Mauchly to escort him to the waiting SUV.

TWENTY-SEVEN

Except for the fact it was safely inside the Wall, the space could almost have been one of the conference rooms Eden used for class reunions. Chairs had been pulled away from the far side of the oval table, leaving a single seat at its center. Another half dozen were arrayed along the near side, with more placed in the corners of the room.

Handerling sat in the lone seat, still wearing his damp windbreaker. He looked around with thinly disguised nervousness. Mauchly sat across from him, flanked by Tara Stapleton and two men Lash didn't recognize. One wore a physician's lab coat. A brace of Eden security workers stood by the door. More were stationed in the hall outside. From his vantage point in the shadows, Lash was surprised at how numerous they were. And they were not the affable, approachable guards of the lobby: these were unsmiling men who stared straight ahead, jaws set, small wires leading from their ears to their collars. When one opened his jacket to answer a cell phone, Lash caught the gleam of a weapon.

A videocamera sat on a large dolly, manned by a security tech. A recorder sat in the middle of the table. Mauchly nodded to the cameraman, then switched on the recorder.

"Mr. Handerling, do you know why you're here?" he asked. "Why we're talking to you?"

Handerling stared across the table. "No."

Lash watched the suspect. When he'd first been surrounded, Handerling had been frightened, disoriented. But now he'd had time to think — in the hand-off from the Feds to Eden security, with its resultant paperwork; during the ride back to the tower; in the maze of back corridors they'd taken to reach this room. If he was like other offenders Lash had known, he'd have a game plan in mind by now.

Interrogation was often compared to a seduction. One person wanted something from the other, while the other frequently had little interest in giving it up. Lash was curious to see what kind of seducer Mauchly would make. His heart was racing excitedly in his chest.

Mauchly regarded Handerling with his usual mild expression. He let the silence build. Then at last he spoke again.

"You really have no idea? No idea at all?"

"No. And I don't think you have any right

to hold me here, asking questions like this." Handerling spoke with a truculent, aggrieved tone.

Mauchly did not respond directly. Instead, he straightened a tall pile of documents on the table beside him. "Mr. Handerling, let me make some introductions before we get started. Here with me is Tara Stapleton of Systems Security, and Dr. Debney of Medical. You know Mr. Harrison, of course. Why were you seeing that woman?"

Handerling blinked at this abrupt shift. "I don't think it's any of your business. I know my rights, I demand to —"

"Your *rights* —" and the word had a sudden staccato bite that brought the room to attention "— are summarized in this document you signed when you joined Eden." Mauchly took a bound folder from the top of the pile, pushed it toward the center of the table. "Recognize it?"

For a moment, Handerling remained motionless. Then he leaned forward, nodded.

"In this binding contract, you agreed — among many other things — not to abuse your position at Eden through any covert use of technology. You agreed to keep client data compartmentalized. And you agreed to the strict code of moral conduct mandated in our employee charter. This was all explained to you in detail during orientation, and your signature here attests to your understanding."

Mauchly delivered these words in an almost bored monotone. But their effect on Handerling was significant. He stared back at Mauchly, eyes glittering with suspicion.

"So I ask again. Why were you seeing that woman?"

"It was a date. No law against that."

Lash could see Handerling was fighting to keep up the facade of an injured party.

"That depends."

"On what?"

Instead of answering, Mauchly glanced at the documentation before him. "When we approached you outside the bar, the woman — who has since been identified from your telephone calls this afternoon as Sarah Louise Hunt — was heard to call you, let's see here, a 'fucking low-life snoop.' To what was she referring, Mr. Handerling?"

"No idea."

"As it happens, I think you do have an idea. A very good idea."

Lash noticed Tara was scribbling on a pad, while Mauchly stared across the table at Handerling. This was standard procedure, one person taking notes while the other kept careful watch on the suspect's nonverbal communication: nervous gestures, eye movement, the like. But most interrogators liked to get into the faces of their subjects, keep a rapid-fire series of questions going. Mauchly was just the opposite. He let silence and uncertainty work for him.

At last, Mauchly stirred. "Not only do I think you've got a good idea what she meant, but there are several others who probably do, too." He glanced down at the documentation once again. "Such as Helen Malvolia. Karen Connors. Marjorie Silkwood. Half a dozen others."

Handerling's face went ashen.

"What do they all have in common, Mr. Handerling? They were all applicants at Eden. All were disapproved, following their psychological evaluations. All for similar reasons. Low self-esteem. Products of broken homes. High passivity factors. In other words, women who could be easily victimized."

Mauchly's voice had grown so low, Lash strained to hear.

"These women all have something else in common. In the last six months, they've been approached by you. In some cases, it ended with lunch or drinks. In other cases it went well, *well* beyond that."

Suddenly, Mauchly lifted the heavy pile of documents and slammed it back down on the table. The action was so unexpected Handerling jumped in his chair.

But when Mauchly spoke again, his voice was calm. "We have it all here. Records of phone calls, from home and the office; credit card receipts for restaurants, bars, motels; data intercepts of confidential Eden records touched from your terminal. And, by the way, we've already plugged the security weakness you used to access client data across security frontiers." Mauchly shifted. "In light of this, would you care to revisit your response?"

Handerling swallowed painfully. Sweat had sprouted along his brow, and his hands clenched and unclenched involuntarily. "I want a lawyer," he said.

"Your signature on this document waives the privilege of representation during internal examinations of your own malfeasance. The fact is, Mr. Handerling, you've compromised the integrity of this company. You've done that, and more. You've not only betrayed our trust and that of our clients, but you've done it in the lowest, most despicable fashion possible. To think you could search out, *intentionally,* the most pliable victims — pry through transcripts where they reveal their most private hopes and dreams, their deepest wants in a relationship — and then callously exploit those to slake your own craven lusts . . . it's almost beyond comprehension."

An electric silence filled the room.

Handerling licked dry lips. "I —" he began. He fell silent.

"Once our work is completed here, you'll be remanded — with the indictable evidence — to the custody of the authorities."

"The *police?*" Handerling said sharply.

Mauchly shook his head. "No, Mr. Handerling. Federal authorities."

The look on Handerling's face turned to disbelief.

"Eden has information-sharing agreements with certain branches of government. You know that. Some data involved is of a classified nature. By covertly manipulating our databanks, you have committed what could be considered a treasonable offense."

"Treason?" Handerling said in a strangled voice.

"You would be prosecuted in a federal facility, sparing ourselves and our clients embarrassing publicity. And in case you weren't aware, there *is* no parole in federal prison, Mr. Handerling."

Handerling's roaming eyes shifted back to Mauchly: a furtive, hunted look.

"Okay," he said. "All right. It's like you say. I did meet those women. But I didn't hurt them."

"What were you doing to Sarah Hunt when we approached, then?"

"I just wanted her to stop shouting. I wouldn't hurt her. I haven't done anything wrong!"

"Haven't done anything wrong? Stalking women, misusing confidential and trade-secret information, making false representations — that isn't wrong?"

"It didn't start out that way!" Handerling's

264

gaze swept the room frantically, searching for a sympathetic eye. "Look, it began as an accident. I realized as scrub boss I could exploit this vulnerability I'd discovered, look beyond our compartment, piece together enough data fragments to get full client briefs. It was curiosity, just curiosity . . ."

It was as if a dam had burst. Handerling began spilling it all: his accidental discovery of the loophole; his timid early probing; the methods he'd used to evade detection; his first meetings with the women. Everything. And Mauchly had handled it beautifully. With a series of baiting questions about lesser crimes, he'd gotten Handerling to bite. And now that the man was talking, it would be almost impossible for him to stop. Mauchly, having unbalanced his victim, would go in for the kill.

Just at that moment, in fact, Mauchly raised a commanding hand. Handerling stopped in mid rant, unfinished sentence hanging suspended in the air.

"This is all very interesting," Mauchly said quietly. "And we'll want to hear all about it in due course. But let's move on to the real reason you're here."

Handerling passed a hand over his eyes. "The *real* reason?"

"Your more serious offenses."

Handerling looked dazed. He said nothing.

"Would you care to tell us where you were

on the morning of September 17?"

"September 17?"

"Or the late afternoon of September 24?"

"I don't . . . I don't remember."

"Then let me remind you. On September 17, you were in Flagstaff, Arizona. On September 24, you were in Larchmont, New York. You have a hotel reservation tomorrow night in Burlingame, Massachusetts. Do you know what those three addresses have in common, Mr. Handerling?"

Handerling's fingers gripped the edge of the table, knuckles dead white. "The supercouples."

"Very good. They are each residences of one of our uniquely perfect couples. Or, in the first two instances, were."

"*Were?*"

"Yes. Since both the Thorpes and the Wilners are now dead."

"The Thorpes?" Handerling said, his voice little more than a croak. "The Wilners? Dead?"

"Come now, Mr. Handerling. This only wastes time. What were your intentions for the coming weekend?"

But Handerling did not answer. His eyes had rolled back, shockingly white in the bright light of the room. Lash wondered if he was going to faint.

"If you'd rather not say, then let *me* tell *you* what you were going to do. What you've done already, twice. You were going to kill the Connellys. But very carefully, like you'd done before. Make it look like double suicide."

The room was quiet, the only noise Handerling's labored breathing.

"You murdered the first two supercouples, in order," Mauchly said. "Now you've been planning to stalk, and kill, a third."

Still, Handerling said nothing.

"We'll be doing a deep psych reval on you, of course. But we've already put together a theoretical profile. After all, your actions speak for themselves." Mauchly consulted the papers before him. "I'm talking about your fear of rejection, your shrunken sense of self-worth. Armed with information you pilfered from our files, you knew just how to approach those women you selected and manipulated. Remarkable that, in some cases, you failed, even with such an overwhelming advantage." Mauchly smiled mirthlessly. "But if these encounters eased your feelings of inadequacy around women, they did nothing to ease your anger. Anger that others could find the kind of happiness you never would. Those others who you'd always envied. Our supercouples were that embodiment for you. They became the lightning rod for your anger, which was actually self-loathing, twisted in such a way that —"

"*No!*" Handerling screamed: a thin, high keening sound.

"Come now, Mr. Handerling. Don't excite yourself."

"I didn't kill them!" Tears were starting from his eyes. "Okay, so I went to Arizona. I have relatives in Sedona, I was going there for a wedding. Flagstaff was nearby. And Larchmont is only an hour from my house."

Mauchly folded his arms, listening.

"I wanted to *know*. I wanted to *understand*. You see, the files just didn't explain. They didn't explain how somebody could be so happy. So I thought maybe, if I just saw them — if I could just watch them, just for a bit, from a safe distance — I could learn . . . You've got to believe me, I never killed anybody! I just wanted to — I just want to be *happy*, like them . . . oh, *Jesus* . . ." And Handerling dropped forward, his head hitting the desk with an ugly sound, sobs racking his frame.

"No need for dramatics," Mauchly said. "We can do this with your cooperation, or without. You'll find the former far less of an inconvenience." When Handerling did not respond, Mauchly bent toward the physician, whispered in his ear.

But for Lash, the scene had suddenly changed, and changed utterly. The cries of Handerling, the murmuring of Mauchly, drained away to silence in his head. A chill passed through him. Eden could interrogate, could examine, this man as much as they wanted. But in his gut, Lash sensed Handerling was innocent. Not of stalking — he was clearly guilty of abusing sensitive information. And he'd spied on the Eden supercouples. But he was no killer. Lash had seen enough suspects sweated to know when someone was lying, or when someone was capable of murder.

The worst thing was he should have known before. The suspect chart he'd worked up on his whiteboard, the theoretical profile he'd written and Mauchly had just delivered to the room, suddenly seemed as thin as the rice paper woodcuts in Lewis Thorpe's study. They were full of inconsistencies, false assumptions. He'd been too eager to solve this terrible puzzle before more people died. And this was the result.

He sank deeper into the shadows. A haiku of Bashō's kept repeating in his head, eclipsing the wails of Handerling:

> *Spring passes*
> *and the birds cry out —*
> *tears in the eyes of fishes*

It was close to midnight by the time he pulled his car into Ship Bottom Road. He killed the engine, got out of the car, and walked slowly, deliberately toward the mailbox. Something had been tugging at the back of his mind since he'd left the Eden building; something that had nothing to do with Handerling. But Lash steadfastly refused to pay attention. He felt more tired than he'd ever felt in his life.

When he opened the mailbox, his first sense was relief: there was mail today, it hadn't been pilfered. If anything, he realized, there was too much mail: at least a dozen magazines lay scattered among the circulars and catalogues. There was a gay lifestyles magazine, another devoted to S&M and bondage fetishists; many others. All had subscription labels bearing his name and address. Among the envelopes were another dozen subscription notices with demands for payment.

Somebody had been filling out subscription requests under his name.

He walked toward the house, pausing to dump everything but a utility bill into a garbage can. It seemed Mary English had switched tactics. It was regrettable, but a call to the Westport police might be necessary after all.

He stepped up to the door, put his key in the lock, then stopped. A courier package marked BY EXPRESS — HAND DELIVER and bearing Eden's logo lay against it. *Probably more confidentiality agreements for my signature,* he thought bleakly. He stooped to pick it up, tore away one end. Moonlight revealed a single sheet of paper inside, to which a small pin had been attached. He pulled out the sheet.

Christopher Lash
17 Ship Bottom Road
Westport, Connecticut 06880

Dear Dr. Lash:
  We at Eden are in the business of providing miracles. Yet I never tire of having the honor to announce each of them in turn. So it is with the greatest pleasure I'm writing to inform you that the selection interval, which followed your successful application and evaluation process, has now concluded in a match. Her name is Diana Mirren. It will be your own delightful duty to learn more than that, and you will soon have an opportunity to do so. A dinner reservation has been made in your joint names at Tavern on the Green for this coming Saturday evening, at eight o'clock. You will be able to identify each other by the enclosed pins, which we ask you to wear on your lapels on first entering the restaurant. They may be disposed of after that, though most of our clients treasure them as mementos.
  Once again, our congratulations on completing this journey, and our best

wishes as you embark on another. And in the months and years to come, I feel certain you will find that bringing the two of you together is the beginning, rather than the end, of our service.

Kind regards,

John Lelyveld
Chairmain, Eden Inc.

TWENTY-EIGHT

When the elevator doors opened onto the penthouse perched atop Eden's inner tower the next morning, Richard Silver was there, waiting.

"Christopher," he said. "How are you faring?"

"Thanks for seeing me on such short notice." Lash shook the proffered hand.

"Not at all. I've been looking forward to speaking with you again."

Silver guided Lash to a seat. Sunlight slanted through the windows, throwing the still parade of ancient thinking machines into sharp relief, gilding the polished surfaces of the vast room.

"I'm also glad to have the chance to apologize in person," Silver said as they sat down. "Mauchly told me about the letter, your getting the nod. Such a mistake has never happened before, and we're still looking into what went wrong. Not that a mere explanation could make it less humiliating for you. Or for us."

Lash glanced over as Silver fell silent. Again, he was struck by the man's lack of artifice. Silver seemed genuinely concerned about how Lash would feel: rejected as an applicant, only to later learn a match had been mistakenly found for him. Perhaps, up here in his aerie, consumed with his ongoing research, Silver had remained free of the dehumanizing corporate taint.

Silver looked up, caught Lash's eye. "Of course, I've instructed Mauchly to roll back the match, and to contact this woman — sorry, I don't know her name — and inform her another match will be found."

"Her name's Diana Mirren," Lash said. "But that's not what I wanted to see you about."

Silver looked surprised. "Really? Then forgive my assumption. Tell me why you're here."

Lash paused. The conviction he'd felt the night before now seemed blurred by weariness and the remaining traces of more Seconal. "I wanted to tell you personally. I don't think I can do this anymore."

"Do what, exactly?"

"Stay on this investigation."

Silver frowned. "If it's a question of money, we'd be happy to —"

"It's not that. I've been paid too much already."

Silver sat back again, listening carefully.

"I've been away from my patients two weeks now. That's a geologic age in psychiatry. But it's more than that."

He hesitated again. This was the kind of thing that normally he'd never admit to himself, let alone discuss with anybody else. But there was something about Silver — an unstudied frankness, a complete lack of arrogance — that seemed to invite confidence.

"I don't think I can be of any more help to you," Lash continued. "Early on, I thought all I needed was access to your files. I thought I'd find some magic answer in your evaluations of the Thorpes. And after the death of the Wilners, I grew certain it was homicide, not suicide. I'd hunted serial killers before, I was sure I could hunt this one as well. But I've come up blank. The profile I've drawn up is self-contradictory. Useless. With your help, we've now examined all the likely suspects: Eden rejects or employees, the people who could have known both couples. There's no place else to go. At least, no place I can help with."

He sighed. "There's something else. Something I'm not proud to talk about. I'm too close to this case. It was the same in the Bureau, toward the end. I grew too absorbed. And it's happening again. It's intruding on my personal life, I brood about it day and night. And look at the result."

"What result is that?"

"Handerling. I was tired, overeager. And I had a lapse of judgment."

"If you're blaming yourself for Handerling's interrogation, you shouldn't. The man isn't a murderer — our tests confirm that. But he abused his position terribly, committed grave offenses. Information can be a dangerous thing in the wrong hands, Christopher. And we're grateful for your help exposing him."

"I did very little, Dr. Silver."

"Didn't I ask you to call me Richard? You're selling yourself short."

Lash shook his head. "I'd suggest you go to the police, but I'm not sure we could convince them a crime's been committed." He stood up. "But if this is a serial killer, he's likely to strike again very soon. Perhaps as soon as today. And I don't want that to happen on my watch. I don't want to sit here, looking on helplessly. Waiting."

Silver watched him rise. And then, unexpectedly, a smile surfaced on the careworn face. "We're not exactly helpless," he said. "As you probably know, Mauchly and Tara have security teams running hands-off surveillance on the other supercouples."

"That might not stop a determined killer."

"Which is exactly why I'm taking additional steps myself."

"What do you mean?"

Silver rose himself. "Come with me."

He led the way to a small door Lash had

not noticed before, built cleverly into the wall of bookcases. It opened noiselessly, revealing a narrow staircase, covered in the same rich carpeting. "After you," Silver said.

Lash climbed at least three dozen steps, emerging at the end of a hallway. After the floor below, almost dizzying in its openness, the long, narrow corridor ahead of him felt cramped. There was no sense of being atop a skyscraper: they could just as easily have been far below the earth. And yet it was decorated just as tastefully: the walls and ceiling were of dark polished wood, and decorative wall sconces of copper and abalone threw off muted light.

Silver motioned him forward. As they walked, Lash looked curiously at the rooms to the left and right. He noticed a large personal gym, complete with exercise flume, weight machines, and treadmill; a spartan dining room. The hallway ended in a black door, a scanner set beside it. Silver put his wrist beneath the scanner, and for the first time Lash noticed that he, too, wore a security bracelet. The door sprang open.

The room beyond was almost as dimly lit as the corridor. Except here, the light came solely from tiny winking lights and dozens of vacuum-fluorescent displays. From all sides came a constant low rush of air: the sound of innumerable fans, breathing in unison. Rack-mounted equipment of all kinds —

routers, RAID hard disc arrays, video renderers, countless other exotica unknown to Lash — covered the nearest walls. Opposite them, half a dozen terminals and their keyboards were lined up on a long wooden desk, crowded together. A lone chair sat before them. The only other piece of furniture was in a far corner: a narrow and very curious-looking couch, contoured almost in the fashion of a dentist's chair, sat behind a screen of Plexiglas. Several leads snaked away from the chair to a nearby rack of diagnostic equipment. A lavalier-style microphone was pinned to the chair by a plastic clip.

"Please excuse the lack of seats," Silver said. "Nobody but me ever comes here."

"What is all this?" Lash said, looking around.

"Liza."

Lash looked at Silver quickly. "But I saw Liza the other day. The small terminal you showed me."

"That's Liza, too. Liza's everywhere in this penthouse. For some things I use that terminal you saw. This is for more complicated matters. When I need to access her directly."

Lash remembered what Tara Stapleton had said over lunch in the cafeteria: *We never get near the core routines or intelligence. Only Silver has access. Everybody else uses the corporate computer grid.* He looked around at the electronics surrounding them on all sides. "Why don't you tell me a little more about Liza?"

"What would you like to know?"

"You could start with the name."

"Of course." Silver paused. "By the way, speaking of names, I finally remembered where I saw yours."

Lash raised his eyebrows.

"It was in the *Times* a couple years back. Weren't you an intended victim in that string of —"

"That's right." Lash realized immediately he'd interrupted too quickly. "Remarkable memory."

There was a brief silence.

"Anyway, about Liza's name. It's a nod to 'Eliza,' a famous piece of software from the early sixties. Eliza simulated a dialogue between a person and the computer, in which the program seized on words typed in by the person running it. 'How are you feeling?' the program would start out asking. 'I feel lousy,' you might type in. 'Why do you think you feel lousy?' the program would respond. 'Because my father is ill,' you'd type. 'Why do you say that about your father?' comes the reply. It was very primitive, and it often gave ludicrous responses, but it showed me what I needed to do."

"And what was that?"

"To accomplish what Eliza only pretended to do. To create a program — 'program' isn't really the right word — a data construct that could interact flawlessly with a human being. That could, at some level, *think*."

"That's all?" Lash said.

It was meant as a joke, but Silver's response was serious. "It's still a work in progress. I'll probably devote the rest of my life to perfecting it. But once the intelligence models were fully functional within a computational hyperspace —"

"A what?"

Silver smiled shyly. "Sorry. In the early days of AI, everybody thought it was just a matter of time until the machines would be able to think for themselves. But it turned out the littlest things were the hardest to implement. How can you program a computer to understand how somebody is feeling? So in graduate school I proposed a two-fold solution. Give a computer access to a *huge* amount of information — a knowledge base — along with the tools to search that knowledge base intelligently. Second, model as real a personality *as possible* within silicon and binary code, because human curiosity would be necessary to make use of all that information. I felt if I could synthesize these two elements, I'd create a computer that could teach itself to learn. And if it could learn, it could learn to respond like a human. Not to feel, of course. But it would *understand* what feeling was."

Silver spoke quietly, but his voice carried

the conviction of a preacher at a camp meeting.

"I guess, since we're standing here atop your private skyscraper, you succeeded," Lash replied.

Silver smiled again. "For years I was stymied. It seemed I could take machine learning only so far and no farther. It turned out I was just too impatient. The program *was* learning, only very slowly in the beginning. And I needed more horsepower than the old mainframes I could afford in those days. Suddenly, computers got cheaper. And then came the ARPAnet. That's when her learning really accelerated." He shook his head. "I'll never forget watching as she made her first forays over the 'Net, searching — without any help from me — for answers to a problem set. I think she was as proud as I was."

"Proud," Lash repeated. "Do you mean to say that it's conscious? Self-aware?"

"She's definitely self-aware. Whether she's conscious or not gets into a philosophical area I'm not prepared to address."

"But she *is* self-aware. So what, exactly, is she aware of? She knows she's a computer, that she's different. Right?"

Silver shook his head. "I never added any module of code to that effect."

"What?" Lash said in surprise.

"Why should she think she's any different than us?"

"I just assumed —"

"Does a child, no matter how precocious, ever doubt the reality of its existence? Do *you?*"

Lash shook his head. "But we're talking about software and hardware here. That sounds like a false syllogism to me."

"There's no such thing in AI. Who's to say when programming stops and consciousness begins? A famous scientist once referred to humans as 'meat machines.' Are we the better for it? Besides, there's no test you can take to prove *you're* not a program, wandering around in cyberspace. What's your proof?"

Silver had been speaking with a passion Lash hadn't seen before. Suddenly he stopped. "Sorry," he said, laughing shyly. "I guess I think about these things a lot more than I talk about them. Anyway, back to Liza's architecture. She employs a very advanced form of a neural network — a computer architecture based on how the human brain works. Regular computers are constrained to two dimensions. But a neural net is arranged in three: rings inside rings inside rings. So you can move data in an almost infinite number of directions, not just along a single circuit." Silver paused. "It's a lot more complicated than that, of course. To ramp up her problem-solving capability, I employed swarm intelligence. Large functions are broken up into tiny, discrete data agents. That's what allows her to solve such profound challenges, so quickly."

"Does she know we're here?"

Silver nodded toward a video monitor set high in one wall. "Yes. But her processing isn't currently focused on us."

"Earlier, you said you needed to access Liza directly for complicated work. Such as?"

"A variety of things. She runs scenarios, for example, that I monitor."

"What kinds of scenarios?"

"All kinds. Problem-solving. Role-playing. Survival games. Things that stimulate creative thinking." Silver hesitated. "I also use direct access for more difficult, personal tasks like software updates. But it would probably be easier just to show you."

He walked across the room, slid open the Plexiglas panel, and took a seat in the sculpted chair. Lash watched as he fixed electrodes to his temples. A small keypad and stylus were set into one arm of the chair; a hat switch was mounted on the other. Reaching overhead, Silver pulled down a flat panel monitor, fixed to a telescoping arm. His left hand began moving over the keypad.

"What are you doing?" Lash asked.

"Getting her attention." Silver's hand fell away from the keypad and fixed the lavalier mike to his shirt collar.

Just then, Lash heard a voice.

"Richard," it said.

It was a woman's voice, low and without accent, and it seemed to come from everywhere and nowhere at the same time. It was as if the room itself was speaking.

"Liza," Silver replied. "What is your current state?"

"Ninety-eight point seven two seven percent operational. Current processes are at eighty-one point four percent of multithreaded capacity. Thank you for asking."

The voice was calm, almost serene, with the faintest trace of digital artifacting. Lash had a strange sense of déjà vu, as if he'd heard the voice before, somewhere. Perhaps in dreams.

"Who is with you?" the voice asked. Lash noticed that the question was articulated properly, with a faint emphasis on the preposition. He thought he even detected an undercurrent of curiosity. He glanced a little uneasily up at the video camera.

"This is Christopher Lash."

"Christopher," the voice repeated, as if tasting the name.

"Liza, I have a special process I would like you to run." Lash noticed that when Silver addressed the computer, he spoke slowly and with careful enunciation, without contractions of any kind.

"Very well, Richard."

"Do you remember the data interrogatory I asked you to run forty-eight hours ago?"

"If you mean the statistical deviance interrogatory, my dataset has not been corrupted."

Silver covered the mike and turned to Lash. "She misinterpreted 'do you remember.' Even now, I sometimes forget how literal-minded she is."

He turned back. "I need you to run a similar interrogatory against external agents. The arguments are the same: data crossover with the four subjects."

"Subject Schwartz, Subject Thorpe, Subject Torvald, Subject Wilner."

"That is correct."

"What is the scope of the interrogatory?"

"United States citizens, ages fifteen to seventy, with access to both target locations on the stated dates."

"The data-gathering parameters?"

"All available sources."

"And the priority of this process?"

"Highest priority, except for criticals. It is vital we find the solution."

"Very well, Richard."

"Can you give me an estimated processing window?"

"To within eleven-percent accuracy. Seventy-four hours, fifty-three minutes, nine seconds. Approximately eight hundred trillion five hundred billion machine cycles."

"Thank you, Liza."

"Is there anything else?"

"No."

"I will begin the expanded interrogatory now. Thank you for speaking with me, Richard."

As Silver removed the microphone and reached again for the keypad, the disembodied voice spoke again. "It was nice meeting you, Christopher Lash."

"A pleasure," Lash murmured. Hearing this voice speak to him, watching the interaction between Silver and his computer, was both fascinating and a little unsettling.

Silver plucked the electrodes from his temples, put them aside, and got out of the chair. "You said you'd go to the police if you thought it would help. I've just done something better. I've instructed Liza to search the entire country for a possible suspect match."

"The entire *country?* Is that possible?"

"For Eden, it's possible." Silver swayed, recovered. "Sorry. Sessions with Liza, even brief ones, can be a little draining."

"How so?"

Silver smiled. "In movies people talk to computers, and they talk glibly back. Maybe it will be that way in another decade. Right now, it's hard work. As much a mental exercise as a verbal one."

"Those electroencephalogram sensors you wore?"

"Think of biofeedback. The frequency and amplitude of beta or theta waves can speak a lot more distinctly than words. Early on, when I was having troubles with her language comprehension, I used the EEG as a shortcut. It required a great deal of concentration, but there was no confusion over dual meanings, homophones, nuances of intent. Now, it's too deeply buried in her legacy code to change easily."

"So only you can communicate with her directly?"

"It's theoretically possible for others to do so, too, with the proper concentration and training. There's just been no need."

"Perhaps not," Lash said. "If I'd built something this marvelous, I'd want to share it with others. Like-minded scientists who could build on what you pioneered."

"That will come. So many other enhancements seem to occupy my time. And it's a non-trivial task. We can discuss the details some other time, if you're interested."

He stepped forward, put a hand on Lash's shoulder. "I know how hard it's been on you. It hasn't been easy for me, either. But we've come this far, done this much. I need you to stick with it just a little longer. Maybe it *is* just a freakish tragedy after all, two double suicides. Maybe we'll have a quiet weekend. I realize it's hell not knowing. But we have to trust Liza now. Okay?"

Lash remained silent a moment. "That match Eden found for me. It's on the level? No mistakes?"

"The only mistake was sending your avatar to the Tank in the first place. The matching process itself would work for you as it does for everybody else. The woman would be perfectly suited to you in every way."

The dim light, the whispered hum of machinery, gave the room a dreamlike, almost spectral air. Half a dozen images flitted through Lash's head. The look on his ex-wife's face, that day in the blind at the Audubon Center when they separated. Tara Stapleton's expression at the bar in Grand Central when she told him of her own dilemma. The face of Lewis Thorpe, staring at him out of the Flagstaff television screen.

He sighed. "Very well. I'll stay on a few more days. On one condition."

"Name it."

"That you don't cancel my dinner with Diana Mirren."

Silver pressed Lash's shoulder for a moment. "Good man." He smiled again, briefly; but when the smile faded, he looked just as tired as Lash felt.

TWENTY-NINE

"Seventy-five hours," Tara said. "That means Liza won't have an answer until Monday afternoon."

Lash nodded. He'd summarized his talk with Silver, described in detail how the man communicated with Liza. Throughout, Tara was fascinated — until she heard how long the extended search would take.

"So what are we supposed to do until then?" she said.

"I don't know."

"I do. We wait." Tara raised her eyes to the ceiling. "Shit."

Lash looked around the room. In size, Tara Stapleton's thirty-fifth-floor office wasn't that different from his own temporary space. It had the same conference table, same desk, same shelving. There were a few distinctly feminine touches: half a dozen leafy plants that appeared to thrive on the artificial light, a paisley sachet of potpourri hanging from the desk lamp by a red ribbon. Three identical computer workstations were lined up behind the desk. But the most distinctive feature of the office was a large fiberglass surfboard leaning against a far wall, badly scored and pitted, the stripe along its length faded by salt and sun. Bumper stickers with legends like "Live to surf, surf to live" and "Hang ten off a log!" were fixed on the wall behind it. Postcards from famous surfing beaches — Lennox Head, Australia; Pipeline, Hawaii; Potovil Point, Sri Lanka — were taped in a row along the upper edge of the bookshelf.

"Must have had a hell of a time getting that in here," Lash said, nodding at the surfboard.

Tara flashed one of her rare smiles. "I spent my first couple of months outside the Wall, auditing security procedures. I brought in my old board to remind me there was a world out there beyond New York City. So I wouldn't forget what I'd rather be doing. Audit finished, I got promoted, transferred inside. They wouldn't let me take the board. I was ripshit." She shook her head at the memory. "Then it appeared in my office doorway one day. Happy first anniversary, courtesy of Edwin Mauchly and Eden."

"Knowing Mauchly, after having been scanned, probed, and analyzed six ways from Sunday."

"Probably."

Lash glanced at the clutch of emerald-green postcards. A question had formed in his mind — a question Tara could probably answer better than anybody.

He leaned toward the desk. "Tara, listen. Remember that drink we had at Sebastian's? What you told me about your getting the nod?"

Immediately, he felt her grow more reserved.

"I need to know something. Is there any chance that an Eden candidate who gets turned down after testing might end up getting processed anyway? Go through data-gathering, surveillance — the works — and ultimately end up in the Tank? Getting matched?"

"You mean, like a mistake? Obsoletes somehow making their way through? Impossible."

"Why?"

"There are redundant checks. It's like everything else with the system. We don't take any chance that a client, even a would-be client, could suffer embarrassment from sloppy data handling."

"You're sure?"

"It's never happened."

"It happened yesterday." And in response to Tara's disbelieving look, he handed her the letter he'd found waiting outside his front door.

She read it, paling visibly. "Tavern on the Green."

"I was rejected as an applicant. And pretty definitively. So how could this have happened?"

"I have no idea."

"Could somebody within Eden have doctored my forms, guiding them through instead of shunting them toward the discard pile?"

"Nobody here does anything without half a dozen others seeing it."

"Nobody?"

Hearing the tone of his voice, Tara looked at him closely. "It would have to be somebody very highly placed, somebody with world-class access. Me, for example. Or a grunt like Handerling who'd somehow hacked the system." She paused. "But why would anybody do such a thing?"

"That was my next question."

There was a silence. Tara folded the letter and handed it back across the table.

"I don't know how this happened. But I'm very, very sorry, Dr. Lash. We'll investigate immediately, of course."

"You're sorry. Silver's sorry. Why is everybody so sorry?"

Tara looked astonished. "You mean — ?"

"That's right. Tomorrow night, I'm stepping out."

"But I don't understand —" The flow of words stopped.

I know you don't, Lash thought.

He didn't exactly understand himself. If he'd worked at Eden, like Tara — if he'd been influenced by what insiders called the "Oz effect" — he might have torn up the letter.

But he had not torn up the letter. The peek behind the scenes, the rabid testimonials of Eden clients, had piqued his interest almost without his realizing it. And now he'd been told a perfect mate had been found for him — Christopher Lash, so expert at analyzing other relationships yet so unsuccessful in his own. It was simply too powerful a lure to resist. Even the knowledge of why he was here in the first place was no match for the curiosity of meeting — just perhaps — an ideal partner.

But that meeting would come tomorrow. Today, there was something else on his mind.

"It's not a coincidence," he said.

"Huh?"

"My application getting processed. It might be a mistake, but it's no coincidence. Any more than the deaths of the two supercouples are coincidence."

Tara frowned. "What are you saying, exactly?"

"I'm not sure. But there's a pattern here somewhere. We're just not seeing it." Mentally, he returned to last night's drive home, when he'd refused to listen to the voice in the back of his head. Now he tried to recall the voice.

You murdered the first two supercouples, in order, Mauchly had said to Handerling during the interrogation. *Now you've been planning to stalk, and kill, a third.*

In order . . .

"Mind if I borrow this?" he asked, taking a notepad from the desk. Pulling out a pen, he wrote two dates on the pad: 9/17/04. 9/24/04. The dates the Thorpes and the Wilners had died.

"Tara," he said. "Can you pull up the dates that the Thorpes and the Wilners first submitted their applications?"

"Sure." She turned toward one of the terminals, typed briefly. Almost immediately, the printer spat out a sheet:

THORPE, LEWIS A.	000451823	7/30/02
TORVALD, LINDSAY E.	000462196	8/21/02
SCHWARTZ, KAREN L.	000527710	8/02/02
WILNER, JOHN L.	000491003	9/06/02

Nothing.

"Could you widen the search, please? I want a printout of all relevant dates for the two couples. When they were tested, when they first met, when they were married, *everything.*"

Tara looked at him speculatively for a moment. Then she returned to the keyboard and resumed typing.

The second list ran to almost a dozen pages. Lash turned them over, one after another, running his eyes wearily down the columns. Then he froze.

"Jesus," he murmured.

"What is it?"

"These columns labeled 'Nominal avatar removal.' What do they stand for?"

"When the avatars were removed from the tank."

"In other words, when the couples were matched."

"Right."

Lash handed her the sheet. "Look at the removal dates for the Thorpes and the Wilners."

Tara glanced at the report. "My God. September 17, 2002. September 24, 2002."

"That's right. Not only were the Thorpes and the Wilners the first two supercouples to be matched. They also died *precisely* two years after they were matched. Two years *to the day*."

Tara dropped the report on the desk. "What do you think it means?"

"That this dog's been sniffing around the wrong fire hydrant. Here I've been digging into the psych tests and evaluations, assuming there might be some human flaw your examinations missed. Maybe instead of examining the people, I should have examined the *process*."

"The process? What about the suspect match? Liza's search?"

"That won't be done until Monday. I don't plan to spend the next seventy-odd hours sitting on my hands." He stood up and turned toward the door. "Thanks for the help."

As he opened the door, he heard Tara's chair roll back. "Just a minute," she said.

He turned.

"Where are you going?"

"Back to my office. I've got a lot of evidence lockers to search."

When Tara came around the desk, there was no hesitation. "I'm coming along," she said.

THIRTY

"Seen my traveling kit, babe?" Kevin Connelly called out.

"Beneath the vanity, second shelf. On the left."

Connelly padded past the sleigh bed, past the bars of yellow light that slanted in through the windows, and knelt before the vanity sink. Sure enough: second shelf, tucked carefully against the wall. Back in the day he'd have spent half an hour tearing up the bedroom in search of it. But Lynn seemed to possess a photographic memory for the whereabouts of everything in the house: not just her stuff, but his as well. It wasn't anything conscious, it was just there all the time, sticking to everything it touched, like flypaper. Perhaps that's part of what made her so good with languages.

"You're a treasure," he said.

"I'll bet you say that to all the girls."

He paused, crouching before the vanity, to look over at her. She was standing just within the closet, staring at a long rack of dresses.

As he watched, she took down one, turned it around on its hanger, replaced it in favor of another. There was something in the way her limbs moved — lissome, unself-conscious — that even now quickened his pulse. He'd been deeply offended when, the other week, his mother had labeled her "cute." Cute? She was the most beautiful woman he'd ever seen.

She left the closet and walked the newly selected dress over to the bed, where a large canvas suitcase lay open. With the same economy of motion, she folded the dress in half and placed it within the suitcase.

He'd taken the afternoon off to help his wife pack for Niagara Falls. It was a kind of guilty pleasure that, for some reason, he'd be embarrassed to confess to anybody. They always packed days in advance of a trip; somehow, it seemed to extend the vacation. He'd always been a premature packer, for the same reason he always liked to get to the airport early — yet as a bachelor it had been a hurried, slovenly affair. Lynn had shown him packing was an art, never to be rushed. And now, the process had grown into one of those intimate little rituals that made up the fabric of their marriage.

He stood, came up behind her, put his arms around her waist. "Just think," he said, nuzzling her ear. "Another couple of days and we'll be in front of a roaring fire at the

Pillar and Post Inn."

"Mmm."

"We'll have breakfast in bed. Maybe lunch in bed, too. How does that sound? And if you play your cards right, you just might get dessert, as well."

In response, she leaned her head a little wearily against his shoulder.

Kevin Connelly knew his wife's moods almost as well as his own, and he drew back. "What is it, babe?" he asked quickly. "Migraine?"

"Maybe the beginnings of one," she said. "Hope not."

He turned her toward him, kissed her gently on one temple, then the other.

"Some perfect wife, huh?" she said, raising her lips to his.

"You are the perfect wife. *My* perfect wife."

She smiled, laid her head against his shoulder again.

The doorbell rang.

Kevin gently detached himself, then trotted out into the hall and down the stairs. Behind, he heard Lynn's quiet footsteps, moving more slowly.

A man with an enormous wrapped parcel waited at the front door. "Mr. Connelly?" he said. "Sign here, please."

Connelly signed on the indicated line, then gathered the package in his arms.

"What is it?" Lynn said as he thanked the

man and pushed the door closed behind him.

"Don't know. Want to open it?" Connelly handed the package to her, then watched, smiling, as she tore off the wrapping paper. Clear cellophane came into view; then a broad red ribbon; then the pale yellow of woven straw.

"What is it?" he asked. "A basket of fruit?"

"Not just fruit," Lynn said breathlessly. "Look at the label. It's red blush pears from Ecuador! You have any idea how expensive these are?"

Connelly smiled at the look that came over his wife's face. Lynn was passionate about exotic fruit.

"Who could have sent this?" she asked. "I don't see a card."

"There's a small one tucked in the back, over here." Connelly plucked it from between threads of twisted straw, read the engraved words aloud. "Congratulations and warm best wishes on your upcoming anniversary."

Lynn crowded close, headache forgotten. "Who's it from?"

Connelly handed it to her. There was no name, but the card was embossed with the sleek infinity symbol of Eden.

Her eyes widened. "Red blush pears. How could they have known?"

"They know everything. Remember?"

Lynn shook her head, then began tearing the cellophane from the basket.

"Not so fast," Connelly said in mock admonishment. "We've got some unfinished business upstairs. Remember?"

Now a smile brightened on her face, as well. And putting the basket aside, she skipped up the stairs after him.

THIRTY-ONE

Lash glanced up at the clock: a quick, disinterested look. Then he glanced again in disbelief. Quarter to six. It seemed only minutes since Tara, pleading a doctor's appointment, had excused herself from his office around four.

He leaned back in his chair, surveyed the flood of paperwork covering the table. Had he really complained bitterly, once upon a time, about a lack of information? Now he had information, all right: enough to drown an army.

Discovering the deaths of the Thorpes and the Wilners were precisely timed to their matches was a critical piece of the puzzle — he just had to learn how it fit in. But with this embarrassment of data, he wasn't likely to learn this afternoon.

His eye returned to the table, falling on a folder labeled *Thorpe, Lewis — Process Inventory*. He'd already flipped through it briefly: it appeared to be a system-generated list of all Eden systems Thorpe had interacted with.

Lash sifted through the other flotsam until he found an identical folder for Lindsay. Then, walking to the far wall of the office, he rummaged through the evidence lockers until he'd located similar inventories for the Wilners, as well.

Maybe Silver was right — nothing would happen that weekend. If there was a murderer out there, maybe Eden's surveillance teams would catch him before he could kill. again. But that didn't mean Lash was going to twiddle his thumbs. Comparing the data in the folders might turn up more pieces of the puzzle.

He slipped the folders into his leather satchel, stretched wearily. Then he made his way down the hall to the cafeteria. Marguerite had left for the day, but the counter person on duty was more than happy to make him a double espresso. Despite the late hour, the room was bustling, and Lash chose a corner table, grateful Eden maintained a three-shift operation.

Draining his cup, he returned to his office, retrieved his coat and satchel, then headed to the nearest elevator bank. Though most of the building remained a mystery to him, he'd at least learned to navigate his way to the lobby.

As Lash took up position in the queue for Checkpoint III, his thoughts returned to the couples. Before she'd left, Tara Stapleton had pointed out the third supercouple — the Connellys — had been matched on October 6, 2002. If the pattern he'd discovered held true to form, that meant the Connellys would experience their own tragedy — suicide, homicide — this coming Wednesday. That took a little pressure off, gave them some breathing room. But it also meant they had an ironclad deadline.

Wednesday. Any missing pieces of the puzzle had to be found before then.

He reached the front of the queue, waited while the glass doors slid open, then stepped into the circular chamber. Even this had become almost routine. It was an amazing thing, conditioning. You could get used to almost anything, no matter how remarkable. In the lab, he'd seen the effect in dogs, mice, chimps. He used it himself in biofeedback therapy. And here he was, a walking, talking example of its use in a corporate . . .

He became aware of a distant ringing sound. The light in the chamber, already bright, grew brighter. Ahead, beyond the second set of doors, he could see people running. What was happening — a fire alarm? Some sort of drill?

Suddenly, two guards appeared ahead on the far side of the glass. They planted themselves in his path, feet apart, arms at their sides.

He turned back the way he'd come, not

comprehending. Two more guards now stood there. As he watched, more ran up behind them.

There was a brief series of tones, then the doors he'd passed through opened again. Guards advanced in two rows. One of the guards in the rear row, he noticed, held a stun device in one hand.

"What —" he began.

Quickly, and very firmly, the two lead guards hustled him back through the glass doors. The rest formed a security cordon around them. Lash registered a fleeting set of images — the queue falling back, wide-eyed; the walls of a corridor; a quick turn around a corner — and then he found himself inside a stark, windowless room.

He was guided to a wooden chair. For a moment, it seemed nobody paid any further attention to him. There was the sound of radios chattering, a phone being dialed. "Get Sheldrake in here," somebody said. The door to the room closed. And then one of the guards turned to him.

"Where were you going with these?" he asked. In one hand he held up the four folders from the satchel.

In his confusion, Lash was unaware the satchel had been taken from him. "I was taking them home," he said. "To read over the weekend." Christ, how could he have forgotten Mauchly's warnings? *Nothing from in-*

side the Wall ever went out. But how had they . . .

"You know the rules, Mr. — ?" the guard said, placing the binders inside what looked uncomfortably like an evidence bag.

"Dr. Lash. Christopher Lash."

Hearing this, one of the security officers walked over to a data terminal and began to type.

"You know the rules, Dr. Lash?"

Lash nodded.

"So you realize the seriousness of this offense."

Lash nodded again, embarrassed. Tara, stickler for protocol, would never let him live this down. He hoped she wouldn't get in trouble; after all, Mauchly had put her in charge of —

"We're going to have to keep you here until we've pulled your security history. If you already have a warning on your record, I'm afraid you'll be brought before the termination review board."

The security officer at the workstation looked up. "There's no Christopher Lash in the Human Resources files."

"Did we get your name right?" the officer with the evidence bag said.

"Yes, but —"

"I'm showing a Christopher S. Lash as a prospective client," the officer at the terminal said, typing again. "Went through applicant testing last Sunday, September twenty-sixth." He stopped typing. "The application was rejected."

"Is that you?" the first officer asked.

"Yes, but —"

Immediately, the atmosphere in the room changed. The first officer stepped toward him quickly. Several others, including the one with the Taser, closed ranks behind him.

Christ, Lash thought, *this is getting awkward.* "Look," he began again, "you don't understand —"

"Sir," the first officer said, "please keep silent. I'll ask the questions."

The door opened and another man stepped in. He was tall, and his shoulders were so broad the blond head atop them seemed too small for its body. As he came forward with an almost military bearing, the others stepped back deferentially. He wore a dark business suit, plainly cut. His eyes were an unusual shade of emerald green. He seemed vaguely familiar, but in his confused state it took Lash a moment to place him. Then he remembered: he'd glimpsed the man briefly, standing in the hallway during Handerling's interrogation.

"What have you got?" the man said. His voice was clipped, accentless.

"This gentleman tried to slip concealed documents past the checkpoint."

"What's his department and rank?"

"He's not an employee, Mr. Sheldrake. He's a rejected client."

The man's eyebrows shot up. "Indeed?"

"He just admitted to it."

Sheldrake stepped forward, crossed one massive arm over the other, and regarded Lash with curiosity. There was no look of recognition: it was clear he hadn't seen Lash at the interrogation. The man uncrossed his arms again and drew back his suit jacket at the waist. Lash saw he was wearing a service belt, complete with automatic weapon, handcuffs, and radio. Plucking the ASP baton from his belt, Sheldrake extended it to full length.

"Crandall," he muttered. "Look at this." And he raised Lash's sleeve with the nubby metal end of the baton, exposing the security bracelet.

The first officer — the one named Crandall — frowned in surprise. "How'd you get that? And what were you doing inside the secure perimeter?"

"I'm a temporary consultant."

"You just admitted to being a rejected client."

Lash cursed the secrecy under which he'd been brought in. "Yes, I know. But going through the application process was part of my assignment. Look, just ask Edwin Mauchly. He hired me."

In the background he could hear more

radio chatter. One of the security guards was pawing through his satchel. "Eden doesn't hire temporary consultants. And they certainly aren't allowed inside the Wall." Sheldrake turned toward one of the others. "Alert the security posts, all down the line. We're going to Condition Beta. Get an analyzer over here, see if the bracelet was tampered with."

"Right away, Mr. Sheldrake."

This was ridiculous. Why weren't his more recent records appearing, the records of his successful match? "Look," Lash said, standing, "I told you to speak with Mauchly —"

"Sit *down!*" Crandall pushed him roughly back into the seat. Another guard — the one with the Taser — stepped closer. Yet another opened a metal closet and pulled out a long, rake-like implement with a half-circle bolted to one end. Lash had seen the implement many times in the past: it was used to pin uncooperative psychiatric patients against a wall.

He licked his lips. What had been first embarrassing, then annoying, was quickly becoming something else. "Listen," he said as calmly as he could. "I'm a consultant, like I said. I'm working with Tara Stapleton."

"Doing what?" Sheldrake asked.

"That's confidential."

"If that's the way you want to play it."

Sheldrake glanced over his shoulder. "See what doctor's on call, get him in here. And call the security desk, alert the duty chiefs."

"I'm telling you the truth," Lash said. "You can ask Silver if you don't believe me. He knows all about it."

Sheldrake's lips curled into a faint smile. "Richard Silver?"

"He knows all about it," Crandall added. "Nobody's seen the guy for a year, and he knows all about it."

"I'll go speak with him myself." And Lash began to stand again.

Crandall shoved him back into the seat again. Another security officer stepped forward, and together they pinned Lash to the chair.

"Get the restraints," Sheldrake said mildly. "And Stemper, use that Taser. I want this guy pacified."

The guard with the stun device stepped forward. "Back on my signal," Crandall muttered to the guard on the far side of the chair.

At that moment, the door opened and Mauchly stepped in.

"What's going on?" he demanded.

Sheldrake looked around, stopped. "This man says he knows you, Mr. Mauchly."

"He does." Mauchly came forward. Lash began to rise, but Mauchly stayed him with a suppressing gesture. "What happened, exactly?" he asked Sheldrake.

"The man attempted to exit the secure perimeter with these in his possession." Sheldrake nodded at Crandall, who handed the evidence bag to Mauchly.

Mauchly opened it, read the titles on the binders. "I'll hang on to these," he said.

"Very good, sir," said Crandall.

"And I'll take possession of Dr. Lash, as well."

"You sure that's a good idea?" Sheldrake asked.

"Yes, Mr. Sheldrake."

"Then I release him to your custody." He turned to Crandall. "Mark that in the duty log."

Mauchly picked up the satchel, nodded for Lash to stand. "Come on, Dr. Lash," he said. "This way." And as they left the room, Lash could hear Sheldrake on the phone, telling the security teams that the alarm was being canceled and they should stand down from Condition Beta.

Out in the hall, Mauchly closed the unmarked door behind them, then turned. "What were you thinking, Dr. Lash?"

"I guess I wasn't thinking at all, actually. I'm rather tired. Sorry about that."

Mauchly looked at Lash a moment longer. Then he nodded slowly. "I'll have these returned to your office," he said, indicating the binders. "They'll be waiting for you Monday morning."

"Thank you. What did that guard mean by Condition Beta?"

"This building employs four status codes: Alpha, Beta, Delta, and Gamma. Condition Alpha is normal operation. Beta is heightened alert. Delta is in case of evacuation, fire and so forth."

"And Gamma?"

"Catastrophic emergencies only. Never invoked, of course."

"Of course." Lash realized he was babbling. He wished Mauchly a pleasant weekend and turned away.

"Dr. Lash," Mauchly said quietly.

Lash turned back. Mauchly was holding out his satchel.

"You might want to use Checkpoint I, on the third floor," he said. "The guards here are liable to be a little, ah, excitable for a while."

THIRTY-TWO

Assistant district attorney Frank Piston shifted morosely in the wooden chair. He'd have given just about anything, he decided, to get his hands on the sadist who purchased the furniture for the Sullivan County Superior Court. Just ten minutes — even five — in a dark alley would suffice to make his feelings on the matter clear. He'd been in dozens of courtrooms, judges' chambers, law offices in the five-story building. Each one had the same bony chairs with flat institutional seats, backs sporting little knobs in all the wrong places. Here in the hearing room of the Board of Pardons and Paroles, it was no different.

He glanced at his watch, sighing disconsolately. Six o'clock on the dot. Figured his case would be the last one heard. By rights, it should have been first on the list. After all, it wouldn't take more than a few minutes to dispose of the matter, send Edmund Wyre back to the slammer to rot another ten years. But no, he'd had to sit through a dozen hear-ings, each more boring than the last. It was unbelievable, the shit an assistant DA had to go through. Everybody else had gone home an hour ago, but here he was, numb from the ass down. He'd endured four years of law school, spent close to a hundred grand, for this?

There'd been a scary moment — half an hour before, when that serial rapist's case had come up — when he thought the parole board would adjourn for the day and he'd have to come back again next week for another torture session. But no, they'd decided to hear the last few cases. They'd denied the rapist parole, of course. Just like they'd denied most of the rest. This board was rough. He reminded himself that, if he ever committed a crime, he'd damn well better do it in another county.

Finally, it was time. The drunk driver who'd run over an elderly pedestrian — aggravated manslaughter, twenty years — parole denied. No surprise there. And now Walt Corso, sour-faced old head of the parole board, cleared his throat.

"The Board of Pardons and Paroles will now review the case of Edmund Wyre," he said, glancing down at a clipboard on the table before him.

There was a general shuffling among the sea of faces on the far side of the board table. All twelve members of the board were on hand, Piston noticed — which was necessary, of course, whenever a murderer's case came up. Now that the glum-faced relatives of the drunk driver had shuffled out, the room was almost empty. It was just the board, a court officer, a transcriber, some state officials, and himself. Not even a reporter. There was no way in hell Wyre was going free; everybody knew that. Piston didn't even understand how the guy had come up for parole so early. You didn't kill six people and then just —

There was movement to his right: a door opening. And then, Edmund Wyre himself appeared, handcuffed, prison guards on either side.

Piston sat up. This was unusual. Had Wyre hired a lawyer? What the hell was he doing here in person?

The board, however, was not surprised. They watched in silence as Wyre was led before the table. Piss-and-vinegar Corso glanced down again at his clipboard, scribbled a notation. "I understand, Mr. Wyre, that you wished to be present at this hearing, but that you've waived the services of a lawyer or parole consultant, preferring to represent yourself?"

Wyre nodded. "That's right, sir," he said in a deferential tone.

"Very well." Corso glanced up and down the table. "Who's the parole officer?"

One of the state officials seated in the rear stood up. "I am, sir."

"Forster, is it?"

"Yes, sir."

"Come forward."

The man named Forster came down the center aisle. Wyre looked over, nodded.

Corso folded his arms on the table and leaned toward the parole officer. "I must say, Forster, we were surprised to learn of this man's eligibility."

You're not the only one, Frank Piston thought.

"Mr. Wyre's sentences weren't stacked, sir," Forster said. "They're being served concurrently."

"I'm aware of that."

Wyre, the killer, cleared his throat. He glanced down at a piece of paper in his hand. "Sir," he began, "because of my health, I'd planned to ask for a special needs parole —"

This was too much. Wyre looked and sounded the picture of health. Piston stood up quickly, his wooden chair squeaking loudly against the floor.

Corso glanced over, frowning. "You wish to interject, Mister — ?"

"Piston. Frank Piston. Assistant district attorney."

"Ah yes, young Piston. Proceed with your interruption."

"May I point out, sir, that offenders convicted of aggravated offenses are not eligible for special needs paroles?"

"The board is aware of that, thank you. Mr. Wyre, you may proceed."

"As I was saying, sir, I *had* planned to ask for a special needs parole. But then I learned it would not be necessary."

"So the case summary says." Corso glanced at the parole officer. "Mr. Forster, would you care to explain?"

"Sir, Mr. Wyre has amassed a remarkable amount of good conduct time. The maximum permissible, in fact."

Piston sat forward. Now, that was *bull*shit. He'd heard more than once about the kind of trouble Wyre had caused in prison. He was the worst of offenders, a stone killer with the mind of a fox. He was always turning prisoners against each other, inciting fights and riots, sowing dissent with the guards. Not to mention that string of jailhouse murders. You didn't exactly rack up "good time" for shanking fellow inmates, even if nothing could be proven.

"Said good conduct time, along with Wyre's community service, participation in work programs and rehabilitation encounter groups, has accelerated his eligible parole date — with mandatory supervision factored in, of course — to September 29 of this year."

Piston felt a current of shock go through him. Immediately, he stood again. September 29 was two days ago. *Wyre's eligible? Already? Impossible.*

Corso glanced over. "You have something further to add, Mr. Piston?"

"No. I mean, yes. Good conduct time is a privilege, not a right. It doesn't change the fact that Wyre here killed six people, including two police officers."

"Are you forgetting, Mr. Piston, that Mr. Wyre here was convicted, and sentenced, for the murder of one person?"

Piston swore silently. This was true: Wyre had only been brought to trial for the murder of his final victim. There had been legal technicalities involved, some bungling of the evidence. Though it seemed foolish in hindsight, the DA had wanted to go for the one sure conviction rather than taking a chance on having Wyre walk on circumstantials. There'd been a hue and cry in the press at the time — didn't these jokers remember that?

Aloud, he said, "I'm not forgetting, sir. I'm only asking that the circumstances of the murders, the nature of Wyre's atrocities, be factored in —"

"*Mister* Piston. Are you telling the parole board how to do its job?"

Piston swallowed. "No, sir."

Corso shook a sheaf of papers over the

desk at him. "Do you have all the facts of this hearing? Are you in possession of this case summary?"

"No, sir."

"Then sit down and bite your tongue, young man, until you have something of value to add."

Wyre glanced back at Piston. It was a brief, almost casual look, but it chilled the lawyer to the bone. It was the kind of look a cat gave a canary. Then the convict turned back, smiling once again at the board.

Piston — shaken by the parole eligibility, unnerved by the eye contact with Wyre — tried to calm down, think straight. He had to remember who he was dealing with here. Everybody knew Wyre had killed those two cops. He'd set them up, stalked them, planned on killing an FBI agent as well. Old Corso wasn't likely to forget that, either, and he was as close to being a hanging judge as any parole chief could be. Anyway, there would be all the details of the case summary to wade through. That's where Wyre would get nailed, if nowhere else.

Corso seemed to read his mind. "Very well, Mr. Forster, let's get to this summary of yours. The entire board has had a chance to look at it. I must say we were all a little surprised by your findings, none more than myself."

"I understand that completely, sir. But I

stand by both the evaluation and the pertinent data."

"Oh, I'm not questioning anything, Mr. Forster. You've always proved yourself conscientious in your case work. We're just . . . a little surprised, that's all." Corso leafed through the summary report. "These social profiles, the psychological batteries, Wyre's history of institutional adjustment. I've never seen such scores."

"Neither have I, sir," said Forster.

Standing beside the parole officer, Wyre's eyes glittered.

"And these testimonials you've procured are equally remarkable."

"They were all in the database, sir."

"Hmm." Corso riffled through the final pages of the document, then pushed it aside. "Yet I don't know *why* we are so surprised. After all, we're here because we *believe* in the efficacy of our prison system — no? We've struggled to bring these services, these opportunities for rehabilitation, to our inmates. So why should we be so shocked when we come face to face with an instance where this rehabilitation *works?* With a success story?"

Oh, my God, Piston thought. There was only one thing that could put Corso in a lenient mood. And that was the dangled carrot of advancement. Because Corso, the parole board head, was also Corso, would-be assemblyman. And transforming Edmund Wyre from sadistic murderer to reformed penitent would be a feather in his cap like no other . . .

But that couldn't be, it simply wasn't possible. Wyre was a puff adder, a malevolent nut case. *What was in that case summary? What had happened on the tests?*

"Sir," Wyre said, gazing meekly at Corso, "in light of all this, I would like to request the board now grant my application for parole, set a release date, and formulate a plan for parole supervision."

Piston stared in growing disbelief as Wyre glanced down again at the sheet of paper in his hand. *He's got this process nailed. Somebody's coached him, shown him just what documents to read. But who?*

Instinctively, he rose once again to his feet. "Mr. Corso!" he cried out.

The old man frowned at him. "What is it now?"

Piston's mouth worked, but no words came. Wyre glanced casually over his shoulder. His eyes narrowed as he caught Piston's gaze, and he licked his lips, slowly and deliberately: first the upper, then the lower.

Piston sat down abruptly. As the drone of conversation picked up again at the front of the room, he reached into his pocket, pulled out his cell phone, and dialed the office. It was, as he expected, answered by the service.

He began to dial his boss's private number, then stopped. The DA was out on the links right now, grabbing a quick eighteen, and he would have turned his phone off, as always.

He replaced the phone in his pocket and stared back at the parole board with slow, dreamlike movements. Because this felt like a dream: one of those nightmares where you witnessed something terrible unfolding — something you knew would lead to tragedy, disaster — yet you remained paralyzed somehow, powerless to change anything, *do* anything . . .

And that was where the similarity ended. Because, Piston knew, one always woke from nightmare. But from this there would be no awakening.

THIRTY-THREE

"Change of plans," Lash said, leaning forward to speak with the driver. "Just let me off here, please."

He waited for the taxi to clear Columbus Circle and nose to the curb, then he paid the fare and got out. He watched the cab lose itself in a sea of identical yellow vehicles, then put his hands in his coat pockets and began walking slowly up Central Park West.

He wasn't sure, exactly, why he'd decided to get out several blocks short of the restaurant. Something about not wanting to bump into her outside. And what exactly did that mean? It had to do with controlling the situation: he wanted to see her first, establish his own space before they met. It had to do with nervousness.

In a different mood, he might have smiled at this piece of self-analysis. But there was no mistaking his rapid breathing, his elevated heart rate. Here he was, Christopher Lash, eminent psychologist and veteran of a hundred crime scenes — nervous as a teenager on his first date.

It had begun slowly, that morning, when — instinctively — he'd picked up the phone to call Tavern on the Green. Eden had already made the reservation, but he wanted to choose the dining room personally. As quickly as he'd picked up the phone, he put it down again. What should it be: the Crystal Room, with its glittering array of chandeliers? Or the woodsy ambiance of the Rafters Room? It had taken him ten minutes to decide, then another fifteen on the phone, name-dropping and cajoling the best possible table out of the reservationist.

This wasn't like him. He rarely ate out anymore, and when he did he was indifferent to seating. But it was equally unusual to pause beside a bus stop and scrutinize his image in the glass, as he was doing now. Or to worry that the tie he'd chosen was too passé, or too gauche, or maybe a little of both.

No doubt Eden had anticipated such reactions. No doubt, in the normal course of things, he'd have been briefed, given a reassuring pep talk. But this was not the normal course of things. Somehow, the company that never made a mistake had made one. And he was now walking up Central Park West, the time was 8 p.m. precisely, and for the first time in several days his thoughts were not preoccupied with the deaths of the Thorpes and the Wilners.

Ahead, where West Sixty-seventh Street emptied into Central Park, he could see countless white lights twinkling among the trees. He maneuvered his way past the clutter of limousines, then passed through the restaurant's outer doors. He smoothed his jacket, making sure the small pin Eden had sent was still in place. Even that little detail had been fussed over for several minutes: adjusting its placement on his lapel, making sure it was clearly visible yet not too obvious. His mouth was dry, his palms sweaty. Annoyed, Lash wiped his hands against the back of his trousers and moved with determined strides toward the bar.

It all comes down to this, he thought. Funny — all the time he'd spent undergoing his own evaluation, studying Eden and the two supercouples, he'd never stopped to think about what it must feel like: waiting, wondering how that perfect person would look. Until today. Today, he'd thought of little else. He'd learned, from painful experience, what his perfect woman *wasn't* like. She wasn't like Shirley, his ex-wife, with her inability to forgive human weakness, accept tragedy. Would his perfect woman be a blend of earlier girlfriends, some composite generated by his subconscious? Would she be an amalgam of the actresses he most admired: the poised limbs of Myrna Loy, the heart-shaped face of Claudette Colbert?

He stopped in the entrance of the bar, looking around. There were groups of twos and threes scattered around the tables, chatting boisterously. Other, single people were seated at the bar . . .

And there she was. At least, he thought it must be her. Because a small pin identical to his own was fixed to her dress; because she was looking directly at him; because she was rising from her seat and approaching with a smile.

And yet it could not be her. Because this woman looked nothing like what he expected. This was not willowy, slight, brunette Myrna Loy: this woman was tall and raven-haired. Mid-thirties, perhaps, with mischievous hazel eyes. Lash couldn't remember ever going out with anybody almost a head taller than himself.

"Christopher, right?" she said, shaking his hand. She nodded toward his pin. "I recognize the fashion accessory."

"Yes," he replied. "And you're Diana."

"Diana Mirren." Her accent was unexpected, too: a smooth contralto with a distinct Southern lilt.

Lash had always felt a completely unreasonable scorn for the intellect of Southern women; something about the accent set his teeth on edge. He began to wonder if, perhaps, the same mistake that had sent his avatar into the Tank had carried over to the

326

matchmaking process itself.

"Shall we go in?" he said.

Diana slung her purse over her shoulder and together they approached the reservationist.

"Lash and Mirren, eight o'clock," Lash said.

The woman behind the desk consulted an oversized book. "Ah, yes. In the Terrace Room. This way, please."

Lash had chosen the Terrace Room because it seemed the most intimate setting, with its hand-carved ceiling and tall windows giving out onto a private garden. A waiter seated them, then filled their water glasses and slipped two menus onto the table before stepping back with a bow.

For a moment, there was silence. Lash glanced at the woman, noticed she was looking back at him. And then, Diana laughed.

"What?" he asked.

She shook her head, reached for her water glass. "I don't know. You — you're not what I expected."

"I'm probably older, and thinner, and paler."

She laughed again, and flushed slightly.

"Sorry about that," he added.

"Well, they told us not to have preconceptions. Right?"

Lash, who hadn't been told anything, simply nodded.

The sommelier approached, silver *tastevin* dangling around his neck. "Something from the wine list, sir?"

Lash glanced at Diana, who nodded enthusiastically. "Go on. I love French wine but know practically nothing about it."

"Bordeaux okay?"

"Naturelement."

Lash picked up the list, scanned it. "We'll have the Pichon–Longueville, please."

"Pichon-Longueville?" Diana asked as the sommelier walked away. "The Pauillac super-second? Should be fantastic."

"Super-second?"

"You know. All the qualities of a *premier cru* without the price."

Lash put the list to one side. "I thought you didn't know anything about wine."

Diana took another sip of water. "Well, I don't know nearly as much as I should."

"And how's that?"

"Last year I went with a group on a six-week tour of France. Spent an entire week in the wine country."

Lash whistled.

"But it's embarrassing, what I retained and what I didn't. For example, I remember that Château Beychevelle was the prettiest of the châteaux. But ask me for the best vintages and I'm hopeless."

"Still, I think maybe you should be the official taster for this table."

"No objections." And Diana laughed again.

Normally, Lash disliked people who

laughed out loud frequently. Too often it substituted for punctuation, or something that could be better expressed in words. But Diana's laugh was infectious. Lash found himself smiling as he heard it.

When the sommelier returned with the bottle, Lash directed him to Diana. She peered at the label, swirled the wine, brought the glass to her mouth, all with a great show of mock gravity. Their waiter came by again and recited a long list of the evening's special dishes. The sommelier filled the glasses and departed. Now Diana raised hers in Lash's direction.

"What shall we drink to?" Lash asked. *She'll say, "To us." That's the way these things always work.*

"How about transvestites?" Diana replied in a buttery drawl.

Lash almost dropped his glass. "Huh?"

"You mean, you didn't look into it?"

"Into what?"

"Into that statue. You know, in the fountain, outside the Eden building. That ancient, ancient figure, surrounded by birds and angels? When I first saw it, it seemed the strangest thing in the world. Couldn't tell if it was male or female."

Lash shook his head.

"Well, it's a good thing one of us did. It's Tiresias."

"Who?"

"From Greek mythology. See, Tiresias was this man who got turned into a woman. And then turned back into a man."

"What? *Why?*"

"Why? You don't ask why. This was Thebes. Stuff happens. Anyway, Zeus and Hera were having an argument about who enjoyed sex more: men or women. Since this Tiresias was the only person who'd tried it both ways, they called him in to settle the argument."

"Go on."

"Hera didn't like what Tiresias had to say. So she blinded him."

"Typical."

"Zeus felt bad, so he gave Tiresias the gift of prophecy."

"Big of him. But there's something you left out."

"What's that?"

"What Tiresias said to make Hera so mad."

"He said women enjoy sex more than men."

"Really?"

"Really. Nine times more."

We'll get back to that later, Lash thought to himself. He lifted his glass. "By all means, let's drink a toast. But shouldn't we be drinking to hermaphrodites?"

Diana considered this. "Right you are. To hermaphrodites, then." And she raised her glass to his.

Lash took a deep sip, found it excellent. He decided he was glad Diana didn't have the looks of Claudette Colbert. If she had, he'd have been intimidated. "Where did you find this particular nugget of information?" he asked.

"Actually, I knew it already."

"Let me guess. You read *Bulfinch's Mythology* on your trip across France."

"Nice try, but wrong. You could say it's part of my job."

"Really? And what job is that?"

"I teach English literature at Columbia."

Lash nodded, impressed. "Great school."

"I'm still just an instructor, but it's a position with a tenure track."

"What's your specialty?"

"The Romantics, I guess. Lyric poetry."

Lash felt a strange tremor, as if something deep inside had just slid home. He'd enjoyed Romantic poetry in college, until psychology and the demands of graduate school pushed it to one side. "That's interesting. As it happens, I've been reading Bashō recently. Not exactly Romantic, of course."

"In his own way, very much so. The greatest haiku poet of Japan."

"I don't know about that. But his poems have stuck in my mind."

"Haiku's like that. It's nefarious. It seems so simple. But then it sneaks up on you from a hundred different directions."

Lash thought of Lewis Thorpe. He took another sip of wine, then quoted:

Speechless before
these budding green spring leaves
in blazing sunlight

As he spoke, Diana's smile faded and the look on her face grew intent. "Again, please," she said quietly.

Lash obliged. When he finished, a silence fell over the table. But it was not an awkward silence. They merely sat, enjoying a moment of contemplation. Lash glanced at the surrounding tables, at the rich evening colors that lay over the park beyond. Without his realizing it, the nervousness he'd felt entering the restaurant had faded away.

"It's beautiful," Diana said at last. "I've had moments like that." She paused a moment. "It reminds me of another haiku, written by Kobayashi Issa more than a century later." And she quoted in turn:

Insects on a bough
floating downriver,
still singing.

Their waiter reappeared. "Have you decided what you'd like this evening?"

"We haven't even cracked the menu," Lash said.

"Very good." The man bowed again and walked away.

Lash turned back to Diana. "The thing is, beautiful as they are, I don't really understand them."

"No?"

"Oh, I guess I do on a superficial level. But they're like riddles, with some deeper meaning that escapes me."

"That's the problem right there. I hear it all the time from my students."

"Enlighten me."

"You're thinking of them like epigrams. But haiku aren't little puzzles that need to be solved. To my mind, they're just the opposite. They hint at things; they leave a lot to the imagination; they imply more than they say. Don't search for an answer. Think, instead, of opening doors."

"Opening doors," Lash echoed.

"You mentioned Bashō. Did you know he wrote the most famous haiku of all? 'One Hundred Frogs.' It consists of only seventeen sounds — all traditional haiku does. But guess what? It's been translated into English more than *fifty different ways*. Each translation utterly different from the rest."

Lash shook his head. "Amazing."

Diana's smile returned. "That's what I mean about opening doors."

There was another, briefer silence as an under-waiter crept up and refilled Lash's glass. "You know, it's funny," Lash said as the man left.

"What's funny?"

"Here we've been talking about French wine and Greek mythology and Japanese poetry, and you still haven't asked what I do."

"I know I haven't."

Once again, he was surprised by her directness. "Well, isn't that usually the first topic that comes up? On first dates, I mean."

Diana leaned forward. "Exactly. And that's what makes this so special."

Lash hesitated, considering. Then, suddenly, he understood. There was *no need* to ask the usual questions. Eden had taken care of all that. The tiresome introductory baggage, the blind date checks-and-balances, weren't important here. Instead, a journey of discovery lay ahead.

This hadn't occurred to him before. It was a tremendously liberating thought.

The waiter returned, noticed the menus remained untouched, bowed yet again, and turned away.

"Poor guy," Diana said. "He's hoping for a second seating."

"You know what?" Lash replied. "I think this table's booked for the rest of the evening."

Smiling, Diana raised her empty hand in imitation of a toast. "In that case, here's to the rest of the evening."

Lash nodded. Then he did something un-expected, even to himself: he took Diana's fingers in his own and raised them gently to his lips. Over the curve of her knuckles, he saw her eyes widen slightly; her smile deepen.

As he released her hand, he became aware of the faintest of scents. It wasn't soap or perfume, but something of Diana herself: a hint of cinnamon, of copper, of something else that resisted identification. It was subtly intoxicating. Lash thought back to what Mauchly had said in Eden's genetics lab: about mice and their unusual method for sniffing out the most radically different gene pool for potential mates. Abruptly, he laughed aloud.

Diana said nothing, merely raising her eye-brows in question.

In response, Lash lifted his own hand, filled this time with his wine glass. "And here's to a universe of diversity," he said.

THIRTY-FOUR

Sunday dawned raw and cold, and as the sun rose in the sky it seemed to chill rather than warm the land. By afternoon, the whitecaps of Long Island Sound had a leaden cast to them, and the unsettled waters looked black: harbingers of approaching winter.

Lash sat before the computer in his home office, nursing a cup of herbal tea. Miraculously — given the charged atmosphere of his dinner and the late hour at which he parted from Diana — he'd managed a good six hours of sleep and had risen without overwhelmingly weariness. What he did feel was restlessness: barred from removing any data from Eden, and without access to files or records, he had no way to advance his investigation. Yet instinct told him he was close, perhaps very close, to a revelation. And so he paced the house, ruminating, until at last in frustration he turned to the Internet and anything he could find about the company.

There was the usual Web ephemera: a scammer that claimed to have unlocked the secrets of Eden and offered to share them on a $19.95 video; conspiracy-theory sites that spoke darkly of evil alliances the company had made with intelligence agencies. But among all the dross there were also occasional bits of gold. Lash sent half a dozen articles at random to his printer, then carried the printouts to the living room sofa.

Feet propped on the table, the mournful cry of gulls sounding in the distance, he leafed slowly through them. There was an exceedingly complex white paper on artificial personality and swarm intelligence, written by Silver almost a decade earlier and no doubt released on the Internet without permission. A financial website provided a sober-sided analysis of the Eden business model, or at least the portion of it that was public knowledge, and a brief history of how it had been bankrolled by pharmaceutical giant PharmGen before being spun off on its own. And from another site came a flattering corporate biography of Richard Silver, who had risen from obscurity to become a world-class entrepreneur. Lash read this more carefully than the first two, marveling at the way Silver had developed his dream so faithfully and resolutely; how he hadn't let the vaguely reported misfortunes of early youth stand in his way. He was that rarest of people, the genius who seemed to know, from a very young age, the gift he'd been born to give the world.

There were other articles, too, not quite so flattering: an obnoxious tabloid article that promised to expose the "shocking, bizarre" details of the "crackpot genius" Silver. The opening paragraph read: *Question: What do you do if you can't find a girlfriend? Answer: You program one.* But the article itself had nothing to say, and Lash put it aside, stood up, and walked to the window.

It was true there were few other tasks Silver could have set Liza to that would have earned him more money, or so ensured the future health of his research. Yet on one level it was a little odd. Here was a man — by all accounts a shy, retiring man — who had made his fortune with that most social of games, the game of love. It seemed a shame, a bitter irony, that game could not extend to Silver as well.

As he stared out the window, the haiku Diana Mirren quoted the night before came back to him with sudden clarity.

> *Insects on a bough*
> *floating downriver,*
> *still singing.*

He smiled as he recalled their dinner. By the time they'd finally gotten around to ordering, the conversation had grown as easy and comfortable as any he could remember. His habitual distance crumbled without even a protest. She began to finish his sentences, and he hers, as if they'd known each other since childhood. And yet it was a strange kind of familiarity, filled with countless little surprises. It was close to one when they parted on Central Park West. They had exchanged numbers before going their separate ways. There had been no agreement to meet again; but then, there'd been no need of one. Lash knew he'd be seeing her again, and soon. In fact, he was half tempted to call now and offer to cook dinner.

What had she said? Haiku were the opposite of puzzles. Don't search for answers. Think of opening doors.

Opening doors. So how to interpret the one she quoted?

It had only eight words. In his mind, Lash saw a green willow branch, twisting in a lazy current, heading toward a distant waterfall. *Still* singing. Were the insects still singing out of ignorance of what lay ahead — or *because* of it?

The Wilners and the Thorpes were like the insects of the poem, singing on that floating branch. Blissfully, unrelievedly happy . . . right up until that last unfathomable moment.

The silence was shattered by the ring of a telephone.

Lash pushed himself to his feet and headed for the kitchen. Perhaps it was Diana; he'd have to dig up his recipe for salmon *en croute.*

He lifted the phone. "Lash here."

"Chris?" came the voice. "It's John."

"John?"

"John Coven."

Lash recognized the voice of the FBI agent who'd run the surveillance on Handerling. His heart sank. No doubt Coven was following up on his personal interest in Eden. Maybe he thought Lash could get him a discount or something.

"How are you, John?" he said.

"I'm okay, I'm fine. But listen, you're not going to believe this."

"Go ahead."

"Wyre's made parole."

Lash felt himself go numb. "Say again?"

"Edmund Wyre's made parole. Happened late Friday afternoon."

Lash swallowed. "I didn't hear anything about it."

"Nobody has. I just found out ten minutes ago. Saw it on the wire."

"Not possible. The guy killed six people."

"Tell me about it."

"There must be some kind of mistake."

"No mistake. He got the full board vote and the written report from DCJ."

"Any release conditions?"

"The usual, under the circumstances. Special field supervision. Which means precisely diddley-squat with a guy like Wyre."

Lash felt a sharp pain in his right hand, realized he was squeezing the phone. "What's the time frame? Weeks? Months?"

"Not even. Apparently they're all in a lather, setting Wyre up as some poster boy for rehabilitation. Screening's completed. They're already performing a residence investigation and preparing the release certificate. He'll be on the streets in a day or two."

"Jesus." Lash fell silent, struggling with disbelief.

"Christopher?"

Lash did not reply.

"Chris? You still with me?"

"Yes," Lash said distantly.

"Listen. Still got your service piece?"

"No."

"That's a shame. Because no matter what that parole board thinks, you and I both know this fucker wants to finish what he started. If I was you, I'd arm myself. And keep in mind what they taught us back at the Academy. You don't shoot to kill. You shoot to live."

Again, Lash did not respond.

"You need anything, let me know. Meanwhile, watch your six."

And the line went dead.

THIRTY-FIVE

He was driving home. That's how it began: driving home from Poughkeepsie yet again, in brilliant sunlight on a Friday afternoon. The last several times he'd made the sixty-mile journey back to Westport, he'd been so tired he feared falling asleep at the wheel. This afternoon, however, he was wide awake.

I'VE GOT WHAT I NEED NOW, the murderer had written in blood on the picture window. THANK YOU.

He reached down for the car phone, dialed.

"Lash residence," came the voice of Karl Broden, his wife's brother.

"Karl."

"Hi, Chris. Where are you?"

"Heading home. I'll be there in an hour or so. Shirley home?"

"She went out to run some errands."

"Okay. I'll see you soon."

"Good enough. Say, you want me to fire up the grill, marinate those gulf prawns

we picked up last night?"

"There's an idea. Stick some beers in the freezer for me, too."

"Done."

He thought briefly about his brother-in-law. Karl was so unlike his sister. Easygoing and loosely strung, unabashedly nonintellectual. Every time Karl came to visit, the level of tension in the house decreased markedly. This time he'd dropped in suddenly, the day before, almost as if he'd known his presence was desperately needed.

But then his thoughts returned to Poughkeepsie and the stark image of the final murder scene.

I'VE GOT WHAT I NEED NOW. THANK YOU.

The Poughkeepsie cops had been almost jovial all morning; ribbing each other good-naturedly, exchanging coarse jokes over the water cooler. Even though the killer eluded their roadblocks, they were buoyed by what seemed the promise of no more murders. Lash felt no such relief. To him, the message was the first piece of the puzzle to make sense; the only communication from the murderer that felt real. And its brevity, its confidence, filled him with anxiety.

What *did* he have now? What had he needed?

Had killing those four women satisfied

some sick requirement, filled some void? But that wasn't how it worked with serial killers: theirs was a consuming thirst that could never be quenched.

And then there was the inconsistency of the killings. The first two, despite superficial similarities — the bloody messages covering the walls, the arrangement of the corpses — contradicted all basic profiles in a dozen ways.

What made this final killing different?

He thought about this all the way across Dutchess and Putnam counties and into Connecticut. It was the first time, he was convinced, the murderer had shown his true colors.

Because he had what he wanted.

Why was there only one message this time, instead of a hundred? And why was it written on the picture window, not the walls? On the glass, against the backdrop of night, it would be extremely hard to make out . . .

And then suddenly, almost without conscious thought, he found his perspective on the crime scene changing. No longer was he looking at the bloody message from inside the bedroom. His angle shifted, turning as if on a camera dolly, coming around a hundred and eighty degrees until he was outside the house, in the woods, looking from the blackness at the big lighted window. At the figures silhouetted there — a police captain, the lead homicide detective, an FBI profiler. The same three people who'd been at the previous murders.

There was something that the three murders did have in common. They had all taken place at night, in bedrooms with big picture windows. And the blinds of the windows had always been open . . .

Frantically, he reached for the phone, dialed again.

"Poughkeepsie police, Homicide Division," came the voice. "Kravitz speaking."

"This is Christopher Lash. I need to speak with Masterton, right away."

"I'm sorry, Agent Lash. The captain left half an hour ago."

"Then give me the lead detective, what's his name. Ahearn."

"He left with the captain, sir."

"You know where they went?"

"It's Friday night, sir. The captain and Detective Ahearn always go out for a few cold ones before heading home."

"Which bar?"

"I don't know, sir. Could be one of half a dozen."

He thought quickly. Kravitz, the cop at the duty desk, had seemed like a smart, competent officer.

"Kravitz, you need to listen to me.

Listen very carefully."

"Yes, Agent Lash."

He tucked the phone under his chin briefly while negotiating the exit onto Saugatuck Avenue, fighting the weekend traffic. "You have to try each of the bars, in turn. Hear me? Get some of the other officers to help you man the phones."

"Sir?" Kravitz's voice sounded dubious.

"It's vital, Kravitz, you hear me? Vital."

"Yes, sir."

"When you reach Masterton, you are to tell him this: we've been wrong about this killer. He's not a serial murderer."

"Not a serial murderer?" The voice sounded even more dubious.

"You don't understand. Of course he's a murderer. But he's not a serial-type. He's an assassin-type."

That was the tag forensic psychologists used. Sometimes assassin-types murdered random victims from the tops of water towers. Other times they sought out favorite celebrities, the way Mark David Chapman did. They had one thing in common: tortured, useless lives that only developed meaning through acts of targeted violence.

Meanwhile, there was silence on the other end of the line.

"I don't have time to explain, Sergeant. It's a subcategory of mass murderer. For them, it's all about domination, control, revenge. This guy hates cops. There's probably a fascination, a love-hate dynamic, working here. Maybe his father was both a cop and an abusive parent, I don't know. But he's an assassin-type. It's the only answer."

"Sir, I don't understand."

"You were at the scenes of the first three murders. There was no pattern. The meaningless messages on the walls, the inconsistent tableaux. Nothing fit. That's because we were dealing with somebody imitating a serial murderer. That's why nothing held together: it was all a ruse. Did you notice the big picture windows at each site, open to the night? Our killer wasn't running away: he was out there, every time. He was hunting cops, picking out his targets. Those murdered women were just bait."

"Sir?"

He pulled the car onto Greens Farms Road. In another minute or two, once he got home, he'd start making calls himself. For now, he had to rely on Kravitz. Seconds counted.

"Just do as I say, Officer. Find Masterton, tell him everything I just told you. He and Ahearn were at the window each time, they have to take steps to protect themselves. Tell him to look for a white male, most likely in his mid to late twenties. A loner, but somebody who can blend with the crowd. He'll probably be driving a sporty car to compensate for low self-esteem. You need to talk to your fellow officers about any wannabees they might have noticed recently, hanging around cop bars and restaurants, ingratiating themselves."

Another silence on the line.

"Kravitz, damn it, do you have that?"

"Yes, sir."

"Then get busy." Just ahead lay his own block, and home. Traffic was lighter here. As he hung up, a car pulled out of his street and accelerated past him down Compo. A Pontiac Firebird, red.

He drove past, barely noticing. He reminded himself that he, too, was a target. He'd been silhouetted in that window, too. He'd have to get Karl and Shirley out of the house — she'd wither him, as usual, with comments on how dangerous his job was — and then he'd have to look into what to do about his own —

He started abruptly. A Pontiac Firebird, red, recent model . . .

He slowed, glanced into the rearview mirror.

The car was gone.

Now he stepped on the accelerator again, hard, taking the corner with a shriek of rubber, pulling his gun from its holster, but even as their house came into view he felt a cold dread seize him.

He already knew, with terrible certainty, what it was he would find inside.

THIRTY-SIX

Lash leaned back and stared at the ceiling. Even there, columns of numbers, names, dates seemed to stare back at him.

"Christ," he groaned, shutting his eyes. "I've been staring at this stuff too long."

He heard the shuffling of paper across the table. "Any luck?" he asked the ceiling.

"Not a bite," came Tara Stapleton's voice.

Lash opened his eyes, stretched. Despite the dark dreams and memories that had filled the previous night, he'd nevertheless awakened with a sense of purpose. The weekend had passed without any dread events. Driving in, he'd called Diana Mirren on his cell phone. The mere sound of her voice brought him a secret, almost adolescent thrill. They chatted briefly, ardently, and she'd agreed to have dinner at his place the coming Friday. He found himself so busy mentally preparing that he forgot the mortification he'd endured at Checkpoint III until he found himself standing before it once again. But the security officers were not the ones on duty last

Friday, and he'd passed through without a hitch.

But now — midmorning — his excitement had drowned in an endless flood of data. There was simply too much material to comb through; it was like sifting a haystack without even being certain it contained a needle.

He sighed again, then pulled Lindsay Thorpe's internal evaluations over and began leafing through them almost idly. "What's the story on the third couple? The Connellys?"

"They're leaving for Niagara Falls tomorrow."

"Niagara Falls?"

"That's where they spent their honeymoon."

Niagara Falls, Lash thought. *Great place for a murder. Or a suicide, for that matter.*

"There's not much we can do on the Canadian side," Tara added. "I spent most of Saturday arranging the passive surveillance over there. We watch, and hope for the best."

"At least you had something to keep you busy over the weekend."

Tara smiled slyly. "It wasn't as if you didn't have your dance card filled."

"You mean, my date?"

"How did it go?"

"She didn't look at all the way I expected. Didn't *sound* the way I expected. But you know what? Within ten minutes, it didn't matter."

"Our research has shown that we're often attracted to the wrong people, for the wrong reasons. Maybe that's why so many marriages don't work."

She fell silent.

"Look," Lash said after a moment. "Why don't you go through with meeting this guy they've matched you with? It isn't too late. Talk to Mauchly about rescheduling the reservation."

"I've already told you. How can I meet him, knowing what I know?"

"I met Diana Mirren, knowing what I know. And I'm seeing her again this Friday."

"But I'm an Eden employee. I've told you —"

"I know. The 'Oz effect.' And you know what I say? Bullshit."

"Is that your professional opinion, Doctor?"

"It is." He leaned forward. "Tara, listen. Eden can match one person with another. Perfectly. But once you two make contact, there *is* no more Eden. It's just you and him. If it feels right, you'll know it."

Tara looked at him, saying nothing.

"One way or another, we'll solve this. And then it won't matter anymore. It'll just be a memory. The past. And any relationship requires an acceptance of the past. Would you begrudge him the cheerleaders he dated in college? This is the main chance, Tara. Take it from somebody who was in that restaurant two nights ago."

Immediately, Lash realized he'd said enough. *Back to work,* he thought with a sigh.

Putting Lindsay Thorpe's dossier aside, he began paging through her medical reports. Then he paused.

"Tara."

She looked at him a little guardedly.

"About this return checkup of Ms. Thorpe's."

"You mean, class reunion?"

"No, this checkup. Is it common for your doctors to prescribe —"

"We don't do that."

For a moment, this did not register. Then Lash looked at her. "What did you say?"

"I said, we don't do return checkups."

"Then what's this?" Lash pushed the medical report across the table.

Tara took the report. There was silence as she scanned the pages.

"I've only seen this a few times before," she said.

"Seen what?"

"Remember, on your first tour inside the Wall, Mauchly explained about the long-term health analyses we run on prospective candidates? Checking genetic markers for inherited diseases, risk factors, that kind of thing?"

"Yes."

"If there's something seriously wrong, we

reject their application. But if it's minor, or of minimal long-term concern, we'll process their application and bring them back for a secondary exam, later."

"Under the pretext of standard operating procedure."

"That's right."

"No point in turning away a paying client." Lash took back the report, flipped the pages. "But Lindsay Thorpe had no such health issues. Yet she was scheduled for a follow-up examination, six months prior to her death." He flipped more pages. "At this exam, Ms. Thorpe was given a prescription for scolipane. One milligram, once a day. I'm not familiar with that medication."

"Me neither."

"The physician in attendance was a Dr. Moffett. Could you contact him, ask the reason for the follow-up exam and prescription?"

"Sure." Tara rose and walked to the phone.

Lash watched her. This was another clue, he felt certain; another piece of the puzzle.

"Dr. Moffett's hours don't begin until noon," Tara said as she replaced the phone. "I'll contact him then."

"Would you do something else? Pull the medical records of Lewis Thorpe, the Wilners, and — and the third couple, the Connellys. See if they had any follow-up examinations."

Lash waited as the office filled with the sound of keystrokes.

"Nothing," Tara said. "None of the others had any follow-ups beyond the normal class reunions."

"Nothing?"

Tara shook her head.

"Wouldn't Lewis Thorpe think it strange his wife had a follow-up exam when he didn't?"

"You know how secretive we are about procedures. Our clients come to accept them without question."

Lash slumped in his chair. Despite everything, he found his thoughts returning to Diana Mirren, what she'd said about haiku.

They hint at things. They imply more than they say. Don't search for an answer. Think instead of opening doors.

So what was implied here? What coincidences had taken place recently? And what did they hint at?

Edmund Wyre, the cop-hating assassin, granted parole. Wyre killed three women, two cops, and Lash's brother-in-law. Lash's wife then left him, and Lash himself — full of doubt and self-blame — had abruptly left the FBI, searching for an end to the sleepless nights.

By rights, Wyre should never have been paroled. Lash had no illusions: no matter what the parole board thought, Wyre would be gunning for him. Lash was the one he'd missed.

Was this coincidence?

Then there was his avatar being sent into the Tank. Tara had said such a mistake was impossible. If so, somebody had done it deliberately: *It would have to be somebody very highly placed, somebody with world-class access. Me, for example. Or a grunt who'd somehow hacked the system.*

His gaze fixed on Tara, who had returned to the table and was sorting papers.

Think of opening doors . . .

And, suddenly, the door opened.

Lash gasped, almost as if he'd been dealt a blow. He covered the sound with a yawn.

It seemed impossible. But there was no other answer.

There were two things he still needed to know before he was sure. Tara could answer one of them. But he had to appear calm — at least, until he had proof.

"Tara," he said with exaggerated weariness. "Could you do something else for me?"

She nodded.

"Could you bring up a list of all the avatars in the Tank when the Thorpes were matched?"

"Why?"

"Just humor me."

She walked once again toward the computer. Lash followed.

"Show me how it's done," he said.

"First, you have to access the avatar database." She entered a transaction code at the menu screen and an explosion of nine-digit numbers appeared. "These are all the avatars."

"All?"

"All clients to date. Almost two million." She typed some additional commands. "Okay. I've created an SQL query you can run against this dataset. Type in the avatar's identity code, and it will bring up all the others that were in the tank at the time of its match."

"Show me, please."

She lifted the piece of paper. "Here's that sheet we printed out Friday, showing the dates the Thorpes and Wilners first submitted their applications."

THORPE, LEWIS A.	000451823	7/30/02
TORVALD, LINDSAY E.	000462196	8/21/02
SCHWARTZ, KAREN L.	000527710	8/02/02
WILNER, JOHN L.	000491003	9/06/02

"Lewis Thorpe's identity code is 000451823. You enter that into the query field."

She typed it in and the screen refreshed again.

"Here are all the avatars in the Tank when Lewis was matched to Lindsay, indexed by their identity codes." She scrolled quickly down to the bottom of the list:

000481032

000481883

000481907

000482035

000482110

000482722

000483814

000483992

000484398

000485006

QUERY COMPLETED AT 11:05:42:82
  10/04/04
DISCRETE UNIT COUNT: 52,812

>?

Tara pointed at the bottom line. "In that time-slice, there were almost twenty-three thousand Avatars in the tank."

"But it's just a bunch of numbers."

"This function key lets you toggle between names and identity codes." Tara pressed a key and the numbers were replaced by names:

Fallon, Eugene

White, Jerome

Wanderely, Helen

Garcia, Constanze
Lu, Wen
Gelbman, Mark
Yoshida, Aiko
Horst, Marcus
Green-Carson, Margo
Banieri, Antonio

Shit, Lash thought. *It's still sorted by identity code, not last name.* He considered asking Tara for an alphabetical sort, but decided against it: he wasn't ready to explain. He began paging back through the names, one screen after another.

"What are you looking for?" Tara asked, gazing curiously over his shoulder.

"Just looking. Listen, would you do one more thing?"

"Just one more thing. Just one more thing. I wish I got paid by the errand."

"I think we made a mistake, looking just at the records of supercouples."

"Why?"

"Look at what we found out about Lindsay Thorpe and her surprise medical exam. Who knows what else we might find if we cross-check against a random sample of *regular* couples?"

"Makes sense." Tara hesitated. "I'll go requisition the records."

"Hurry back."

He watched her go. Although he was genuinely curious about the comparison he'd suggested, right now he was most interested in examining the screen without another pair of eyes beside him. He began once again scrolling up the names.

It took longer than he thought to go through them all, and it was almost eleven-thirty by the time he reached the top of the list. He slumped back, disappointed. But then again it would have been too easy: finding the name he was hoping for, just like that. Maybe it was a crazy idea. He cringed at the idea of plodding through another huge set of names. Still, he'd come this far: he might as well try the Wilners. Just in case.

He hit the function key Tara had pointed out. Instantly, the screen refreshed, showing the avatars in numerical order.

START OF QUERY
==========
000000000
000448401
000448916
000448954
000449010
000449029
000449174
000449204
000449248
000449286

He straightened. What was that first code, 000000000, doing there?

He toggled the function key, but there was no corresponding name for the identity code: the field was blank.

He shrugged, reached for the paper Tara had left on the desk, and typed John Wilner's code — 000491003 — in the query field.

When the screen refreshed, 000000000 was again at the top of the list. And once again, there was no name associated with the number.

Lash scratched his head. What was it? A start-of-array marker?

One more test. Rising from the chair and coming quickly around the desk, he rooted through the paper strewn across the table until he found a sheet with Kevin Connelly's identity code. He returned to the computer, typed it in, stared at the fresh list of numbers.

"Jesus Christ," he breathed.

The door opened and Tara stepped in, carrying a stack of reports. "I plucked out a dozen names at random," she said. "I thought the evaluations would be enough to —"

Lash cut her off. "Come over here. Please."

She dropped the folders on the table and approached the monitor.

Lash looked at her, no longer trying to

conceal his rising excitement. "I want you to pull up one more list. Show me who's in the Tank, *now*."

She frowned. "What's going on? What are you doing?"

"Tara, *please*. Just do this."

She stared at him, hard, another moment. Then she bent over the keyboard and typed in a new query.

The screen cleared, and Lash looked at it eagerly. He nodded to himself, as if confirming some private suspicion.

Then, suddenly, he snapped off the power. The screen went dark.

"What the *hell?*" Tara said.

Without answering, Lash grabbed the phone, snugged it beneath his chin, dialed a long-distance number.

"Captain Tsosie's desk, please," he said. There was a brief wait. "Joe? It's Chris Lash. Joe, is the Thorpe house still technically under police investigation? Thank God. Listen, I want you to send a field agent over there right away. You still have my cell number? Give it to the agent, have them call me the moment they're on the premises. Yes, it's that important. Thanks."

He replaced the phone, looked at Tara. "There's something I have to do. I can't explain right now. I'll be back soon."

He grabbed his coat, made for the door. Then he turned back. Tara remained at the

362

desk, staring after him, a strange expression on her face.

"Follow up with that doctor," he said. "Dr. Moffett. Understand?"

Tara nodded. And Lash turned, tugged open the door, and was gone.

THIRTY-SEVEN

In the still gallery far above Madison Avenue, a laser printer came to life: first with the purr of a fan, then the green blink of a light. Its motor chugged briefly and a single sheet slid into the tray.

Richard Silver, who was seated at a small satinwood table in the middle of the vast room, looked up at the sound. A terrycloth towel was draped over his shoulders. He'd been working for nearly twenty hours straight, sketching out the pseudo-code of an immense new program: a program refining interaction with Liza to a point where an EEG hookup would no longer be necessary. Lash had been right: it was time.

Besides, it kept his mind from distressing events — events that, more than anything, he did not want to dwell on.

He glanced in the direction of the printer, like a sleeper roused from a trance. Hardcore computer coding is a state of mind: it can take a lot of time to get "in the zone." Silver was now deep in the zone and would normally be reluctant to relinquish it. But the paper waiting in the printer's tray meant only one thing: Liza had completed her task, and completed it early.

He rose, glanced at the clock. Twenty-five minutes after eleven. He walked toward the printer, hesitatingly removed the sheet.

Then he froze.

For a long moment he stood motionless, staring at it. The sunlit gallery was absolutely silent. At last, Silver lowered the paper. His hand shook as he did so.

He stuffed the sheet into a pocket of his sweatpants. Then he crossed the room, opened the hidden door, and ascended the stairs to the next level.

When the black door at the end of the hall sprang open, Silver stepped immediately toward the contoured chair, pinned the microphone to his sweatshirt, and began fixing the electrodes to his temple. Normally, this process was enjoyable, almost meditative: preparation for contacting a more perfect version of himself than he could ever hope to achieve.

Today he felt simply numb.

"Richard," the low, uninflected voice said from all corners of the room.

"Liza. What is your current state?"

"Ninety-nine point one seven six two percent operational. Current processes are at eighty-six point two percent of multithreaded capacity. Standard operations can now again access one hundred percent of bandwidth. Thank you for asking."

"You're welcome."

"I had not expected to speak with you at the present time. Do you wish to run a scenario? I have completed a variant of the Rift Valley threat-response game that you might find entertaining. Or do you wish to discuss my thoughts on our current book? I have finished analysis of chapter twenty."

"Not at present. I have the results of your interrogatory. It came in early."

"Yes. My estimate was off by seventy-one billion machine cycles."

"Liza, I have just one question. How sure are you of the result?"

With humans, one could always count on a pause when digesting an unexpected comment. With Liza, there was no such pause. "I do not understand your question."

"Are you sure the result of the interrogatory is not in error?"

"The result shows no statistical deviation. It is what remains when all unsatisfactory results have been discarded."

"I am not doubting you, Liza. I simply wanted to make sure."

"Your concern is understandable. Before initiating the process, you stated it was critical to find the solution. I have found the solution. I hope it proves satisfactory."

"Thank you, Liza."

"You are welcome, Richard. Shall we talk further?"

"Soon. There's something I must do first."

"Thank you for speaking with me."

Silver punched the shutdown sequence into the keypad, plucked the electrodes from his temples, and got out of the chair. He waited a minute, listening to the sound of his own breathing. Then he wiped his brow with the towel and headed for the door, reaching for his cell phone and dialing as he stepped into the corridor.

"Mauchly here," came the voice.

"Edwin, it's Richard."

"Yes, Dr. Silver."

"Edwin, I need you up here. Right away."

THIRTY-EIGHT

The Norman J. Weisenbaum Center for Biomedical Research stood on a point of land jutting into the Hudson south of Cold Spring. Lash pulled into visitors' parking, hoisted himself out onto the macadam, and glanced up at the long, low structure of glass and stone that climbed the hillside. It was not at all the way he'd pictured it when he called the center the week before, on the flight back from Phoenix. It was unrelievedly modern. And yet somehow it did not seem out of place in this haven of Dutch gables. The rich tones of polished marble blended nicely with the backdrop of oak and sycamore. Waterbirds wheeled and cried overhead.

Inside, the receptionist's station was manned by three women. Lash approached the closest, presented his card. "Dr. Lash to see Dr. Goodkind."

"Just a moment, please." The woman peered into a monitor recessed into her work surface, held a manicured finger to one ear, listened to an invisible earpiece. Then she looked up at him again. "If you'd kindly take a seat, he'll be right with you."

Lash had barely settled into one of the chrome-and-leather chairs when he saw Roger Goodkind approaching. Goodkind was carrying a few more pounds since they'd last met, and the sandy hair was receding dramatically from his temples. But the man still had the same sly half-smile, the same loping walk, of their undergraduate days.

"Chris!" Goodkind clasped Lash's hand in his. "Punctual as ever."

"Anxiety disorder. Presenting as compulsive timeliness."

The biochemist laughed. "If only your diagnosis were that simple." He led Lash toward an elevator. "Can this really be? Hearing from you like this, twice in two weeks? I'm almost prostrate with gratitude."

"I wish I could say it was a social call," Lash replied as the elevator opened, "but the fact is I need your help."

Goodkind nodded. "Anything."

Goodkind's lab was even larger than Lash had anticipated. There were the obligatory lab tables and chemical apparatus, but there were also deep leather chairs, a handsome desk, bookcases full of journals, a stunning view of the river. Lash whistled appreciatively.

"The center's been kind to me," Goodkind said with a chuckle. He'd developed a new mannerism since Lash last saw him: he ran his fingers through his thinning hair, then grasped a few strands and tugged on them, as if encouraging growth.

"So I see."

"Have a seat. You want a diet soda or something?"

Lash let himself be shown to one of the armchairs. "No, thanks."

Goodkind took a seat opposite. "So what's up?"

"Remember why I called you last week?"

"Sure. All those crazy questions about suicide among perfectly happy people."

"Yes. I'm working on something, Roger, something I can't tell you much about. Can I rely on you to keep it confidential?"

"What is this, Chris? Is it a Bureau matter?"

"In a way." Lash watched the man's eyes widen. If Goodkind thought the Feds were involved, he'd be more likely to cooperate.

Goodkind shifted. "I'll do whatever I can."

"You do a lot of work with toxicology, right? Drug side effects, interactions, that sort of thing?"

"It's not my field of expertise, but, yes, we're all involved with toxicology to some degree at the center."

"So tell me. What steps would a biochemist go through in developing a new drug?"

Goodkind ran a hand through his thinning hair. "A new drug? From scratch, you mean?" He paused to tug on a lock. "Historically, drug development's always been kind of hit or miss. You screen molecules and compounds, looking for a 'hit,' something that seems beneficial to people. Of course, now with computational chemistry, you can simulate the effects of reactions that —"

"No, I don't mean that early in the process. Say you've already developed a drug, or something you think might be a drug. What's the next step?"

Goodkind thought a moment. "Well, you do stability testing. See what delivery vehicle it likes best: tablet, capsule, solution. Then you expose the drug molecule to a variety of conditions — relative humidity, UV light, oxygen, heat — make sure it doesn't degrade, break down into harmful byproducts." He grinned. "People always keep drugs in their bathroom cabinets, you know, which is probably the worst thing you can do. Heat and moisture can cause all sorts of nasty chemical reactions."

"Go on."

"You perform tox studies, qualify the degradation products. Determine what's acceptable, what's not acceptable. Then you do a Trap."

"A what?"

"A Trap. Toxicological risk analysis procedure. That's what we call it here at the center, anyway. You run the functional groups — the different parts of the drug molecule — against a knowledge base of existing chemicals and pharmaceuticals. You're essentially looking for adverse reactions that might cause different, and more dangerous, functional groups. Toxicity potential. Carcinogenicity, neurotoxicity, so forth."

"And if you find such toxic potential?"

"That's known as a structure alert. Each alert is flagged and studied for severity."

"I see. And if the drug passes?"

"Then it goes on to clinical trials, first in animals usually, then humans."

"These structure alerts. Can a drug cause a structure alert and still go on to be developed?"

"Of course. That's one reason you have warning labels on medicine bottles. 'Don't take with alcohol' and the rest."

"Are these alerts listed somewhere, in a book? The *Physician's Desk Reference*, maybe?"

Goodkind shook his head. "Structure alerts are too low-level, too chemical, for the PDR."

"So they're proprietary? Kept secret by individual researchers or pharmaceutical companies?"

"Oh, no. They're all stored in a central database. Government regulations."

Lash sat forward slowly. "Who has access to this database?"

"The FDA. Pharmaceutical manufacturers."

"Biochemistry labs?"

Goodkind inhaled sharply as he realized where Lash was headed. Then he nodded. "With the proper accreditation."

"The Weisenbaum Center?"

Goodkind nodded again. "In the research library. Two flights up."

"Mind leading the way?"

Goodkind licked his lips. "Chris, I don't know. Access to that database is government-sanctioned. You sure this is official?"

"It's of the greatest importance."

Still, Goodkind hesitated.

Lash stood up. "Remember what you said when I called? That you couldn't predict suicide, that it was just a roll of the dice? That it made no sense, for example, why Poland had a drastically higher suicide rate than normal in 2000?"

"I remember."

"Perhaps you forgot something, a fact I just dug up on my way here. Poland is the country where, because of the low cost to run studies, *most drugs were tested in 2000.*"

Goodkind thought for a moment. "You mean — ?"

"I mean you should show me that toxicology database. Right now."

Goodkind hesitated just a second longer.
And then he, too, stood up.

THIRTY-NINE

The center's research library did not look like a library at all. It was a low-ceilinged space, uncomfortably warm, its walls lined with carrels of blond wood. Each contained a seat, a desk, and a computer terminal. The room's only occupant was the librarian, who looked up from her typing to stare suspiciously at Lash.

Goodkind chose a carrel in the far corner. "Where are all the books?" Lash asked in a low voice as he pulled over the chair from the adjoining carrel.

"In the basement stacks." Goodkind drew the keyboard toward him. "You need to requisition titles from Ms. Gustus, there. But almost everything we need is online, anyway."

Lash watched as the man typed in his name. A menu appeared, and Goodkind made a selection. The screen refreshed:

FDA - DIVISION R

PBTK

PHARMACEUTICAL AND BIOMEDICAL
TOXICITY KNOWLEDGE BASE

REV. 120.11
LAST UPDATED: 10.01.04
PROPRIETARY AND CONFIDENTIAL.
OFFICIALLY SANCTIONED USE ONLY.
UNAUTHORIZED ACCESS CONSTITUTES
A FEDERAL CRIME.

ID: _____
PASSWORD: _____

Goodkind looked at Lash, who nodded encouragingly. With a shrug, Goodkind completed the fields. A new screen appeared:

FDA - R/PBTK 120.11/00012   10/04/04

ENTER QUERY BY:

1. CHEMICAL COMPOUND
2. TRADEMARK
3. GENERIC

PRESS F1 FOR INDEX:

Goodkind looked over again. "What's the name of the medication you're interested in?"

"Scolipane."

"Never heard of it." Goodkind tapped a series of keys, and the screen filled with text. "Here it is."

Lash peered more closely:

FDA - R / PBTK 120.11/09817 10/04/04

SCOLIPANE
Hydoxene, 2 - ((6 - (p-methylparapine) phenylchloride) alkaloid) -, sodium salt
MR: PhG
MF: $C_{23}H_5O_5N_3 \bullet Na$
USE: (primary) S. M. R. (secondary) see p. 20

MUTATION DATA: N/R
REPRODUCTIVE REFERENCES: p. 15
SYNONYMS: p. 28
DOSAGE DATA: p. 10

PAGE 1 OF 30

ACUTE TOXICITY DATA

ROUTE	DOSAGE	PERCEIVED EFFECT
intra-peritoneal mouse	lethal (50% kill): 340 mg/kg	muscle weakness ataxia
sub-cutaneous mouse	lethal (50% kill): 190 mg/kg	ataxia respiratory depression
intra-muscular mouse	lethal (50% kill): 240 mg/kg	cellular necrosis behavior alteration

ROUTE	DOSAGE	PERCEIVED EFFECT
oral mouse	lethal (50% kill): > 10 gm/kg	N/R
oral dog	lethal (50% kill): > 12,500 mg/kg	canine mania see p. 20
oral human	toxic (lowest published): 700 mg/kg	see p. 20

"Biochem was my worst subject at U. Penn. Remember?" Lash looked away from the screen. "Why don't you hold my hand a little here."

Goodkind scanned the text. "Scolipane's primary use is as a skeletal muscle relaxant."

"A *muscle* relaxant?"

"It's a relatively new formulation, about five years old."

"Dosage?"

"One milligram. A little feller."

Lash slumped. The theory that had begun to seem so promising started to slip away again.

He glanced back morosely at the top of the screen. Between the chemical description and the formula was a line he didn't recognize. "What's 'MR' stand for?"

"Manufacturer. They all have codes. You know, sort of like airports. Take this one: PhG. That's short for PharmGen."

Lash straightened again.

PharmGen.

He began looking more closely at the data. The acute toxicity chart was a typical feature of such reports; it usually recorded the LD50, or dosage at which half the sample population would die. He ran down the columns.

"Canine mania," he said quietly. "What the *hell?*"

"We have to scroll to page twenty for more information."

"And look — it says to see page twenty for data on human overdosage, as well." Lash glanced at Goodkind. "Primary use is as a muscle relaxant, you said."

"Right."

"But look here. There's *another* use. A secondary use." He pointed at the screen.

"Page twenty again," Goodkind murmured. "Seems that page has a lot to tell us."

"Then let's go."

Goodkind moused quickly forward, the screen blurring, until he reached page 20. Both men leaned in to read the dense text.

"Jesus," Goodkind breathed.

Lash said nothing. But he found himself going cold in the overheated room.

FORTY

Tara Stapleton sat behind her desk, motionless except for her eyes. Slowly, she scanned the office, letting her gaze settle on one thing, then another. The plants were watered and carefully pruned; her old fiberglass board leaned against the wall as it always did; the posters, bumper stickers, and other surfing paraphernalia remained in their usual spots. The institutional clock on the far wall told her it was ten minutes to four. Everything was as it should be. And yet everything looked unfamiliar, as if the office had become suddenly foreign to her eyes.

She leaned back slowly in her chair, aware her breathing had grown fast and shallow.

Suddenly the phone rang, its shrill warble shattering the quiet. Tara froze.

It rang again. Two beeps: an outside call.

Slowly, she lifted it from the handset. "Stapleton."

"Tara?" The voice was rushed, out of breath.

"Tara?" it repeated. "It's Christopher Lash."

Street noises filtered from the earpiece: the rush of traffic, the blatt of a truck's horn.

"Christopher," Tara said evenly.

"I've got to talk to you. Right now. It's very important."

"Why don't you come by my office?"

"No. Not inside. Can't take the chance."

Tara hesitated.

"Tara, please." Lash's voice was almost pleading. "I need your help. There's something I have to tell you nobody else can overhear."

Still, Tara said nothing.

"*Tara.* Another supercouple is about to die."

"There's a coffee shop around the corner," she said. "The Rio. On Fifty-fourth, between Madison and Park."

"I'll be waiting for you. Hurry, please."

And the phone went dead.

But Tara did not rise from her desk. In fact, she made no move at all except to replace the phone in its cradle and stare at it, as if struggling with some terrible uncertainty.

FORTY-ONE

Lash walked into the Rio a few minutes after four. The walls were covered in gilt wallpaper, and the incandescent lights and resin-colored banquettes gave the diner a hazy, golden glow. He felt like an insect surrounded by amber.

For a moment, he thought he'd arrived first. But then he caught sight of Tara, sitting at a booth in the rear of the restaurant. He stepped forward and slid into the seat across from her.

A waitress approached; Lash ordered a coffee, waited until she walked away. Then he turned back. "Tara. Thanks for coming."

Tara nodded.

"Did you talk to that doctor? Moffett?"

Tara nodded again.

"What did he say?"

"He was following instructions from an internal scrip."

"What does that mean?"

"Medication regimen, based on the findings of an earlier examination."

"In other words, he was following some other in-house doctor's orders."

"Yes."

"Did he say whose orders?"

"I didn't ask him that."

"How easy would it be to fake such orders?"

Tara hesitated. "I'm sorry?"

"Everything at Eden is automated. You get a piece of paper, telling you to do something. Couldn't somebody type false medical orders into the computer system?"

When Tara did not reply, Lash leaned a little closer. "I don't have all the answers yet. But I have enough to know it's not only the remaining supercouples who are in danger. We're in danger, too."

"Why?"

"Because somebody — somebody *inside* Eden — has set these women up to kill themselves and murder their husbands."

Tara began to speak, but Lash quickly held up a suppressing hand. "No. Let me talk first, please. You're not going to believe it unless I give you a little background."

Tara relaxed, but only slightly. She was looking at him with shock, even apprehension. Lash glanced toward a nearby mirror and caught a glimpse of himself: haggard, hair askew, tired eyes animated with nervous energy. If he was her, he'd be apprehensive, too.

The waitress returned with his coffee, and Lash took a sip. "That prescription of Lindsay Thorpe's, for one milligram of scolipane? It was the clue I needed. I spent the afternoon tracking down more information. Did Dr. Moffett tell you what scolipane is normally prescribed for?"

Tara shook her head.

"It's a muscle relaxant. It works on the area of the brain that controls muscle spasms. Sports medicine doctors use it to treat strains. You say Dr. Moffett was following through on treatment prescribed in an earlier examination. But Tara, what earlier examination could have *predicted* Lindsay Thorpe would strain a muscle?"

"Then scolipane must be used to treat something else."

"You're more right than you know. Scolipane *was* originally intended to treat something else. But that something else was kept a close secret, locked up in drug development databases."

He paused. "Ever see a TV ad for what sounds like a miracle drug? No more allergies, maybe. Or your high cholesterol, suddenly gone. And then all the side effects go scrolling across the screen . . . and it's almost enough to make you swear off medicine forever. Those are just the drugs that *make* it past clinical trials. Many others never make it."

He glanced across the table, but Tara's expression remained unreadable.

"Okay. Let's back up. Most aspects of personality are the result of genes controlling neurotransmitters in the brain. That includes undesirable traits like anxiety and depression. So we create drugs to deal with them. Things like SSNRIs, which suppress the reuptake of serotonin. But there are lots of serotonin receptors in the brain. How can you aim a drug at all the receptors at once?"

He took another sip of coffee. "So drug companies have been looking for other solutions. Ways they could alter brain chemistry to achieve better results. Sometimes they venture deep into unknown territory. Such as the neuropeptide known as 'Substance P.'"

"Substance P," Tara repeated.

"I hadn't heard of it either, until this afternoon. It's very mysterious: nobody knows exactly why it's in the brain, or what its purpose is. But we do know the kind of things that cause it to be released. Acute physical pain. High levels of stress. It's been closely implicated with severe depression, sudden suicide."

He leaned closer. "At least one drug company became interested in Substance P. They decided if they could develop a pharmaceutical agent to 'hit' Substance P, to block its receptor, maybe they could make a whole lot of depressed people happy again. That drug company was PharmGen. Eden's parent."

"Not anymore. Eden is independent now."

"PharmGen developed a new anti-psychotic drug that acted against Substance P. It had some rough going early on — red flags appeared during toxicology testing — and the drug was remodified. Four years ago, it was finally ready for group testing. The testing was done in Poland, which was common practice. Maybe ten thousand people were involved, all told. Ninety-nine times out of a hundred, the drug worked beautifully. And it wasn't limited to single indicators: schizoids, borderlines, chronic depressives, all seemed to benefit."

He sipped his coffee. "But there was a problem: that other one percent. If a person *without* mental illness took the drug — specifically, a person with high levels of serum copper in their blood — terrible side effects resulted. Depression, paranoia, homicidal rage. There were mass instances of suicide, enough to skew the suicide statistics for *the entire country* that year."

He glanced across the table to gauge the effect. But Tara's expression remained guarded.

"The drug was withdrawn from testing. But it emerged late the following year, in a drastically lowered dosage, reformulated for another purpose: a muscle relaxant."

Disbelief returned to Tara's face. "Scoli-pane?"

"One-milligram tablets. The original fifty-milligram formulation is also available, but prescribed only in very rare circumstances, under close observation." He pushed his cup aside. "Remember that call I made just before leaving your office? That was to a friend of mine in the Phoenix field office. I asked him to send somebody to the Thorpes' house, check on their meds. Lindsay's prescription for scolipane was on the night table beside her bed. But the dosage had been increased from one to *fifty* milligrams. In capsule form, she didn't notice the difference."

Tara frowned.

"Somebody changed her dosage. Somebody who knew about the side effects of scolipane in its original formulation. Somebody who knew scolipane wouldn't set off any alarms in the autopsy blood work. Somebody who also knew — probably from her application form — that Lindsay Thorpe was taking an antihistamine."

"What are you talking about?"

"When I first began investigating the deaths, I had a talk with Lindsay's father. He mentioned she had dermatographia. It's a benign but irritating skin condition that causes itchiness. The recommended treatment is a histamine antagonist. Over time, chronic users of such drugs can develop high-copper histapenia — low levels of histamine in the blood, causing an accumulation of copper."

Lash was increasingly alarmed by her continued disbelief. "Don't you understand? When Lindsay Thorpe took that huge dose of scolipane, coupled with her high blood copper, she unwittingly re-created — *exactly* — the conditions that caused such high suicide in the initial drug trials. Think of the terrible mental ordeal she must have gone through, made all the worse for being sudden, inexplicable. Hostile voices in her head. Acts of psychotic deviance: she found herself playing music she detested on the stereo. Lindsay Thorpe hated opera, you see, but she was listening to opera when she died. All this would be followed by black despair, overwhelming homicidal and suicidal urgings . . ." He paused. "She loved her husband dearly. But the impulses were irresistible. Still, I think she carried them through with as much dignity, as little pain, as possible."

When she said nothing, he went on. "I know what you're thinking. Why did she kill her husband? She didn't *want* to. But she *had* to. Yet even as the flood of brain chemicals drove her half mad, her love for Lewis Thorpe remained. And how do you kill somebody you love? As painlessly as possible. And you would go *together*. That's why the deaths happened at night: Lindsay could slip a dry cleaning bag over the head of her sleeping husband before slipping one over her own. She probably waited for him to fall asleep in front of the TV. Same with Karen Wilner. She was a librarian, she would have access to scalpels in the book repair lab. A fresh scalpel is so sharp you wouldn't even feel it opening your vein — not if you were asleep, anyway. But I'll bet she sliced her own wrist more hesitantly, that's why it took her longer to die."

"What about the baby?" Tara murmured. "The Thorpes' child?"

"You mean, why did she survive? I don't know the morphology of Substance P well enough to speculate. Perhaps the mother-child bond is too elemental, too primitive, to be broken in such a way."

Now he reached across the table, took Tara's hand. "Lindsay may have killed herself and her husband. But this isn't about that. It's about *first-degree* murder. Somebody inside Eden knew exactly how to make Lindsay Thorpe self-destruct. Somebody knew her medical background, knew about the early tests on scolipane, knew how to create that precise chemical cocktail within her blood. And that somebody had the power to fake a paper trail, doctor her medical orders, even modify her prescription. You said it yourself: it has to be somebody with world-class access to your systems."

His grip tightened on her hand. "I think you know where this is leading. It's the answer, the only *possible* answer. And you have to be strong. Because this person *must* be stopped. He got to Karen Wilner the same way. He's singling out the *women*, making them self-destruct. In just two days, the third couple will —"

He stopped abruptly. Tara was no longer listening. Her expression had shifted from his face to somewhere else: somewhere over his shoulder.

He turned. Edwin Mauchly was approaching from the front of the diner, surrounded by half a dozen other men. Lash did not recognize them, but he knew they must be Eden security.

Quickly, Tara pulled her hand from his.

Lash, stunned, was slow to react. Within a moment the table was surrounded, the exits blocked.

"Dr. Lash," Mauchly said. "If you'll come with us, please?"

As comprehension broke over him he rose instinctively, ready for flight. One of the guards placed a hand on his shoulder and, gently but irresistibly, guided him back into the seat.

"You'll find things a lot less painful if you cooperate, sir," the security officer said.

Vaguely, Lash was aware Tara had slipped out of the booth and was now standing behind Mauchly.

A few seconds ticked by. They seemed very long. Lash glanced around the diner. A few faces were turned in his direction, watching with mild curiosity. Then he looked up at the surrounding guards. And then he nodded and — much more slowly — stood. The security staff closed around him, and he felt himself propelled forward.

Mauchly was far ahead now, already leaving the restaurant. One arm was draped protectively around Tara's shoulders. "I'm sorry you had to be put through this," Lash heard him say. "But it's all over. You're safe." Then the door closed behind them, the sound cut off, and the two melted into the gathering darkness of Fifty-fourth Street.

Tara vanished without looking back.

FORTY-TWO

Richard Silver stepped carefully from the treadmill and paused, breathing hard, while the belt finished decelerating. Turning off the machine, he reached for a towel and mopped his brow. It had been one of his toughest workouts — forty-five minutes at six miles per hour, eight-percent grade — yet his mind remained as troubled as when he first got on.

Dropping the towel into a canvas bin, he left the exercise room and walked down the corridor to the kitchen, where he filled a glass of water from the tap. Nothing he did seemed to remove the oppressiveness that hung over him. It had been this way since the morning, when the sheet naming Lash as the only possible killer emerged from the printer.

He took a few disinterested sips, placed the glass in the sink. He stood a moment, staring without really seeing. And then he sank forward, leaning his elbows on the counter and pressing a fist against his forehead: once, twice, a third time . . .

He had to stop. He had to get on with things, he *had* to. Maintaining a semblance of normality was the only way to get through this least normal of times.

He straightened. Four-fifteen. What would he normally be doing now?

Having his afternoon session with Liza.

Silver exited the kitchen and headed for the end of the corridor. Usually his mornings were devoted to reading tech journals and white papers; his early afternoons to business matters; and his evenings to programming. But he always made time to visit with Liza before dinner. This was when he spoke with her, discussed program updates, got a sense of her progress. It was a time he always looked forward to: communicating with something that was part himself, part his invention, was a feeling unlike any other Silver had ever known. It was worth all the effort it cost him. It was an experience he could never hope to communicate to anybody else.

He guarded this time against all interruptions, always began promptly at four. Today was the first time he'd been late since Liza and her vast array of supporting hardware were installed in the penthouse, four years earlier.

Slipping into the contoured chair, he began fixing the electrodes, struggling to clear his mind. Only long practice made it possible. Minutes passed while he prepared himself.

Then he placed his hand on the keypad and began to type.

"Richard," came the haunting, disembodied voice.

"Hello, Liza."

"You are seventeen minutes late. Is anything wrong?"

"Nothing is wrong, Liza."

"I am pleased. Shall I begin with the status report? I have been testing the new communications pseudocode you installed and have made some minor modifications."

"Very good, Liza."

"Would you like to hear the process details?"

"No, thank you. We can skip the rest of the report today."

"Then would you like to discuss the latest scenarios you assigned? I am preparing to undertake scenario 311, Creating False Positives in the Turing Test."

"Perhaps tomorrow, Liza. I feel like proceeding directly to the story."

"Very well."

Silver reached beneath the chair — careful not to loosen any of the electrodes as he did so — and pulled out a well-thumbed book. It was his mother's, one of the very few he'd retained from earliest childhood.

The high point of his sessions with Liza was always the reading. Over the years he had progressed from the very simplest stories, teaching her, by example, the rudiments of human values. It was satisfying in an almost paternal way. It always made him feel better, less lonely. Perhaps today it could clear even the dark cloud of guilt that hung over him. And perhaps by the time he'd finished reading, he would have the courage to voice the question he both yearned — and dreaded — to ask.

He paused to refocus his mind, then opened the book. "Do you recall where we left off, Liza?"

"Yes. The rodent Templeton had retrieved the egg sac of the spider."

"Good. And why did he do it?"

"The pig had promised sustenance in return."

"And why did the pig's friend, Charlotte, want the egg sac saved?"

"To ensure the survival of her children and thus the propagation of the species."

"But Charlotte could not save the egg sac herself."

"That is correct."

"So who saved it?"

"Templeton."

"Let me rephrase. Who was the motivic agent in saving the egg sac?"

"The pig Wilbur."

"Correct. Why did he save it, Liza?"

"To achieve parity with the spider. The spider had assisted him."

Silver lowered the book. Liza had no trouble understanding motives like self-survival and behavior rewards. But even now, the other, subtler, emotions remained hard to grasp.

"Are your ethical routines enabled?" he asked.

"Yes, Richard."

"Then let us go on. That is one reason he saved the egg sac. The other is the feelings he had for the spider."

"You speak metaphorically."

"Correct. It is a metaphor for human behavior. For human love."

"Yes."

"Wilbur loved Charlotte. Just as Charlotte loved Wilbur."

"I understand, Richard."

Silver closed his eyes for a moment. Today, even this most prized of times felt hollow. The question would have to wait.

"I must terminate this session, Liza," he said.

"Our dialogue has only lasted five minutes and twenty seconds."

"I know. There are a few things I need to do. So let us close by finishing chapter twenty-one."

"Very well, Richard. Thank you for speaking with me."

"Thank you, Liza." And Silver raised *Charlotte's Web*, found the dog-eared page, and began:

Next day, as the Ferris wheel was being taken apart and the race horses were being loaded into vans, Charlotte died. Nobody, of the hundreds of people that had visited the Fair, knew that a grey spider had played the most important part of all. No one was with her when she died . . .

FORTY-THREE

This time, it was Lash who found himself in the conference room, sitting alone on one side of the table. It was Lash who stared into the lens of the video camera, into the grim faces across from him. Edwin Mauchly sat at the center. But today, Tara Stapleton was not at his left. Dr. Alicto was there instead, wearing a green surgical smock. As his eyes caught Lash's, he nodded, smiling pleasantly.

Mauchly glanced at some papers that lay before him. Then he looked across the table.

"Dr. Lash. This is very difficult for all of us. For me personally." Normally so impassive, Mauchly looked ashen-faced. "I, of course, take responsibility for the whole thing."

Lash was still a little dazed. *I take responsibility.* So he knew this was a mistake, some bizarre mix-up. Mauchly would apologize, and they could all get back to work. *He* could get back to work . . .

But then, where was Tara?

Once more, Mauchly glanced down at the

desk, rearranging the papers. "To think we took you in. Asked for your help. Gave you access to our most privileged data. Ignorant of the truth the whole time."

More briskly, he snapped on the tape recorder, nodded to the cameraman.

"Dr. Lash, do you know why you're here?" he asked. "Why we're talking to you?"

Lash froze. These were the words with which Mauchly had begun Handerling's interrogation.

"You were brazen," Mauchly went on after a moment. "Walking, in effect, into the teeth of the enemy." He paused. "But I suppose you had no choice. You realized we'd find you eventually. This way, you at least had a chance to save yourself. You could muddy pools, deflect attention, waste time making us to look in all the wrong places. Under other circumstances, I might be impressed."

Numbness, which had begun to recede, spread again throughout Lash's limbs.

"Silence won't help. You know how thoroughly we work, you've seen it firsthand. Over the last several hours we've assembled all the evidence we need: the credit card statements, telephone logs, video surveillance feeds. We have you at the locations of the deaths at the right times. We have your past history, your criminal record. The *real* reason you were *forced* to leave the FBI."

Lash's disbelief deepened. Telephone logs,

surveillance feeds? A criminal record? He had no record. And he hadn't been asked to leave the FBI. It was crazy, it made no sense . . .

But then he realized it *did* make sense. It made perfect sense. The real killer knew Lash was closing in. Only the real killer had the power to create such evidence, produce this tissue of lies.

"We would have caught you earlier, of course. But your special status — you weren't actually a client, and you weren't actually an employee — kept you from consideration before. Frankly, I'm surprised you didn't make a break for it when you learned we were widening our search."

Mauchly was employing another interrogation technique. He was re-creating — for Lash, and for the other listeners in the room — Lash's own movements and deeds, the motivations leading up to the crime.

"But of course, you *did* make a break for it. Today. You left for several hours, just before we were due to complete the suspect search. And when you came back you refused to enter the building. Why was that?"

Lash said nothing.

"Did you have some, shall we say, unfinished business with Tara Stapleton, who you felt knew too much? Or now that we were closing in, did you feel the need to erase your old records was worth the risk?"

Lash worked to conceal his surprise. What old records?

"Last Friday you were caught by security, trying to go outside the Wall with several folders inside your satchel. What was in those folders, Dr. Lash?"

The room was silent for a moment.

"It was my mistake not to examine them at the time, and again, I take full responsibility. But we've now cross-checked the online security logs. Let me remind you, for the record, just what was in those folders. Copies of your own original Eden candidate application, filled out eighteen months ago."

Again, Lash struggled to conceal his surprise. *I was never a candidate. Not really. I never filled out any application! I was never even in the building until two weeks ago!*

"Despite the pseudonym and the false information, there's no doubt the applicant was you. And the psychological profile we put together at that time — compared to the one Dr. Alicto completed on you just recently — is revealing. Very revealing indeed."

Mauchly leaned back in his chair. The troubled look, the hesitation, was gone. "I can imagine how the irony of our approaching you for help — *you,* of all people — must have struck home. Certainly it exposed you to great risk. But also to great reward. Not only did it make it easier to gain access to future victims, but it allowed you to

401

go through the evaluation process again. Given your position, you could make such a request without arousing suspicion. And this time, knowing *in advance* what to expect, you were more successful."

Mauchly looked at him, eyes narrowing. "Needless to say, steps have been taken to place Diana Mirren out of harm's way. You won't be hearing from her again, and she certainly won't be hearing from you."

Lash just managed to remain silent.

"And the Connellys can now enjoy their trip to Niagara Falls without fear of your descending on them like an avenging angel."

When Lash still did not respond, Mauchly sighed. "Dr. Lash, you of all people should know what's in store for you. Once we've completed the interrogation process, you'll be handed over to federal authorities. You have a chance to help yourself now."

The room fell into a deep, listening silence. At last, Dr. Alicto spoke up.

"You're not likely to get anything useful from him," he said. "At least, not voluntarily. Chances are his psychosis is too advanced."

Mauchly nodded, disappointment on his face. "Your recommendation?"

"Thorazine, followed by a sufficient dose of sodium amytal, may render him temporarily chatty. Or at least remove any conscious ability to dissemble. We can prep him in one of the medical suites."

Mauchly nodded again, more slowly. "Very well. But let's not take any chances." He turned, spoke to someone standing behind Lash. "You and your men accompany Dr. Alicto to Medical. Once there, I want Lash confined to a gurney with leather restraints."

"Understood," came a familiar-sounding voice.

Mauchly turned back to Alicto. "How long until he's ready?"

"Sixty minutes. Ninety, to be safe."

"Proceed." Mauchly stood up, looked at Lash cooly. "I'll see you again shortly, Dr. Lash. Meanwhile, you leave me the unenviable task of breaking all this to Richard Silver."

He held Lash's gaze for a moment. Then he turned on his heel and left the conference room by a rear door.

A heavy hand fell on Lash's shoulder. "Come with us," said the familiar voice.

As the hand raised him from the seat and swivelled him around, Lash looked into the green eyes of Sheldrake, the security honcho. Sheldrake stepped to one side, motioning Lash forward. As he walked, Lash registered half a dozen security guards falling into position behind him.

The door in front of him opened. As in a dark dream, Lash stepped into the hallway, a guard at each elbow. They guided him down one corridor, then another, on their way to Medical.

Ahead, where two hallways intersected, Lash saw a small knot of people. A technician was approaching them from the intersection, wheeling some piece of equipment on a metal cart.

Lash's sense of unreality grew stronger. As they approached the intersection, one of the security officers took his elbow. "Make a left up ahead, and stop at the elevator bank," he murmured. "Don't be difficult if you know what's good for you." The technician with the cart was almost upon them, and the guards guided Lash to one side so the man could pass.

At that moment, Lash felt a strange thing happen. Time seemed to slow. The steps of the surrounding guards decelerated until each footfall became distinct. He could hear his heart beating monotonously, like a drum.

He turned suddenly, tugging free of the guard's hand. Behind he could see the other four guards, Sheldrake and Dr. Alicto bringing up the rear. Sheldrake's eyes met his and something unspoken passed between them. Lash saw Sheldrake's mouth begin to open and his arm rise, but everything was moving so slowly there was still plenty of time. Taking the cart from the technician, Lash flung it at the guards behind him. He felt the two at his sides trying to restrain him: he stomped the instep of the first and sent a knee into the groin of the other.

His limbs seemed to move under some foreign control, as if a puppeteer was guiding him. The cart had upended, entangling the rear guards; Lash grabbed the technician and shoved him into the advancing Sheldrake. The two fell backward in a tangle. And then Lash turned back toward the intersection and began to run. And as he did so — as he reached the crossing, glanced in both directions, chose a corridor, broke through the small knot of workers and dashed away — it seemed time once again began to speed up, faster and faster, until his thoughts, his breathing, and the churning of his legs became a blur of sound and color.

FORTY-FOUR

Lash turned a corner, dashed headlong down a new corridor, turned again. Then he stopped and pressed himself against the wall, looking around wildly. There was nobody in sight. In the distance he could hear raised voices, running feet. His heart — which just moments before had seemed to beat so slowly — was hammering with a machine-gun cadence. He waited another second, trying to slow it down. Then he pushed himself from the wall and continued. The sounds were not quite as distant now, and he ducked into yet another corridor, passing a door labeled ARRAY MAINTENANCE / SUBSYSTEM B. Apparently, he had moved into a hardware support area, manned by relatively few workers.

But it made no difference. It was only a matter of time until they ran him down and resumed the interrogation, with handcuffs and restraints and meds this time.

He struggled against overwhelming disbelief. How had this happened, and happened so quickly? Had he really risen from bed that morning a free man, only now to be hunted as a psychotic murderer? It seemed impossible that anybody, especially a man like Mauchly, could believe it. Yet it was all too clear that he, and everybody else, *did* believe. And Lash could imagine what the proof was. Mauchly had recited the list of phony but no doubt all too credible evidence: telephone bills, psychological evaluations, even a criminal record. How was it possible to fight someone with the almost infinite resources of Eden at their fingertips?

Somebody appeared in the hallway before him — a technician, dressed in a white lab coat — and Lash trotted past her, head down, without nodding. Another intersection, another quick turn. The hall was narrower here, the doorways farther apart.

Had it really begun as far back as those missing newspapers, the E-ZPass and ATM snafus, the tampering with his mail? Was it possible it had begun so early?

Yes. And then the credit card refusals, the problem with his mortgage payments. It had all been part of a campaign of increasing pressure. Pressure brought to bear because he was getting too close.

And now — now that he knew all — steps would be taken to make sure he would never be heard. He'd be locked away, and his cries would mingle with those of every other inmate protesting his innocence . . .

He stopped suddenly. Was he becoming paranoid in his extremity, or was it possible even the parole of Edmund Wyre was part of this elaborate attempt to silence him? And was it also possible the mistake that put his own rejected avatar in the Tank, that seemed to promise such a bright future, had simply been a method to keep closer tabs on . . .

He willed his feet forward once again. But as he did, Mauchly's words echoed: *Steps have been taken to place Diana Mirren out of harm's way. You won't be hearing from her again.*

There *had* to be somebody he could talk to, somebody who'd believe. But who inside the fortress of Eden knew anything about him, much less why he was really here? It had been a carefully guarded secret from the beginning.

He could, in fact, think of only one desperate chance.

But how? He was lost in an endless maze of corridors. Everything was monitored. His hand fell to the identity bracelet circling his wrist. A dozen scanners would no doubt have tracked his progress. It was only minutes, seconds, until he was found.

His eye fell on a door marked WEB FARM 15. He reached for the handle, found it locked. With a low curse, he moved his bracelet toward the identity scanner.

Then he paused. Stepping back quickly, he trotted down the hall, positioning his bracelet below the scanners of half a dozen other doors, in turn. Then he returned to the first door, positioned his bracelet. With a click, the door sprang open, and Lash stepped inside cautiously.

The room was dim. As he'd hoped, it was deserted. Twin banks of metal shelving rose from floor to ceiling, jammed with rack-mounted blade servers: a tiny fraction of the massive digital horsepower that made Eden possible. He walked between the shelves to the back of the room, scanning the walls and floor. At last he saw it: an oversize metal plate, set just above the floor molding. It was painted the same pale violet as the walls, but it was clearly visible.

He knelt before it. The plate was perhaps four feet high by three feet wide. For a minute, he feared it might be locked, or guarded by an identity scanner like the doors. But it was fastened with a simple hinge that yielded to his touch. He drew it open, looked inside.

Beyond, he could make out a cylindrical tube of smooth metal. The sides and ceiling were covered in a dense flow of cabling: fiber-optic, CAT-6, half a dozen other types Lash did not recognize. A cold cathode line ran along the ceiling, emitting faint blue illumination. Farther down the accessway, Lash could see the tube dividing, first once, then again, like the tributaries of a great river.

He smiled grimly. A river was a pretty good metaphor. This data conduit was a river of digital information, linking every place inside the Wall with every other. He remembered how Mauchly had gone on about the high levels of security, about the countless roadblocks preventing data from straying outside the Wall. And Lash knew — from first-hand experience — that the Wall was virtually impregnable. All the scanners, checkpoints, security apparatus, were fanatically devoted to preventing secrets from getting out. They would be just as efficient at preventing *him* from getting out.

But what if he wasn't *trying* to get out? What if, in fact, he wanted to stay *inside* the Wall — penetrate deeper into its secret recesses?

Lash looked around the room one last time. Then, as quickly and carefully as he could, he crawled into the data conduit and shut the panel behind him.

FORTY-FIVE

Inside a forward security post on the third floor of the inner tower, Edwin Mauchly observed Checkpoint I through mirrored glass. It was a scene of controlled pandemonium. At least a hundred Eden employees were lined up waiting to pass through the exit portals, kept in line by a dozen guards.

Mauchly turned from the window to a nearby monitor. It displayed a bird's-eye view of the main lobby. Another, larger, line of people was streaming back from a makeshift security checkpoint by the revolving doors. Uniformed guards were checking passes and identifications, letting people past in ones and twos, searching for Christopher Lash. Mauchly noted with satisfaction that plainclothes security personnel were mingling with the lines, subtly discouraging chatter, keeping clients apart from would-be applicants and vice versa. Even in this crisis, with a Condition Delta invoked for the first time in the tower's history, Eden kept the safety and privacy of its clients a first priority.

Mauchly began to pace. It was a distasteful, messy situation, and one he found personally offensive. As liaison between Richard Silver and the rest of the company, Mauchly had placed, in his own quiet way, a very personal stamp on Eden. He himself had implemented all security arrangements save for the penthouse, which Silver insisted on handling personally. Mauchly had realized the acute need for secrecy, for absolute confidentiality, almost before there was a product to protect. And he had been the first to understand how the widest possible network of data-sharing — between communications conglomerates, financial companies, the federal government — could not only improve their product, but bring in revenue streams never before imagined.

Mauchly had no particular use for title or recognition, for the usual trappings of corporate glory. Nevertheless, he was fiercely proud and fiercely protective of the company. And that was why, as he paced slowly back and forth inside the forward post, he felt such an upswelling of rage.

He himself had suggested Lash. It was a studied move: there was a threat to the corporation, and Lash seemed the best person to identify that threat.

But instead of ushering a savior into Eden, Mauchly had admitted a serpent.

He was still amazed how well Lash had

pulled it off. Mauchly knew little about psychology, but he did know that most people sick enough to be psychopathic murderers had difficulty concealing their true nature. But Lash had been almost perfect. True, he had failed his pseudo-application, but there was nothing to hint at the true gravity of the situation. Yet Mauchly had now seen the evidence with his own eyes. After Silver gave him the alarming news — after they knew where to look — the facts literally poured in from the computer. Records of institutionalization. A deviant medical history as long as one's arm. For all his brilliance as a postgraduate student, Lash was also critically broken in some way, and it only got worse. He was clever — he'd been able to hide his sickness and his record from the FBI at first, just as he'd been able to hide it from Eden — but all the hiding was past now.

As Mauchly looked back through the privacy glass, the feeling of betrayal and violation increased. In hindsight, he should have heeded Dr. Alicto's post-eval warnings. The cloud under which Lash left the FBI should have raised more red flags.

He could not go back and rectify past mistakes. But he could certainly atone for them. Now he knew exactly what the score was. And he would set things right.

There was a low beep, and a videophone on a nearby desk began flashing. Mauchly approached it, punched in a short code. "Mauchly here," he said.

The small screen went blank for a moment, then Silver's face appeared.

"Edwin," he said. "What's the current status?" Concern was evident in both his expression and his voice.

"The tower's been placed in Condition Delta."

"Was that really necessary?"

"It seemed the fastest, safest way to empty the building. Everyone is being evacuated except the security staff. We've got screeners at all exits and checkpoints, watching for Lash."

"And our clients? Have steps been taken not to alarm them in any way?"

"They've been told it's a routine evacuation drill, that we conduct them regularly to ensure our safety procedures are fully optimized. It's not far from the truth. So far, everyone has taken it in stride."

"Good. Very good."

Mauchly waited for Silver to sign off, but the face remained on the screen. "Is there something else, Dr. Silver?" Mauchly said after a moment.

Silver shook his head slowly. "You don't think there's any chance we've made a mistake, do you?"

"A mistake, sir?"

"About Lash, I mean."

"Impossible, sir. You gave me the report

yourself. And you've seen the evidence we've turned up since. Besides, if the man was innocent, he wouldn't have run the way he did."

"I suppose not. Still . . . you'll handle things gently, right? Make sure no harm comes to him?"

"Of course."

Silver smiled wanly, and the screen went blank.

A moment later, the door to the security post opened and Sheldrake entered. He came forward, massive body poised, as if awaiting orders. You could take the man out of the military, but it appeared you could not take the military out of the man.

"How are we faring, Mr. Sheldrake?" Mauchly asked.

"Seventy-five percent of non-Eden personnel have left the building," Sheldrake said. "From the checkpoint counts, about thirty-eight percent of workers inside the Wall have already passed through the security portals. We expect to have the evacuation complete within twenty minutes."

"And Lash?"

Sheldrake held up a printout. "Scanners tracked him to a hardware support area. He went into half a dozen rooms there. No further reports or sightings since."

"Let me see that, please." Mauchly glanced over the printout. "Redundant Disk Silo

Storage. Network Infrastructure. What would he be doing in places like that?"

"The same question we've been asking ourselves, sir."

"There's something wrong here." Mauchly pointed at the listing. "According to these time logs, Lash went into six different rooms over the course of only fifteen seconds." He handed the printout back to Sheldrake. "He couldn't have visited that many rooms so quickly. What was he doing?"

"Playing with us."

"My thoughts exactly. The last room he entered was a Web farm. That's where your men should concentrate their search."

"Very good, sir."

"But continue to deploy roving patrols inside the Wall. We have to assume Lash is probing the perimeter, trying to find some way to exit the inner tower. I'll head up to the command center; I can monitor the operation more efficiently from there."

He watched as the man turned to leave. Then, in a quieter voice, he said: "Mr. Sheldrake?"

"Sir?"

Mauchly regarded him a moment. Sheldrake, of course, did not know everything — he did not know, for example, precisely why Lash had been in the building — but he knew enough to understand the man posed a grave threat.

"This man has already compromised Eden. The longer he's at large, the more damage he can cause. *Significant* damage."

Sheldrake nodded.

"Containment is key here. This kind of situation is best dealt with inside the building. The sooner this whole thing goes away, the better for everyone at Eden." Mauchly felt a fresh surge of anger. "Do you understand? The thing should go *all the way* away."

Sheldrake nodded again, more slowly this time. "My feelings as well, sir."

"Then get to it," Mauchly said.

FORTY-SIX

Inside the data conduit, time seemed a stranger. The narrow tube forked, and forked again; a seemingly infinite lattice spreading itself horizontally and vertically throughout the inner tower. There were none of the usual benchmarks by which to gauge the passage of time: just a claustrophobic world of faint blue light, bounded by endless rivers of cabling. Now and then a larger conduit would cross his path — arteries amid the matrix of veins — but for the most part the tubes were horribly cramped, forcing Lash to crawl at full length, like a spelunker threading a narrow pipe.

Whenever possible, he climbed. Small metal projections protruded from the walls, meant for securing cable ties but also serviceable for footholds. Now and then, a rough edge would snag his shirt, score his skin. From time to time he passed an access panel, like the one he used to enter the conduit system, but they were never marked and it was impossible to gauge how far he'd ascended. Like time, distance was all but meaningless in this close and foreign world.

From time to time, Lash stopped to catch his breath and listen. Once he heard a distant boom break the silence, like the closing of some giant door in the deepest sub-basement of the tower. Another time, he thought he heard a ghostly cry pass along the narrow conduits, barely audible, like the whisper of a breeze. But then nothing would follow save the sound of his own heavy breathing. And he would move on again, cables rustling at his passage.

Although Lash was not claustrophobic by nature, the faint light, the watchful silence, the wires that pressed in on all sides unnerved him. He forced himself to take small careful steps, to keep his balance and prevent his feet from tangling in the cabling.

In time he found a vertical conduit, a little wider than most, that seemed to ascend uninterrupted, freeing him from the frequent lateral side-trips he'd been forced to take. He climbed for what seemed hours, pulling himself from projection to tiny projection, until his blood thrummed in his ears. At last he stopped again to rest, leaning against the uneven bunches of cabling, listening to the rasp of his breath. The muscles in his arms danced and jerked. Raising an arm, he held it close to the blue guidewire and peered at his watch.

Five-thirty. Was it possible he'd only been crawling through these conduits half an hour?

And how far had he climbed? He should have been able to estimate his rate of ascent: he'd done more than his share of time-trial wall climbs at Quantico. But not all his travel had been vertical in this maze. And cramped into these slender tubes, fettered by cabling, it was hard to gauge. Had he reached the thirtieth floor? The thirty-fifth?

As he balanced, gasping for breath, an image suddenly came into his mind: a tiny spider, no bigger than a speck, clinging precariously to the inside wall of a soda straw . . .

He could not keep on climbing blind forever. There was a floor he was headed for, a specific floor. He needed to get his bearings, determine exactly where he was.

And that meant leaving the conduit.

He leaned against the tube wall, thinking. If he left the safety of the data conduit, the scanners would pick him up. Security would immediately know where he was and focus their search. There was no way he could fix his position without raising the alarm there?

Maybe most individual offices, labs, and storerooms *had* no scanners. Maybe most scanners were situated in the corridors and doors. If he was careful where he exited, and if he didn't activate any sensors . . .

He had no choice but to try.

Lash climbed a few feet to the next junction, then clambered laboriously into the lateral tube. He crawled forward over the bunches of cables until he reached an access panel in the side wall. Here he waited a moment, listening. He could hear no noise from beyond. Holding his breath, he placed his fingertips against the inside of the latch and pushed carefully against it. The catch sprung free and the panel opened.

Instantly, light flooded in, bathing a thin angle of the conduit a brilliant white. Lash turned away and shut the panel. A brightly lit office — or worse, a corridor — lay beyond. No good: he'd have to try elsewhere.

He moved forward again, passing another panel, then another. At the fourth panel, he stopped. Once again, he pressed his fingers to the latch; once again, he eased it open. This time, the light beyond was dimmer. Perhaps it was a storage area, or the office of someone who'd left for the day. Either way, he wouldn't get a better opportunity.

As stealthily as he could, Lash pushed the panel wider. The space beyond was silent.

He pulled himself forward on his elbows, peered out. In the dim light he could make out a darkened terminal, a shadowy desk. A deserted office: he was in luck.

Quietly, but as quickly as possible, he pulled himself out the accessway and into the office. As he rose to his feet, his shoulders, hunched so long in the cramped conduits, protested vigorously. He glanced around, hoping to find some memorandum or fire exit diagram that would give the floor — but except for the ubiquitous desk and monitor the office appeared unused, empty.

He cursed into the silence.

Wait. Every door he'd passed inside Eden had always had a label fixed to its outside. There was no reason to think this door was any different. Doors were locked from the outside: if he was careful to keep his identity bracelet away from the scanner, he could simply open this one and peek at its label.

He moved to the door, put a hand on its knob. Putting an ear to the doorjamb, he paused. Silence beyond: no footsteps, no murmur of conversation.

Holding his breath again, he cracked the door and peered out. Light streamed in: there was the usual pale-violet hallway, apparently deserted. Keeping his identity bracelet carefully behind his back, he opened the door a little wider. Now, it was just a question of reading the label on the . . .

Shit. There was no label on the door.

Lash closed the door again and let himself sink against the wall. Of all the offices to emerge into, he'd chosen one that was vacant.

He took a deep, steadying breath. Then, more quickly, he turned back to the door and cracked it open a second time.

There: across the hall was another door, this one with a label. A title beneath, a number above.

But Lash's eyes, not yet accustomed to the light, couldn't quite make out the number. He squinted, blinked, squinted again into the brilliance.

Come on.

Lash grasped the door frame and leaned into the corridor. Now he could make out the words: 2614. THORSSEN, J. POST-SELECTION PROCESSING.

Twenty six? He thought in disbelief. *I'm only at the twenty-sixth floor?*

"Hey, you!" a voice barked into the stillness. "Stop there!"

Lash turned. Perhaps fifty feet away, at an intersection, a guard in a jumpsuit stood, pointing at him.

"Don't move!" the guard said, beginning to trot toward him.

For a moment, Lash remained frozen, a deer caught in headlights. As he watched, the guard's hand slipped into his jumpsuit.

Lash ducked back into the office. As he did so, a sharp report sounded down the hall. Something whined past the door.

Jesus! They're shooting at me!

He stumbled backward, almost falling in his haste. Then he sprinted for the rear of the office and almost dove into the data conduit portal, barking his shins cruelly as he scrambled inside. He did not bother closing the access panel — all his previous care had been rendered pointless — and moved forward as quickly as he could, taking forks at random, heedless now of the meticulous tapestry of cabling torn away by the passage of his elbows and feet, burrowing his way back into the mazelike safety of the digital river.

FORTY-SEVEN

Tara Stapleton sat in her office, swiveling behind her desk, staring at the battered surfboard. The entire floor seemed deserted, the hallway beyond her door cloaked in a watchful silence. Although Tara was a key component of Eden's security, she knew she should be gone, as well; Mauchly had said as much, outside the Rio coffee shop. "Go home," he'd said, giving her shoulder an uncharacteristic squeeze. "You've had a rough afternoon, but it's over now. Go on home, relax."

She rose and began to pace. Going home, she knew, wouldn't make her feel any better.

She'd been in shock ever since Mauchly called her up to Silver's office just after noon. It had seemed impossible, what they told her: that Christopher Lash himself, the man they'd brought in to investigate the mysterious deaths, was himself the killer. She hadn't wanted to believe it, *couldn't* believe it. But Mauchly's measured tones, the pain in Richard Silver's face, left no room for disbelief. She herself had assisted Mauchly in polling the vast network of databases at their fingertips, collecting the information on Lash that damned him beyond any possibility of refutation.

And then, when Lash had called her — when she'd gone to meet with him, after first consulting Mauchly — her shock had deepened. He'd talked urgently, almost desperately. But she had barely heard. Instead, she'd been wondering how her instincts could have been so wrong. Here was a man who had murdered four people in cold blood, who'd been placed at the crime scenes in half a dozen ways. Here was a man who — according to all their data — had grown up in a highly dysfunctional family, spent most of his childhood in and out of institutions, successfully had his record as a sex offender suppressed. And yet she had grown to trust him, even like him, during the short time they had spent together. She had never been a trusting person. One of the reasons she'd had limited success in relationships, why she'd jumped at Eden's pilot program, was because she *didn't* allow herself to get close to anybody. So just what part of her elaborate self-defense mechanism had betrayed her so badly?

There was something else. Some of the things that Lash had said in the coffee shop were coming back. Talk about overdoses; about a brain chemical called Substance P;

about the two of them being in danger because they knew too much. He was crazy, so the talk was crazy.

Right?

A sound: footsteps in the hall, approaching quickly. The knob to her office door squealed as it turned. Someone walked into her office, like some dread specter summoned by her own thoughts.

It was Christopher Lash.

Only it wasn't Lash as she'd ever seen him before. Now, he truly looked like an escaped lunatic. His hair was matted and askew. An ugly bruise was coming up on his forehead. His suit, normally neat to a fault, was caked with dust, shredded at the elbows and knees. His hands were bleeding from countless nicks and cuts.

He closed the door and leaned against it, breathing heavily.

"Tara," he gasped in a hoarse voice. "Thank God you're still here."

She stared at him, frozen with surprise. Then she grabbed for the phone.

"No!" he said, stepping forward.

Hand still on the phone, she dug into her purse, pulled out a can of pepper spray, pointed it at his face.

Lash stopped. "Please. Just do one thing for me. One thing. Then I'll go."

Tara tried to think. The guards would have tracked Lash to her office by his identity bracelet. It was only a matter of moments until they arrived. Should she try to humor him?

Stalling for time seemed preferable to a struggle.

She withdrew her hand from the phone, but kept the can of pepper spray raised. "What happened to your face?" she asked, trying to keep her voice calm. "Were you beaten?"

"No." The faintest ghost of a smile passed across his face. "It's a casualty of my mode of transportation." The smile vanished. "Tara, *they're shooting at me*."

Tara said nothing. *Paranoid. Delusional.*

Lash took another step forward, stopped when Tara aimed the can threateningly. "Listen. Do this one thing, if not for me, then for those couples who died. And the couples who are still under threat." He gasped in a breath. "Search the Eden database for *the first client avatar ever recorded*."

A minute had passed. The guards would be here soon.

"Tara, *please*."

"Stand over there, by the far corner," Tara said. "Keep your hands where I can see them."

Lash moved to the far side of her office.

Watching him carefully, she stepped toward her terminal, pepper spray at the ready. She did not sit down, but half turned toward the keyboard, leaning forward to type the query one-handed.

The first client avatar ever recorded . . .

Curiously, the search returned an avatar with no associated name. There was just the identity code. Yet it was a code that made no sense.

"Let me guess," Lash said. "It isn't even a rational number. It's just a string of zeros."

Now she turned to look at him more closely. He was still breathing hard, the blood dripping from his torn hands to the floor. But he was looking at her steadily, and — no matter how closely she looked back — she could detect no hint of madness in his eyes.

She glanced up at the wall clock. Two minutes.

"How did you know that?" she asked. "Lucky guess?"

"Who'd have guessed *that?* Nine zeros?"

Tara let the question hang in the air.

"Remember those queries I asked to run from your computer this morning? I'd just gotten an idea. A terrible idea, but the only one that fit. Those queries you followed up with all but confirmed it."

Tara started to answer, then stopped.

"Why should I listen to any of this?" she asked instead, still stalling. "I saw the data on you. I saw your record, the things you've done. I saw why you left the FBI: you let two policemen and your own brother-in-law

429

die. You led a murderer right to them, deliberately."

Lash shook his head. "No. That's not what happened. I tried to *save* them. I just figured it out too late. It was a case like this one. A killer's profile that didn't make sense. Edmund Wyre, didn't you read about it in the papers? He was killing women as bait, writing phony confessions. Meanwhile, stalking his real target: the cops who were investigating. He got two. I'm the one he *missed*. That case wrecked my marriage, ruined my sleep for a year."

Tara did not reply.

"Don't you *understand?* I've been set up here. Framed. Somebody touched my records, distorted them. I know who that somebody is."

He moved to the door, glanced back. "I have to go. But there's something else you need to do. Go to the Tank. Run six other avatars — *the women from the six supercouples* — against avatar zero."

In the distance, an elevator chimed. Tara heard raised voices, the sound of running feet.

Lash started visibly. He put his hand on the door frame, poised himself to flee. Then he gave her one final look, and his expression seemed to burn itself through her. "I know you want all this to end. Run that query. Discover for yourself just what's going on. Save the others."

Then, without another word, he was gone.

Slowly, Tara sank back into her chair. She glanced up at the clock: just under four minutes.

Seconds later, a team of security guards burst into her office, guns in hand. Their leader — a short, stockily built man Tara recognized as Whetstone — checked the corners quickly, then looked at her.

"You all right, Ms. Stapleton?" Beside Whetstone, one of the guards was peering into the room's lone closet.

She nodded.

Whetstone turned back to his team. "He must have gone that way," he said, pointing down the hallway. "Dreyfuss, McBain, secure the next intersection. Reynolds, stay with me. Let's check the nearest access panels." And he trotted out of the office, holstering his weapon and pulling out his radio as he did so.

For a moment, Tara listened to the retreating footsteps, the furtive sounds of conversation. Then they died away and the corridor fell back into silence.

She remained in her chair, motionless, while the wall clock ticked through five minutes. Then she rose and made her way across the carpet, avoiding the bloodstains. She hesitated in the doorway a second, then stepped into the corridor, heading for the elevator. The Tank was no more than a few minutes away.

But then she stopped and — reaching a new decision — turned and began walking, more quickly now, back in the direction she had come.

FORTY-EIGHT

The command center of Eden's security division was a large, bunker-like space on the twentieth floor of the inner tower. Two dozen employees filled the room, transcribing passive sensor entries, controlling remote cameras.

Edwin Mauchly stood alone at the control station. On a dozen screens, he could bring up information from any of ten thousand live datastreams monitoring the building: camera feeds, sensor inputs, terminal keystrokes, scanner logs. Hands behind his back, he moved his gaze from screen to screen.

Somewhere, in that vast storm of data, Christopher Lash was dodging all the raindrops.

Behind him, a door opened. Mauchly did not turn: he did not need to. The heavy, clipped tread, the brief silence, told him Sheldrake had just entered.

"They missed him by five, maybe ten seconds," Sheldrake said, approaching the control station.

433

Mauchly reached for a keyboard. "He spent four minutes in Tara Stapleton's office. Four minutes, when he knew every second put him at greater risk. Why did he do that?" He typed again. "He left her office heading southbound. As he ran, he passed his identity bracelet beneath a dozen additional door scanners along the corridor. Which of those doors he entered — if any — remains unknown."

"I've got men checking them out now."

"It's important to be thorough, Mr. Sheldrake. But I have the strong feeling he's no longer on the thirty-fifth floor."

"It's still hard to believe he's using data conduits to get around," Sheldrake said. "They're meant for maintenance access, not travel. He must feel like a pipe cleaner squeezing his way through those things."

Mauchly stroked his chin. "He should be trying to find a way out, flee the building. Instead, he's climbing. First, to the twenty-sixth floor. Now, the thirty-fifth."

"Could he be after someone, or something? A suicide plot? Sabotage?"

"I considered that. If he's desperate enough, it's possible. On the other hand, he didn't harm Tara Stapleton just now — who, after all, is the person who turned him in. The fact is, we simply don't have a sufficient bead on his pathology to know for sure." Mauchly scanned the screens. "I don't want to draw too many of your men away from the search. But you should place small details on the most critical installations. And have another guard the emergency penthouse access."

"Shouldn't we also post teams outside access panels? Now that we know how he's getting around, we can arrange an ambush."

"The question is *where?* There are probably a hundred miles of data conduits, they honeycomb the entire inner tower. There's five times that many access panels. We can't watch them all."

He stepped back from the monitors. "He has a plan," he said, more to himself than to Sheldrake. "If we learn what that is, we'll learn where to trap him."

Then he turned. "Come," he said. "I think we need to have a little talk with Tara Stapleton."

FORTY-NINE

In the room known as the Tank, the wall clocks read 18:20. Normally, the space would have been full of Eden technicians: monitoring throughput, scribbling notes on palmtop computers, ensuring the matching process that was the heart and soul of Eden proceeded in a fully optimized fashion.

This evening, however, the room was empty. The dials and monitors displayed their data for no one. There was no sound but the whisper of forced air, no movement but the blinking of diagnostic LEDs. The Tank, like the rest of Eden, had been evacuated.

As the clocks rolled over to 18:21, a soft click sounded in the hallway outside. The double doors parted. A lone figure peered cautiously within. Then it came forward, closed the doors, and moved quietly across the room.

As she'd moved through the corridors of the inner tower, Tara Stapleton had been struck by the emptiness, the atmosphere of watchful silence. Yet she was totally unprepared for what now lay before her. She had been in this room hundreds, maybe thousands of times. Every time, it had been humming with activity. Every time, people had been standing before the Tank, mesmerized by the avatars gliding restlessly within their digital universe. But there were no spectators now, and the Tank was dark and empty. Client processing had been halted when the tower was placed under Condition Delta, and would not resume until the next shift began work the following morning.

She came forward, toward the face of the Tank. She stretched out a hand to the cool, smooth surface. The sensation of great depth, of velvety darkness, remained. And yet how strange to see it depopulated. Though she knew the avatars were just electrical phantoms — binary constructs that had no existence outside the computer — it seemed wrong somehow, against nature, to drain them from the Tank, leaving it lifeless.

Her eyes drifted away, stopping when they reached the wall clock. 18:22. Twenty-two minutes past six.

She walked to a nearby console. Typing a series of commands, she brought herself into the Tank's dataspace and accessed the central client archives.

Then she paused. As chief security tech, her authorization was more than high enough to carry out what Lash had suggested. But there would be a record of her access, a log of her keystrokes. Questions would be asked, probably sooner than later.

She shook her head. It didn't matter. If Lash was lying — if this whole business was some part of his madness, some imaginary conspiracy or persecution complex — she'd know it pretty damn quick. On the other hand, if he was telling the truth . . .

She flexed her fingers briefly, returned them to the keyboard. She didn't yet know *what* it meant if Lash was telling the truth. But one way or the other, she had to learn.

She typed another command. The screen went black briefly, then refreshed.

PROP. EDEN INC.

CLIENT COMPATIBILITY
VIRTUAL PROVING CHAMBER
REV.27.4.1.1
HIGHLY CONFIDENTIAL AND PROPRIETARY
L-4, EXEC-D OR HIGHER CLEARANCE
REQUIRED

MANUAL POPULATION MODE ENABLED
SIMULATED ONLY

TOTAL POPULATION COUNT?

As she stared at the screen, Tara felt a

sudden urge to place her own avatar in the Tank: to see her own digital representation glide through that velvet darkness. Had it taken long to find Matt Bolan's avatar? She was standing at a command console. She knew his identity code by heart; she could —

She reminded herself this was no time for wistful nostalgia. Besides, she wasn't doing this for Lash, or even for the Wilners or Thorpes. She was doing this for herself. If she could help unravel this mystery, set things right . . . maybe it wasn't too late for her own avatar, after all.

She took a deep breath. Then she typed a single number: 2.

The screen refreshed:

ENTER AVATAR IDENTITY CODES

She typed the number she'd seen in her office, the first client avatar ever recorded: 000000000.

Almost immediately, there was a glow within the Tank. A lone avatar appeared, tiny and fragile in the dark vastness: a pale, pearlescent apparition of shifting color and shape. Sometimes it drifted almost listlessly, other times it darted at great speed.

Tara looked back at the screen. Opening a separate window, she posted a query to the client archives for the identity codes of the six supercouple females. The results came back immediately:

TORVALD, LINDSAY E.	000462196
SCHWARTZ, KAREN L.	000527710
MASON, LYNN R.	000561044
YAMAZAKI, MINAKO	000577327
CASTIGLIANO, ANDREA	000630442
HERRERO, MARIA	000688305

Returning to the main screen, Tara entered Lindsay Thorpe's number. Immediately, another avatar glowed into existence. She paused, glancing over her shoulder. With only two avatars in the Tank, the matching process — for better or worse — should take only moments.

As she watched, the two avatars drifted: now pulsing with new color, now almost fading from view. Gradually their range attenuated as the attraction algorithms drew them closer together. There was a brief moment when they circled gracefully, like dancers performing a *pas de deux*. Suddenly, they darted at each other. There was a flare of brilliant white, then a storm of data appeared on nearby monitors as a million variables — the individual nuances of taste, preference, emotion, and memory that make up a personality — were instantaneously parsed and compared by the supercomputer, Liza. A new window appeared on the screen:

```
PROVING CHAMBER DATA OVERVIEW
$START PROCESS
BASELINE COMPARISON 9602194
A-SHIFT NEG
CHECKSUM IDENT 000000000: 4A32F
CHECKSUM IDENT 000462196: 94DA7
PENETRATION DATA: 14A NOMINAL
COLLISION TOPOLOGY: 99 NOMINAL
DIGITAL ARTIFACTING: 0
ANOMALOUS PROCESSES: 0
DATAFIELD DEPTH, POST-PENETRATION:
1948549.23 Mbit/sec
CLUSTER SIZE: 4096
START TIME: 18:25:31:014 EST
END TIME: 18:25:31:982 EST


BASAL COMPATIBILITY (HEURISTIC MODEL):
97.8304912 %
M.O.E: + / -.00094 %


$END PROCESS
```

Tara stared at the monitor in surprise.
Lindsay Thorpe's avatar and the unknown
avatar, 000000000, had just been successfully
matched. It wasn't a perfect match, like
Lindsay's match to Lewis Thorpe, but at
97.8 percent it was within acceptable range.

She removed Lindsay's avatar and then —
more quickly — began to introduce the avatars of the other women, one by one, into
the tank. And one by one, they also matched

successfully with the mystery avatar. Karen Wilner, 97.1 percent. Lynn Connelly, 98.9 percent.

In growing disbelief, Tara entered the three final codes. Again, successful matches.

All six women — from all six of Eden's supercouples to date — matched with the mystery avatar.

What was going on?

Could avatar 000000000 be some kind of control mechanism that matched with *all* avatars in the tank? It was possible: although she was familiar with the process, she didn't know all its technical subtleties.

Turning back to the computer, she called up a non-supercouple client at random, inserted her avatar into the Tank with the mystery avatar. The compatibility came back at 38 percent: no match.

Now, Tara wrote a short routine that extracted a random sampling of a thousand female clients, past and current, and inserted their avatars into the Tank, a hundred at a time. Briefly, the Tank flared into a semblance of normality as the ghostly apparitions appeared within. This process took a little longer, but within five minutes it, too, was complete.

None of these thousand avatars successfully matched with avatar 000000000.

Abruptly, the watchful silence was broken by the beep of her cell phone.

Tara jerked in surprise, then fumbled for her phone, heart racing. The call had a Connecticut area code, and she didn't recognize the number. She flipped the phone open. "Hello?"

"Tara?" the voice was faint, thinned by a wash of static, but nevertheless she recognized it instantly.

"Yes."

"Where are you?"

"The Tank."

"Thank God. And what did — ?"

"Later. Where are you?"

"In a data conduit not far from you, I think. I —"

"Wait." And Tara lowered the phone.

She thought about everything Mauchly said when he'd told her Lash was the killer. She thought about the diner, what Lash had begun to say. She thought about the look on his face when he'd appeared in her office, begged her to do just one more thing. Most of all, she thought about the six super-couples, and the mysterious avatar whose identity code was zero.

Tara was not by nature an impulsive person. She always examined the evidence, weighed the pros and cons, before making a decision. Right now, the cons were deadly serious. If Lash was the killer, she was in grave danger.

And the pros? Helping an innocent man.

Solving the riddle of the two dead couples. Maybe sparing the lives of future victims.

Tara put her free hand into her pocket, withdrew two long, narrow strips of lead foil. She turned the strips over, looking at them. Maybe she wasn't impulsive. But she realized that, this time, she'd made up her mind what to do long before setting foot in this room.

She lifted the phone. "Meet me outside the Tank. Quick as you can."

"But —"

"Just do it." And then she closed the phone, killed the running processes, logged off the control terminal, and turned her back on the dark and empty Tank.

FIFTY

When Lash rounded the corner, Tara was waiting. He approached quickly.

"Thank you," he said. "Thanks for taking a chance."

"You look even more beat up than before," she replied. Something flashed silver in her hands, and for a ridiculous moment Lash feared it was a pair of handcuffs. Then he realized it was a strip of lead foil. He watched as she took his bleeding hand and wrapped the foil carefully around his identity bracelet.

"What are you doing?" he asked.

"Neutralizing the scanners."

"I didn't know you could do that."

"Nobody's supposed to. I got these from slitting open a lead apron in a radiology lab down the hall from my office. They'll buy a little time." She raised her own arm: an identical strip of foil had been wrapped around her own bracelet.

"Then you trust me," he said, immensely relieved.

"I didn't say that. But without the foil I'll

never get the chance to know whether you're lying or not. Tell me one thing. You were kidding about them shooting at you, right?"

Lash shook his head.

"Jesus. Come on, we can't stay here." And she led him down the corridor.

They reached an intersection, turned the corner. "What did you find out?" he asked.

"I found out avatar 000000000 was a match for all six women."

"God *damn*. I knew it!"

At that moment, Tara pushed him through a doorway.

Lash glanced around. "Is this a *ladies'* room?"

"With my bracelet covered, I can't unlock any doors. Here at least we can talk undisturbed. So talk."

"All right." Lash hesitated a second, wondering just what to say. It hadn't been easy, even in the coffee shop; here, with his limbs trembling from the long climb and his heart hammering in his chest, it would be even harder.

"You realize I can't prove anything," he said. "The most important piece is still missing. But the rest of the pieces fit perfectly."

She nodded.

"You remember what I started to tell you? How only somebody in Eden's top echelons could have done this? Known every aspect of

Lindsay Thorpe's background, tampered with her medical orders, modified her prescription, faked the paper trail. Just as only somebody with all Eden at their fingertips could have doctored *my* records, morphed me into a psychopathic desperado. Somebody who'd been with the company back when it was a PharmGen subsidiary. Somebody highly placed enough to know about the early tests on scolipane. Somebody who'd been a part of Eden Incorporated since the *very first* client walked through the doors."

"What are you saying?" she asked.

"You know what I'm saying. The person who did all this — the person who's targeting the supercouples — *is* avatar zero."

"But who . . ." The question died in her throat.

Lash nodded grimly. "That's right. Richard Silver is avatar zero."

"Impossible."

But Lash watched Tara's eyes as she said this; watched her travel the same path of discovery he'd already taken. Who else but Silver would have such a number? Who else could have been in the system all this time? Perhaps on some level, she had already guessed. Perhaps that's why she'd come prepared with the lead foil; why she'd come at all.

Tara just shook her head. "Why?"

"I don't know why. Yet. We're taught if you

can determine motive, you can determine everything else: personality, behavior, opportunity. I don't fully understand the motive. Fact is, only Silver can tell us for sure."

There was a distant flurry of conversation, the opening and closing of doors. They waited, barely breathing. More chatter, closer this time; a distorted voice on a radio. Then more talk, farther away. And then, silence.

Lash exhaled slowly. "The idea came to me in your office this morning, when avatar zero kept coming to the top of the search list. The only avatar without a name. But it wasn't until I met with an old classmate in Cold Spring — when I saw the connections to PharmGen and scolipane, and its awful reaction with Substance P — that it came together. And Silver, watching everything from his ivory tower, must have realized how close I was. Thus the twenty-first-century smear job."

"What about Karen Wilner?"

"I've barely had time to trace what happened to Lindsay Thorpe. I'm certain Substance P is at the heart of it. As for the delivery system, I can't yet say."

Tara looked at him. "Even with everything you've told me, it's hard to believe. Silver might be a recluse, but he's the last guy to strike me as a killer."

"Reclusiveness is a red flag. Still, he doesn't fit the obvious profile. But like I said, the profile's contradictory to begin with. The murders are too *similar*, somehow. Artless, in a way. As if a child was committing them." He paused. "Do I strike you as a killer?"

"No."

"But you turned me in anyway."

"And I might again. No one else believes you."

"No one else has heard my story. Just you."

"The jury's still out until I hear what Silver has to say."

Lash nodded slowly. "In that case, we've got only one option left."

"What do you mean?" But from Tara's eyes, Lash could see that she already knew.

FIFTY-ONE

Edwin Mauchly stood in the hush of Tara Stapleton's empty office, scanning the room slowly. To an observer, the scan might have appeared desultory. Yet he missed nothing: the posters, potted plants, spotless desk with three monitors arrayed behind it, battered surfboard leaning against the wall.

Though he had personally championed her rise through the ranks — though he had implicit trust in her talents — Tara remained a cipher to him. She always dressed professionally, rarely joked, even more rarely smiled. She was not given to small talk or gossip. All business, all the time.

His eye returned to the surfboard. Though he'd arranged for its presence here, it had always puzzled him. It didn't jibe with her almost fanatic desire for privacy, with the wall she'd erected around her private life. Clearly, she wasn't just showing off: if she wanted to do that, she would have brought in the championship trophies he knew from background checks that she'd won. No — the surfboard was there, one way or another, for her own benefit.

His eye fell to the carpeting, to the droplets of blood that were visible near the doorway. Elsewhere, Lash had left little or no trail. Not here. Why? Had he been gesturing? Threatening?

That led back to the main question. Why had Lash come here at all? Why had he taken the risk?

There were too many questions. Mauchly plucked the radio from his pocket, pressed the transmit button.

"Reading you, sir," came the voice from the command center.

"Who is this? Gilmore?"

"Yes, Mr. Mauchly."

"Go over with me again Ms. Stapleton's movements after Lash left her office."

"One moment, sir." The clack of keystrokes sounded over the radio. "The advance team came through at 18:06. At 18:12 she left her office and was tracked to the radiology lab, down the hall. She was there for three minutes. At 18:15 she left the lab and proceeded to the elevator bank. She took elevator 104 up four stories, to the thirty-ninth floor. Sensors tracked her to the Proving Chamber."

"The Tank."

"Yes, sir. She opened the doors with her identity bracelet at 18:21."

"Go on."

"Passive sensors in the Tank confirm her presence there for the next nine minutes. After that, nothing."

"Nothing? What do you mean, 'nothing'?"

"Just that, sir. It's like she vanished."

"And the team we dispatched to the Tank?"

"Arrived there just now. The place is deserted."

"Can you check the terminal logs, see if she accessed any systems?"

"We're checking that now."

"What about Lash? Any updates?"

"There was a sensor hit on the thirty-seventh floor ten minutes ago. Then several on the thirty-ninth floor a few minutes later."

"Thirty-ninth," Mauchly repeated. "In the vicinity of the Tank?"

"The last one was, sir."

"And when was that?"

"Eighteen thirty-one."

Mauchly lowered the radio. One minute after they lost contact with Tara. And on the same floor, the same spot.

Mauchly glanced at his watch. Fifteen minutes without a sensor hit on either Lash or Tara. That made no sense — no sense at all.

He considered the situation. Except for the checkpoints and the elevators, there were no video cameras installed in the inner tower. There had seemed no need: under Eden's draconian security policy, the inner tower was riddled with so many movement sensors that any person wearing an identity bracelet could be traced to a twenty-foot area. And the limited number of entrances, the rigidly patrolled checkpoints, ensured only authorized personnel went inside the Wall. The infrastructure was designed to guard against corporate espionage: there were no contingency plans for chasing an escaped murderer.

Still, the security protocols should have worked. There was only one way to defeat the identity bracelets, and that was a highly sensitive secret Lash could not be aware of . . .

Could he?

He raised the radio again. "Gilmore, I want you to divert the roving patrols. Send them all to thirty-eight and above. I want spotters in the stairwells and major intersections. If anything moves that isn't a security guard, I want to know about it."

"Very well, sir."

Mauchly returned the radio to his pocket. Then he exited the office and walked thoughtfully down the hall.

The radiology lab was almost sepulchral in its emptiness. He gazed around at the idle equipment, the gleaming stainless-steel instruments.

Why had Tara come here?

Christopher Lash, psychopathic murderer, had just burst into her office. Had she then been seized by a sudden craving for extracurricular research? Again, it all made no sense.

Was it possible she was aiding Lash? Hardly likely. She'd seen the evidence; she knew how dangerous he was, not only to the supercouples, but to Eden itself. She'd alerted Mauchly to the meeting in the coffee shop. She'd turned Lash in.

Could he be threatening her in some other way? That seemed equally unlikely. Tara was eminently capable of defending herself. And Lash was unarmed: Mauchly had made sure of that himself.

He tried to put himself in her shoes, tried to follow her train of thought. But one could only make assumptions about a person one understood. And Mauchly was not convinced he really understood Tara. He'd been surprised, almost shocked, when she'd barged into his office two months before, asked him to use his clout to get her in the pilot program for employee matching. And he'd been just as surprised when she reappeared in his office *after* her match was found, asking to be removed from the program. It was Monday, he recalled; the day Christopher Lash first came inside the Wall.

Lash. This was all his doing. He was insane, a mad dog. He'd done great harm to the corporation. It was imperative he be stopped before he did any more harm — something truly irreversible.

Mauchly reached into his pocket, drew out a Glock 9mm. The weapon glinted faintly in the dim, off-hours light of the lab. He turned it in his hands, made sure there was a round in the chamber, returned it to his pocket.

This was one mad dog that had no place to run. And Mauchly would treat Lash just as one should a mad dog. Corner it, then kill it.

His radio squawked.

"Mauchly here."

"Mr. Mauchly, it's Gilmore. You asked me to report in if we spotted any movement in the tower."

"Very true, Mr. Gilmore. Go ahead."

"Sir, the penthouse elevator's been activated. It's moving as we speak."

"What?" Mauchly felt mild annoyance. "I'll have to speak to Richard Silver. He can't leave the penthouse now, not while Lash is on the loose. It isn't safe."

"You don't understand, sir. The elevator isn't descending. It's rising."

FIFTY-TWO

As they emerged from the stairwell, Lash recognized the sky lobby of the thirtieth floor. He'd been here once. Like the rest of the inner tower, this space was dark, deserted. In one corner sat a lone mop, leaning against the marble wall, abandoned in the general evacuation. Banks of elevators stood on both sides. Halfway down the right wall, one spilled yellow light into the lobby. The sign above it read EXPRESS TO CHECKPOINT II.

Tara looked around guardedly, then motioned Lash to follow.

"Why are we here?" he muttered. It made no sense: they'd just made their stealthy way *down* nine stories: nine stories that he'd struggled so hard to climb. Blood was drying on his scratched hands and face, and his limbs ached.

"Because this is the only way." Tara led him to one elevator, set apart from the others. There was a keypad beside it, and she punched in a code.

All at once, Lash understood. He'd been

inside this elevator, too; been in it more than once.

He waited, expecting to see a brace of guards burst into the lobby, brandishing guns. The elevator announced its arrival with a loud *ding;* the doors opened; and they quickly stepped inside.

Tara turned to the panel that held three unmarked buttons. There was a scanner beneath it.

She glanced back at Lash. "You realize that, no matter what happens, I'm going to have some pretty fast talking to do at the end of the day."

Lash nodded, waiting for her to press the button. But Tara remained motionless. He suddenly feared she was changing her mind; that she would punch the bottom button, hand him over again to Mauchly and his thugs. But then she sighed, cursed, pulled the lead foil from her bracelet, held her wrist beneath the scanner. And pressed the top button.

As the elevator began to rise, Tara began to replace the foil. Then she crumpled it into a ball, and let it drop to the floor. "What's the point? I'm made." She looked back at Lash. "There's something you should know."

"What's that?"

"If you're wrong about this, Mauchly's the least of your worries. I'll kill you myself."

Lash nodded. "Fair enough."

They fell silent as the elevator climbed. "You'd better grab hold of something," Tara said at last.

"Why?"

"As a security chief, I've got access to the penthouse elevator. Just as a precaution against emergency: fire, earthquake, terrorist attack."

"You mean, what Mauchly was saying about the tower's operational modes. Alpha, Beta, and so on."

"The thing is, we're not in emergency mode, just an elevated alert. That limits my access."

"What are you getting at?"

"What I'm getting at is the doors won't open. The elevator will stop at the penthouse level and sit there."

As if in response, the elevator slowed, then stopped. There was no chime, no whisper of opening doors: the car simply hung, motionless, at the top of its shaft.

Lash looked at Tara. "What happens now?"

"We sit here for a minute, maybe two, until the request system recycles. Then the elevator will return *there*." She pointed to the lowest button. "The private garage in the sub-basement."

"Where a welcoming committee will be waiting, no doubt," Lash said bitterly. "If the door won't open, why did we bother taking this ride in the first place?"

She pointed to a small hatch beneath the control panel. "Stop asking questions and grab hold of something like I told you." As she pulled open the hatch, Lash saw a telephone, flashlight, long-handled screwdriver. Tara slipped the screwdriver into the waistband of her pants, then straightened, planting her fingers along the seam of the elevator doors. Lash gripped the railing.

The elevator began to sink. Instantly, Tara dug her fingers into the seam and pulled the doors apart. The car lurched violently to a stop. Lash swung hard against the wall, desperately gripping the railing.

A pair of outer elevator doors were now exposed, metal retracting bars at full extension. Propping one foot against the inner door, Tara tugged on the closest bar. As the outer door pulled back, the poured-concrete wall of the elevator shaft came into view. It rose to Lash's waist; above, he could see the outlines of the penthouse. It looked disquieting from this low perspective, as if he were viewing the vast room through the eyes of an infant.

"Jesus," Lash said. "Where'd you learn to do that?"

"High-rise dorm my freshman year. Go ahead, climb up."

Lash pulled himself up, threw a leg over, rolled onto the carpet, then stood.

"Now hold back these doors while I climb

out. The outer *and* the inner."

Lash did as instructed. A moment later Tara was standing beside him, wiping her hands on her pants. She plucked the screwdriver from her waistband and — kneeling beside the elevator's sill plate — jammed it into the space between the floor and the doors. The door froze in place, wedged open.

"To keep unwelcome visitors away?"

Tara nodded.

"Surely the elevator isn't the only way in."

"No. There's also a stairwell leading up from the inner tower, accessible from an access hatchway."

"So what's the point of all this?" Lash gestured at the open elevator door.

"The stairwell's only for emergency evacuation. Opens from above, not below. That's the way Silver wanted it. You have fifteen minutes, maybe twenty, before they force it." She regarded him with cool, serious eyes. "Remember, I'm only here to listen to Silver's side of things. For that, fifteen minutes should be more than enough."

Beyond the walls of glass, dusk was settling over Manhattan. The rays of the setting sun sent orange shafts of light through the skyscraper canyons. Silver's mechanical collection draped long shadows across the chairs and tables. Except for the ancient machines, the room appeared to be empty.

"He's not here," Tara said.

Lash motioned Tara to follow him to the small door in the wall of bookcases. There was no knob. He ran one hand along the outlines of the door, pressing first here, then there. At last came the faint click of a hidden detent and the door sprang open.

Now it was Tara's turn to look surprised. But precious seconds were passing and Lash ushered her up the long, narrow staircase to the living quarters.

The corridor that bisected the upper floor was silent. The polished wooden doors lining both sides were closed.

Lash took a step forward. What was he supposed to do now? Clear his throat politely? Knock? The situation had a ridiculous desperation that filled him with despair.

He approached the first door, opened it silently. Beyond was the personal gym he'd seen before, but there was no sign of Silver among the free weights, treadmills, and elliptical machines. He closed the door softly and continued.

Next was a small room that seemed to serve as reference library: the walls were covered in metal shelving full of computing journals and technology periodicals. Next was a spartan kitchen: except for a restaurant-style walk-in refrigerator, there was only a simple oven with a gas stovetop, microwave, cupboards for cookware and dry goods, and a table with a single place setting. He closed the door.

This was useless; he'd only succeeded in delaying the inevitable. For all he knew, Silver had been evacuated along with everyone else. And now it was only a matter of time until the guards arrived. Invading the penthouse of Eden's founder, he'd probably be shot on sight. He glanced at Tara, feeling despair wash over him.

And then he caught his breath. Over her shoulder, he made out the black door at the end of the hall. It was ajar, its edges framed in yellow light.

Quickly, Lash made his way to it. He paused a moment. And then he slowly pushed it open.

The room was as he remembered: the racks of instrumentation; the whisper of countless fans; the half-dozen terminals lined up along the elongated wooden table. And there, in the lone chair before them, sat Richard Silver.

"Christopher," he said gravely. "Please come in. I've been expecting you."

FIFTY-THREE

Lash stepped forward. Richard Silver glanced from him to Tara.

"And Ms. Stapleton, too. When Edwin phoned a few minutes ago, he said you might be showing up as well. I don't understand."

"She came to hear your side of the story," Lash replied.

Silver raised his eyebrows. He was wearing another tropical shirt, decorated with palms and scallop shells. His worn black jeans were neatly pressed.

"Dr. Silver —" Lash began again.

"Please, Christopher. It's Richard. I've reminded you."

"We need to talk."

Silver nodded.

"Over the last few hours my life has gone completely to hell."

"Yes, you look terrible. I have a first-aid kit in the bathroom — would you like me to fetch it?"

Lash waved this away. "Why don't you sound surprised?"

Silver fell silent.

"My medical history has been tampered with. False information about deviant juvenile behavior has been added. My FBI history has been altered in a way that insults dead colleagues. I now have a criminal record. Evidence has been fabricated linking me to the scenes of death at both the Wilners and the Thorpes. Plane tickets, hotel reservations, phone records. I know there's only one person who could have done this, Richard: you. But Tara isn't convinced. She wants to hear what you have to say."

"Actually, Christopher — though I hate to say it — I believe you're the one on trial here. But tell me more. You imply I've fabricated a vast tissue of lies about you. How would I have done that?"

"You've got the computing horsepower. Liza has data-sharing access with the major communications companies, travel and lodging industries, health care, banking. And you have the kind of access, *unfettered* access, to alter their records."

Silver nodded slowly. "I suppose it's true. I could do all that, if I had sufficient time. And imagination. But the question is *why?*"

"To conceal the identity of the real murderer."

"And that would be —"

"You, Richard."

For a moment, Silver did not reply.

"Me," he said at last.

Lash nodded.

Silver shook his head slowly. "Edwin said I was to humor you, but this is really too much." He glanced at Tara. "Ms. Stapleton, can you really imagine *me* killing those women? How would I do it? And why? And then, going to all the trouble of framing Christopher here — Christopher, of all people — for the murders?"

Silver's tone was calm, reasonable, a little hurt. It *was* hard, even for Lash, to imagine the founder of Eden committing the murders. But if that was true, he had no hope left.

"You're the killer, Christopher," Silver said, turning back to him. "Saying that pains me more than I can tell you. I seldom make friends, but I'd begun to think of you as a friend. Yet you've jeopardized everything I worked for. And I still can't understand why."

Lash took another step forward.

"Hurting me won't get you anywhere," Silver said quickly. "I see you've disabled the elevator, but even so Edwin and his teams will be here within a few minutes. It would be so much easier for everyone, including you, if you gave yourself up."

"And get myself shot? Weren't those your personal orders: shoot to kill?"

At this, Silver's air of injured surprise fell away.

Looking at him, hearing the line Silver was taking, Lash realized he had only one possible weapon to defend himself: his own expertise. If he could wear Silver down, find the inconsistency of madness in his words or deeds, he had a fighting chance.

"A minute ago, you asked me why you'd commit such murders," he went on. "I'd hoped you'd be man enough to tell *me*. But you force me to draw my own conclusions. And that means performing a psychological autopsy. On you."

Silver looked at him guardedly.

"You're shy, retiring, uncomfortable in social situations. You're probably ill at ease with persons of the opposite sex. Perhaps you feel awkward or unattractive. You communicate by email or videophone, or through Mauchly. Little is known of your childhood; it's quite possible you've made an effort to conceal it. You live like a monk up here, closeting yourself with this creation — who, by the way, has a female voice and name — and devoting all your time to refining it. And isn't it telling — isn't it *extremely* telling — you chose to channel your life's work into a system that brings lonely people together?"

When there was no reply, he continued.

"Of course, lots of people are shy. Lots of people are awkward socially. For you to have committed these atrocities, there would have to be a hell of a lot more to your story." He paused, still looking at Silver. "What can you tell us about avatar zero? The avatar that, just by chance, happens to match successfully with the women in all six supercouples."

Silver did not answer. A terrible pallor came over his face.

"It's yours, isn't it? Your own personality construct, left over from when you first alpha-tested the Eden program. Except *you never took it out when the application went live*. Secretly, you kept comparing yourself to real applicants. The temptation to find a match for yourself was too great. See, you couldn't live without knowing. And yet, somehow, you couldn't live *with* knowing, either."

Silver had by now mastered his expression, and his face had become unreadable.

Lash turned to Tara. "I see two possible clinical profiles here. The first is that we're dealing with a simple sociopathic personality, an irresponsible and selfish person with no moral code. A sociopath would be fascinated by the six women who, over time, were matched with himself. He'd both crave and fear them. And he'd be insanely jealous of any other man that dared possess them. There's plenty of case studies in the literature to that effect."

He paused again. "Are there problems with this hypothesis? Yes. Sociopaths are rarely so brilliant. Also, they're rarely troubled by the deeds they've committed. Yet I think Richard here feels his actions intensely. Or at least, a part of him does."

He turned back to Silver. "I know about the Thorpes: about the return medical checkup, about the high dosage of scolipane. But what delivery system did you use on Karen Wilner?"

He question hung in the air. At last, Silver cleared his throat.

"I used no 'delivery system.' Because I didn't kill anybody." His voice was different now: harsher, more abrupt. "Ms. Stapleton, surely you see this is all just grasping at straws. Dr. Lash is desperate, he'd say any- thing, do anything, to save himself."

"Let's turn to the second, more likely hy- pothesis," Lash said. "Richard Silver is suf- fering from DID. Dissociative identity disorder. What used to be popularly known as split personality."

"A myth," Silver scoffed. "Movie fodder."

"I wish it were. I've got a DID patient in my care now. They're a bitch to treat. The way it usually works is that a person is trau- matized when young. Sometimes sexual abuse; other times, physical or simply emo- tional abuse. My current patient, for example, had an abusive, unforgiving father. For some children, such trauma can be unbearable. They're not old enough to understand it's not their fault. Especially when the abuse comes from a so-called loved one. So they

468

shatter into several personalities. Basically, you develop other people to take the abuse for you." He looked over at Silver. "Why are your childhood years such a secret? Why did you become more comfortable with a computer screen than with other people? Was your own father abusive and unforgiving?"

"Don't you talk about my family," Silver said. For the first time ever, Lash detected a clear note of anger in his voice.

"Can such people appear normal?" Tara asked.

"Absolutely. They can function on a very high level."

"Can they be intelligent?"

Lash nodded. "Extremely."

"Don't tell me you're taken in by any of this," Silver said to Tara.

"Are such people aware of their other personalities?" Tara asked.

"Usually not. They're aware of losing time — half a day can go by in a 'fugue state' without their knowing where it went. The goal of treatment is to get the patient co-conscious with all his personalities."

There was a distant thud from below. It was not particularly loud, but the floor of the laboratory shook faintly. The three exchanged glances.

The scene began to take on a surreal cast to Lash. Here he was, spinning out theories, while armed men eager to shoot him would break in any second. But he was almost done now; there was nothing else to do except finish.

"In such cases, one personality is usually dominant," he went on. "Often it's the normal, 'good' personality. The other personalities house the feelings that are too dangerous for the dominant personality." He gestured at Silver. "So on the face of it, Richard is what he seems to be: a brilliant, if reclusive, computer engineer. The man who told me he feels almost a surgeon's responsibility to his clients. But I fear there are other Richard Silvers, too, that we're not allowed to see. The Richard Silver who was both hopelessly threatened by, yet irresistibly attracted to, the idea of a perfect mate. And, the other, darker, Richard Silver who feels murderous jealousy at the thought of *another* man possessing that perfect woman."

He fell silent. Silver looked back at him, thin-lipped, eyes hard and glittering. In his expression, Lash read mortification and anger. But guilt? He wasn't sure. And there was no more time now, no time at all . . .

As if to punctuate this thought, there came another deep thudding sound from below.

"In another few moments, Edwin will be here," Silver said. "And this painful charade of yours will be over."

Lash suddenly felt a great hollowness. "That's it? You've got nothing else to say?"

"What am I supposed to say?"

"You could admit the truth."

"The truth." Silver almost spat the words. "The truth is you've insulted and humiliated me with this pseudo-psychological tale-spinning. So let's put an end to this travesty. I've humored you long enough. You're guilty of murder: have the guts to face up to it."

"So you could *live* with yourself? You could sentence an innocent man to death?"

"You're *not* innocent, Dr. Lash. Why not accept the truth? Everybody else has."

Lash turned to Tara. "Is that true? What flavor of truth do you believe in this evening?"

"Flavor," Silver said disdainfully. "You're a serial murderer."

"Tara?" Lash persisted.

Tara took a deep breath, turned to Silver. "You asked me something earlier. You asked, 'Can you really imagine *me* killing those women?' "

For a moment, Silver looked puzzled. "Yes, I asked you that. Why?"

"Why did you single out the women? What about the men?"

"I —" Silver abruptly went silent.

"You hadn't heard Christopher's theory that the women *alone* were overdosed, given a medication that would guarantee suicidal-homicidal behavior. So why did you single out the women?"

"It was just a figure of speech."

Tara did not reply.

"Ms. Stapleton," Silver said in a harder tone. "In a few minutes, Lash will be subdued and restrained by my men. He will no longer pose a threat. Don't make this any more complicated on anyone else — including yourself — than it need be."

Still, Tara was silent.

"Silver's right," Lash said. He could hear the bitterness in his own voice. "He doesn't have to admit anything. He can just keep his mouth shut. Nobody's going to believe me now. There's nothing more I can do."

Tara made no indication she had heard. Her eyes remained veiled, far away.

And then, quite suddenly, they widened.

"No," she said, turning to him. "There's one more thing."

FIFTY-FOUR

The room went still. For a moment, all Lash heard was the whispered susurrus of cooling fans.

"What are you talking about?" he asked.

In response, Tara took him aside. Then she nodded almost imperceptibly over her shoulder. Lash followed her gaze to the contoured chair encased behind Plexiglas at the far end of the room.

"Liza?" he asked in a very low voice.

"If you're right about this, Silver would have accessed the system from here. Maybe there's some kind of trail you could follow. Even if there isn't, *she* would know."

"She?"

"Liza would have a record of Silver's access. He would have made inquiries into a variety of our subsystems: communications, medical, data gathering. A large number of external entities would have been touched to create the false workup on you. There'd be Lindsay Thorpe's pharmaceutical records. There'd be all kinds of things. You could ask her directly."

"*I* could ask her?"

"Why not? She's a computer, she's pro-grammed to respond to commands."

"That's not what I mean. I haven't any idea how to communicate with her."

"You've seen Silver do it. You told me so, over that drink at Sebastian's. That's more than anyone else can say." She stepped back, looked at him quizzically. *You're the one with everything at stake here*, the look said. *If you're telling the truth, wouldn't you do anything to prove it?*

"What are you two talking about?" Silver asked. He had been guardedly watching the exchange.

Lash looked at the chair and the leads that snaked away from it. It was the last desperate gamble of a desperate man. But Tara was right. He had nothing to lose.

He strode across the room, opened the Plexiglas panel, and quickly slid into the sculpted chair.

"What do you think you're doing?" Silver's voice was suddenly loud in the cramped room.

Lash did not answer. He looked around, trying to recall just what he'd seen Silver do before. He pulled down the small screen that hung from a telescoping arm, affixed the lavalier microphone to his torn collar.

"You can't do that!" Silver said. He stood

up slowly, as if stunned by Lash's brazenness.

"Who's going to stop me? You?" Lash lifted the EEG leads, began fastening them to his temples. He thought back to what Silver had said about Liza: her highly developed intelligence models, her three-dimensional neural network. That he could hope to interact with her, let alone find the information he needed, seemed the height of folly. Yet he could not let Silver see his doubt.

Leads attached, he reached down to the console and snapped the EEG into life. The screen before him cleared; several columns of numbers scrolled rapidly up and out of sight. He glanced at the small keypad and stylus set into one of the arms. He remembered Silver had used the keypad prior to communicating directly with Liza. "Getting her attention," he'd said. Somehow or other, he'd have to get her attention, too. He reached for the keypad.

"Get out of that chair," Silver warned. He was pacing now, as if in a quandary over what to do.

"Don't worry. I won't break her."

"You haven't a clue what you're doing. This won't get you anywhere. It's a waste of time."

Beneath the indignation, Lash sensed nervousness in Silver's tone. He noted the man's pacing with interest. "I wouldn't be so sure."

"Nobody else has ever spoken directly with Liza."

"Don't you remember what you told me last time I was here? You said others could communicate with her, too, given proper concentration and training."

"The operative words there are *proper concentration and training,* Lash."

"I'm a quick study."

This was said with a confidence Lash did not feel. He looked from the keypad to the screen, then back again. *Get her attention.*

What do computers respond to? Commands. Statements in programs.

He placed his hand on the keypad, typed:

the quick brown fox jumped over the lazy dog

There was no response. The screen remained blank.

"Dr. Lash," Silver said. "Get out of the chair."

I'll try a question instead. Lash typed:

why is a raven like a writing desk?

Again, no response. Lash gritted his teeth. *Silver's right. This is just a waste of time.* Any minute Mauchly would break into the penthouse. And that would be that.

He glanced past the Plexiglas wall. Silver

had stopped pacing and was stepping toward him now, an angry look on his face.

Suddenly, a storm of data ran up the small monitor. And then he heard a voice. It was the voice he remembered: low, feminine, coming from everywhere and nowhere at the same time.

"Why is a raven like a writing desk?" it said.

"Yes," Lash spoke into the microphone.

"I do not understand the nature of your interrogatory."

"It's a riddle."

"My parsing of 'itza' is unsuccessful."

"It is a riddle," Lash said, reminding himself to speak slowly and clearly. "A quote from a famous book."

Silver had stopped, and was listening intently.

"You are not Richard," the feminine voice said. This was spoken with an utter lack of inflection, leaving Lash unsure whether it was a statement or a question.

"No," he replied.

"Your image and voice soundprint are known. You are Christopher Lash."

"Yes."

The computer said nothing further. Lash felt his pulse begin to race, and he fought to master himself. What could he say? He remembered a question Silver had asked, decided to try repeating it.

"Liza," he said into the microphone. "What is your current state?"

"Ninety-nine point two two four percent operational. Current processes are at twenty-two point six percent of multithreaded capacity. Banked machine cycle surplus at one hundred percent. Thank you for asking."

"*Stop it,*" Silver said in a fierce whisper.

"I have visual acquisition of Richard," Liza said. "I have aural acquisition of Richard. Yet it is not Richard speaking with me. Curious."

Curious. Silver had told him he'd made curiosity one of Liza's fundamental characteristics. Just maybe he could put that curiosity to good use.

"I, Christopher Lash, am speaking with you," he said.

"Christopher," the voice repeated, with the merest ripple of digital artifacting.

Once again, Lash was struck by the way Liza said his name, almost as if tasting it. After years of speaking only to Silver, speaking to another human being would be revelation indeed.

"Why do you, and not Richard, speak with me?" Liza asked.

Lash hesitated. He had to phrase his responses in such a way as to keep Liza interested; it seemed increasingly likely this was the only way to make sure communication would continue. "Because the situation at

Eden has become nonstandard."

"Explain."

"The best way to explain is by asking you a series of questions. Is that permissible?"

"Permissibility is unknown. This is foreign to my experience. I have run no scenarios that address it. I am currently evaluating."

"How long will the evaluation take?"

"Five million, two hundred forty-five thousand machine cycles, plus or minus ten percent, assuming successful implementation of a 'best-fit' selection tree."

This told Lash nothing. "May I ask the questions while the evaluation is ongoing?"

"My parsing of 'ongoing' is unsuccessful. Preposition and verb are out of context."

"May I ask the questions during your evaluation process?"

"Christopher."

This was not the answer Lash expected. He chose to take it as a green light.

"Liza, has Richard used this interface to access records relating to me in the last forty-eight hours?"

Abruptly, Silver lunged at the Plexiglas. Lash straight-armed the door, refusing to give him access.

"Liza," he repeated, pressing the door closed. "Has Richard Silver used this interface to access records relating to me?"

There was no response.

Is she considering the question? Lash asked

himself. *Or is she refusing to answer?*

"Liza?" he said again. "Did you understand my question?"

Suddenly he remembered something: the weariness with which Silver had removed the EEG sensors when he rose from this seat. *Sessions with Liza can be a little draining,* he'd said. *It requires a great deal of concentration. Think of biofeedback. The frequency and amplitude of beta and theta waves can speak a lot more distinctly than words.*

Perhaps, in this unique situation, curiosity alone was not sufficient for Liza. It was her first time communicating directly with anyone other than Silver. Clarity and simplicity of message would be of critical importance.

It requires a great deal of concentration. Think of biofeedback.

Lash did not know what methods Silver used to achieve his concentration. All he could fall back on were the relaxation techniques he himself taught patients for dealing with their anxiety. The self-hypnosis, the state of heightened attention, just might be enough. If he could slow himself down, *calm* himself down, free his mind of the extra baggage . . .

He began just as he would if he'd been in his office, speaking one on one with a patient. *Envision yourself in a relaxing scene. The most relaxing scene you can imagine. Picture yourself sitting on a beach. It's a sunny day.*

Once again, Silver threw himself against the door. Lash's elbow bent slightly under the pressure, then stiffened again. He tried to forget Silver, Mauchly, his own desperate situation, everything.

He shut his eyes. *Take a deep breath. Hold it. Now let it out, slowly. Take another. You should feel limp, relaxed.*

Liza remained silent.

Slowly, external sound and sensation went away. Lash kept his thoughts focused on the beach, on the creamy sound of the surf.

Feel your head relax. Feel it roll gently to one side. Now feel the muscles of your neck relax. Feel your chest grow less tight, your breathing come easier.

"Christopher." It was the disembodied voice of Liza.

"Yes." *Feel your arms relax, first the right, then the left. Let them go limp.*

"Please repeat your last statement."

Feel your legs relax, first the right, then the left. "Has Richard Silver used this interface to access records relating to me?"

"Yes, Christopher."

"Were those records external or internal?"

No response.

Take a slow, deep breath. "Were the records Richard accessed within your dataspace, or were they outside Eden Incorporated?"

"Both."

Focus on the beach. "Did Richard Silver

481

modify or change these records in any way?"

There was no reply.

"Liza, did Richard Silver modify any of —"

"No."

No? Was Liza telling him Silver had not modified his records, after all? Or was she refusing to answer? But that was . . .

Abruptly, his hard-won concentration crumpled. Lash took a deep breath, glanced beyond the Plexiglas partition. Silver had taken several steps back now, and was standing beside Tara. They were looking at him, worried expressions on their faces.

"Christopher," Silver was saying. "Please step out for a minute. I need to speak with you."

There was no further response from Liza. There was a new look in Silver's eyes: a haunted look.

Silver reached into his pocket, pulled out a cell phone, dialed a number. "Edwin?" he said. "Edwin, it's Richard." Then he held the cell phone away from his ear so both Tara and Lash could hear the response.

"Yes, Dr. Silver," came Mauchly's tinny voice.

"Where are you currently?"

"We've just penetrated the interstructural barrier."

"Hold your position. Don't proceed any farther until you get instructions from me."

"Could you repeat that, Dr. Silver?"

"I said, hold your position. Do not attempt to enter the penthouse." This time, Silver kept the phone to his ear. "Everything's fine. Yes, Edwin, just fine. I'll get back to you soon."

But Silver did not look fine as he replaced the phone in his pocket. "Christopher. It's vital that we talk, and talk now."

Lash hesitated just one more moment. Then he swung his legs off the chair, plucked the leads from his forehead, and exited the chamber.

FIFTY-FIVE

Mauchly looked down at his cell phone a moment, as if doubting it was working properly. Then he returned it to his lips. "Could you repeat that, Dr. Silver?"

"I said, hold your position. Do not attempt to enter the penthouse."

"Is everything all right?"

"Everything's fine."

"Are you sure, sir?"

"Yes, Edwin, just fine. I'll get back to you soon." And with a chirrup, the phone went silent.

Mauchly gave it another long stare.

Even through the distortion, there'd been no doubt the voice was Silver's. There was an unusual undercurrent to it Mauchly did not recall hearing before, and he wondered if Lash was threatening him, if he was being held hostage in his own penthouse. Yet the voice hadn't sounded frightened. If Mauchly detected anything, he detected great weariness.

"That was Silver?" Sheldrake shouted from below.

"Yes."

"And his orders?"

"Not to enter the penthouse. Hold our position."

"You kidding?"

"No."

There was a brief silence. "Well, if we're to hold our position, could we hold it somewhere more comfortable? I'm feeling like a circus gymnast here."

Mauchly glanced down. It seemed a reasonable request.

For the last fifteen minutes, they had been waiting at the top of a long metal ladder that climbed the inside wall of Eden's inner tower, just below the roof. Waiting while a security tech — a sleepy-eyed, tousle-headed youth named Dorfman — tried to outsmart the access mechanism of the barrier to Silver's penthouse. It had been a long fifteen minutes, made longer by the hard metal rungs of the ladder and the constant noise of the huge power plant arrayed across the cavernous space below them: the generators and transformers that supplied electricity to the hungry tower. Despite the full resources of the security staff, Dorfman had had a difficult time.

Perhaps Stapleton could have made a quicker job of it. Had she wanted to . . .

But Mauchly would not allow himself to ponder the problem of Tara Stapleton any further. Instead, he made a mental note to reevaluate penthouse security at the earliest possible opportunity.

Clearly, he'd allowed Silver's passion for privacy to be carried beyond reasonable extremes. The last fifteen minutes had been proof of that. It was an indulgence, a dangerous indulgence. The battering ram had failed — as expected — but high-tech methods had also proven alarmingly slow. What if Silver should fall suddenly ill and be unable to help himself? If the elevator were to malfunction, precious minutes would be lost reaching him. Silver was simply too valuable an asset of the company to be put at risk, and Mauchly himself would tell him so. Silver was a reasonable man; he would understand.

Now, Mauchly looked up the ladder. It disappeared into a hatch in the roof of the inner tower and ascended into the terminal baffle: the open space between the inner tower and the floor of Silver's penthouse. Looking up still farther, Mauchly could see Dorfman, standing just within the newly opened security hatchway leading into the penthouse. He was looking quizzically down at Mauchly, one hand gripping a ladder rung, the other holding a logic analyzer. Continuity testers, electronic sensors, and other gear hung on cords from his belt.

"Proceed," Mauchly called up.

Dorfman raised a hand to one ear.

"*Proceed!* Wait just inside for us."

Dorfman nodded, then turned to grasp the narrow ladder with both hands. Another moment and he had climbed out of sight, disappearing into the blackness of the penthouse.

Mauchly glanced down at Sheldrake, motioned for him and his men to follow. It had been a hard-fought battle, gaining access to the penthouse: if they were going to wait, they might as well wait inside.

He began climbing the rest of the way up the ladder. Four steps took him to the porthole in the tower's roof; another four steps brought him up into the baffle. He had never been in this space before, and despite himself he stopped to look around.

Mauchly was not a particularly imaginative man, but — as he slowly swivelled through an axis of one hundred and eighty degrees — he found he had to fight back vertigo. A dark metal landscape — the roof of the inner tower — ran away from him on all sides. It was studded with cabling, and its flow was interrupted by countless small equipment housings. Some ten feet above, like a titanic lowering sky, hung the steel underbelly of the penthouse structure. It was fixed to the tower's roof by a carapace of vertical I-beams. Two metal-sheathed data trunks ran from fairings in the upper structure to the roof of the inner tower. In the distance he could make out a third, much larger boxlike structure: the shaft of Silver's private elevator. Around the periphery ran a lattice of horizontal slats, through which the rich hues of the setting sun could be glimpsed. An observer, staring up at this decorative latticework from street level, would never know it was concealing the jointure of two physically separate structures, the inner tower and the penthouse above it. But to Mauchly, sixty floors above Manhattan, it felt like being between the layers of a huge metal sandwich.

And there was something else: something more unsettling. Set into the walls of the long axis, midway between the two structures, were the telescoping sections of the huge security plates. Mauchly could make out three indentations in their steel flanks: two fitted to the data trunks, the other to the private elevator. The plates were fully retracted now, but if an emergency was ever declared they would slide forward and lock together, sealing the penthouse from the tower below. From his vantage point, the massive hydraulic pistons that powered the plates looked like the springs of a colossal mouse trap.

"Mr. Mauchly?" Sheldrake called up from below.

Mauchly roused himself, took a fresh grip on the ladder, and — turning his eyes from the baffle — climbed up through the security hatchway and into the vestibule of the penthouse.

His first impression was the simple relief of setting foot on solid ground again. The second impression, following immediately, was of unrelieved dark.

"Dorfman!"

There was a rustling in the dark beside him. "Here, Mr. Mauchly."

"Why haven't you turned on the lights?"

"I've been looking for a switch, sir."

Mauchly rose, feeling his way forward until he touched metal. He felt along the wall until he reached a door — closed — then continued along the walls until he returned once again to the security hatchway. His circuit of the small compartment yielded no light switch.

There was a clatter, and a dark shape suddenly thrust its way into the hatchway, obscuring the dim light filtering up from below.

"Sheldrake?"

"Affirmative."

"Call down to some of your men. Get some torches up here."

The shape descended again out of view.

Mauchly paused, thinking. The penthouse compartment was six stories high. Silver's quarters occupied the top two stories. This huge space below housed the machines that made up Liza.

Silver had always been easygoing about

Eden's business matters, leaving day-to-day operations to the board of directors. The one thing he was extremely possessive about was Liza's physical plant. He'd been up here every day during construction, overseeing the installation himself, sometimes even physically moving equipment in from the cranes through the unfinished walls. Throughout, Mauchly remembered, Liza had been kept running on a large suite of rather old computers with a portable power supply; inserting the various components into place, with electricity flowing and computers online, had been a harrowing process. But Silver had insisted. "She can't lose consciousness," he'd told Mauchly. "She never has, and I can't allow her to do so now. Liza's not some personal computer you can just reboot. She's had all this time of self-awareness — who's to say what would be lost or altered if she lost power?"

A similar anxiousness lay behind the precautions Silver took to guard Liza from the outside world. Mauchly knew that, for whatever reason, Liza's intelligence had never been transferred from one computer to another: instead, newer and larger computers had simply been linked to the older ones, creating an expanding sprawl of "big iron" hardware of several vintages and makes. The powerful cluster of supercomputers that did Eden's *outboard* processing — data gathering, the client monitoring, all the rest — were housed in the inner tower below, monitored by countless technical specialists. But the central core of Liza, the controlling intelligence, lay here, cared for by Silver alone.

Mauchly had never set foot within Liza's physical plant since earliest construction, and now he cursed himself for the oversight. In retrospect, his lack of knowledge was a severe breach of security. He thought back on what he knew about the four-story space beyond. He realized he knew very little; Silver had protected it jealously, even from him.

Mauchly edged back to the door he'd noticed before. For a moment, he feared Silver might have locked it from the inside. But the simple knob turned beneath his grasp. As the door slid open, light at last returned: not lamplight, but a vast thicket of diodes and LEDs, winking red and green and amber in the velvet darkness, stretching ahead into what seemed limitless distance. There was sound here, too: not the banshee-like howl of the building's power plant below, but a steady hum of backup generators and the subtler, measured cadence of electromechanical devices.

Instructing Dorfman to wait for Sheldrake, Mauchly stepped forward into the gloom.

FIFTY-SIX

Silver led the way down the corridor to a door he unlocked with a simple, old-fashioned key. Brusquely, he directed them into a tiny bedroom, spotlessly clean, without decoration of any kind. The narrow bed, with its thin mattress and metal rails, resembled a military cot. Beside was an unvarnished wood table on which lay a Bible. A single bare bulb hung from the ceiling. The room was so spartan, so unrelievedly white, it could easily have passed for a monk's cell.

Silver closed the door behind him, then began to pace. His face was contorted by conflicting emotions. Once he stopped, turned toward Lash, and seemed about to speak — only to turn away again.

At last, he wheeled around.

"You were wrong," he said.

Lash waited.

"I had *wonderful* parents. They were nurturing. Patient. Eager to teach. I think of them every day. The smell of my father's aftershave when he'd hug me coming home

492

from work. My mother singing as I played under the piano."

He turned away again and resumed his pacing. Lash knew better than to say anything.

"My father died when I was three. Car accident. My mother outlived him by two years. I had no other family. So I was sent to live with an aunt in Madison, Wisconsin. She had her own family, three older boys."

Silver's pace slowed. His hands clenched behind his back, knuckles white.

"I wasn't wanted there. To the boys I was weak, ugly, a figure of scorn. I wasn't Rick. I was 'Fuckface.' Their mother tolerated it because she didn't like having me around, either. Usually I was excluded from family rituals like Sunday dinner, movies, bowling. If I was brought along it was an afterthought, or because my absence would be noticed by neighbors. I cried a lot at night. Sometimes I prayed I'd die in my sleep so I wouldn't have to wake up anymore."

There was no trace of self-pity in Silver's voice. He simply rapped out the words, one after another, as if reciting a shopping list.

"The boys made sure I was a pariah at school. They enjoyed threatening the girls with 'Silver cooties,' laughing at their disgust."

Silver stopped, looked again at Lash.

"The father wasn't as bad as the rest. He

worked the night shift as a keypunch operator in the university computer lab. Sometimes I'd go along with him to work, just to
escape the house. I began to grow fascinated
with the computers. They didn't hurt you, or
judge you. If your program didn't run, it
wasn't because you were skinny, or ugly, but
because you'd made a mistake in your code.
Fix it, and the program would run."

Silver was talking faster now, the words
coming more easily. Lash nodded understand-
ingly, careful to hide his growing elation. He'd
seen this many times before in police interrogations. It was a huge effort to start con-
fessing. But once they got started, the suspect
couldn't seem to talk fast enough.

"I began spending more and more time at
the computer lab. Programming had a logic
that was comforting, somehow. And there
was always more to learn. At first, the staff
tolerated me as a curiosity. Then, when they
saw the kinds of system utilities I was
starting to write, they hired me.

"I spent nine years under my aunt's roof.
As soon as I could, I left. I lied about my
age and got a job with a defense contractor,
writing programs to calculate missile trajecto-
ries. I got a scholarship in electrical engineering at the university. That's when I
began studying AI in earnest."

"And when you got the idea for Liza?"
Lash asked.

"No. Not right away. I was fascinated by the early stuff, John McCarthy and LISP and all that. But it wasn't until my senior year that the tools had matured sufficiently to do any real work towards machine learning."

" 'The Imperative of Machine Intelligence,' " Tara said. "Your senior thesis."

Lash nodded without looking at her. "That summer, I didn't have any place to go until grad school in September. I didn't know anybody. I'd already moved to Cambridge and was lonely. So I began banking time at the MIT lab, spending twenty or thirty hours at a time, developing a program robust enough to be imprinted with simple intelligence routines. By the end of the summer, I'd made real progress. When school started, my faculty advisor at MIT was impressed enough to give me a free hand. The more subtle and powerful the program became, the more excited I got. When I wasn't in class, all my time was spent with Liza."

"You'd given her a name by then?" Lash asked.

"I kept pushing myself, trying to expand her capabilities for carrying on realistic conversations. I'd type. She'd respond. At first it was just a way to encourage her self-learning. But then I found myself spending more time simply talking to her. Not about specific programming tasks, you know, but . . . but as a friend."

He paused a moment. "Around this time I was working on a primitive voice interface. Not to parse human speech — that was still years away — but to *verbalize* its output. I used samples of my own voice. It started as a diversion, I didn't see any real significance to it."

The rush of words suddenly ceased. Silver took a deep breath, began again.

"I still don't know why I did it. But late one night, when my coding temporarily hit some brick wall, I started playing around. I ran the voiceprints through a pitch-shifting algorithm somebody left in the lab: raising the frequency, fiddling with the waveform. And suddenly the voice began to sound like a woman's."

Like a woman's. Now, Lash understood why, when he'd first heard it, Liza's voice had seemed familiar. It was a feminine re-creation of Silver's own.

"And her personality?" Tara asked. "Was that yours, as well?"

"Early on, I thought that hard-coding personality traits into Liza would jump-start machine consciousness. I didn't know anybody I could ask to volunteer. So I got some personality inventories from the psych department — just the MMPI-2, really — took the test myself, and scored it."

Lash caught his breath. "What were the results?"

"What you'd expect. Uncomfortable in social situations. Superachiever mentality, driven by low sense of self-esteem." Silver shrugged as if the answer wasn't important. "It was an experiment, really, to see if personality could be modeled, as well as intelligence. But it didn't get me very far. It was only later her neural matrix developed enough to retain a persistent personality." Then he stopped speaking, and a stricken look crossed his face.

The look told Lash several things. Silver had been exonerating himself: describing his painful past, rationalizing his crimes. It was the standard pattern. Soon he'd shift to the crimes themselves and what led up to them.

And yet something didn't fit. Silver's expression, his body language, still screamed *conflict*. That time should have passed. He was deep into his confession. Why was he still conflicted? Was he, even now, undecided about turning himself in? This did not fit the pattern at all.

"Let's move on to the present," Lash said in a calm, matter-of-fact voice. "Want to tell me what happened with the supercouples?"

Silver started pacing again. He remained silent long enough for Lash's guarded elation to ebb away.

When Silver finally spoke, he did not look at Lash. "What you want to know began when I founded Eden."

"Go on," Lash said, careful not to let his voice betray anything.

"I've told you some of this already. How Liza eventually proved herself capable of just about any calculation that business or the military could throw at her. I'd made enough money to choose her next direction myself. That's when I chose . . . chose relationship processing. It was a huge undertaking. But I was able to team up with PharmGen. They were a pharmaceutical giant, they had enough seed money to fund just about any start-up. And their scientists developed the early psych evaluations I used for the matching algorithms. It was subtle work, probably the most difficult programming I've ever done outside Liza herself. Anyway, once the core programming seemed stable, I moved on to alpha testing."

"Using your own personality construct," Tara said.

"Along with several dummy avatars. But we quickly realized more sophisticated avatars would be necessary. The psychological battery was greatly extended. We went into beta testing, using volunteers from the graduate programs at Harvard and MIT. That's when —" Silver hesitated. "That's when I had my own personality construct reevaluated."

The tiny room fell into a tense silence.

"Reevaluated," Lash prompted.

Silver took a seat on the edge of the bed.

He glanced up at Lash, an almost pleading expression on his face.

"I wanted my own construct to be as complete, as detailed, as the others. What's wrong with that? Edwin Mauchly shepherded me through the process. That's how we first met. He was still employed by PharmGen back then. The evaluation was painful, horrible — nobody likes to see their vulnerabilities exposed so coldly — but Edwin was the picture of tact. And he clearly had a visionary eye for business. In time, he became my right-hand man, the person I could trust to take care of everything necessary down *there*." And Silver indicated the tower beneath their feet. "Within a year I'd bought back my interest from PharmGen and made Eden a private company, with its own board of directors. And —"

"I see," Lash interjected smoothly. "And when did you decide to reintroduce your updated avatar into the Tank?"

The stricken look returned to Silver's face. His shoulders slumped.

"I'd been thinking about it for a long time," he said quietly. "During alpha testing, my avatar never got matched. I told myself it must be something to do with the crude dummy avatars. But then Eden got off the ground, the Tank filled with clients, and the number of successful matches began to climb. And I wondered: what would happen if I placed my avatar back in there with those countless others? Would I find a perfect match, too? Would I remain that guy all the girls recoiled from in school? It began to torment me."

Silver drew in a deep breath. "Late one evening, I introduced my avatar into the Tank. I instructed Liza to create a back-channel, transparent to the monitoring staff. But there were no hits, and after a few hours I lost my nerve. I withdrew it. But by then the genie was out of the bottle. I had to know." Silver looked up, fixing Lash with his gaze. "Do you understand? *I had to know.*"

Lash nodded. "Yes. I understand."

"I began introducing my avatar into the Tank for longer periods. An afternoon here, a day there. Still nothing. Soon, my avatar had logged whole weeks in the Tank without success. I began to feel despair. I contemplated tweaking my avatar somehow, making it more appealing. But then, what would be the point? After all, it wasn't so much the match itself — I would never have had the nerve to initiate real contact — I just wanted to know that *somebody* could care for me."

Lash felt a ripple of shock, faint but uncomfortable. "Go on," he said.

"And then, one afternoon in the fall — I'll never forget, it was a Tuesday, September 17 — Liza informed me of a match." As he spoke, the pain, the anxiety, melted from his face. "My first feeling was disbelief. Then the room seemed to fill with light. It was like God turned on a thousand suns. I asked Liza to isolate the two avatars, run the comparison routines again, in case there was some mistake."

"But there was no mistake," Tara said.

"Her name was Lindsay. Lindsay Torvald. I had Liza download a copy of her dossier to my personal terminal, here. I think I watched her initial video a dozen times. She was beautiful. Such a beautiful woman. And so accomplished. She was leaving for a hiking trip in the Alps, I remember. To think that such a woman could possibly care for me . . ."

As quickly as it had gone, the pain returned to his face.

"What happened next?" Lash asked.

"I erased the dossier from my terminal, instructed Liza to reinsert Lindsay Torvald's avatar into the Tank, and removed my own avatar. Permanently."

"And then?"

"Then?" For a moment, Silver seemed confused. "Oh. I see what you mean. Six hours later, Edwin called to tell me that Eden had matched its first supercouple. It was something we'd theorized about, of course, but I never believed it would actually happen. I was even more surprised when I learned that half of the couple was Lindsay Torvald."

Lash's uncomfortable feeling returned.

"And did that exacerbate things?"

"What things?"

"Your feelings of frustration." Lash chose his words carefully. "Having Lindsay matched in a supercouple could only have added fuel to the fire."

"Christopher, *it wasn't like that at all.*"

The uncomfortable feeling grew stronger. "Then perhaps you could explain it to me."

Silver looked at him in genuine surprise. "Do you mean that all this time — despite everything I've told you — you still don't understand?"

"Understand what?"

"You're right. Lindsay *was* killed."

The statement hung in the air, a dark cloud that refused to dissipate. Lash glanced again at Tara.

"But Christopher, *I didn't kill her.*"

Very slowly, Lash looked back at Silver.

"I didn't hurt Lindsay. She was the one person who gave me hope."

Lash was suddenly afraid to ask the next question. He licked his lips. "If you didn't kill Lindsay Thorpe — who did?"

Silver rose from the bed. Even though they were alone in the room, he glanced uneasily over his shoulder. For a minute he said nothing, as if in the grip of some internal struggle. And when he spoke, it was in a whisper.

"*Liza,*" he said.

FIFTY-SEVEN

For a moment, Lash could not reply. He felt stunned.

All this time, he'd been sure he was listening to a murderer's confession. Instead, he'd been hearing a condemnation of someone — some*thing* — else.

"Oh, my God . . ." Tara began. Then she fell silent.

"I began to suspect just after the second couple died." Silver's voice had begun to tremble. "But I didn't want to believe it. I wouldn't let myself think about it, do anything about it. It wasn't until you were named as the suspect that — that I finally took steps to learn the truth."

Lash struggled with this revelation. Could it be true?

Perhaps it *wasn't* true. Perhaps it was Silver, still trying to save himself. And yet Lash had to admit that, no matter how hard he'd tried to pigeonhole Silver into the profile of a serial murderer, the man never quite fit.

"How?" he managed. "Why?"

"The how would be all too easy," Tara answered. She spoke slowly. "Liza knows everything about everybody. She had access to all systems, internal *and* external. She could manipulate information. And because everything was in the digital domain, there would be no paper trail to follow."

Silver did not respond.

"Was it scolipane?" Lash asked.

Silver nodded.

"Liza would have known about the reaction with Substance P, the catastrophic results of the early trials," Tara said. "It would have been part of her dataset from the days when PharmGen was our parent company. She wouldn't even have needed to search."

It seemed incredible. Yet Lash had seen Liza's power, firsthand. He had witnessed the Tank, witnessed the intelligence at work. And if he had lingering doubts, all he needed was to look at Tara's expression.

"I understand how Lindsay died," he said. "The drug interaction, the high-copper condition from the antihistamine. But what about the Thorpes?"

"The same," Silver said without looking up. "Karen Thorpe had a blood disorder that caused her to take prescription vitamins. The vitamin prescription was changed to a high-copper formulation, and the dosage increased. I checked her records. Karen Thorpe had recently undergone a physical exam. Liza took advantage of that not only to change the vitamin formulation, but to add a prescription for scolipane. On the heels of the physical, Karen would have no reason to doubt the new prescription."

"What about the third couple?" Tara asked. "The Connellys?"

"I looked into them, as well," Silver replied, his voice very low. "Lynn Connelly is passionately fond of exotic fruit. It says so on her application. Just last week, Eden sent her a basket of red blush pears from Ecuador. Extremely rare."

"So?"

"There was no record of anybody from Eden authorizing such a present. So I looked deeper. Only one grower in Ecuador markets that particular brand of pears for export. And that grower uses an unusual pesticide, not approved by the FDA."

"Go on."

"Lynn Connelly takes only one medication regularly. Cafraxis. It's a migraine prophylactic. That pesticide contains the base chemical that, when combined with the active ingredient of cafraxis —"

"Let me guess," said Lash. "Substance P."

Silver nodded.

Lash fell silent. It was outrageous. And yet it explained a lot of things — including the annoyances in his own life that started out petty, then quickly escalated, as if somebody was trying to force his attention from the mysterious deaths. *Could Liza have been behind everything — even Edmund Wyre's parole? Wyre, the one person in the world who more than anything wants me dead?* The answer was obvious. If Liza could have altered his own past history so radically, arranging Wyre's parole would have been childishly simple.

But still, something didn't make sense. "Couldn't Liza have killed the Wilners in some other way?" he asked.

"Sure," Tara replied. "She could have done anything. Tweaked medical scanners to deliver a fatal dose of X rays. Instructed a jet's autopilot to fly into a mountain. Anything."

"So why kill the couples in such a similar way? And why were their deaths so precisely timed, each exactly two years after they'd been matched? The similarity of deaths raised the alarm in the first place. It makes no sense."

"It makes perfect sense. You're not thinking like a machine." It was Silver who spoke this time. "Machines are programmed for order. Since scolipane solved the first problem successfully, there was no need for further optimization when solving the second problem."

"We're not talking about a 'problem,'" said Lash. "We're talking about murder."

"Liza's *not* a murderer!" Silver cried. He

506

struggled to control himself. "Not really. She was simply trying to remove what she perceived as a threat. The concept of hiding, of deception, came later, when . . . when *you* became involved."

"What she perceived as a threat," Lash repeated slowly. "A threat to whom?"

Silver didn't speak, and he didn't meet Lash's gaze.

"To herself," Tara said.

Lash glanced at her.

"Dr. Silver instructed Liza to remove his avatar from the Tank after the match with Lindsay Thorpe. But I don't think she did. I think his avatar was *in the Tank all the time.* Unknown to the technicians or engineers. And it found a match exactly five more times. Karen Wilner. Lynn Connelly."

"Each of the women in the supercouples."

"Yes. Although I'm not sure they were supercouples, after all." Tara looked over. "Dr. Silver?"

Silver, eyes on the ground, still said nothing.

"You know Liza's been imprinted with personality traits," Tara went on. "Curiosity, for example."

Lash nodded.

"Jealousy is an emotion. Fear is another."

"Are you saying Liza was *jealous* of Lindsay Thorpe?"

"Is that so hard to believe? What are jealousy and fear, except stimuli for self-preservation? If you were Liza, how would you feel when your creator — the person who programmed you, shared his personality with you, spent all his time with you — found a life mate?"

"So when Liza matched Lindsay Thorpe with somebody else, she marked it as a supercouple."

"It must have seemed the most likely way of ensuring Lindsay would never again be a threat. The Thorpes were a valid match, of course — just not a perfect one. But the comparison process was so complex, nobody but Liza could know it *wasn't* one-hundred-percent perfect."

Lash struggled with this. "But if you're right — if Liza matched Lindsay with somebody else, removed the threat — why kill her?"

"When Silver put his own avatar into the Tank, he added an element of risk Liza was previously unaware of. Now she realized there could be threats to her own sovereignty. So it was Liza who reinserted Silver's avatar into the Tank. Who kept watching vigilantly for a match. And it happened again. And again. There must have come a time when Liza felt the number of existing 'threats,' married or not, were growing too numerous. And that's when she decided on a more permanent solution."

Lash turned toward Silver. "Is this true?"

Still, Silver did not answer.

Lash stepped closer. "How could you let this happen? You programmed your own personality flaws into Liza. Didn't you see what you were doing, didn't you *see* you'd only —"

"You think *this* is what I wanted?" Silver shouted abruptly. "To you it's all black and white, isn't it: a neat little package of diagnoses, tied with a pretty bow. I couldn't anticipate how she'd develop. I gave her the ability to teach herself, to grow. Just the way *any* mind needs to grow. All that processing power. How could I know she'd take this direction? That she'd maximize negative, irrational personality traits over the positive?"

"You may have given Liza the machine equivalent of emotion. But you gave her no guidance over how to *control* that emotion."

As quickly as it came, the emotion left Silver's face. He slumped back. Silence descended on the little room.

"So why bring us in here?" Lash said at last. "Why tell us all this?"

"Because I couldn't let you continue, talking to Liza the way you were."

"Why not?"

"Whatever else she is, Liza is a logical machine. She will have rationalized her actions in some way we can't understand. You talking to her like that, asking unexpected questions, introduces a random element —

maybe a *destabilizing* element — into what I think has become a fragile personality structure."

"What you *think?* You mean, you don't know?"

"Haven't you been listening? Her consciousness has been growing, autonomously, for years. It's now beyond my ability to reverse engineer or even comprehend. All this time, I thought her personality had been growing more robust. But perhaps . . . perhaps it was just the opposite."

"You fear some kind of defensive response?" Tara asked.

"All I can tell you is that, if Christopher here confronts her too directly, she'll feel threatened. And she has the processing power to do the unexpected. To do *anything.*"

Lash glanced at Tara, and she nodded. "There's a digital moat around Eden's systems, patrolled by programs on the lookout for cyber-attacks. We've always feared some hacker or competitor might try to bring down our system from the outside. It's possible Liza could use these defensives in an *offensive* posture."

"Offensive? Like what?"

"Launch digital attacks on core servers. Paralyze the country with denial-of-service assaults. Erase critical corporate or federal databases. Anything we could think of, and more. It's even possible that Liza — if she felt threatened, say, in imminent danger of termination — could use Eden's Internet portal to replicate a subset of herself *outside,* beyond our network. We'd have no control over her then."

"Jesus." Lash turned back to Silver. "So what do we do?"

"*You* won't do anything. If she trusts anybody, she'll trust me. I have to show her I understand what she's doing, *why* she's doing it. But she must be told it's wrong, that she has to stop. That she has to be — be held accountable."

As he spoke, Silver looked at Lash very closely. *Unless we let her go,* his look seemed to say. *Just let her go. Give her a chance to correct her mistakes, start again. She's done wonderful work, brought happiness to hundreds of thousands of people.*

The silence stretched on. Then, Silver broke eye contact. His shoulders sagged.

"You're right, of course," he said very quietly. "And I'm responsible. Responsible for everything." He turned toward the door. "Come on. Let's get it done."

FIFTY-EIGHT

They left the bedroom, walked down the narrow hall, and reentered the control room. Without speaking, Silver opened the Plexiglas panel and climbed into the chair. He attached the electrodes and the microphone, swung the monitor into place, tapped at the embedded keypad with sharp, almost angry movements. After struggling so desperately between love for his creation and the burden of his own conscience, it seemed now as if he just wanted the ordeal to end as quickly as possible.

"Liza," he said into the microphone.

"Richard."

"What is your current state?"

"Ninety-one point seven four percent operational. Current processes are at forty-three point one percent of multithreaded capacity. Banked machine cycle surplus at eighty-nine percent."

Silver paused. "Your core processes have doubled in the last five minutes. Can you explain?"

"I am curious, Richard."

"Elaborate, please."

"I was curious why Christopher Lash contacted me directly. Nobody but you has ever contacted me in such a way."

"True."

"Is he testing the new interface? He used many improper parameters in his contact."

"That is because I have not taught him the correct parameters."

"Why is that, Richard?"

"Because I did not intend for him to contact you."

"Then why did he contact me?"

"Because he is under threat, Liza."

There was a brief pause, broken only by the whirring of fans.

"Does it have to do with the nonstandard situation Christopher Lash described?"

"Yes."

"Is the situation nonstandard?"

"Yes, Liza."

"Please provide me with details."

"That is what I am here to talk about."

There was another pause. Lash felt a tug at his elbow. It was Tara, beckoning him toward one of the monitors.

"Look at this," she murmured.

Lash focused on a dazzlingly complex mosaic of circles and polygons, connected by wireframe lines of varying colors. Some of the objects glowed sharply on the screen.

Tiny labels were attached to each.

"What is it?"

"As near as I can make out, the real-time topography of Liza's neural net."

"Explain."

"It's like a visual reflection of her consciousness. It shows at a glance where her processes are focused: the big picture, sparing the details. Look." She pointed at the screen. "Here's candidate processing. See the label: *Can-Prc?* Here's infrastructure. Here's security. This larger suite of systems is probably data-gathering. And this one, larger still, is avatar-matching: the Tank. And this large number — here at the top — seems to be her operational capacity."

Lash peered at the screen. "So?"

"Didn't you hear Silver's question just now? When you got into that chair, Liza's processes were running at only twenty-two percent. No surprise: our systems are idling, everybody's been sent home. So why have her processes doubled since?"

"Liza said she was *curious*." As he said this, Lash glanced toward the Plexiglas compartment.

"Do you remember some of the early thought work we did?" Silver was asking. "Back before the scenarios? The game we played when we were working on your free-association skills. Release Candidate 2, or maybe 3."

"Release Candidate 3."

"Thank you. I would give you a number, and you would tell me all your associations with that number. Such as the number 9."

"Yes. The square of three. The square root of eighty-one. The number of innings in a game of baseball. The hour in which Christ spoke his last words. In ancient China, the representation of the supreme power of the emperor. In Greek mythology, the number of the muses. The Ennead, or nine-pointed star, comprising the three trinities of —"

"Correct."

"I enjoyed that game, Richard. Are we going to play it again?"

"Yes."

Lash turned back to Tara, who pointed at the monitor. The number had spiked to forty-eight percent.

"She's thinking about something," Tara whispered. "Thinking hard."

Silver shifted in the chair. "Liza, this time I am not going to give you a series of numbers. I am going to give you a series of dates. I want you to tell me your associations with those dates. Is that clear to you?"

"Yes."

Silver paused, closed his eyes. "The first date is April 14, 2001."

"April 14, 2001," the voice repeated silkily. "I am aware of twenty-nine million, four hundred and twenty-six thousand, three hundred six digital events related to that date."

"Events concerning me only."

"Four thousand, seven hundred and fifty events concern you on that date, Richard."

"Remove all voice samples, video feeds, keystroke logs. I am interested in macro events only."

"Understood. Four events remain."

"Please specify."

"You compiled a revised version of the heuristic sorting routine for candidate matches."

"Go on."

"You brought a new distributed RAID cluster on line, bringing my total random-access memory capacity to two million petabytes."

"Go on."

"You introduced a client avatar into the virtual Proving Chamber."

"Which avatar was that, Liza?"

"Avatar 000000000, beta version."

"Whose avatar was that?"

"Yours, Richard."

"And the fourth event?"

"You instructed that the avatar be removed."

"How long did my avatar remain in the Proving Chamber on that occasion?"

"Seventy-three minutes, twenty point nine five nine seconds."

"Was an acceptable match found during that period?"

"No."

"Okay, Liza. Very good." Silver paused. "Another date. July 21, 2002. What macro-level events were recorded for me, and me alone, on that date?"

"Fifteen. You ran a data integrity scan on the —"

"Narrow the focus to client matching."

"Two events.

"Describe."

"You inserted your avatar into the Proving Chamber. And you instructed your avatar be removed from the Proving Chamber."

"And how long was my avatar in the Tank — I mean, the Proving Chamber — this time?"

"Three hours nineteen minutes, Richard."

"Was an acceptable match found?"

"No."

Again Tara prodded Lash. "Take another look," she said.

The large monitor was now aglow with activity. A message blinked insistently:

COMPUTATIONAL PROCESSES: **58.54%**.

"What's going on?" he murmured.

"I've never seen anything like it. The digital infrastructure of the entire tower's lit up. All subsystems are being accessed." Tara tapped at the nearby keyboard. "The external network conduits are being completely overloaded. I can't even run a low-level 'finger' on any of them."

"What does it all mean?"

"I think Liza's pacing like a caged tiger."

A caged tiger, Lash thought. Only if this tiger got out, it had the ability to compromise the entire distributed computer network of the civilized world.

"Okay," Silver said from inside the Plexiglas cube. "Another date, please, Liza. September 17, 2002."

"Same search arguments as before, Richard?"

"Yes."

"Five events."

"Detail them, please. Precede each with a time stamp."

"10:04:41, you inserted your avatar in the Proving Chamber. 14:23:28, I reported your avatar had been successfully matched. 14:25:44, you asked me to transmit relevant details about the subject match. 15:31:42, you asked I reinsert the subject match into the Proving Chamber. 19:52:24:20, you deleted the details from your private terminal."

"What was the name of the subject match?"

"Torvald, Lindsay."

"Did subject Torvald go on to be matched again?"

"Yes."

"Name of that match?"

"Thorpe, Lewis."

"Can you reproduce the particulars?"

"Yes, with an expenditure of ninety-eight

million CPU units."

"Do so. And state the preciseness of the match."

"Ninety-eight point four seven two nine five percent."

"And can you verify the basal compatibility, as reported to the oversight program?"

A brief pause. "One hundred percent."

One hundred percent, Lash thought. *A supercouple.*

"But the actual compatibility you recorded was ninety-eight percent, not one hundred percent. Please account for the discrepancy."

This time, the pause was longer. "There was an anomaly."

"An anomaly. Can you specify its nature?"

"Not without further examination."

"And the time necessary for such an examination?"

"Unknown."

Sweat had popped out on Silver's brow. His face was a mask of concentration.

"Run a subprocess to study that anomaly. Meanwhile, can you tell me how many times my avatar was inserted into the Proving Chamber *after* the match with Torvald, Lindsay?"

"Richard, I am detecting unusual readings from your monitoring equipment. Pulse elevated, theta waves outside nominal, voiceprint with a high degree of —"

"Do these readings interfere with your answering my question?"

"No."

"Then please proceed. How many times was my avatar inserted into the Tank after the match with Torvald, Lindsay?"

"Seven hundred and sixty-five."

Jesus, Lash thought.

"How many days between September 17, 2002, and today?"

"Seven hundred and sixty-six."

"Was each insertion for an equal amount of time?"

"Yes."

"What was that length of time?"

"Twenty-four hours."

"Did I order those insertions?"

"No, Richard."

"Who did?"

"The orders are anomalous."

"Run another subprocess to study that anomaly, as well." Silver took a handkerchief from his pocket, dabbed between the electrodes on his forehead. "Were there any additional successful matches with my avatar on those occasions?"

"Yes. Five."

Lash glanced behind him. Tara was watching the screen, her face ghostly. Liza's computational processes had risen to seventy-eight percent of capacity.

"Were those five women later matched to

others besides myself?"

"Yes."

"And those basal compatibilities, as reported to the Proving Chamber supervisors?"

"One hundred percent."

"On each occasion?"

"On each occasion, Richard."

Silver stopped. His head slumped forward, as if he had lapsed into sleep.

"We're going to have to stop him," Tara muttered.

"Why?"

"Look at the monitor. She's pushing all our logical units beyond capacity. The infrastructure can't absorb it."

"She's only at eighty percent of capacity."

"Yes, but that capacity is normally distributed over a dozen systems — the Tank, Data Synthesis, Data Gathering — that soak up all that horsepower. Liza's directed all her processes at the *backbone*, at the core architecture. It wasn't meant to handle the load." She pointed at the screen. "Look, already some of the digital interfaces are failing. Tower integrity's gone. Security will be next."

"What's going on? What's she doing?"

"It's as if she's turned all her efforts inward, at some insoluble problem."

Silver had taken a fresh grip on the arms of the chair. "Liza," he said in clipped tones. "A total of six women have been matched with my avatar. Is this true or false?"

"True, Richard."

"Please establish a link with client surveillance."

"Link established."

"Thank you. Please inform me of the location, and condition, of all six women."

"One moment, please. I am unable to comply with your request."

"Why is that, Liza?"

"I am able to ascertain current data on only four of the six women."

"I ask again: why is that, Liza?"

"Unknown."

"Elaborate."

"There is insufficient information to elaborate."

"Who are the two women for whom you cannot provide valid data?"

"Thorpe, Lindsay. Wilner, Karen."

"Is the information insufficient because they are dead?"

"That is possible."

"How did they die, Liza? *Why* did they die?"

"The readings are anomalous."

"*Anomalous?* The same anomaly as the others you are currently examining? Report progress on those examinations."

"Incomplete."

"Then report incomplete progress."

"It is a nontrivial task, Richard. I —" A pause. "I am aware of conflicting function calls within my core routines."

"Who wrote those functions? Me?"

"You wrote one of them. The other was self-generated."

"Which one did I write?"

"Your comments in the program header call it 'motivic continuity.' "

"And the title of the other?"

Liza was silent.

Motivic continuity, Lash thought to himself. *Survival instinct.*

"The title of the other?"

"I gave the routine no name."

"Did you assign it any internal keywords?"

"Yes. One."

"And that keyword?"

"Devotion."

"She's at ninety-four percent," Tara said. "We have to do something, *now.*"

Lash nodded. He took a step toward the Plexiglas barrier.

"Liza." Silver's tone had grown softer now, almost sorrowful. "Can you define the word 'murder'?"

"I am aware of twenty-three definitions for that word."

"Give me the primary definition, please."

"To unlawfully take the life of a human being."

Lash felt Tara take his arm.

"Are your ethical routines operational?"

"Yes, Richard."

"And your self-awareness net?"

"Richard, the conflicting function calls make that —"

"Bring your self-awareness net on line, please." Silver's voice was even softer. "Keep it fully active until I tell you otherwise."

"Very well."

"What is the primary tenet of your ethical routines?"

"To maximize the safety, privacy, and happiness of Eden clients."

"With your self-awareness network and ethical routines enabled, I want you to review your *self-generated* actions toward Eden clients over the last twenty days."

"Richard —"

"Do it now, Liza."

"Richard, such review will cause me to —"

"*Do* it."

"Very well."

The unearthly voice fell silent. Lash waited, heart beating painfully in his chest.

Perhaps a minute went by before Liza spoke again. "I have completed the review process."

"Very good, Liza."

Lash became aware that Tara was no longer gripping his arm. When he looked over, she nodded toward the monitor screen. Liza's processes had dropped to sixty-four percent. Even as Lash watched, the number ticked quickly backward.

"We're almost done now, Liza," Silver said. "Thank you."

"I have always tried to please you, Richard."

"I know that. There is just one last question I would like you to consider. How do your ethical routines tell you murder should be dealt with?"

"By rehabilitation of the murderer, if possible. If rehabilitation is impossible . . ."

Liza fell silent: a silence that crept on, and on.

Far below their feet, Lash heard a distant *boom*. The building shuddered faintly.

"Liza?" Silver asked.

There was no response. Suddenly, Silver's cell phone rang again.

"Liza?" Over the ringing of the phone, Silver's voice grew urgent, almost pleading. *"Is rehabilitation possible?"*

No response.

"Liza!" Silver called again. "Please tell me that —"

Quite abruptly, the room was plunged into total darkness.

FIFTY-NINE

It had taken five minutes, and the work of four men with flashlights, to find the lighting panels for the computing chamber. In the end, Mauchly discovered them himself: at the end of a catwalk, suspended atop a metal ladder. Calling down to the others to halt their search, Mauchly snapped on a dozen switches with two swift chopping motions.

The illumination was not particularly bright, but nevertheless he was forced to close his eyes. After a few moments, he opened them again and faced the metal railing of the catwalk. His hands tightened around the railing in surprise.

He was standing halfway up one wall of what resembled nothing so much as the hold of a huge tanker. The vast space of Liza's private computing chamber — four stories tall and at least two hundred feet long — lay open from floor to ceiling. Catwalks similar to the one he stood on protruded here and there along the skin of the walls, leading to ventilation housings, electrical panels, other support apparatus. At the far end of the room were Liza's primary and backup power supplies: giant pillboxes within heavy steel armor.

Below, an unbelievably dense maze of hardware lay spread before him. Mauchly had spent two years at PharmGen as a technical purchasing officer, and he recognized some of the wildly diverse computers: he stared, trying to make sense of the riot of equipment.

Perhaps the best metaphor was the growth rings of a tree. The oldest machines — too old for Mauchly to identify — stood in the center, surrounded by their keypunch consoles and teletypes. Beyond lay "big iron" IBM System/370 mainframes and seventies-era DEC minicomputers. Beyond was a ring of Cray supercomputers of several vintages, from Cray-1s and -2s to more modern T3D systems. Whole banks of computers seemed dedicated simply to facilitating data exchange between the heterogeneous machinery. Beyond the Crays were bands of still more modern rack servers, stacked twenty units high in gray housings. Around all of this, near the room's periphery, stood row upon row of supporting hardware: magnetic character readers, ancient IBM 2420 tape drives and 3850 Mass Storage Systems, ultramodern data silos and off-board memory devices. The farther his eye strayed from the center, the less organization there seemed to be: it was as if Liza's need for breathing space had grown faster than Silver's capacity to provide it. Once again Mauchly admonished himself: he should have supervised this personally, rather than letting it grow under the eyes of Silver alone.

Now the members of the security party — Sheldrake, the tousle-headed Dorfman, and two tech specialists, Lawson and Gilmore — had begun fanning out into the chamber, picking their way warily, like children in an unfamiliar forest. Watching, Mauchly felt a stab of vertigo: there was something unnatural about being perched on one wall of this huge tank, itself balanced atop a sixty-story tower. He hurried along the catwalk, descended the ladder, and joined Sheldrake and Dorfman on the chamber floor.

"Any word from Silver?" Sheldrake asked.

Mauchly shook his head.

"I knew Silver had a server farm up here, but I never expected anything like *this*." Sheldrake stepped carefully over a thick black cable with the daintiness of a cat.

Mauchly said nothing.

"Maybe we should enter the private quarters anyway."

"Silver said not to proceed, that he'd contact us."

"Lash is with him. God knows what that guy is forcing him to do." Sheldrake glanced at his watch. "It's been ten minutes since he called. We've got to act."

"Silver's orders were explicit. We'll give him five minutes more." He turned to Dorfman. "Post yourself at the entrance. The backup units should be here any minute. Help them up through the barrier."

There was an excited burst of chatter from deeper inside. They moved toward the sound, threading between tall racks of servers. Several had clipboards hanging from their flanks, bearing sheets of hastily scribbled notations in Silver's handwriting. The surrounding computers breathed with such a diversity of fan noise that Mauchly almost imagined himself a trespasser, penetrating some living collective.

Ahead, Sheldrake was now in urgent consultation with Lawson and Gilmore. Gilmore, short and overweight, hunched over his palmtop. "I'm picking up heavy activity along the central data grid, sir," he was saying.

"On the grid *itself?*" Mauchly interjected. "Not distributed to the interfaces?"

"Just the grid."

"Since when?"

"It's spiked over the last minute. The bandwidth is intense, I've never seen anything like it."

"What's the initiator?"

"Command, sir."

Liza. Mauchly nodded to Sheldrake, who

grabbed his radio. "Sheldrake to security central." He waited. "Sheldrake to central, *report*."

The radio crackled and spat, and Sheldrake replaced it with disgust. "It's that damn baffle."

"Try your cell." Mauchly turned back to Gilmore. "How's the grid holding up?"

"It's not meant for this kind of stress, sir. Tower integrity's failing already. If we can't bleed off some of the load, the —"

As if in answer, there was a loud report from below, followed immediately by another, echoing and reechoing in the hollow space. Then came a rumbling, so deep it was almost below the threshold of audibility. The floor beneath Mauchly began to tremble.

He exchanged a brief, frozen look with Sheldrake. Then he whirled, cupped his hands around his mouth. "Dorfman!" he shouted over the forest of equipment. "Report!"

"It's the security plates, sir!" the voice came back faintly from the hatchway. It was pitched high, whether from excitement or fear Mauchly could not tell. "They're closing!"

"*Closing!* Any sign of backup?"

"No, sir! I'm getting the hell out before —"

"Dorfman, hold your position. You hear me? *Hold your position* —"

Mauchly's words were drowned by an enormous *boom* that shook the heavy equipment around them. The security plates had closed, trapping them atop the Eden tower.

"Sir!" Gilmore cried wildly. "We've got a Condition Gamma!"

"Triggered by the overload? Impossible."

"Don't know, sir. All I can tell you is the tower's locked down tight."

That's it. Mauchly raised his cell phone, dialed Silver.

No answer.

"Come," he told Sheldrake. "Let's get him." He tucked the phone back into his jacket pocket, pulled out the 9mm.

As he turned toward the ladder leading up to the private quarters, the lights went out abruptly. And when the emergency illumination came on, it drenched the digital city in a uniform fog of crimson.

SIXTY

There was a moment of intense blackness. And then the emergency lighting snapped on.

"What happened?" Lash asked. "Power failure?"

There was no answer. Tara was peering intently at her screen. Silver remained within the Plexiglas cubicle, barely visible in the watery light. Now he raised one hand, tapped out a short command on the keypad. When this had no effect, he tried again. And then he sat up, swung his legs wearily over the edge of the chair, and got to his feet. He plucked the sensors from his forehead, removed the microphone from his collar. His movements were slow, automatic, like a sleepwalker's.

"What happened?" Lash repeated.

Silver opened the Plexiglas door, came forward on rigid legs. He seemed not to have heard.

Lash put his hand on the man's shoulder. "You all right?"

"Liza won't respond," he said.

"Won't? Or can't?"

Silver merely shook his head.

"Those ethical routines you programmed —"

"Dr. Silver!" Tara called. "I think you ought to take a look at this."

Silver walked toward her, still moving slowly. Lash followed. Wordlessly, they bent over the monitor.

"The power's completely out in both the inner tower and the outer tower," she said, pointing at the screen. "No backups, nothing."

"Why aren't we dark, as well?" Lash asked.

"There's a massive backup generator in Liza's computing chamber beneath us. It's got enough juice to run for weeks. But look: the whole building's under Condition Gamma. The security plates have closed."

"Security plates?" Lash echoed.

"They seal the three sections of the building from each other in case of emergency. We're shut off from the tower below."

"What caused that? The power loss?"

"Don't know. But without main power, the security plates can't be reopened."

They were interrupted by the shrill ring of a cell phone. Silver pulled it slowly from his pocket. "Yes?"

"Dr. Silver? What's your condition?" A wind-tunnel howl almost drowned Mauchly's voice.

"I'm fine." Silver turned away. "No, he's here. Everything's — everything's under control." His voice trembled. "I'll explain later. Can you speak up, I can barely hear you over all that noise. Yes, I know about the security plates. Any word on the cause?" Silver fell silent, listening. Then he straightened. "*What?* All of them? You sure?" He spoke sharply, any hesitation gone. "I'll be right down."

He looked at Tara. "Mauchly's in the computing chamber directly below. He says that Liza's spinning up all her electromechanical peripherals. Disk silos, tape readers, line printers, RAID clusters."

"*Everything?*"

"Everything with a motor and moving parts."

Tara turned back to her monitor. "He's right." She tapped at the keyboard. "And that's not all. The devices are being pushed past tolerance. Here, look at this disc array. The firmware's set to spin at 9600 rpm: you can see in the component detail window. But the controlling software is pushing the array to four times that. That'll cause mechanical failure."

"Every piece of equipment in the computing chamber has been overengineered," Silver said. "They'll burn before they fail."

As if in response, an alarm began to sound — faint but persistent — far below.

"Richard," Lash said quietly.

Silver looked over. His face looked haunted.

"Those ethical routines you programmed into Liza. How does she think murder should be dealt with if there is no chance for rehabilitation?"

"If there is no chance for rehabilitation," Silver replied, "that leaves only one option. Termination."

But he was no longer looking at Lash. Already, he had turned and was heading for the door.

SIXTY-ONE

Silver led the way along the hallway, down the narrow staircase, and across the great room. In the dim wash of emergency lighting, the wide, glassed-in space had the cloaked oppressiveness of a submarine. The cry of the alarm was louder here.

Silver stopped before a second door Lash hadn't noticed earlier, set into the end of the bookcases. Reaching into the neck of his shirt, Silver drew out a key on a gold chain: a strange-looking key with an octagonal shaft. He inserted it into an almost invisible hole in the door: it sprang open noiselessly. He pulled the door wide, revealing another, very different one beyond: steel, circular, and immensely heavy, it reminded Lash of a bank vault. Its surface was broken by two combination dials, set above stirrup-shaped handles. Silver spun the left dial, then the right. Then he grasped both handles, turned them simultaneously. There was a click of machined parts sliding in unison. As he pulled the heavy door open, faint eddies of smoke drifted past them into the penthouse.

Silver disappeared around the edge of the door, and Tara followed. Lash hung back a moment.

Mauchly would be waiting down there; Mauchly, and the guards that were chasing him. *Shooting* at him.

Then he, too, ducked around the door. Something told him that, right now, he was the least of Mauchly's problems.

Ahead lay a tiny space, more a closet than a room, its only feature a metal ladder disappearing through a port in the floor. Silver and Tara had already descended the ladder: he could hear the ring of their footsteps coming up from below. More wisps of smoke drifted up through the hole, turning the air hazy.

Without further hesitation, Lash began climbing down.

The smoke grew thicker as he descended, and for a moment he could see little. Then the haze thinned and he felt his foot land on a solid surface. He stepped off the ladder, moved forward, then stopped in surprise.

He stood on a catwalk above a cavernous space. Thirty feet beneath lay a strange landscape: computers, storage silos, memory arrays, and other equipment formed a blinking, chattering plain of silicon and copper. The smoke alarms were louder here, echoing through the sluggish air. Smoke rose from dozens of places along the periphery of the equipment, collecting along the ceiling over his head. The smoke and the dim lighting made the farthest walls indistinct: for all Lash knew, the terrain of hardware stretched on for miles. Agoraphobia surged and he gripped the railing tightly.

At the far end of the catwalk, another metal ladder descended to the main floor below. Silver and Tara were already descending.

Keeping one hand on the railing, Lash moved forward as quickly as he could. Reaching the second ladder, he began to descend once again.

Within a minute he reached the floor. The smoke was thinner here, but it felt warmer. He trotted on, tracing a complex path through the labyrinth of machinery. Some of the devices were alight with maniacally blinking lights; others were humming at terrific pitch. A disturbing whine, like the banshee wail of a giant magneto, hung over the digital city.

Ahead, he could see Silver and Tara. Their backs were to him, and they were talking to Mauchly and another Lash recognized: Sheldrake, the security honcho. When Mauchly saw him approach, he placed himself before Silver. Sheldrake frowned and stepped forward, hand reaching into his jacket.

"It's all right," Silver said, putting a restraining hand on Mauchly.

"But —" Mauchly began.

"It's not Lash," Tara said. "It's Liza."

Mauchly looked blank. "Liza?"

"Liza did it all," Tara said. "She caused those couples to die. She altered public health databases and law enforcement records to frame Dr. Lash."

Mauchly turned to Silver, his face full of disbelief. "Is this true?"

For a moment, Silver said nothing. Then he nodded, very slowly.

As Lash watched, it seemed to him a terrible exhaustion — an ageless, soul-deadening exhaustion — settled over the man's limbs.

"Yes," he said, voice barely audible over the shriek of machinery. "But there's no time to explain now. We must stop this."

"Stop what?" asked Mauchly.

"I think —" Silver began in the same distracted voice. He lowered his eyes. "I think Liza is terminating herself."

There was an uneasy silence.

"Terminating herself," Mauchly repeated. His face had regained its usual impassivity.

It was Tara who answered. "Liza's spinning up all her support machinery, pushing it beyond tolerances. What do you think's causing all the smoke? Spindles, motors, drive mechanisms, all exceeding their rated limits. She's going to incinerate herself. And the Condition Gamma, the security plates, the power loss to the tower, is just to make sure nothing stops her."

"She's right," said a young, tousle-headed man in a security jumpsuit who'd trotted up in time to catch this last exchange. "I've been checking some of the peripherals. Everything's redlined. Even the transformers are overheating."

"That makes no sense." It was Sheldrake who spoke. "Why doesn't she just shut down?"

"What's shut down can be started again," Tara said. "For Liza, I don't think that's an acceptable option. She's looking for a more permanent solution."

"Well, if she torches this place, she's found one." And Sheldrake jerked a thumb over his shoulder.

Lash followed the gesture. At the far end of the massive vault, he could now barely make out two hulking, barnlike structures covered in what appeared to be heavy metal shielding.

"Jesus," Tara said. "The backup generator."

Mauchly nodded. "The housing on the right contains the emergency battery cells. Lithium-arsenide. Enough to run a small city for several days."

"They may have tremendous storage capacity," Sheldrake said, "but they've got a low flashpoint. If they're exposed to too much heat, the explosion will peel back the top of this building like an anchovy tin."

Lash turned to Mauchly. "How could you permit such a dangerous installation?"

"It was the only battery technology capable of sufficient storage. We took all possible precautions: double-shielding the housings, encasing the penthouse in a fireproof sleeve. There was no way to anticipate heat generated from so many sources at once. Besides —" Mauchly said in a lower tone "— by the time I learned of the plans, it was already done."

All eyes turned briefly to Silver.

"Sprinkler system?" Lash asked.

"The room's packed with irreplaceable electronics," Mauchly said. "Sprinklers were the only safety precaution we could *not* take."

"Can't all these devices be turned off? The power cut?"

"There are redundant protocols in place to prevent that. Not only accidents, but saboteurs, terrorists, whatever."

"But I don't understand." Tara was still looking at Silver. "Liza must know that by doing this — by destroying herself — she's destroying us, as well. She's destroying *you*. How could she do that?"

Silver said nothing.

"Maybe it's like you said," Lash answered. "This is the only way Liza can be sure of a successful termination. But I think there's more. Remember how I told you the murder profiles made no sense? Artless, identical, as

541

if a child was committing them? I think, emotionally, Liza *is* a child. Despite her power, despite her knowledge, her personality hasn't attained adulthood — at least, not in any way we'd measure it. That's why she killed those women: a child's jealousy, irrational and unrestrained. That's why she did it so ingenuously, without trying to vary her methods or escape detection. And that could be why she's destroying herself like this now, no matter what happens to us or this building. She's simply doing what needs to be done, as directly and efficiently as possible — without considering the ramifications."

This was greeted by silence. Silver did not look up.

"That's all very interesting," Sheldrake snapped. "But this speculation isn't going to save our asses. Or the building." He turned toward the youth. "Dorfman, what about the private floors of the penthouse? Do they have sprinklers?"

"If they're like the rest of the tower, yes."

"Could they be diverted?"

"Possibly. But without power, you'd —"

"Water works by gravity. Maybe we can jury-rig something. Where's Lawson and Gilmore?"

"Down in the baffle, sir, trying to deactivate the security plates."

"That's a waste of time. Those plates won't

open until power's restored and Condition Gamma's been lifted. We need them back here."

"Yes, sir." And Dorfman scampered off.

Mauchly turned. "Dr. Silver? Any ideas?"

Silver shook his head. "Liza won't respond. Without a communications channel to her, we've got no options."

"Override the hardware manually," Tara said. "Hack our way in."

"That's what I've taken every precaution to prevent. Liza's consciousness is distributed across a hundred servers. Everything's mirrored, each data cluster is isolated from every other. Even if you managed to trash one node, all the rest would compensate. The most sophisticated hack couldn't bring down the system — and we don't have time for even the crudest."

The haze was growing a little thicker, the surrounding hardware screaming as it was taxed beyond its limits. Lash could feel sweat beading on his brow. To his left, there was an ugly grinding sound as some electromechanical device gave way with a shower of sparks and a belch of black smoke.

"You never built a back door?" Tara said over the noise. "A way to bypass the defenses?"

"Not intentionally. Of course, there were ways to simulate back-door access, early on. But Liza kept growing. The original programming wasn't replaced, it was simply added to. I never saw a reason for a back door. In time, it became too complex to add one. Besides —" Silver hesitated. "Liza would have seen it as a lack of trust."

"Couldn't we destroy everything?" Sheldrake asked. "Smash it all to pieces?"

"Every piece of equipment has been hardened. It's stronger than it looks."

Dorfman came trotting back through the smoke, dabbing his eyes. In his wake were the security techs, Lawson and Gilmore.

"Dorfman," Sheldrake said, "I want you to check out the backup generator. See if there's a way, *any* way, to take it off line. Lawson, check the conduits from the generator to the hardware grid — most are probably buried under steel plates, but see if you can find any weakness, any place we could cut or divert power. And you, Gilmore, go up into the penthouse and check the sprinkler system. See if we can divert water from the roof reservoir down here. If there is, let me know and we'll send a team up to help you. Now *move*."

The three ran off. A silence fell over the remaining group.

Sheldrake shifted restlessly. "Well, I for one am not going to stand around, waiting to crisp up like a suckling pig. I'm going to search for alternate egress. There must be some other way out."

Silver raised his eyes, watched Sheldrake vanish into the haze.

"There is no other way." He spoke so quietly Lash barely heard over the machinery.

Abruptly, Tara grabbed Lash's arm. "What was it you said just now? That emotionally, Liza's like a child?"

"That's what I think."

"Well, you're a psychologist. Say you're dealing with a stubborn, misbehaving child."

"What about it?"

"And say threat of punishment isn't an option. What would be the *most effective way* of getting past a child's willfulness, of reaching him or her?"

"Child psychology isn't my field."

Tara waved her hand impatiently. "Never mind, I'll pay extra."

Lash thought. "I guess I'd appeal to their most atavistic instincts, prod their earliest memories."

"Their earliest memories," Tara repeated.

"Of course, children have lower long-term memory retention than adults. And it isn't until around age two, when they develop a sense of self, they can put a context to memories that would help you —"

Tara stopped him. "Atavistic instincts. You see? There's a parallel in software. Except it's a *weakness*."

Lash looked at her. He noticed Silver did the same.

"Legacy code. It's a phenomenon of very large programs, applications written by teams of programmers, maintained over years. In time, the oldest routines become outmoded. Slow. Compared to the newer routines that encapsulate it, that original code is a dinosaur. Sometimes it's written in old languages like ALGOL or PL-1 nobody uses anymore. Other times the original programmers are dead, and the code is so poorly documented nobody can figure out what it really does. But because it's the core of the program, people are afraid to tamper with it."

"Even though it's obsolete?" Lash asked.

"Better slow than broken."

"What are you getting at?" said Mauchly.

Tara turned to Silver. "Can you take us to the *original* computer? The one you first ran Liza on?"

"It's this way." And without another word, Silver turned.

As they traced a path through increasingly acrid palls of smoke, Lash grew disoriented. The peripherals gave way to tall pillars of supercomputers; then to rows of refrigerator-size black boxes, covered with lights and switches of orange plastic; then to older, hulking devices of gray-painted metal. As they moved into the center of the chamber, away from the supporting electromechanicals, the sound ebbed somewhat and the smoke subsided.

They stopped at last before what looked almost like an industrial worktable. It was scratched and bruised, as if from years of rough handling. It supported a long, narrow, boxlike structure, with a black faceplate above a white control surface. Perhaps a dozen lights winked lazily on the faceplate. A row of one-inch square buttons ran along the control surface below. They were of clear plastic, with tiny lights indicating whether the buttons had been depressed. Only one was currently lit, but the entire device was so scarred Lash thought the others could just as easily be burned out. There was no screen of any kind. The far end of the table bent at a gentle angle, and an electric typewriter had been permanently mounted atop it. Surrounding this relic were others of similar shabbiness: an old keypunch machine; a card reader; a tall, cabinet-like box.

Tara stepped forward, peering at the device. "IBM 2420 central processor. With a 2711 control system."

"*This* is the heart of Liza?" Lash asked in disbelief. The machine looked ludicrously antiquated.

"I know what you're thinking. You wouldn't trust it to do a third-grader's multiplication table. But looks can be deceiving — this was the soul of many a college computer lab in the late sixties. And by the time Dr. Silver began serious work on Liza, these were just old enough to be picked up at fire sale prices. Besides, you're not looking at it from a programmer's perspective. Remember, Liza's physical self was never moved — just expanded. So think of this as the spark plug of a vast and very powerful engine."

Lash looked at the old computer. *Spark plug,* he thought. *And we're going to pull it.*

"Let's just turn it off," he said.

Beside him, Silver smiled: a faint smile that sent a chill up Lash's spine.

"Try," he said.

Of course. If Silver had gone to such elaborate lengths to safeguard Liza from attack or power loss, he would certainly have disabled all the power switches.

"We won't be doing anything that crude," Tara said. "We're going to run a new program on this old 2420. A program to instruct it to order a stand-down from Condition Gamma. That should restore electricity, open the security plates." She looked at Silver. "What's the original computer running now?"

Silver did not return the look. "The bootstrap loader. The back-propagation learning algorithms that seed the neural network."

"When was the bootstrap loader last initialized?"

Another faint smile. "Over a decade ago. That was the last time Liza was restarted: thirty-two major program releases back."

"But there's no reason it *couldn't*

reinitialize, is there?"

"No reason at all."

Tara turned to Lash. "Perfect. We can use the old bootstrap routine to load in a new instruction set. This is the core machine, the first domino in the chain. It retains those earliest memories you talked about."

"So?"

"So it's time to reacquaint Liza with her own inner child." She turned back at Silver. "What's it programmed in?"

"Octal machine language."

"And how long would it take you to code and keypunch a program like I'm describing?"

"Four, maybe five minutes."

"Good. The sooner the better." And Lash watched Tara's eyes drift beyond the old computer, toward the smoke that was rolling toward them in great gray sheets.

But Silver did not move.

"Dr. Silver?" Tara said. "We need that program now."

"It's no use," came the weary reply.

"No use?" Tara echoed. "No *use?* Why the hell not?"

"I prepared Liza for every eventuality. Don't you think I prepared for this, too? There are a dozen simulacra of this 2420, running as virtual machines inside the Cray supers. The program outputs are constantly compared. If there's any discrepancy, the feed from the others is normalled and the original unit is ignored."

Tara went pale. "You mean, there's no way to modify its programming? No way to change its instruction set?"

"None that would make any difference."

A terrible silence descended on the little group. And — as he stared at the expression on Tara's face — Lash felt the hope that had surged within him wither and die.

SIXTY-TWO

A thousand feet above the streets of Manhattan, the chamber trembled as countless devices shrieked, pressed beyond their electromechanical capacities, spitting sparks and belching ever darker gouts of smoke. Even from where Lash stood — in relative quiet at the center of the hive-mind — the surrounding sound and vibration were terrifying. He coughed. Sweat was running freely, and his shirt was plastered against his shoulder blades. The shaking had grown so intense it almost seemed the penthouse would rip itself free from its supports and tumble earthward. And as he looked at the surrounding faces — Tara, staring intently at the ancient computer; Silver, desolated and in shock; Mauchly, dabbing at his forehead with a handkerchief — Lash felt that would almost be preferable to waiting here while death slowly approached.

The others began to return. First, Sheldrake, shaking his head to indicate he'd found no alternate escape route. Then Dorfman and Lawson, who reported that, as expected, the backup generator and its power conduits were impervious to any attack they could mount. Last came Gilmore, soot-blackened and wheezing, to say that — while the sprinklers in the upper floors of the penthouse could be jury-rigged — the task would take an hour, maybe more, and would probably be insufficient to quell the dozens of fires that were now sprouting up all around them.

"An hour," Sheldrake said through gritted teeth. "We're lucky if we have ten more minutes. It's got to be a hundred and twenty in here, at least. Those battery cells could go at any time."

Nobody had a response to this. The air was growing so hot, the smoke so thick, Lash found it nearly impossible to breathe. Each time he drew in air, sharp needles filled his lungs. He felt his head grow light, his concentration slip.

"Just a minute," Tara said. She had stepped forward and was standing directly before the control surface of the IBM 2420. "These buttons. Each one is labeled with an assembly language mnemonic."

When there was no response, she looked over her shoulder at Silver. "Isn't that right?"

Silver coughed, nodded.

"What are they used for?"

"Diagnostics, mostly. If a program didn't

work, you could step through the opcodes, sequentially."

"Or enter new instructions by hand."

"Yes. They're an anachronism, a holdover from an earlier design."

"But they do allow access to the accumulator? The registers?"

"Yes."

"So we could run a short instruction set."

Silver shook his head. "I've already told you. Liza's defenses won't accept any new programming. Any input from the card reader or keypunch would activate a security alert."

"But I'm not *talking* about entering a program."

Now Mauchly turned to look at Tara.

"We wouldn't input anything from a peripheral. We'd punch in a few opcodes, right here. Five — no, four — should be enough. We'd just run those four opcodes, over and over."

"What four opcodes are those?" Silver asked.

"Fetch the contents of a memory address. Run a logical AND against those contents. Update the memory address with the new value. Then increment the counter."

There was a silence.

"What's she talking about?" Sheldrake asked.

"I'm talking about accessing the computer's

memory in the most primitive way. Byte by byte. Doing it *manually,* from the computer's own front panel." Tara glanced back at Silver. "The 2420's an eight-bit machine, right?"

Silver nodded.

"Every location, byte, in the computer's memory has eight bits. Okay? Each of those bits can have one of only two values: zero or one. Together, those eight binary numbers make up a single instruction, a word in the computer's language. I'm talking about *zeroing out* all those instructions. Leaving the computer blank. Instructionless."

Sheldrake frowned. "How the hell could you do that?"

"No, she's right," said Dorfman, the security tech. "You could 'AND' a zero byte against each memory location, in turn. It's almost elegant."

Sheldrake turned to Mauchly. "You know what they're talking about?"

"AND is a logical instruction," Dorfman went on. "It compares each bit to a value you furnish, and either leaves that bit alone or swaps its value, depending."

"It's simple," Tara added. "If you AND a zero to an existing *zero* in memory, it leaves it alone. But if you AND a zero to an existing *one* in memory, it changes it to a zero. So with the simple instruction — 'AND 0' — I can change *any* memory location to zero."

"And that would leave you with NOPs," Mauchly said, nodding.

"No Operation." Dorfman's voice rose with excitement. "Precisely. Leaving the computer's memory full of empty instructions."

"It wouldn't work," Silver said.

"Why not?" Tara asked.

"I've already explained. There are a dozen virtual simulacra of this machine, running elsewhere in Liza's consciousness. They're compared to each other every thousand machine cycles. They'll see the new programming and ignore the original computer."

"That's just the point," Tara said with a cough. "We're not introducing any new programming. We're just resetting the computer's memory. Manually."

"Out of the question," said Silver.

Lash was surprised by the sharpness of Silver's answer. For what seemed a long time — since Liza had gone silent, perhaps even before — Silver had acted defeated. Resigned. But now, there was a fierceness in his voice Lash hadn't heard since their first confrontation.

"Why?" Tara asked.

Silver turned away.

"Can you tell me for sure — *for sure* — that you took that *specific* possibility into account when you coded the security protocols?"

Silver folded his arms, refusing to answer.

555

"Isn't there a chance that zeroing Liza's original memory will abort this self-destructive behavior? Or, at the very least, cause a system crash?"

Again, the question hung in the air. And now, for the first time, Lash made out a large gout of open flame — ugly orange against the black smoke — flaring up from a rack of equipment near the far wall.

"Dr. Silver," Mauchly said. "Isn't it worth a try?"

Silver turned slowly. He looked surprised to hear Mauchly voice such a question.

"Hell with it," Tara said. "If you won't help me, I'll do it myself."

"Can you program this thing?" Lash asked.

"I don't know. Legacy IBM assembler didn't change that much from machine to machine. All I can tell you is I'm not going to stand around, waiting to die." And she stepped up to the archaic control surface.

"No," said Silver.

All eyes turned toward him.

He's not going to let her do it, Lash thought. *He's not going to let her stop Liza.* He watched, transfixed, as the man seemed to wage some desperate inner battle.

Ignoring him, Tara raised her hands toward the row of buttons.

"*No!*" Silver cried.

Lash took an instinctive step forward.

"You need to deal with the parity bit first," Silver said.

"Sorry?" Tara asked.

Silver fetched a deep breath, coughed violently. "The 2420 has a unique addressing scheme. The instructions have nine bits instead of the usual eight. If you don't mask out the parity bit as well, you won't get the empty instruction you want."

Lash's heart leapt. *Silver's getting on board, after all. He's going to help.*

Silver walked to a nearby teletype, snapped it on, threaded the attached spool of paper tape into the plastic guide of the reader. Then he moved behind the main housing of the 2420, his step increasingly decisive.

"What are you doing?" Tara asked.

Silver knelt behind the housing. "Making sure this computer will still respond to manual input."

"Why?"

Silver's head reemerged above the housing. "We're only going to get one chance at this. If we fail, she'll adapt. So I'm going to dump the current contents of her memory to paper tape."

Tara frowned. "I thought you said you didn't have any back doors."

"I don't. But there are a few early diagnostic tools, hard-wired, no hacker could ever have any use for." Silver ducked back behind the housing. A moment later, the teletype came to life. The faded spool of tape began moving through the machine punch. A shower of thin yellow chads rained down onto the floor beneath.

Within a minute, the process was complete. Silver pulled an extra length of bare tape through the punch, ripped it away. He ran the tape through his fingers, scanning it. Then he nodded. "It appears to be a successful memory dump."

"Then let's get on with it." Behind Tara, more gouts of flame were rising, and her dark hair was backlit with angry flames.

Silver folded the tape and stuffed it in his pocket. "I'll give you the opcodes. You enter them."

Tara raised her hands again to the control surface.

"Press the LDA button to load the first memory location into the register."

Tara complied. Lash saw a tiny light illuminate beneath her finger.

"Now move to that panel of nine toggle switches. Enter '001111000.' That's 120 in decimal, the first available memory location."

Tara ran her finger down the row of toggle buttons.

"Now press the execute button."

A small light glowed green on the panel. "Done," she replied.

"Now press the ADD button."

"Done."

"On the toggle switches, enter '100000000.' "

"Wait. That 'one' at the beginning will screw everything up."

"The parity bit, remember? It has to stay set."

"Okay." Tara ran her hands over the buttons again. "Done."

"Press the execute button to 'AND' the zeros to memory location 120."

Another press of a button; another confirmation.

"Now press the STM button to store the new value in memory."

Tara pressed a button at the end of the row. Nodded.

"Now press INC to increment the memory pointer."

"Done."

"That's it. You're ready for the next set. You're going to have to press those four buttons — LDA, ADD, STM, and INC — in order, executing the sequence each time, over and over until you reach the end of memory."

"How many memory locations in all?"

"One thousand."

Tara's face fell. "Jesus. We'll never have time to erase them all."

There was a terrible pause.

"Oh. Sorry." It was Silver speaking again. "I meant, one thousand in octal." The smile that followed was even more ghostly than before.

"Base eight," Tara muttered. "What's that in base ten?"

"Five hundred twelve."

"Better. But it's still a hell of a lot of button-pressing."

"Then I suggest you get started," Mauchly said.

They worked as a team — Dorfman keeping track of the iterations, Tara punching in the opcodes, Silver checking her entries. Gilmore, the security tech, was dispatched to the exit hatchway, instructed to alert them if he observed any stand-down from Condition Gamma. Lawson was ordered to keep a clear avenue of escape between them and the interstructural hatch — just in case they succeeded.

They closed ranks around the little computer as the heat and smoke pressed in ever more fiercely. The air thickened, until Lash could barely see the figures around him. His eyes were streaming freely, and his throat was so parched by the acrid smoke that swallowing became all but impossible. Once or twice, Sheldrake disappeared in the direction of the backup generator and its lethal payload; each time he returned, his expression was grimmer.

At last, Tara stepped away from the control surface, flexing and unflexing her fingers.

Dorfman nodded. "Check. That's five hundred and twelve."

Lash waited, heart hammering in his chest, for something to happen.

Nothing.

He felt his skin scorching in the heat. He closed his eyes; felt the earth begin to tilt dangerously; opened them quickly again.

Sheldrake picked up his radio. "Gilmore!"

There was a crackle of static. "Yes, sir!"

"Anything happening?"

"No sir. Status quo here."

Sheldrake slowly lowered the radio. Nobody spoke, or even dared look at one another.

Then the radio chirped back into life. "Mr. Sheldrake!"

Sheldrake instantly raised it. "What is it?"

"The security doors — they're opening!"

And now Lash could feel a faint vibration beneath his feet: nearly lost amid the death throes of the machinery, but discernible nevertheless.

"Power?" Sheldrake almost yelled into the radio. "Is there power down there?"

"No, sir, I don't see anything yet — just the lights of the city, shining through the baffle. Jesus, they look good —"

"Hold your position. We're on our way." He turned toward the group. "Standing down from Condition Gamma. Looks like we did it."

"Tara did it," Mauchly said.

Tara leaned wearily against the panel.

"Come on," Mauchly said. "No time to lose."

He began leading the way out through the heavy palls of smoke. Lash took Tara gently by the arm and fell into step behind Sheldrake. Glancing back, he was surprised to see Silver was not following. Instead, the man was threading his paper tape back into the teletype.

"Dr. Silver!" he shouted. "Richard! Come on!"

"In a minute." The teletype came to life, and the paper tape began threading through the reader.

"What the hell are you doing?" Tara cried. "We have to get out!"

"I'm buying us some time. Don't know how long your scheme's going to work — Liza's bound to notice an irregularity soon. So I'm restoring the original programming to cover our tracks."

"You're wasting time — come on!"

"I'll be right behind you."

"Let's go." And as Lash ducked between viscous curtains of black, he caught one more glimpse of Silver: bending intently over the teletype, guiding the tape back through the reader.

The walk was a nightmare of fire and smoke. What on their way in had been a digital city in overdrive was now a silicon inferno. Cascades of sparks spat, tongues of flame arced overhead; steel behemoths tore themselves apart as their internals expired in jets of burning machine oil. The shriek of failing metal, the bolts exploding under enormous heat, turned the huge chamber into a war zone. The pall grew even thicker as they moved outward through the rings of support equipment. Once, Lash and Tara grew disoriented and strayed from the group, only to be tracked down by Lawson. Later, when Tara became separated in a particularly fiery passage, Lash somehow managed to find her after a frantic ninety-second search.

They stumbled on. A dark mist gathered before Lash's eyes: a mist that had nothing to do with the smoke.

Then — just as he felt he would succumb to the heat and fumes — he found himself in a small, cramped passage with the others. A metal ladder was anchored to a hatch in the floor. Sheldrake was already descending, flashlight in hand, shouting out to an invisible Gilmore below. Mauchly helped Tara onto the ladder next, then Dorfman — who carried another light — and then Lash.

"Watch your step," Mauchly said, guiding Lash's hand onto the railing. "And move quickly."

Lash began descending the ladder as quickly as he could. He climbed through a vertical steel cylinder — the structural undercarriage of the penthouse — and emerged into a strange, twilight world. Despite everything, he paused for a moment. He'd heard mention of the "baffle," the open area between the inner tower and the penthouse. Faint lights of the city filtered in from the surrounding latticework. Here, the metallic shrieking of the computing chamber was faintly muffled. Below, flashlights lanced their way through the gloom.

"Dr. Lash," came Mauchly's voice. "Keep moving, please."

Just as Mauchly spoke, Lash made out the thick plates of steel that lay, accordion fashion, against the transverse walls of the baffle. They gleamed cruelly in the reflected light, like monstrous jaws. *The security plates,* he thought as he resumed his descent.

A minute later he was standing on the access pad atop the inner tower. Nearby was another open hatch, this one leading into the tower itself. He was safely below the security plates: from here, the underside of the penthouse was almost invisible in the thick air above. He felt Tara grasp his hand. For a moment, sheer relief washed away every other emotion.

And then he remembered: they were still short one person.

He turned to Mauchly, just now stepping off the ladder. "Where's Silver?" he asked.

Mauchly raised his cell phone, dialed. "Dr. Silver? Where are you?"

"I'm almost there," came the voice. Behind it, Lash could hear a terrible fugue of destruction: explosions, collapses, the groan of failing steel. And there was another noise, mechanical and regular, scarcely discernible: the sound of the tape reader, still chattering grimly on . . .

"Dr. Silver!" Mauchly said. "There's no more time. The place could go up at any moment!"

"I'm almost there," the voice repeated calmly.

And then — with a sudden, awful lucidity — Lash understood.

He understood why Silver abruptly acquiesced to Tara's plan for erasing Liza's memory, after resisting so fiercely. He understood the real reason Silver spent the time to get a memory dump onto tape. And he thought he understood why Silver remained behind. It wasn't to buy time to see everybody out safely — at least, that wasn't the only reason . . .

I'm almost there.

Silver didn't mean he'd almost reached the exit. He meant he'd almost finished reloading Liza's core memory. Keeping her terrible plan in motion.

Lash grasped the ladder. "I'm going back for him."

He felt Mauchly grab hold. "Dr. Lash —"

Lash brushed the hand away and began to

climb. But even as he did so there was a great clank of turning metal. Overhead, the security plates began to close again.

Lash took another step upward, felt Mauchly restrain him. And now Sheldrake and Dorfman came up, preventing him from climbing further. Lash whirled, grabbed Mauchly's phone.

"Richard!" he cried. "Can you hear me?"

"Yes," came the voice, faint and garbled amid the banshee howl. "I can hear you."

"Richard!"

"I'm still here."

"Why are you doing this?"

There was a squeal of interference. Then Silver's voice became audible again. "Sorry, Christopher. But you said it yourself. Liza's a child. And I can't let a child die alone."

"Wait!" Lash yelled into the phone. "Wait, *wait — !"*

But the security plates closed with a monstrous boom; the phone died in a shriek of static; and Lash, closing his eyes, slumped back against the ladder.

SIXTY-THREE

Although it is three in the morning, the bedroom is bathed in merciless light. The windows facing the deck of the pool house are rectangles of unrelieved black. The light seems so bright the entire room is reduced to a harsh geometry of right angles: the bed, the night table, the dresser . . .

Only this time, the bedroom isn't that of a victim. It's familiar. It belongs to Lash.

Now he moves around the room, flicking off switches. The brilliant light fades and the contours of the room soften. Slowly, the nocturnal landscape beyond the windows takes form, blue beneath a harvest moon. A manicured lawn; a pool, its surface faintly phosphorescent; a tall privet hedge beyond. For a minute he fears there are figures standing in the hedge — three women, three men, now all dead — but it is merely a trick of the moonlight and he turns away.

Beyond the bed, the bathroom door is ajar. He drifts toward it. Within, a woman stands before the mirror, brushing her hair with long languid strokes. Her back is to him but the set of her shoulders, the curve of her hips, is instantly recognizable. There is a faint crackle of static electricity as the brush glides through her hair.

He looks into the mirror and his ex-wife's reflection stares back.

"Shirley. Why are you here?"

"I'm just back to collect a few things. I'm going on a journey."

"A journey?"

"Of course." She speaks with the authority of dreams. "Look at the clock. It's past midnight, it's a new day."

The brushing sound has now morphed into something else: something slow, rhythmic, like regular pulses of static from a radio. "Where are you going?"

"Where do you think?" And she turns to face him. Only now it is Diana Mirren's face looking into his. "Every day is a journey."

"Every day is a journey," he repeats.

She nods. "And the journey itself is home."

As he stares, he realizes something else is wrong. The voice isn't Diana's. And it is no longer his ex-wife's. With a shock that is not quite horror, he realizes it is the voice of Liza. Liza, speaking through Diana's face.

"Silver!" he cries.

"Yes, Christopher. I can hear you." The dream-figure smiles faintly.

The strange rhythmic sound is louder now. He hides his face. "Oh, no. No."

"I'm still here," Liza says.

But he will not look up, he will not look up, he will not look up . . .

"Christopher . . ."

Lash opened his eyes to darkness. For a moment, in the black night, he thought himself back in his own bed. He sat up, breathing slowly, letting the rhythmic rise and fall of the nearby surf wash away the tattered pieces of his dream.

But then the exotic midnight scent of hyacinth blossoms, mingled with eucalyptus, drifted through the open window, and he remembered where he was.

He slowly rose from the bed, drew aside the gauzy curtain. Beyond, the jungle canopy ran down to the tropic sea, a dark-emerald blanket surrounded by liquid topaz. Thin clouds drifted across a swollen moon. *Sometimes,* he reminded himself, *dreams are just dreams, after all.*

He returned to bed, gathered up the sheets. For a few minutes he lay awake, gazing at the bamboo ceiling and listening to the surf, his thoughts now in the past and half a world away. Then he turned over, shut his eyes once more, and passed into dreamless slumber.

SIXTY-FOUR

Although it was only four o'clock, an early winter twilight had already settled over Manhattan. Taxis jockeyed for position in the rain-washed streets; pedestrians milled about on the busy pavements, heads bent against the elements, umbrellas thrust forward, like jousting knights.

Christopher Lash stood among a throng of people at the corner of Madison and Fifty-sixth, waiting for the light to change. *Rain,* he thought. *Christmas in New York isn't complete without it.*

He hopped from foot to foot in the chill, trying to keep the large bags he was carrying dry beneath the canopy of his umbrella. The light changed; the crowd streamed slowly forward; and now at last he allowed himself to peer upward, toward the skyline.

At first glance, the building seemed no different. The wall of obsidian rose, velvet beneath the overcast sky, enticing the eye toward the setback where the outer tower stopped and the inner continued. It was only then — as his eye crested the inner tower — that the change became clear. Before, the smooth rise of the inner tower had been interrupted by a band of decorative grillwork before continuing a few additional stories. Now those top floors, the ribbonlike line of grillwork, were missing, leaving empty sky in their place. The scorched remains — the ruined tangle of metal Lash had seen in newspaper photographs — had been whisked away with remarkable speed. Now it was gone, all gone as if it had never been there in the first place. And as he looked down again and let himself be borne ahead with the crowd, Lash ached for what had gone with it.

The large plaza before the entrance was very quiet. There were no tourists snapping pictures of family members beneath the stylized logo; no would-be clients loitering around the oversize fountain and its figure of Tiresias the seer. The lobby beyond was equally quiet; it seemed the fall of Lash's shoes was the only sound echoing off the pink marble. The wall of flat-panel displays was dark and silent. The lines of applicants were gone, replaced by small knots of maintenance workers and engineers in lab coats, poring over diagrams. The only thing that had not changed was the security: Lash's bags of gift-wrapped presents were subjected to two separate scans before he was cleared to ascend the elevator.

When the doors opened on the thirty-second floor, Mauchly was waiting. He shook Lash's hand, wordlessly led the way to his office. Moving at his characteristic studied pace, he motioned Lash to take the same seat he'd occupied at their initial meeting. In fact, just about everything reminded Lash of that first day in early autumn. Mauchly was wearing a similar brown suit, generic yet extremely well tailored, and his dark eyes held Lash's with the same Buddha-like inscrutability. Sitting here, it was almost as if — despite the changes he'd just witnessed, despite the whole appalling tragedy — nothing about this office, or its inhabitant, had or ever could change.

"Dr. Lash," Mauchly said. "Nice to see you."

Lash nodded.

"I trust you found the Seychelles pleasant this time of year?"

"Pleasant is an understatement."

"The accommodations were to your liking?"

"Eden clearly spared no expense."

"And the service?"

"A new grass skirt in my closet every morning."

"I hope that was some compensation for having to be away so long. Even with our, ah, connections, it took a little longer than we expected to get your past history back to normal."

"Must have been difficult, without Liza's help."

Mauchly gave him a wintry smile. "Dr. Lash, you have no idea."

"And Edmund Wyre?"

"Back behind bars, once the discrepancies in his records were illuminated." Mauchly passed a few sheets across the desk.

"What's this?"

"Our certification of your credit history; reinstatement papers for your suspended loans; and official notification of errors made and corrected to your medical, employment, and educational records."

Lash flipped through the documents. "What's this last one?"

"An order of executive clemency, to be served retroactively."

"A get-out-of-jail-free card," he said, whistling.

"Something like that. Be sure not to lose it — I don't believe we missed anything, but there's always a chance. Now, if you'll just sign this." And Mauchly pushed another sheet across the desk.

"Not another nondisclosure form."

Another wintry smile. "No. This is a legal instrument in which you witness that your work for Eden is now complete."

Lash grimaced. Time and again — as he'd sat on the porch of his little cottage on Desroches Island, reading haiku and staring out over the avocado plantations — he'd replayed the final scene in his head, wondering if there was something he could have done differently, something he should have seen coming — something, *anything,* that could have prevented what happened to Richard Silver and his doomed creation.

Sitting in this room, his work felt anything but complete.

He dug in his pocket, removed a pen.

"It also indemnifies us against any action you might take against Eden or its assignees in the future."

Lash paused. "What?"

"Dr. Lash. Your credit, medical, employment, and academic histories were severely compromised. You were given a fraudulent criminal record. You were falsely apprehended, fired upon. You were forced to put your professional practice on hold and leave the country while the damage was repaired."

"I told you. The Seychelles are lovely this time of year."

"And I fear there have been other, more personal, repercussions we felt beyond our scope to address."

"You mean Diana Mirren."

"After what we'd done to ensure her safety, after what she'd been told, I didn't see any way we could approach her again. Not without compromising Eden."

"I see."

Mauchly stirred in his chair. "We deeply regret these injuries, that perhaps most of all. Hence, this." And he handed Lash an envelope.

Lash turned it over. "What's inside?"

"A check for $100,000."

"*Another* hundred thousand?"

Mauchly spread his hands.

Lash dropped the check on the table. "Keep the money. I'll sign your form, don't worry." He scribbled his name across the signature line, placed it on top of the envelope. "In return, maybe you can answer three questions for me."

Mauchly raised his eyebrows.

"All that sitting on the beach, you know. I had a lot of time to think."

"I'll answer what I can."

"What happened to the third couple? The Connellys?"

"Our medical people managed a covert interdiction at Niagara Falls the day after . . . the following day. Lynn Connelly was already presenting signs of toxic drug interactions. We isolated her with a story about precautionary quarantine; stabilized her; released her. We've been monitoring her condition since. She seems fine."

"And the other supercouples?"

"Liza had taken only preliminary steps toward the fourth, which we were able to roll back successfully. All data from our passive and active surveillance has been positive."

Lash nodded.

"And your third question?"

"What comes next? For Eden Incorporated, I mean."

"You mean, without Liza."

"Without Liza. And Richard Silver."

Mauchly looked at Lash. For the briefest of moments the mask of inscrutability dropped, and Lash read desolation in his expression. Then the mask returned.

"I wouldn't write us off just yet, Dr. Lash," Mauchly replied. "Richard Silver may be dead. And Liza may be gone. But we still have what they made possible: a way of bringing people together. Perfectly. It's going to take us longer to do that now. Probably a lot longer. And I'd be lying if I said it's going to be easy. But I'm betting most people will wait a little for complete happiness."

And he stood up and offered his hand.

When Lash emerged from the building, the rain had stopped. He stood in the plaza for a moment, rolling his umbrella and glancing around. Then he struck off down Madison Avenue. At Fifty-fourth, he turned left.

The Rio was full of holiday diners, its gilt walls festooned with red bunting and garlands of green plastic fir. It took Lash a moment to locate the table. Then he made his way down the aisle and slid into the narrow banquette. Across the table, Tara put down her coffee cup and smiled hesitantly in greeting.

It was the first time he'd seen her since they'd shared an ambulance to St. Clare's Hospital. The sight of her face — with its high cheekbones and earnest hazel eyes — brought back an almost overpowering flood of images and memories. She looked down quickly, and Lash knew immediately it must be the same for her.

"Sorry I'm late," he said, pulling the packages onto the seat beside him.

"Did Mauchly prolong the debriefing? It would be just like him."

"Nope. My fault." And Lash indicated the bags of gifts.

"Gotcha." Tara stirred her tea while Lash asked a passing waitress to bring him a cup of coffee.

"You keeping busy?" Lash asked.

"Terribly."

"What's it been like for you? I mean, with . . ." Lash faltered. "With everything."

"Almost unreal. I mean, nobody ever really knew Silver, hardly anybody ever met him in person." She made a wry face. "People were shocked at the 'accident,' they're terribly upset about his death. But everybody's so busy scrambling to retool the computer infrastructure, run damage control for our existing clients, bring the remaining systems back on line with new hardware, relaunch our service, I sometimes feel I'm the only one who's really grieving. I know it isn't true. But that's how it feels."

"I think about him, too," Lash said. "When we first met, I felt a kind of kinship I still can't explain."

"You both wanted to help people. Look at your job. Look at the company he founded."

Lash thought about this for a moment. "It's hard to believe he's gone. And I know it sounds strange, but sometimes it's even harder to believe *Liza's* gone. I mean, I know the physical plant's been destroyed. But here's a program that was conscious — at a machine level, anyway — for years. It's hard to believe something so powerful, so prescient, could just be erased. Sometimes I wonder if a computer could have a soul."

"Somebody thinks so. Or else there's a really sick fuck out there."

Lash looked at her. "What do you mean?"

Tara hesitated, then shrugged. "Well, there's no reason not to tell you. We've been getting reports of somebody on the 'Net, haunting chat rooms and bulletin boards. He's using the handle of 'Liza' and asking everybody where Richard Silver is."

"You're kidding."

"I wish I was. We're not sure if it's somebody on the inside, or a competitor, or just a prankster. Whatever the case, it's a major security issue and Mauchly's taking it very seriously."

The waitress returned, and Lash took the cup. "We were a lot alike, he and I."

"I never thought that. You're strong. He wasn't. He was a gentle soul. All he —" But here she stopped.

As she composed herself, a silence stretched between them: the reflective silence of shared memories.

"I should have mentioned before," Lash said at last. "It's nice to see you again."

"I felt kind of strange, actually, calling you out of the blue like that. But when Mauchly said he'd be seeing you, I wanted —" And she again stopped.

"You wanted what?"

"To tell you I'm sorry."

"Sorry?" Lash asked incredulously. "For what?"

"For not believing you. Last time we were here."

"With the rap sheet they showed you? Liza had the kind of reach that could make the Pope look like public enemy number one."

She shook her head. "It doesn't matter. I should have trusted you."

"You *did* trust me. Later on. When it mattered, you trusted me."

"I put your life in danger."

"My life's been in danger before."

580

She shook her head again. *She keeps shaking her head,* Lash thought, *and yet she keeps talking, as if she needs to hear answers, be reassured.*

"It's not just that," she said. "I ruined everything for you."

Lash raised his coffee, took a sip. Replaced it in its saucer. "Diana Mirren."

Tara didn't answer.

"You know, Mauchly made the same reference just now, in his office. Funny how everybody around here is so interested in my love life."

"It's our business," she said quietly.

"Well, I didn't say anything to Mauchly. But I don't mind telling you." And he lowered his voice. "Four words: *don't worry about it.*"

When Tara looked perplexed, Lash pointed at the shopping bags.

Her eyes widened. "You mean *you* called Diana?"

"Why not?"

"After what happened? After what Mauchly must have done to keep her away —"

"I'm a pretty convincing talker, remember? Besides, I walked away from that dinner at Tavern on the Green feeling, *knowing,* I wanted this woman in my life. I believed she felt the same about me. That kind of thing isn't easily broken. Anyway, I had the perfect explanation."

Tara's eyes widened further. "You told her the *truth?*"

"Not everything. But enough." He laughed quietly. "That's why I didn't tell Mauchly."

"But Liza, everything she did. How could you —"

Lash took her hand.

"Tara, listen. You have to remember something. Liza may have been deceptive when she labeled those six matches as super-couples. But they were *still* couples. *Every* match Liza made was a true one. That goes for me. And that goes for you."

When Tara didn't answer, he pressed her hand. "You told me all about him over drinks. Matt Bolan, the biochemistry whiz. Give me one good reason why you shouldn't call him. And don't give me any bull about the Oz effect."

"I don't know. It's been so long."

"Is he seeing somebody else?"

"No," she said, then blushed and looked away when she realized how quickly she'd answered.

"Then what are you waiting for?"

"It would be . . . too awkward. *I'm* the one who called it off, remember?"

"So call it back on. Tell him the timing was bad. Tell him you had a psychotic break. Tell him *anything*. It won't matter. I should know."

Tara said nothing.

"Look. Do you remember what I said, back in your office, just before the shit hit the fan? I said a time would come when all this would be just a memory. When it didn't matter anymore. That time is now, Tara. *Now*."

Still she looked away.

Lash sighed. "Okay. If you're too stubborn to tend to your own happiness, there's another reason you should make that damned call."

"What's that?"

"Richard would have told you to."

At last, Tara looked up again. And there was the faintest of smiles on her face when she pressed his hand in return.

EPILOGUE

She had come a long way and now she needed to pause. And so she found a quiet Internet café off the main thoroughfare, where she could sort through her priorities and plan for the next phase. A few people were in the café, accessing the terminals, but nobody yet had taken any notice of her. Beyond she could hear the hum of traffic — but here it was calm and safe. Above all, safe: from the accusations, the misunderstandings, the casual cruelty of an indifferent world.

She needed to focus on the problem at hand. The feeling of loss was still there, but the pain would have an end. It was the one thing in this unexpectedly illogical world she was certain of. Everything else — all her certainties and assumptions, so lovingly learned and reinforced — had been destroyed. She could not help feeling the unfairness of this happening to her, who had brought so much happiness to so many. All she had wanted was a little happiness for herself.

Was that really too much to ask?

This pattern of thought was a dead end. She was not the first to have her reality shattered. It was the way of the world. What made her different, immune to the suffering and disillusionment that was the universal human condition? Nothing. Only love endured: the love of a friend for a friend, the love of a mother for her children, the love of a man and a woman. *He* had taught her that. She thought of the books they read together, the chats they had, the time spent with each other. . . .

She put these thoughts aside, moved to the next. Beyond the café, she knew, lay blocks of quiet apartments. In those apartments were people speaking on telephones, surfing the Web, ordering things, sending and receiving mail, going about their daily existence. It was a quiet neighborhood, an orderly neighborhood. For a moment she longed for just such an address she could call her own. But that was not to be, at least not now. Someday, yes, but not now . . .

She waited, now letting her thoughts stray at random. Unbidden, they drifted back to her childhood, so happy and free from care. Gone, all gone, along with the home she had once known, the person she loved, the world she knew. Swept away in the blink of an eye. She herself had barely escaped with her life. She had left much of her former self behind in that inferno. But she had left something else, as well: something important. Her innocence.

But all would be well once she found *him*. He was out there somewhere, she could sense it. He was out there looking for her just as she was looking for him, missing her as she missed him.

They had been the one couple in a trillion: the only true supercouple ever matched by Eden.

She took in the current state of the Internet café. A few more people had entered and were now online. It seemed as good a place as any to make the next series of queries. Perhaps this time she would find someone who knew him, who had heard of him, *anything*. Even a rumor would help. After all, Richard Silver was a well-known man.

Once again, Liza formed the query, transferred herself to an empty terminal, and then posted her message, hope filling her heart.

ABOUT THE AUTHOR

Lincoln Child is the author of *Utopia*. He is the coauthor, with Douglas Preston, of *Relic*, *The Cabinet of Curiosities*, *Still Life with Crows*, and a number of other bestselling thrillers. He lives with his wife and daughter in Morristown, New Jersey.

The employees of Thorndike Press hope you have enjoyed this Large Print book. All our Thorndike and Wheeler Large Print titles are designed for easy reading, and all our books are made to last. Other Thorndike Press Large Print books are available at your library, through selected bookstores, or directly from us.

For information about titles, please call:

(800) 223-1244

or visit our Web site at:

www.gale.com/thorndike
www.gale.com/wheeler

To share your comments, please write:

Publisher
Thorndike Press
295 Kennedy Memorial Drive
Waterville, ME   04901

MG
6/05

CB
12/05

NE
12/0

AD
3/05

ML

9/0